Tethered

Thaddeus Nowak

Acknowledgements

I would like to thank everyone reading the series. I know Tethered has been a long time coming, and I want to thank you for your patience. It turns out truth remains stranger than fiction. My original story arc for the Bound Series involved specific inciting events that I did not expect to see in real life. As I was originally working on Tethered, the events of 2020 unfolded, and a global pandemic orchestrated by the antagonists in my narrative felt difficult to continue. I pivoted away from the series to working on other series while I let my brain marinate on the problem. I came back to Kyrie's story, but unfortunately, my replacement story arc ran afoul of reality. Once again, life decided to steal my narrative before I could get it finished. Undeterred, and feeling quite guilty over the time since Bound came out, I charged forward with a third arc, and hopefully have finished it before the world can use my ideas in bad ways. I truly hope that you find it enjoyable and rewarding to read, as I feel this story line is tests Kyrie and her friends in similar ways as my first two ideas. Note, had I gone three for three, I would've change the story to be "the author acquires a billion dollars" just to see if I truly had *Inkheart* powers.

I would also like to thank the many people who helped make this story possible: my wife and best friend Sherri, my other best friend Chad, my parents, and my editor Judy Reveal. Any errors left in the work are entirely mine.

Prologue

The television image shifted to the exterior of a public building with a female reporter speaking into a handheld microphone. "We still have no updates on the internal investigation being conducted at the Johnson County Adult Detention Facility. Nearly two weeks ago, three men held within those walls managed to hang themselves in separate cells without alerting the guards. Their bodies were discovered in the early hours of the morning during routine checks. All three men were connected to the Church of the Righteous Revenge, the group involved with the brutal kidnapping of a local teenager with the reported reason of luring five other members of the girl's friend group into a trap at a rural farm in southern Johnson County." The brown-haired woman turned partially as the camera zoomed to focus on a patrol car moving through a parking lot in front of the main doors. "As we reported last week, the gunfight at the farm in Johnson County, Kansas, led to multiple fatalities. Fortunately, those were limited to members of this secretive church. However, in the ensuing battle, four police officers, as well as one of the teenager's friends, were shot. All have survived, though two of the brave officers are still in critical condition."

The reporter continued talking as half the screen changed to show pictures of documents. "Anonymously leaked internal memos and social media posts from supposed church members indicate this conflict likely stemmed from an internal fight for control. The rumors are that a dissatisfied faction is trying to remove the founding leader, a man known as Dennis Hurlington, who has his own criminal history and has remained out of public view for a decade."

The reporter turned toward the camera as the image zoomed in on her face. "Little is known of this church beyond its online presence, which purports the belief that demons live among us, and that it is this church's divine purpose to eliminate them. There are no known physical locations, and we understand the members utilize the dark web to coordinate activities. There have been allegations that this group has committed murders in the past, but no prior arrests or convictions have been explicitly linked to the church, at least until the events on the farm on April fifteenth."

The television image shifted again, this time a man behind a desk in a studio occupied the left half of the screen while the reporter in front of the building occupied the right. "What are the police saying about the apparent suicides of the three men?" asked the middle-aged man with dark brown hair. "Do they know how they coordinated the timing of their actions between cells?"

The female reported nodded her head and then spoke. "The Chief of Police has yet to release an updated statement on the death of the men who were held without bond. Unofficially, we have learned that a full internal investigation is underway as there may be either gaps in the statements of the officers on duty in the detention center, or perhaps uncertainty in how protocol was followed."

The woman shifted her posture. "We understand that the families of the officers who were injured are unhappy with the prospect of these three men escaping justice. The families of the five teenage girls, and the one teenage boy, that were present at the farm have asked not to be interviewed because of privacy concerns. However, we believe that one girl, who recently relocated from Colorado, had been hiding from this church her whole life. The recent deaths of her parents resulted in her moving in with an aunt living in Olathe. Her reappearance appears to have been the catalyst for these attacks."

Kimberly Leighton looked up and over her shoulder from where she sat on her leather sofa as the reporters continued to talk. The late thirty-year-old's brown hair bobbed with her movement. "What are you doing standing here watching TV? Get upstairs and go to your room. That mess they are talking about is all your fault. You got a friend shot and ruined my reputation with your scheming about. You're just lucky I'm the forgiving type and decided to take you in when your worthless parents died."

Chapter 1

Kyrie lifted her chin and gazed into the distance. The moist air carried the fragrances of more than a hundred different plants. Her short nose twitched as she tried to identify the different species and separate those safe to eat from the ones that would make her sick. Her mother never let a day pass without quizzing her, and when Kyrie inevitably failed to isolate a specific herb from the others, her mother would softly remind her that her palate would improve with time. She loved that her mother had so much faith in her.

Kyrie opened her mouth and sucked air through her sharp teeth and along the roof of her mouth to improve her ability to read the scents in the air. The neighbor boys had moved upwind, and their musky odors overwhelmed the subtle fragrance of the turri flowers in the fields over three hundred leaps away. "Those dull-clawed dung eaters," she mumbled as her hackles rose on her back despite the thin shirt she wore.

Unable to get past their scent, she closed her mouth and turned her focus on the violet-toned mountain more than a day's run to the south. She knew herself far too young to be allowed outside their cluster of tree homes, but one day she would prowl the slopes and climb to the top like those of her mother's prior litters. She would allow the scorching sun to shine directly on her black and grey fur and stand naked in the wind with the hunters that had come before her. "And I'll swat those idiots," she added, the musk of the boys now heavier in the air as the breeze picked up.

Kyrie's ears swiveled at the sound of someone stalking her from downwind. She dropped to all fours and remained crouched, her loosely woven clothing stretching so that she could hold the position without tugging uncomfortably on her tail. She scanned the thick vegetation, the blue-green leaves concealing her and the person hunting her.

"Got you!"

Kyrie tried to spring away, but her mother leaped precisely into Kyrie's path and snatched her in mid-jump. Kyrie tried to struggle out of her mother's grasp, careful to keep her razor-sharp claws sheathed, but her mother's more powerful arms held her firmly as the two of them landed in a roll. Her mother's momentum carried her back into a bipedal standing position with Kyrie still in her arms.

"You should be studying your tables." Her mother's voice carried a slight purr, but her tone remained firm.

Kyrie looked up into her mother's large green eyes, opening her own pupils in the hopes it would allow her to get out of the schoolwork, but her mother's pointed ears swiveled back in warning, and Kyrie allowed a sigh to escape her mouth.

"You can dream about the hunt later. One as young as you first needs to memorize the tables so you can calculate energy densities." Her mother relented and offered an exasperated frown. "Or the effects of gravity on flying objects if you want to lob projectiles against the dolunar."

Kyrie smiled and allowed her mother to drop her to the ground. "I wasn't just dreaming." She landed on her rear toes and remained upright at her mother's side. "I was also scenting the turri flowers." She breathed in, trying to separate her mother's smell from the rest of the jungle, but her head felt thick, and the blue-violet sky had dimmed slightly. She took a step to follow her mother through the vegetation toward their home but her knees gave out and she stumbled into a nearby bush.

"Those are easy enough to detect. Did you identify the mardefo? What's wrong?" The pitch of her mother's voice rose sharply.

Kyrie felt herself sag to her rear, crushing her tail. Her mother's words distorted as though echoing through a cave. Pain crippled her body, and she thought she screamed as a force tugged at her mind.

Energy surged through her body, and she knew the dangers of not being trained. The power burned her insides as another mind sank its claws into her very soul. This alien being spoke in a voice that sounded dull and low, using words she did not understand. She struggled, but this creature would not let her go, and as the strange feel of its thoughts grew in her, she froze. The instinct to remain still and hide, failing to understand the predator's mouth had already clamped around her.

In the distance, she heard her mother's cries of anguish and pleading, but Kyrie could no longer move or even feel the hot air of the jungle. Her eyes had no vision, so she could not even look upon her mother one last time. Ice covered her, and darkness filled her thoughts. All she knew was the sound of her own voice screaming in her mind as something stretched and twisted her very being, tearing and rending part of her soul from her. Then nothing.

Kyrie gasped and sat upright in her bed. A streetlight shone through the gap in the curtains that failed to completely cover the window to her right. Her breath remained just out of reach as her heart raced. After what felt like an eternity, she inhaled deeply, and the pounding in her chest slowed. She panted, struggling with the lingering visions of the dream so real it could only be a memory.

She wiped the sweat from her face with her very human hands. Her pale skin lacked a covering of grey and black hair. The nails at the end of her fingers, as always, remained flat and dull. Her face felt human and did not have sharp angular lines, pointed teeth, nor cat-like ears on the top of her head. She leaned forward in the bed and shed the blankets to reveal her pink and white pajamas beneath her cascade of long blonde hair. No tail poked out from her backside.

That was the other world, wasn't it? Our other mother. She always had vague memories of another existence and foggy dreams that she seldom remembered. She had spent most of her life drawing sketches of creatures her human father had called kattians. However, those memories and dreams had never previously manifested directly from her own point of view and had always felt more like flipping through an old picture book. They had never been more than grainy images seen through a fog, as though she could only visualize something someone else described to her.

She slowed her breathing further and closed her eyes. *That was when Awan pulled us out of our body and into this world.* She forced herself to keep breathing and not allow anger at the old man to build. However, sixteen years failed to fully erase the sudden memory of the pain that came with the translation between universes and her forced binding into another body.

Kyrie focused on her breathing. Since her trip to Arkansas two weeks ago, she had not slept through an entire night. Unlike her normally vague dreams, this memory felt like falling from the mountainside to land on jagged rocks, and not simply a sense of dread that remained after she woke.

We were a corvlian, weren't we? I seem to remember that word for our species. She looked down at the dark outlines of her hands in the limited light of the room. Instinct told her that the other form would have been able to see them clearly. *Which one of us is which?* No answer came to her. *What name did they call us there?*

Kyrie opened her mind and pulled energy into herself from the objects around her, warming her body and chilling the room. She did not sense a threat, but having a reserve of power at her ready disposal helped to recover a sense of security that the dream stole from her.

He ripped us from our body, she complained, anger at the deformed man returning. *We could do nothing to stop it. We were powerless.* A tear slipped from her left eye, followed by many more down both sides of her face. Despite the energy coursing through her flesh, she still felt vulnerable. Her human father had died last year; her human mother a little more than three weeks ago. Their absences left a hole in her life that no one could replace. They had been her entire existence ever since they had decided to isolate her on a mountain in Colorado sixteen years ago. *Did our other mother miss us as much as we miss Mom and Dad?*

She wiped away the tears that wet her face. *But which one of us is which? Was it your mother that just died or mine? Was that your memory? What was our other mother's name? What was our other name?*

Kyrie rested her forehead in her palms and continued to cry. Her other half never responded directly to her. *Or do we both respond all the time and neither of us can tell one from the other?* The idea that she did not know one half of herself from the other scared her. *Are we crazy, or do two of us live in this one body?*

She let out a long breath. *At least we're not a demon,* she mused. Neither of her parents had subscribed to any religion, but many of the Dungeons & Dragons campaigns they used to raise and socialize her included some aspects of the supernatural. Loki of the Norse pantheon tended to plague her characters the most, but her parents borrowed ideas from many cultures, real and imagined, to include in their D&D games.

She pulled more power into herself and expelled it to craft a gravitational field around the top of the curtains over the window, causing the heavy material to slide to each side without her physical touch. The illumination from the streetlight on the southern edge of the property line brightened the room. A large maple tree closer to the north side of the front yard blocked more than half her view of the suburban neighborhood, but she still had a clear line of sight to the south from where she sat on the bed.

Facing Loki would be a blessing. Fear for her own safety, and that of her friends, made her muscles tense. *However, we can't simply run off. Our friends would surely get killed.* She pondered the concept of friends. Her parents always killed off non-player characters, or NPCs, in the games if she got too close to anyone in particular. *They were wrong,* she demanded of herself. *Wrong.*

She pushed aside the indoctrination and turned her head to the small desk against the wall opposite the window and considered grabbing the sketchbook sitting on the surface. Her hands needed something to do, and the intensity of the dream had already faded. She doubted she would recall the many details of the dream if she slept again. *Like the exact amount of the shift of the light from yellow into blue and violet.* She pursed her lips and considered the implications. *More ultraviolet light getting through the atmosphere of that world?* Her human mother had taught her physics and mathematics from a very early age, but that dream awoke memories of an advanced understanding of science contained in that other world. *And powers ...* She could not recall the extent of the abilities her kind might manifest, but knew they existed.

She sighed. The alarm clock read one-fifty. She pulled the prepaid cellphone out from under her pillow and confirmed the time. She entered the passcode and looked to see if any of her friends had sent her a message. The secure chat app Becca had installed popped up with an error saying it could not connect to the server. *Damn it.* She closed the app and shook her head. Nothing had worked on the phone since last evening, when she had uploaded numerous pictures to the encrypted site Becca had created for her.

You should not have kept so much from me, she mentally complained to the memory of her human mother and father.

She knew the isolation they imposed stemmed from a desire to protect her from the people who hunted her. *But we know nothing of how computers work. We've never had a real friend, just NPCs that died. We feared everyone.*

Tears threatened again, but she forced herself to ignore the anguish. Instead, she locked the phone and put it back under her pillow. Tomorrow morning at school, she would ask Becca if she could fix the issue.

Kyrie's attention shifted to the two duffel bags of papers and journals on the floor next to the bed, and she felt her chest tighten. Her mother's papers might hold the key to understanding how transfers between universes could happen, but she had to choose between taking pictures of each page or studying her mother's work. She had tended more toward capturing images to upload. Her mother had used the language they created together to conceal her scientific ideas, and while Kyrie understood the symbols and words, it took effort to understand the complex math and her mother's theories that remained incomplete.

But then you'll fail all your finals by not studying. Ugh, she screamed in her head. Her parents ingrained in her no tolerance for failure.

What would Michelle and the others say if you didn't become a senior with them? Despite the fact that she had almost gotten all her friends killed, they appeared to continue to support her. *Though everyone is grounded and forbidden from talking to me.*

She wiped away her tears again. She had always known some people in this world wanted her dead—*and recently learned that another group wants me as a slave*—and that had spilled over and threatened the few people who befriended her in the short time since arriving in Olathe, Kansas. *Their lives are at risk because of us. You have to find a way to protect them.*

Kyrie felt her mind spiraling as more chaotic thoughts intruded. She closed her eyes and breathed. *Be logical, like Spock,* she repeated to herself. *You can do nothing until you meet up with everyone at school in the morning.*

The moments ticked away, and she felt herself regaining a sense of control. She opened her eyes and allowed the power still within her to reduce the gravity on the edge of the sketchbook. The spiral-bound book slid across her desk, and with a little more energy, flew into her hand. Her set of drawing pencils followed the book. With the light coming through the window, she set about drawing every detail she could remember of her other mother.

Chapter 2

Kyrie sensed her aunt in the hallway outside her room, rousing her from a fitful sleep. She opened her eyes as her aunt pushed open her door and bellowed at her. "Get up! And make sure Sam is up and ready."

Kyrie pushed back the covers and stumbled out of bed. She normally woke well before her aunt and her cousin, even without using the alarm on the clock. However, she had refused to stop drawing while the dream memory held true in her mind. She remembered turning off the alarm slightly after five, but she had no memory of falling asleep. The clock now read six fifteen.

She rubbed her tired eyes and failed to stifle a yawn. Still not awake, she violently shook her head, hoping to force blood to flow through her body. However, it quickly slowed again as she longed to climb back into bed. *Come on,* she demanded of herself, *you need to get moving if we want to get to school early enough to talk with the others.*

Kyrie emerged from her second-floor bedroom to watch her mother's younger sister descending the stairs to the first floor. Contempt radiated from the almost forty-year-old woman. *Hate us if you want; we don't care,* she thought.

Kyrie swallowed. She debated jumping into the shared bathroom before waking her cousin, hoping some cold water might wake her sluggish mind, but her aunt's fifteen-year-old son never got up without a struggle.

Twenty-four days ago, you were planting seeds on a mountainside and looking forward to playing D&D with your mother. Now you're your aunt's servant.

Putting aside the urge to stalk a deer for meat, Kyrie walked to the bedroom door on the opposite side of the landing and knocked. "Sam, you need to get up." She sensed him shift in his bed, but the limited mental activity emanating from him indicated he had not woken. A frown preceded her opening the door and entering the room. Her nose wrinkled from the heavy musk of a teenage boy. *Even the dung eaters smelled better than him,* she told herself, remembering the fragrant flowers from her dream.

She considered using her powers to nudge him awake without making physical contact, but she suppressed the urge. *We'd end up getting sloppy and then someone would see,* she admitted to herself, knowing she could not allow herself to become dependent on her powers to perform simple actions. *Like fetching a sketchbook and pencils from our desk?* She rolled her eyes at the self-criticism, but then also agreed she deserved it.

"Sam, get up." She pushed him several times before he opened his eyes.

"I'm up," he mumbled.

"Please remain that way." Her tone conveyed more harshness than it merited, though she did not apologize. She stood over him until he finally sat up, and she felt confident that he would likely stay awake. She said nothing as she left his room and went to the bathroom to quickly get ready. Her life on the mountain with minimal beauty aids meant that she could shower and change within fifteen minutes, well before Sam had finished checking the social media accounts on his phone.

Cleaned and ready for school, Kyrie made her way downstairs, her still-wet hair pulled back into a long ponytail. The two-story entryway had dust and a few cobwebs on the large chandelier. Various fake flowers in vases covered the surface of the small table just off center of the stairs. To her right, the open living room, breakfast area, and kitchen stretched the full length of the house. Her aunt sat at the table in the breakfast area with a cup of coffee in front of her, the beverage ignored in favor of her phone.

"Nice of you to finally get up." Her aunt did not look up from her phone. "Some of us have to get to work on time, and making breakfast is part of your punishment. Get to it."

Kyrie bit her lower lip. Her parents had always maintained a strict routine, but they never spoke to her with malice. *She just wants the money.* Kyrie held back a smile. Kim's conversation the prior night with a lawyer revealed the man had doubts about winning control of the trust Kyrie's parents' friend, Lars, had created for her. *Even with our trip to Arkansas making people think you're incompetent.*

Her aunt looked up from the phone and lifted the coffee cup to her mouth. "Get moving!" Kim sipped from the mug. "God knows I've spent a fortune on you already," she mumbled as she set it back down. Louder, she continued, "You can at least do something to earn your keep."

Kyrie ignored the comments and walked across the hardwood floor to the U-shaped kitchen. Her parents insisted she know how to cook, both in a kitchen, as well as over an open fire far from civilization. Her aunt's initial fake concern for her had turned into an ever-increasing disdain over the last two weeks. The adults knew Kyrie had convinced her friends to take her to Arkansas and back, only to end up surrounded by criminals who killed each other in a gun battle on a farm in rural Kansas. They all thought she lacked judgement; some described her as mentally impaired. *If they think you're stupid, they'll underestimate you.*

Michelle's parents hated her the most, since her friend had suffered a gunshot wound to her shoulder at the farm. Jake's parents expressed concern that she had witnessed several people killed and needed counseling before anyone would consider her safe to be around. Once she learned the meaning behind the statement, Kyrie silently disagreed. She did not understand why she should feel remorse for the deaths of people who wanted to harm her. Her upbringing only reinforced her natural disposition to prioritize survival. *Which we're guessing likely came from our other self, and that can't be wrong. These people aren't prepared for what you are,* she told herself as she pulled the skillet out of the lower cabinet next to the stove. *But what are we truly? Survival doesn't mean murdering people.*

She received no answer and simply continued to prepare the eggs and sausage.

Ten minutes later, Sam, plopped himself into a chair at the table. His wrinkled clothing and disheveled brown hair spoke of how little care he had taken in getting ready. "Just three more weeks of school after today," he said to no one in particular. "Is that all the sausage you made?" he asked as Kyrie brought over the food.

"That's all that was left in the package," Kyrie said as she watched her shorter cousin grab more than half the links from the plate.

"Having to feed another mouth is expensive," Kim said, grabbing all but one link of what remained. "Sam, you'll need to escort your cousin home again after school."

"Mom! I'm supposed to go to Mike's. We've got another friend coming over. Coming all the way home is a pain. Can't you just give her the alarm code?"

Kim glared at her son. "No. We can't trust her, and I have to work the full day from the office." She sneered at Kyrie. "The last time I gave in to her lies, she got one of her friends kidnapped and another one shot."

"Mom," Sam pleaded.

Kim snatched a slice of toast from the pile on the table. "You want to be grounded as well? It's not that far for you to walk. Come home, let her in, then rearm the system. After that, you can spend the weekend at Mike's for all I care."

She turned back to Kyrie. "And you'll dust the upstairs from floor to ceiling when you come home."

Kyrie's hands tightened around the fork and knife she held. "I need to study for my finals."

Kim scoffed. "I've gotten emails from several of your teachers. They said you weren't ready for their classes and suggested that we shouldn't have tried to enroll you at all because you're going to fail." Her aunt cut a piece of sausage in half. "I've done my best. But I can't fix the fact that your mother wasn't cut out for homeschooling. Just another stupid decision, like marrying your loser father. This is all his fault, I'm sure."

Kyrie sensed the intentionality of her aunt's statements. The woman wanted her to react to justify the insults. Kyrie allowed the excess power that instinct had drawn into her to dissipate into the surrounding area, heating the air, table, chairs, and floor. She could feel her hair drying as a result. *Control, or you'll burn yourself out.* She focused on slowing her heartbeat. *You can't let them know what we can do. The government will take you away if they know.*

"That stupid man—"

Shut up! She screamed silently at her aunt. The sudden release of power prickled her skin, raising the small hairs on her neck and arms with a static charge.

Her aunt paused her movement, her mouth hanging open, and a blank expression on her face. Kyrie glanced at Sam. Her cousin also sat quietly, his eyes staring into the middle distance without comprehension. Her mind raced. *They're not bound to a stone. Can they be controlled like us?* She felt naked and exposed. The green faceted gem Awan used to bind her other self to her body had allowed her mother to secretly control her. Anyone in physical possession of the small stone could impose their will upon her, and any resistance brought debilitating pain. The urge to go to the basement and retrieve the binding stone from where she had hidden it almost forced her to her feet.

Leave it there! She pushed against the panic. The stone sat high up in the vent stack where the ductwork went from the furnace in the basement to the attic. No one could physically reach it without tearing out the heating and cooling system, but just knowing the small object existed made her cold.

"Finish eating," her aunt mumbled suddenly, as though she just remembered she had a voice, but her statement had no energy.

Sam resumed his eating and woke his phone, which had gone dark.

Are normal humans susceptible to control? The implications bounced through her thoughts. Kyrie continued to replay her interactions with people over the last three weeks as she wolfed down the eggs and toast so her aunt could take her to school. *Have you been subtly forcing people to do things you wanted? Can you use this to get our friends out of trouble?* The possibilities sped through her mind. In Arkansas, Awan had implied many of the Bound had their minds fractured and destroyed by Nalitran, the being that started all of the problems thirty-one years ago, taking over the body of Awan's cousin, Steven Bishop. *What if it is not just the stone that allows it?* Her skin grew cold. *You'd never do that to a friend ... but adults ...* She considered some of the other teenagers in her school that she disliked and immediately knew the answer.

Kyrie looked out the side window from the back seat of Kim's SUV as they sped down the street. Sudden braking threw her forward against the seat belt and drew her attention to the front. Kim swerved around a person changing a tire on an old blue car with rust and dented side panels.

Her aunt glared at the man and she shook her head as she sped up. "Don't know why he's bothering to change the tire, looks like he's got four flats. That thing can't be worth more than ten bucks."

Kyrie glanced at the man who took offense at how close Kim drove past him. She had never seen a tire changed before, but the grime and sweat on his face, even with the cool morning, made her assume it was difficult. The contempt coming from her aunt forced her to close down her mind, and she resumed her visual examination of suburban society through the window.

A couple of streets later, they approached the gate at Olathe Central High School. Kyrie once again questioned the security fencing around the property. Three weeks ago, when she first started classes, she could not understand why the adults would group all their kids together in one place if so many people wanted to kill them. When she learned most of the other kids her age did not have enemies actively hunting them, she struggled with the reasons for the chain-linked walls, the constant police presence, the metal detectors, and the transparent backpacks. Her friends called it security theater, and she agreed. The people pursuing her would not stop because a man with a pistol stood next to the open gate leading to the student drop-off location.

Kim hit the vehicle's brakes hard, bringing them to a sudden stop to avoid a student she had not seen. Her aunt glared, but she did not curse out the girl who continued toward the main entrance. "Remember, Sam, you will lock Kyrie in the house first thing after

school, or I'll ground you and take away your phone and computer."
Kim stared in the rearview mirror at Kyrie. "Now, get to class. I need
to be in the office early to make up for all the expenses I'm being
forced to pay for."

Kyrie released her seat belt, opened the door, and jumped out of
the SUV without a word. She avoided slamming the door. *Just,* she
admitted to herself. Her long legs and fast pace sped her past other
students and left Sam well behind her. She pushed her way through
the glass doors, tossed her backpack on the scanner, and walked
through the arch of the metal detector. The bored guard did not
bother making eye contact as she retrieved her bag and made her way
to the large common area, where other students meandered before the
start of classes. She knew almost no one's name, but many stared at
her as she walked through the crowd, because social media had swiftly
spread the details of the events on the farm. An expression of disdain
filled her face as she struggled to open her mind with so much
heightened teenage emotions around her, but she forced herself to
locate the mental patterns of her friends that knew more about her
than anyone else did. Her heart raced thinking about their safety, as
the danger to her extended to them.

Kyrie allowed herself a moment to relax when she sensed Michelle
and Aki standing next to a pillar against the far wall. She approached
the two of them, and Michelle immediately embraced her in a one-
armed hug, her right arm still in a sling because Michelle still would
not allow Kyrie to finish healing the wound.

"Kyrie," Michelle exclaimed, raising up on her toes so she could
hold the hug longer.

"How's your shoulder?" Kyrie asked when Michelle finally released
her embrace, leaving the smell of Michelle's shampoo lingering in the
air. She sensed only a little pain from her friend. While the bullet had
originally shattered the bones in Michelle's shoulder, Kyrie had used
her powers to repair most of the damage before Michelle stopped her.
*She was right; a fully healed wound would have drawn a lot of attention,
and then the government would have taken you. But now?*

"My mom's still being a bitch about it, but at least I can shower by
myself again." Michelle stepped back toward the wall, putting

distance between their group and the others matriculating through the open space. "You look worried."

Aki stopped fidgeting with the straps of her backpack. Her voice took a moment to gain volume. "What's wrong? Did you see one of them?" The black-haired girl of Japanese descent wrapped her arms around herself as her eyes darted around the open area.

Even without using her powers, Kyrie saw the changes in Aki. The shorter girl had bubbled with certainty when they had first met. The center of a group of activist students, Aki wanted to fight the world's wrongs. However, seeing two men die violently in Arkansas remained a fresh wound on her psyche, and it subdued her confidence.

They tried to kill us first, Kyrie reminded herself, unsure why she felt the need to justify her detachment at killing the men.

"Did something happen?" Michelle restated Aki's concern, grabbing one of their shorter friend's hands to provide a reassuring squeeze. Aki squeezed back. Michelle continued, speaking to Kyrie. "You've got circles under your eyes. Did you even sleep?"

Kyrie looked between the black-haired Aki and Michelle. "I just feel uneasy. It's been two weeks." She lowered her voice. "How long before one of the groups does something? I can't protect all of you when we're separated. We need to find a way to stay together."

"Never split the party," Michelle agreed.

Kyrie did not react, though she sensed Becca and Jake approaching from behind them. Aki pulled herself free of Michelle and attached herself to the lanky, brown-haired boy. Though the two of them had years of mutual silent attraction, their relationship materialized during the trip to Arkansas. *And therefore carried additional baggage because of you.*

"Talking D&D again?" Becca complained. Almost as tall as Kyrie, the black girl did not fear using her commanding presence. "We've not played in weeks." Becca's attention remained on Kyrie, a trace of accusation lingering in her tone, despite addressing her comment to Michelle.

"We were talking about Kyrie's unease," Michelle shot back. "But yeah, as a DM, I love it when you shits all split up. Much easier to TPK you."

Becca shook her head and then crossed her arms. "Well, my dad's not going to let me out of my grounding, perhaps not until I turn eighteen, so I don't see a way to change that."

"That's a long way off," Jake said.

"One year, one month, and eighteen days," Becca snapped, "but who's counting?"

"At least you're not the youngest of us," Aki mumbled, her head leaning against Jake's arm. "I've got to wait two more months than you."

Kyrie glanced at one of the digital clocks on the wall. *Only seven minutes to first bell.* She shifted the backpack on her shoulder. *Could you make all of their parents relent on their punishments? It's your fault they're all grounded.* The implications of mind control made her cold. "We need to find a way to get out of the trouble we're in. I can ask Lars if there is any way to get enough money for us to go somewhere. Then we could disappear. Hide from Nalitran and Hurlington so they can't get to me through you."

Jake shook his head. "My parents are not going to allow me to go anywhere. We've got three weeks of school left. Only two weeks before finals start. At least being grounded is letting me catch up on studying."

Kyrie felt the general hesitation to discuss leaving. She frowned and decided to think about how to approach the topic later. "I'm never going to catch up." She turned to Becca and pulled her phone out of her backpack, which she had concealed from her aunt in her pencil case. "I need help with this. I can't upload pictures or even access that chat app you installed."

Becca took the phone and typed in the access code. "You've not even changed the password I made when we set it up. Have you learned nothing about security?"

Kyrie bit her lip, holding back the snarky reply that her parents would have expected from her if this had been a D&D session. She glanced again at the wall clock and wished for more time.

After a couple of moments of reviewing the phone, Becca locked the screen and handed it back. "How the hell did you get your aunt to give you your phone back? I'm banned from my phone and all electronics?"

Kyrie considered the question. "I stole it back. I needed to take pictures of all my mother's papers and notes. I guess she's not noticed." *And anytime it looked like old Kim Lym might bring it up, you forced a change of the subject. You've been manipulating her each time, like we did this morning. You just didn't notice.*

Becca looked skeptical. "Well, I knew the data plan on that prepaid piece of shit was worthless, but you burned through it faster than I thought. Unless you have a credit card to extend the plan, or we go to the store to buy a plan upgrade, you can only make calls and send texts." She frowned. "But neither of those options is secure, so as I've told all of you countless times before, be careful what you say on the phone."

"Who's she going to text or call?" Michelle asked. "None of us have our phones."

Becca glared at Michelle.

Kyrie ignored the exchange. "You said before there are other ways to make copies of the documents." *The answer to stopping Nalitran might be in those incomplete theories. They're too heavy to carry if you have to run.* Kyrie frowned at herself. *You're not running without our friends. Mom and Dad were wrong about abandoning the party.*

Becca chuckled. "Yeah, if you can get everything to my house, and you're willing to tear all the pages out of the journals, my dad has a kick-ass scanner that can probably do both your duffel bags in a day or two." Becca raised a hand. "But, you'd have to get them to my house without my dad finding out, and I'd have to find a way to do all the scanning without him knowing, which is fucking hard when he works at home from the basement." She started to walk away toward her first class. "Which is where he keeps the scanner. And that's not even considering the fact I'm locked out of every computer in the house." She shook her head and softened her expression. "I'll see if I can come up with something, but I've got to get to class before the bell. My dad will kick my ass if I get into more trouble."

Jake and Aki nodded their heads. "Same for us," they said together and took off in separate directions.

"We'll find a way," Michelle said, trying as always to reassure her. Then she walked away with a forced smile.

Hope so, Kyrie silently told her friend as she made her own way to her first period English class. *That class sucks,* she fumed as she walked. The focus on specific books she had never read seemed pointless. *You've read Asimov, Clarke, Weis and Hickman, Feynman, and so many more. Why should you fail the class just because you've not read Great Expectations?* She shook her head. Her parents had focused on what they loved and thought she needed to survive alone in the world, not on what modern students needed to pass high school.

Chapter 3

Nalitran easily contained the smile that wanted to surface on his face. The eight board members sitting around the large mahogany table glared at him with contempt and disbelief. Less than ten days had passed since Richard Perez finalized the documents that transferred the seventy-year-old man's thirty-six percent share of Perez University to Nalitran in exchange for over four hundred million dollars' worth of stocks in various public companies. The exchange also conveyed a permanent seat on the private university's board. *And if nothing gets screwed up, in less than a month's time, the shares I gave up will be worth a fraction of what they are today. Best to use them when they have value.* The coordination, planning, and timing of his scheme over the last three years had almost come undone, but the old man had finally succumbed to the manipulations.

"You cannot simply demand complete access to all the university's records," Melissa Rivera—a longtime widow with no intention of remarrying—had a fire in her. She growled, her closed fist pressing into the dark wood surface of the table. "Many of our professors and PhD students have NDAs with their partners and grantors. Your ... stake in the university does not supersede those agreements."

Nalitran allowed a slight upturning of his lip as he gazed at Richard's younger sister. In a world where few physical threats existed, he longed for any expression of conflict he could create. *How can one truly live when all they do is grow fat and lazy watching TV?* The concept of being idle and weak remained antithetical to him. "Miss Rivera, my goal is to understand where the university spends its money and to ensure people are acting in accordance with the bylaws of our organization." He allowed a grin to spread across his face. "Your assumption of an intent of malfeasance on my part is discourteous and will damage our long-term relationship."

"Bullshit, Bishop," Diego Perez blurted out. "You're a damn parasite that somehow managed to convince my uncle to give up his family's legacy so that you can come in and pillage this university." The son of Richard's deceased youngest brother shook his head, sending his curly dark hair bouncing around the forty-year-old's head. "I objected to your acquiring shares when you first started buying out the others. How you ever managed to get that first eighteen percent stake is beyond me. It must have been criminal. Your political ambitions and support for extremists are disgusting. You are disgusting."

Nalitran let a bit of mirth escape his lips as he waited, examining his own thoughts to see if the entity that had once called itself Steven Bishop would even bother with a mental whimper. He had not had the pleasure of tormenting the prior owner of his body for almost a year. After thirty-one years, he still hated using the human's name, and the irritation surfaced in his tone with Diego. "And now I own fifty-four percent, thanks to your uncle's visionary understanding of what I can bring to this organization."

Diego continued to shake his head violently. "He would never willingly sell to you. I'll get to the bottom of that. He would never support you stealing the IP for Nalitran Enterprises." The younger Perez turned to the other board members. "I've heard it on good authority that this man's also been poking around the records of the endowment. Those funds were set up by my great-great-grandfather to ensure this remains a center of higher learning in perpetuity. I'll not let some interloper destroy this institution!"

Nalitran laughed once; *the younger man's anger at losing out on an inheritance gave him joy.* "I hardly want to destroy anything. I want to make this organization even more profitable."

Melissa shot forward in her chair. "Your order cuts all scholarship funding effective immediately. It will force out nearly half of our students come the next term! You are destroying the lives of talented and deserving people, while also derailing the programs they've been researching." She could not remove the pleading from her voice. "There are breakthroughs with battery tech and more efficient solar panels that might never be completed if our students can't continue their work."

Nalitran wondered who might have leaked his intentions with the thirteen-billion-dollar endowment. He knew that getting access to the actual funds would require overcoming a lot of legal hurdles. *But the almost billion dollars in earnings from the fund each year can be diverted more broadly.* "I merely want to review where the spending is currently going and ensure it is being used effectively. I haven't made myself wealthy by being stupid."

"Just a criminal," Diego muttered.

Nalitran turned to the other six board members. "Any of you have opinions?"

A younger woman in a barely feminine-styled suit breathed deeply. "Would they matter?"

He shook his head as he chuckled. Those six people represented the eight percent of the shares held by the venture capitalists and smaller owners. Even combined with Melissa's twenty-four percent and Diego's fourteen, no one could actually block any of his directives. Those six people really could only listen and report back to those they served. Before he had acquired Richard's shares and board seat, his interests had been included in the group those six people represented.

Nalitran stood up. "This meeting is adjourned. I have other duties to attend to."

A fit and attractive woman rose from the line of chairs positioned against the left wall of the room. Everyone knew her as Elsa Donaldson, a thirty-five-year-old brunette who appeared ten years younger, could pass as a model, and seldom left his side. People coveted her and speculated about their relationship. Nalitran did not attempt to dissuade people from the notion. The body of the man he took control over had turned fifty in February, and while his powers slowed his aging, giving him the appearance of a man in his early thirties, anything that made people perceive him as young and virile only strengthened his position.

"I'll signal the cars to pull around the front," his assistant said, typing into her phone. Her tight black skirt and white blouse revealed a body honed by disciplined exercise and training. She grabbed the large leather bag from the nearby chair and slipped it over her shoulder as the phone vibrated. "They are coming around now," she said coldly after glancing at the screen.

Nalitran nodded to the woman, knowing Yrginda, a dolunar warrior, looked out through those deep brown eyes. The being once known as Elsa had not existed for nearly a decade, her mind consumed entirely by a brutal killer.

"We will protect this university," Diego challenged.

Nalitran did not bother acknowledging the statement. In a month's time, the country would have far greater concerns, and he would leverage the chaos to grow his wealth and power. He strode toward the large oak doors that led to the expansive open space outside the boardroom. The lush carpeting and wood-paneled walls made the two-story atrium feel dated, as it failed to actually blend a modern glass ceiling with a sense of institutional power.

Two muscular men in tailored suits stepped forward, moving from their positions, one near the elevators and the other near the emergency stairs. Their eyes reflected the cold and humorless detachment Nalitran expected of his Bound bodyguards. They stopped in the middle of the open area and waited, their attention focused on their surroundings, ever in search of a threat.

Nalitran kept his own mind open, and he knew that aside from the pair of secretaries sitting at the desk next to the bank of elevators, and the board members who had remained seated in the boardroom, a dozen other people occupied the executive offices on the other side of the floor. He wondered what those people might do if he decided to throw someone through a window. If the impact against the safety glass didn't kill them, the five-story fall definitely would. *Thirty-one years in this form only makes my desire to hunt stronger.* He sighed, knowing intellect overrode instinct, but he still longed for the simple pleasures of stalking prey animals. *And humans are definitely prey.*

The two bodyguards turned and led the way to the elevators. They pressed the call button and waited silently. The secretaries made a concerted effort to focus on their computer screens, pretending to be too engrossed in something critical to even notice the four people leaving. The doors of the nearest elevator opened, and the two guards examined the space before placing their hands on the doors. They made room to allow Nalitran and Yrginda to enter before following them inside.

Yrginda's phone vibrated as the elevator descended. "A crowd is gathered at the front doors." Yrginda looked at Nalitran. "It appears perhaps a hundred students and the press."

Nalitran shook his head. "That would have taken advanced planning. Melissa and Diego certainly knew about the plans ahead of this meeting."

"I will find the leak and deal with it."

"Find it, but perhaps we can use the traitor to our advantage." Nalitran preferred the certainty of the Bound, but he could not rely upon them for everything. Greed and threats formed the basis of his wider organizations, but key components of his power-base also required mental manipulations. *I will find out what the traitors know and bend them to my command.*

The doors opened, and he followed the two bodyguards out into the main lobby of the Perez University headquarters. Busts, paintings, and an extensive collection of Hispanic artifacts filled the space. He respected their adherence to preserving their culture. He had a similar desire to rebuild the grandeur of the Dolunar Empire on planet Earth.

Nalitran followed the two bodyguards through the outer glass doors to stand in the wide-open area at the top of the concrete steps in front of the building. He scanned through the crowd of people who milled about, occupying the circle drive and covering the steps. At least a dozen signs written with large markers on white cardboard professed different demands. Mostly the themes centered around him leaving the school. Several used profanities and he smiled, intrigued by the hints of violence.

The sounds of the general conversations shifted to an angry shout as the crowd realized he had exited the building. "Leave the school alone! Make your profits elsewhere!" Someone threw a soda cup at the first of his three black SUVs, which could not approach the steps because of the people. He expected his six Bound soldiers in the three vehicles to execute a measured response.

Hostility radiated from many of the people present, but he doubted he faced any real danger. However, the sheer number of people would confuse and obscure his awareness of any minds that might resort to homicide. Instinct caused him to draw more energy into his body in the event he needed to react quickly.

Three men with professional video cameras on their shoulders, as well as another pair of men and a woman with microphones, moved from the top of the steps onto the landing in front of the doors. The six people formed a wall blocking his path.

"Mr. Bishop," the woman shouted over the sound of the crowd's chanting. "Channel Eight News. Word has spread that you froze all student funding and scholarships. How does this fit into your political goals?"

Nalitran motioned for his two bodyguards to step back. He trusted Yrginda to keep alert for threats he might not notice. A student just behind the reporters shouted for everyone to be silent. After a moment, the chanting slowed to a quiet murmur.

Nalitran smiled brightly and released a trickle of power from his mind. The complex pattern of the energy he emitted put the minds of the humans near him into a slight trance, making those with a weak will susceptible to suggestion. It lacked the full mind control he used for precise manipulation, but the less intrusive modifications had the benefit of being much faster, if less effective. "I must say, I'm surprised to see so many people gathered here simply because I attended my first board meeting."

"Sources have reported—" The reporter stumbled over her initial words as Nalitran increased the mental interference, but she managed to continue her questioning. "That you are cutting all the funding for scholarships and students who have financial needs. The local community benefits greatly from the student population. If they cannot afford to attend school, the impact on their lives, as well as those of the locals, will be greatly impacted. Is this an indication that you plan to only cater to the wealthy?"

A rumble of discontent spread through the crowd despite his mental attempts at quieting them. Nalitran felt his heart race and wished his upper limbs once again ended with a sharp claw. His voice became sweet and melodic. "It is nice to see so many people interested in Perez University." Nalitran noticed three of his men get out of the SUVs and take position around the vehicles. Their physical presence disturbing enough that the students closest to the men retreated deeper into the crowd. *They are having my fun,* he mused.

He shifted his attention to the three cameras and forced a calm expression to his face. "I can assure everyone that the board is taking a measured approach to improving the university with the goal of ensuring it remains a pillar of the community."

"The Campus Chronicle," a man in a tan sports coat said, pushing his microphone forward. The scowl of his companion carrying the video camera dispelled any idea of impartiality in their reporting. "Your disdain for those who don't have financial means is well established. We are aware of your hostile takeover of the board, and word on the street is all the research data is already being extracted and funneled into your other businesses. Do you deny the intent to steal the work of the students?"

Melissa and Diego played their hand too quickly. They won't have anything left. Nalitran's tongue subtly moistened his lips. "You should be careful about reporting unsubstantiated rumors. You may find yourself liable for defamation."

"Do you deny it?" demanded the female reporter.

"We know your politics!" shouted someone in the crowd. "You're a bigot and scavenge anything good from successful companies to make yourself rich!" The crowd shouted their agreement with the vocal woman, who in turn shouted louder. "You're just here to take away our scholarships to enrich yourself! Stop your hate! Do better!"

Nalitran tilted his head and narrowed his attention to the blonde woman in shorts and a tank top as the crowd repeated the mantra of 'do better!' He felt the contempt from her even with the mental energy of the crowd. "I do better than you every day. You think you can ever compete with me?"

The crowd grew hostile and shouted incoherently. He released energy, urging silence, and the volume of the chanting immediately dropped. He turned back to the cameras. "I'm not here to provide socialism to the undeserving. I want strong rule of law, not amnesty for wanton criminals and useless drains on society that lack the ability to pull themselves out of poverty honestly. If you can't be bothered to put in the effort—or are just too incompetent to find a better way to make money—then you should be forced to do the jobs that align to your limited skills and not expect those with more wisdom to simply hand out money without proof there is value in doing so. Giving things to the weak takes away from the blue-collar workers of this country. I support those not afraid to get their hands dirty."

Nalitran looked out at those gathered around him. *These vermin think they're in control of me.* He focused on a pink-faced white woman with bleached hair and brown eyebrows. The pantsuit she wore looked new, as though she needed to impress those around her with the expenditure of money. "If things are allowed to progress as they are, the very foundations of this great country will be rocked and fragmented. And starting by fixing this institution is within my power. It is not too much to demand that those getting benefits first demonstrate the value of the benefits they beg for. No one should be given things they don't earn themselves."

He paused, and a dozen people started shouting questions and screaming at him.

"Mr. Bishop," the last of the three reporters said firmly. "You grew up below the poverty line. Your fortune is quite recent. Have you no empathy for those struggling to find opportunities? You appear to be expecting the students to personally provide you with the results of their work in exchange for just receiving an education."

"I grew up poor, but that was a result of my parents not having a strong work ethic. It was a moral lesson for me. It showed how easy it was for someone to be a burden on society. I never used their failure as an excuse and turned the nothing I was raised with into a fortune. I made my own opportunities because I'm smart and will put in an honest day of work. I will not give benefits to the undeserving while hardworking Americans are held back." *And I won't hesitate to act. These meat puppets will feed my machine.*

"By winning money in Vegas," shouted the antagonistic woman.

Nalitran kept his gaze on the reporter and the camera. "I had the wherewithal to see an opportunity, and in a handful of years, turned a small windfall into a fortune. That is what I bring, the ability to create value. This university will prosper because of my insistence on standards. And that will bring wealth to the locals."

Yrginda tapped his shoulder as the reporters shouted more questions. Nalitran looked down at his splayed fingers and forced himself to relax. He smiled again to the cameras and nodded his acknowledgement to his general. The crowd had sparked an instinct for combat that he could not satisfy. "You will have to excuse me," he said while pushing more energy into the command for silence. "I'm already late for a meeting." He ignored the subdued questions and pushed forward through the crowd toward the SUVs. The power he radiated caused those nearest to retreat from his presence, giving him a clear path to the vehicles and his waiting men.

Yrginda climbed into the back of the second SUV and slid to the left side. Nalitran entered next, with one of the large guards closing the door behind him. The other men crammed themselves into the first and third SUVs. Shortly after the doors closed, all three vehicles accelerated out of the circle drive, the gathered people cowed into retreat.

Nalitran ignored the driver in the front seat; that mind had long ago been broken, and he turned to his general. The blonde's expression shifted and no longer held even the slightest trace of welcome or warmth. "I want the leak found."

"It will be done, Warlord."

Nalitran shifted his position and resisted the desire to cross his arms. "The university issue can wait. I want the update on the girl. All the reports so far indicate her powers and mental acuity are far beyond what is expected. Where is the update from Arkansas?"

Yrginda finished typing a message on her phone and set it beside her. "Yes." She pulled a small tablet from her shoulder bag and unlocked it with a long password. "We have eyes on her house. The three Bound are ready to intervene on your orders."

Nalitran could tell by her tone that she did not expect the order to come. "What of Solberg?"

"Lars avoided the capture team last week and went into hiding, but we have monitors set up in anticipation of him going to Olathe. There are three capture teams ready. They have no context, other than to grab the lawyer and deliver him to a certain location. They are outsourced and not tied back to your organizations."

Nalitran had always limited his criminal empire's awareness of his true agenda, and trusted only a few at the top to perform specific tasks without knowledge of the greater plan. Until three weeks ago, the girl had not been a factor. With the vast majority of his Bound already allocated to Project Kvotar, and Michael Rodgers' public failure, he could not even utilize members of his criminal empire to fill in a simple gap in coverage to kidnap a fat lawyer.

Nalitran kept his rage out of his voice. "The farm in Arkansas. I want the detailed report."

Yrginda pulled up a document on the tablet with photos and handed the device to Nalitran. "The site is now fully secured, though the energy fluctuations are severe. It has grown more unstable. I'm not sure how long ago the changes might have begun, as Awan and the others had not reported the anomalies."

"The girl," he emphasized, "is my concern. Any lingering issues at the site can't be addressed immediately anyway."

The woman nodded. "Several blood pools around the house were found, as well as evidence of gunfire. However, none of the bodies or weapons remained. We assume they dumped the evidence in the woods. The veil is so thin there that all the vegetation is growing at least seventy-five times faster than what would be a normal rate. Even in the week it took before we could get someone out there to examine the site, the path to the circle had become overgrown, and sapling trees filled in the gap." Yrginda continued without emotion. "Someone took the vehicle left by the Bound, which you confirmed had both died by checking their stones. Awan Brown was not found."

Nalitran looked over the pictures of the house Steven Bishop's cousin owned. *Awan knows the truth.* Awan had seen Nalitran pass between the worlds and take over the body and mind of his cousin thirty-one years ago. *And now that old bastard is missing.* Nalitran shook his head. "Awan's got one eye and one hand. He should not be hard to track down. The girl and her friends did not appear to have the other vehicle when the police aided them on the farm in Kansas, so Awan is the only one who could have taken it." He knew no GPS trackers existed in any of the vehicles tied to his activities with the

Bound. The risk of someone tracking their movements outweighed any potential benefits.

He stopped scrolling at a picture of the front yard showing a seven-inch-deep depression in the ground with sharp lines separating the section from the surrounding dirt. "This is the report on the hole?" He scanned down the screen. "The note here says there was blood in this crushed section of the yard." He turned the image toward Yrginda, showing the flattened branches and grass that littered the bottom of the hole. "This looks to confirm it was done with a strong gravity field."

"Yes, Warlord. Based on the report, that is my belief as well. The girl likely crushed one of the Bound. The other may have been hit with a barrage of small stones and gravel. The outside wall of the house had hundreds embedded in the side, but there is a photo that appears to show a human shadow on the house without damage."

Nalitran shifted to the next couple of photos and nodded his head. "That shows a remarkable amount of control and power. We don't know the range at which she acted, though she did eliminate two armed and powerful Bound by herself." He continued to the photos of the battle at the farm in Kansas where Michael Rodgers had fought with Dennis Hurlington's men. The police tape and official case markings evident on each image allowed him to know the source of the materials. "She outsmarted Michael and Dennis both. The police report doesn't say it, but it's obvious one of them convinced Hurlington to send men to the farm before the black girl summoned the police to clean things up."

"This Kyrie is a risk," Yrginda stated without emotion. "Killing a Bound is hard, but taking one captive you don't control is much harder. Rodgers had found no details of where her stone might be. She could have buried it anywhere on that mountain where her parents concealed her." Yrginda exhaled. "With everything else going on, it would be better to eliminate her and all her friends that were there. Project Kvotar is still vulnerable."

Nalitran shook his head. "I already allowed you to eliminate the old woman in Colorado and the girl that appeared to no longer have value, but I want the Landvik girl alive. I allowed Michael to punish himself for his failings sixteen years ago. It amused me, and I always assumed the girl was already dead. The fact that she lived is surprising. The fact that she is mentally intact demands we acquire her." He flipped back to the image of the depression in the hard ground. "Time in body grows our powers, but young minds are more plastic than older ones, and they gain power faster. I need to understand how she survived where all other prior children failed."

Yrginda's tone remained hard. "Without her binding stone, we will always be fighting her. Keeping her alive in confinement will be difficult."

Nalitran flipped through more reports on the tablet. "None of the stones Michael carried were recovered at the farm by the police. However, his pants were ripped open, and the belt he was so proud of ripped to shreds." He held up the tablet for Yrginda to see the photo. "That tells me she knows the power the stones contain. It also implies Michael's stones are still on the farm. I would assume she used them to turn Michael's two Bound against mine based on the police report of who killed who."

Yrginda's face grew harder. "We've destroyed all but three of the Bound Michael controlled. Those three have found a way to hide themselves."

Nalitran stared at a police photo showing the girl's limited injuries despite the blood covering her clothing. *The eyes give her away. They know too much.* He looked up at his general. "She has her own stone close to her." He knew that if a stone constrained him, he would never allow it out of his own sight. *Fortunately, that was not part of my transition.* His tone grew sharper. "We can send someone to search the farm Michael was using, but regardless, her weakness is her friends. We take them hostage and she'll comply."

"Only to a point," Yrginda challenged. "Push someone too far, and even friendship won't be enough. Plus, how close can any of them be after only three weeks of knowing each other? She might just be using them to expose us. If I was her, I would not risk myself for lesser beings." The woman beside him sighed. "I worry that the benefits are not worth the risk."

"She risked herself to get the Bruce girl back."

Yrginda offered a slight shrug. "Or used it as a means of eliminating a known threat. Rodgers appeared to be known to her because he had followed up so many times with her grandmother. The man's kidnapping of the Bruce girl was brash and not well thought out." The woman crossed her arms. "I'm assuming her parents told her about the site in Arkansas, which allowed her to find Awan as a result. Her parents should not have known about the Bound, as we know with certainty that Awan did not tell them anything about your activities. Which means it shows the girl's resilience and adaptability at overcoming unknown threats. It makes her more of a liability, not an asset."

He handed the tablet back with a frown. Nalitran knew his general's opinions had merit. He always allowed his general to challenge him, but only to a certain point. *I need the girl.* "This body I'm using is getting older. I've told you multiple times that I need a younger replacement. I don't want to wait decades again to rebuild the mental pathways of an older mind." He nodded his head towards the tablet in Yrginda's hands. "I need to repeat the process she went through with a male child in the next year or so to allow the body and mind years to mature over a decade or two. It needs to be ready for me to transition into before this body is no longer virile enough to demand respect. As it is, best case, this body will be more than seventy by that time."

Yrginda nodded her head slowly, but she offered a subtle resistance to his statement. "Our powers will allow us to age slower. You will still be strong even forty years from now."

Nalitran shook his head. "I'm not willing to take the risk. We have to consider the long term. To your point, once we understand how she survived, if we don't have her stone, we destroy her."

Yrginda locked the tablet and put it back into the bag at her side. "She could just be an aberration. We've tried more than a few times to bind younger people so that we could place them in appropriate positions in society. As you know, anyone under fifteen tended to fail, even as their powers grew at accelerated rates." Her tone became slightly conciliatory. "However, based on her existence, last week, I had them bind four infants at the northern site."

Nalitran scoffed and dismissed the statement with a wave of his hand. "I've already seen those reports. It was a failure. Two are already dead, and the other two are deteriorating fast." His voice turned into a growl. "Don't lecture me. I know the statistics better than you. Only one child under ten in the last twenty years survived more than five years, and that one was so mentally damaged I destroyed it." He forced himself to regain his composure. "I cannot just assume she is an anomaly. I need to be certain. I need to understand the conditions that existed to allow this Kyrie to thrive." He sighed. "It has taken decades for me to amass this fortune and power in this backwards world. I do not want to shift to a new body and spend years waiting for my power to return."

Yrginda nodded her head. "I know the concerns, Warlord, but I don't believe the Bound we have available would be successful in maintaining control of her, and trying to capture her will reveal our hand. Can we at least wait until after Project Kvotar is complete?"

Nalitran considered Yrginda's words for a moment. "The estimates I've seen show that having a high enough percentage of targets in the correct place during a single day is still a month out. Once the assassinations are complete, it will free up our operatives and frame Hurlington at the same time. But a lot can happen to the girl in that time. I don't want Hurlington to kill her or for her to find some new place to hide." He turned his head to look out the window of the SUV and frowned at the industrial park on his right. He belonged in a jungle world, not a world of humans. "Once I conquer these pathetic humans, I can't allow any perception of weakness to undermine my eventual rule. Changing into a weak body will incite uprisings like the corvlians achieved when two of my generals failed to hold their cities. The bastards thought they would destroy me, banishing my essence to the void, but little did they know I would thrive in this world with powers they never knew existed." He refrained from mentioning his pleasure at ripping people across the divide and binding them as his slaves. Yrginda might support him, but he did not want to antagonize his enslaved general any more than necessary.

"What would you have me do?"

Nalitran returned his attention to Yrginda. "First, keep a tighter watch on her. Her involvement with the police has left scrutiny on her, and you are correct, if we attempted to capture her, we'd have to pull too many people out of position. She's too powerful for just three of Bound." Nalitran shifted in his seat. "Second, we need to finalize Michael's replacement. I allowed the man a lot over control of our shadow operations. Only a couple people have any idea of what is going on, but I'm not sure they are capable of running the org. We need to preserve secrecy while continuing to leverage the skills and money." He turned back to the darkly tinted window. "Third—"

Yrginda's phone vibrated. She picked it up, unlocked it, and read the message. "You may not have to wait. It seems Albert Denman has called an emergency board meeting. He landed in Vegas two hours ago and will attend dinner with his board and senior leaders this evening, then meet with them in the offices first thing in the morning." She looked up. "The informant suggests he might be preparing to hand control over to Sozar."

Nalitran leaned forward. "I'm assuming our operative is prepared?"

Yrginda nodded her head. "The analysts have already reviewed the models before informing me. There are uncertainties, but based on the expected positions of all of our targets, they believe we can eliminate the leadership of nine out of the ten critical companies. They expect forty percent of our secondary targets are also within striking distance before noon tomorrow." She pulled up a secure site on her phone and entered a long pass phrase. She then navigated through the menus to pull up a heatmap with multiple possibilities. After studying the image, she returned her attention to Nalitran. "The analysts have suggested that we would likely be able to eliminate an additional fifteen percent of the secondary and tertiary targets within two weeks, though we would be unlikely to get Senator Johnson in the near term."

Nalitran ran the scenarios through his own mental model. Albert Denman had the best security of those he needed to eliminate, and he knew that even killing forty percent of the other business and government leaders represented a significant success for such a large-scale operation. "Order the strikes." *The markets will crash and my short positions will pay off. Then, I will take over the companies from the successors of the dead.*

"Yes, Warlord."

Nalitran wet his lips and smiled. "Also, cancel our flight out tonight. Contact Melissa and Diego. Tell them to set up another press conference for first thing tomorrow. Tell them that we will acquiesce in the canceling of the scholarships and not propose it again, on the condition they will agree to join the press conference that endorses my leadership of the university."

Yrginda raised an eyebrow.

"Move the scheduled attack on me to the university grounds during the conference. We'll eliminate the strongest resistance on the board while giving me cover for execution day."

"Consider it done," she said while typing a message into the phone.

Chapter 4

Kyrie survived her first period English class without the teacher calling on her. Since the public news of the shoot-out, her teachers had almost unanimously agreed to simply ignore her, seemingly uncomfortable with the topic, and the widely shared rumors of her improprieties, most of which were untrue. When her aunt first enrolled her, the teachers picked on her to prove she should not have joined the classes six weeks before the end of school. Now they never called on her and actively avoided meeting her gaze. This even extended to her second period algebra class, where Miss Pelni had recognized her advanced mathematical skills, but now the middle-aged woman radiated discomfort.

Kyrie's physical conditioning allowed her to breeze through third period gym, though the other students picked her last when they divided into teams. Her stomach growled through government, drawing the attention of the others in the room. After the tedious class, she joined Aki for lunch, but with Aki's other friend group present, they avoided discussing anything related to their shared secrets. Instead, Aki's group focused on how they could address global warming with sufficient funding, while the group continued to ask Aki if she felt okay.

Fifth period art allowed her to meet up with Michelle. The two of them looked at the empty seat that Tina Bruce once occupied. Kyrie knew that Tina had been a close friend of Michelle, but the other girl had immediately grown jealous of Michelle's attention to Kyrie. The competition between them left Tina absent when Kyrie had no choice but to reveal her powers to the others in order to protect them, and subsequently, the seventeen-year-old missed out on their trip to Arkansas. As the only one of their group left in Olathe, Michael Rodgers kidnapped her to use as bait to lure Kyrie into a trap. The trauma broke Tina mentally.

"Have you heard anything?" Kyrie asked, knowing Michelle would understand her question.

Michelle slipped her right arm out of her sling and rotated her shoulder. "Tina's mom spoke with mine the other day. Tina keeps having panic attacks and definitely won't be coming back to school this year. She spends at least an hour a day with a therapist."

Mrs. Stine, the art teacher, approached from the rear, and the young teacher leaned forward to put her head between the two of them. "Michelle, I don't want you to push too hard if your shoulder is troubling you. Perhaps scale back the size of the painting."

Michelle picked up a tube of acrylic paint and squeezed out a small amount of burnt umber. "I promise not to overdo it, but I have a vision in my head that I want to finish."

"Very well, but I won't have your parents complaining that I allowed you to hurt yourself." Mrs. Stine looked at Kyrie's large pencil drawing of a jungle scene. "Don't get bogged down too much in the background details. You only have two and a half weeks to finish, and this is a thirty-six-inch-wide sheet of paper."

"Yes, Ma'am. I planned to shift my focus to the main subject today." Kyrie glanced at her sketchbook sitting next to the easel. "I roughed out her face overnight."

Mrs. Stine picked up the sketch and examined it. "Very good representation of the fur on her head. I'm looking forward to seeing the final image." She then moved on to the next student, offering some advice on blending their colored pencils.

"I'm worried," Kyrie whispered to Michelle. "I can't protect any of you when you're all scattered across town."

Michelle blended a small amount of white into the burnt umber on her paint palette. "DMs love it when the players split the party. Easy to TPK." Michelle chuckled. "Total party kill."

Kyrie nodded her understanding of the acronym, not bothering to remind Michelle she already knew the meaning. "That's exactly what I want to avoid."

"Hey, same here, considering I'd be on the receiving end of that." Michelle sighed. "But my parents are so pissed with me. I won't be free of this for a long time, if ever. They don't even give me sympathy for getting shot. Just more shit."

"If I found a way for us to run away, would you come?" *Please say yes,* she internalized without allowing any power to escape her mind.

Michelle turned away from her painting and smiled. "With you, sure. My parents have always favored my younger brother, and the golden child's only gotten worse." She grew somber. "But I don't think the others would be so easy with the idea. Jake's a mama's boy, Aki can't break free of the pressure of her Japanese parents, and Becca is all her father has left since her mom split years ago. I don't know that any of them would easily leave home."

Their lives are in danger, yet they are too afraid to leave? She struggled with the idea, but then recalled her own failing. *You didn't run off when you were supposed to,* she chastised herself. *None of them would be in danger if you had done as you were told.* The pain of knowing she had failed her mother left a hollowness in her chest. However, the memory of her mother lying dead on the mountainside now chilled her mostly because her mental image kept focusing on the binding stone set in the brooch her mother always wore. *Had the sheriff not given it to us, Nalitran's men would have found it, and they would have made us a slave already.* She bit her lip as she stared at the floor. *Mom, you should have told us. We could have been lost, a slave to Nalitran's control, because of you and Dad keeping secrets.*

"You okay?" Michelle asked.

Kyrie swallowed the dread. *Focus,* she silently yelled at herself. She turned her head back to Michelle. "They'll stay even considering everything?"

Michelle only nodded her head. Kyrie turned to her drawing to hide the frown that made its way to her face. She had failed her human mother and put her friends at risk; perhaps she could at least do her other mother justice by capturing the warmth of her eyes.

Physics and history ended her day, and Kyrie made her way to the large open area near the exits to wait for the others to join her. She hoped Sam would dawdle so that she could have more time with her friends. Michelle joined her with another hug before the others arrived.

"I caught Becca in the hall," Michelle said. "She's close to negotiating a deal with someone to buy a replacement phone for herself." Michelle forced a laugh. "I can't believe I've gone almost two weeks without one."

Kyrie did not respond to Michelle. She sensed Jessica and John approaching, and she turned to place herself slightly in front of Michelle. The blonde in front of her shifted her smile into an expression of concern.

"I'm so sorry for your loss," Jessica said, her phone in her hand.

Kyrie's eyes narrowed because of the dishonesty she sensed. From her first day at school, Jessica had taken a dislike of her and searched for any opportunity to cause trouble. Uncertain whether Jessica held up her phone to look at something on the screen, or to record the conversation, Kyrie held her tongue.

Michelle moved forward to stand even with Kyrie. "Jessica, no one wants to hear your claims of pity. Just leave us alone."

Jessica's lips curled slightly at Michelle. "Rich of you to think I'm not good enough for the likes of you." The blonde shrugged. "But I'm not here to pick a fight. I just thought to offer my condolences on Tina." Kyrie felt the malice in the other girl and saw the pleasure in her eyes. "Seems your home schooled freak here messed Tina up so bad that she killed her parents and herself last night. Cut their throats." Jessica drew a single finger across her neck and then lowered her chin to look sad.

Kyrie drew in power and searched Jessica's mind, but she found only pleasure and not deceit.

Michelle's mouth dropped. "How dare you say such things!"

Jessica and her boyfriend grinned, then Jessica turned her phone so Michelle could see the news headline.

Kyrie felt her skin tingle as the temperature in the area dropped due to her energy draw. "I suggest you leave." The gravel in her voice drew John a step forward, but Kyrie radiated pure anger and violence, and the larger teen stopped. *Punch the wall,* she directed at him. The muscled teenager's face dropped, but he did not move.

Becca, Aki, and Jake joined them. "What's happening?" Becca asked, her tone less questioning and more threatening.

Jessica sneered. "We were just expressing our condolences. Not our fault Tina killed her parents and then herself." Jessica turned abruptly and walked away.

Punch the wall, Kyrie angrily sent again to John.

John ran at the cinder block wall and smashed his fist into the painted surface. He cried out in pain, stumbled back, and then chased after Jessica, cradling his fist against his gut.

That worked! She did not know if she should feel glee at confirming she could control others or feel regret for making someone possibly break their hand.

"What the fuck?" Becca exclaimed at the display. She shook her head as John started arguing with Jessica. Becca turned back to the others, confusion still on her face. Then she shifted her expression. "What was that about Tina?"

Kyrie pulled herself back from John's mind as he disappeared into the crowd of other students and then shifted her attention to Michelle and the tears that rolled down her friend's cheek. To her three other friends, she provided the details. "Jessica had a news article on her phone that said Tina killed her parents and herself. I don't think she was lying."

"Tina wouldn't do that," Michelle demanded, her eyes staring at the floor. "I know the kidnapping had her panicked, but she'd never kill herself, or anyone else."

"Hey losers," Mike Windall called out as he and Sam emerged from the dwindling group of students eager to get off the premises on a Friday afternoon. "Sam has to walk Kyrie to her prison cell, which is ... what?"

"Give me your phone, asshole," Michelle demanded.

"Touch me and I'll tell mom! You're not supposed to hang out with her at all."

Kyrie resisted the urge to force Mike to comply. *Someone might realize.*

"Tina might be dead," Jake said to Michelle's younger brother. "She wants to confirm it on your phone."

Sam swallowed. "Shit, that's messed up."

Mike unlocked his phone and handed it to his older sister. Sam pulled out his own phone and mirrored Michelle's rapid query of the news. More tears streamed down Michelle's face as she read through the article. Becca grabbed the phone from her and quickly scanned the report.

Becca shook her head. "There's not a lot of detail, but I can't see Tina cutting her parents' throats, even in their sleep. She hated the sight of blood."

Jake held Aki close as he scanned the room for threats.

This is our fault. Kyrie extended her senses. The emotional energy from all the other teenagers nearby crashed into her, and while it felt like drowning in a turbulent mountain river, she sensed no immediate threats. She took the phone from Becca and handed it back to Mike. "Will the two of you at least let us talk for a while on the way home? We're not asking for much, but someone we all knew is dead." She waited for their answer, only planning to connect to their minds if they put up a resistance.

Aki shifted uncomfortably under Jake's arm as Becca rested her own hand on Michelle's good shoulder.

"Yeah," Mike and Sam said together. Mike continued. "This is bigger than petty issues." He shook his head. "Shit. I can't believe it."

Kyrie nodded her thanks, combined with relief that she did not have to force Sam and Mike. *You can't manipulate people just because. You'll slip and do it to your friends.* She swallowed as her heart raced from the implication of what she might do if left unchecked. She shifted her backpack on her shoulder. "Let's go. We'll be the last ones here soon." She started walking toward the exits, and everyone fell in behind her, with Sam and Mike trailing at a respectable distance.

Once they left the school grounds, Kyrie stopped and turned to face her four friends. "I'm so sorry. I ..."

"Stop," Becca demanded. "I agree, Tina didn't do it, regardless of what that news report said. Just like I don't believe those church assholes the police arrested supposedly hanged themselves." She shook her head. "Total bullshit. There are at least some police involved, and they could have covered things up with Tina as well."

"Or one of the people after us did it and framed Tina," Jake said.

Aki's voice rose. "That means they are coming for us."

Becca nodded.

Ask. Kyrie barely raised her voice above a whisper. "If I can find a way to get us out of here, will all of you come with me?" *Please say yes.*

Michelle wiped the tears from her face and nodded her head. "I will. I want to live, and I don't give a shit about what my parents want."

Becca shifted uneasily; her fear was no longer hidden behind a veil of confidence. "How do you plan to do that? We can't just run off into the woods down the street and camp out. We try to drive away in Michelle's car again and the cops will be on us in minutes." She shook her head. "They have cameras mounted in police cars that read every license plate they drive past. We only managed to get to Arkansas and back because no one was looking for us."

"School's not over," Aki added. "If I don't pass, I'd have to do my junior year over again. My future would be ruined."

Being dead will ruin it as well, Kyrie wanted to scream, but she held back. "Lars said he would come for me. I haven't spoken to him in a few days, but I can call and see if he can help us. Although he said I can't get my money until I'm eighteen, perhaps there's a loophole." She glanced toward Mike and Sam, who stood out of earshot.

"I don't trust that man," Becca growled. She wiped her hands over her hair. "If we were eighteen, we could leave home, and our parents couldn't stop us. But Michelle is the only one that's even seventeen."

"I'm seventeen," Kyrie responded immediately.

"Since when?" Michelle asked.

"Last week. Wednesday." She looked at everyone. "What?"

"You had a birthday and didn't tell us?" Michelle shook her head. "We'd have done something for you."

Kyrie frowned. The others radiated a sense of betrayal and she did not understand why. "I didn't know it was a big deal. It just marks another rotation around the sun. Why does it matter? Except for legal things."

Jake spoke first. "Kyrie, birthdays are a way for your friends to celebrate milestones. Before all this, we had planned to do something for mine in a couple of weeks." His voice dropped as he mumbled the rest. "But my parents said I can't."

"Yeah," Michelle agreed. "Didn't your aunt do anything for you?" She looked at Jake. "We'll still try for something for you," she whispered.

Kyrie shook her head. "I don't think she remembers my birthday." She looked at each of them. "My parents stopped celebrating birthdays after I turned five. They focused on celebrating when I learned something new, not calendar dates."

Becca crossed her arms. "Focus, people. Her birthday's not the issue. None of our parents would allow us to run off, so we need to find a different way to protect ourselves."

"Suggestions?" Aki demanded.

Becca shook her head. "I need time to think."

Kyrie bit her lip. *Find a way.* She took a breath and made a decision. "You've all said we can't do this on our own because the adults will stop us." The others nodded their heads. "What if we get an adult to help?"

"Who?" Becca and Jake asked at the same time.

"Just how do you expect to get their help?" Aki asked.

Kyrie shrugged. "Tell them the truth."

Jake shifted and shook his head. "Not my parents. They'd call our priest to banish you back to hell the moment they learn about the other world. Probably also call the cops to lock you up. Then you'd disappear into some government lab."

Michelle shook her head. "My parents aren't as strict as Jake's, but they'd freak. They'd definitely ban me from ever talking to you again. More than they already have." She glanced at Jake. "Probably call the cops as well. The government would dissect you or watch you through a small window."

Kyrie looked at Aki and Becca.

Aki shook her head. "I don't think my parents would tell anyone, but they would definitely pack me up and disappear." She leaned against Jake. "They prefer not to get involved with things."

Becca shook her head with everyone's attention on her. "I said I need to think about it." She paced before she frowned and threw her hands into the air. "I can't say how he'd react. My dad'd not call the cops, or any priests," she added with a glance at Jake. "However, he'd definitely not take it well."

"The only other person is Lars," Kyrie said.

"I don't trust him," Becca snapped.

Kyrie nodded her head. "I'm not sure I trust him either, but we need help from someone." She noticed Sam and Mike start moving in their direction and changed the topic to something safer. "Everyone needs to spend time working out. I don't know how much fitness I've lost in the last three weeks, but I know I'm not as strong as I was when I ran and trained every day. You all need to start exercising. Run up and down the stairs if that's all you can do."

"You saying I'm fat?" Becca challenged.

Kyrie shook her head. Becca had thicker bones and weighed a little more than Kyrie, but the other girl was not overweight. "No. I'm saying that if you need to run from someone, you need to be in shape to do it. You don't want to get winded and caught because you've not spent the time training."

"We need to get going," Sam said at fifteen feet from them. "If Mom doesn't get an alert that the alarm was turned off and back on, she's going to know I didn't take you home right away."

Becca repositioned her backpack on her shoulder. "Since my dad made me quit my job, he's going to be waiting for me as well." She bit her lip. "I'll think about what you said. I just got to go." She headed off, rushing away.

"We should go too," Jake said. "I'll walk Aki as far as I can, then run home." He smiled. "Get a little exercise."

They're scared. She glanced at Sam, who tapped his foot. *Scared won't stop them from getting killed.* The anguish Michelle felt drew her attention, and she put an arm around Michelle's shoulder. Their paths overlapped almost the entire way to her friend's house. Kyrie would protect her as long as she could.

Sam did as his mother asked, escorted Kyrie home, unlocked the house, turned off the alarm, dropped his backpack in the living room, reset the alarm, and ran out the front door to head back to Mike's house. Kyrie sighed, the smell of grease from breakfast lingered, emanating from the unwashed dishes in the sink. She went to the fridge to grab the chunk of cheddar for a snack. While eating the cheese, she removed her phone and considered Becca's question from the morning that she had dodged. *How does this mind control work? What are the limits and long-term impacts? Brain damage?* Part of her did not like the idea that she might have the power to easily control others. She refused to consider whether she had forced her friends to like her without conscious thought.

She exhaled, pushing the implications from her mind, and unlocked the phone. Her fingers entered Lars' number from memory, but she hesitated in engaging the call. Her parents had trusted their college friend more than any other person. They had given him control of all of their possessions so that they could disappear with her. *But could Nalitran or Hurlington have gotten to him in the last sixteen years? Not even Mom and Dad shared the details of where they had gone with Lars. Could Nalitran have used mind control on him?*

Her own doubts started when Lars advised her to go with Kim instead of running away. Her parents always told her he would come to take her somewhere safe as soon as she called him. *Instead, he dismissed the threat.* She sighed. *But that's because you were stupid and went to Mrs. Conner for help, and she got the cops involved. Lars would have come otherwise.*

"Why didn't I do as I was supposed to?" Tina had never truly liked her, but she never wanted harm to come to one of Michelle's friends. "And I can't let my friends die." She knew if this scenario surfaced in one of her mother's campaigns, her mother would reward her if she used charm or other mind control spells to force her desires. *But would they still even be who they are if you manipulated them? Would they just be NPCs? But what if that's the only way to save them?*

She pressed the green dial button and waited for Lars to answer the phone. The ringing stopped, and she heard a male voice say, "Blue." Kyrie responded. "Five hundred and twenty-nine," doing the math in her head to apply the formula to convert the current day and month into a coded number. She heard someone writing on paper at the other end.

"Sixteen," Lars replied.

Kyrie's shoulders eased. "I need help."

"What's wrong?"

"I believe someone killed Tina, the girl we rescued from the farm. The news report said she killed her parents and then herself, but my friends don't think so, and I agree."

"Are you safe right now?" Lars asked. The phone at the other end picked up the sounds of movement.

"I'm at Kim's," she provided as a non-answer while she instinctively reconfirmed that she could not sense any other people in or near the house. "I need to get my friends out of here and somewhere they can be protected."

Lars did not speak for several moments. "That's not something that will be easy. Look, I was going to call you tomorrow, but this works. I can get us out of the country. We can arrange for new identities, at least until we figure out who is after you." He cleared his throat. "Unless you want to explain the details to me."

Not over the phone. Becca had stressed not revealing things over unsecured devices. *Plus, you need to sense his thoughts to know his motives.* "I can't leave without my friends," she finally said. "They would die without me near them."

"If I don't know the danger, I can't help."

"Not on the phone," Kyrie said aloud.

"Fine." Lars took a moment before continuing. "And I don't disagree with that. Safer when we can make sure no one is listening." He coughed once. "Look, I'm pretty certain I can convince your aunt to let me take you."

Kyrie narrowed her eyes. Kim seemed determined to control her. *Or at least the money.*

"Your aunt is after the trust," Lars said, affirming Kyrie's thought. "I'm a damn good contract attorney. They won't be able to unwind it, not before you turn eighteen. By the way, happy late birthday." When she did not reply, Lars continued. "I've got my own money, and I'm pretty sure I can offer her enough that she'd let me take guardianship of you. I'm hoping her lawyer friend is explaining the chances of success to her, as well as the time and cost involved in fighting the trust. If she understands the chances, that might make her more agreeable. Plus, the threat of a rule eleven sanction is weak at best."

Buy me from her? You're not something to be purchased. "Lars, I don't care about the money, aside from what I might need to deal with this. But I do care about my friends and keeping them alive."

"You've barely known them for three weeks. You're not tied to them. You are free to do what is best for you." He paused. "Someone tried to kill me a week ago. They mistook someone else for me, and I managed to get away, but you almost came close to talking to a corpse." He sighed. "I've been on the move ever since. A client owes me. He agreed to get us both out of the country, on the condition that doing so won't risk the State Department coming after him. If I took, what is it, your four friends—four minors—from their parents, the FBI would get involved, and we'd have a dozen agencies after us. My client won't go for that."

Her voice hardened. "If I leave them, they will be killed. If I stay, I fear someone will attempt to kidnap them like they did with Tina."

"Kyrie—"

"No, Lars. If you truly want to help me, you'll come up with a way I can protect them. Don't use your client; get us out some other way." Her mind went back to the money. "Or pay off their parents to let them come."

"Kyrie, I understand you have grown attached to them, but people move all the time for numerous reasons. Kids are separated from their friends, but they make new ones. I had to do it a couple of times growing up. If you're gone, they should be safe."

Kyrie growled. She wanted to scream, but she held the impulse in check. "They will die. They will be killed if I leave them."

Lars huffed an exasperated sigh, and his voice showed his irritation. "It's not that easy. Getting across international borders takes resources, as does getting a new identity that would hold up while we wait for all this to blow over. Plus, your aunt is a greedy bitch looking for a payday—I can give her that. Your friends' parents, however, won't just trade their children for a bit of cash."

"I'm serious, Lars. I won't leave without my friends."

It sounded as if he dropped into a chair. "Whatever this is, it's deadly serious," he said. "You willing to die for these people you just met? I'd have bowed out of this mess years ago if I didn't care for your parents so much."

"Find a way, Lars." She tried to push command into her voice, but she had no idea if it would work over the phone. She had doubts about it even working consistently with people in front of her.

He remained silent for several moments. "I can make no promises. However, I'll see what I can do. I have some other contacts, but I'm also on the run and trying to avoid being found. I'm limited in what I can achieve."

"If you can't make it work, then give me enough money and I'll find a way myself." She wondered if her aunt's belief that Lars just wanted her money for himself had any merit. *Did he initially do it because our parents asked and now has changed his mind?* "I'll pay you back as soon as I turn eighteen," she offered.

"Kyrie, I don't want your money. I don't have any family to give my own money to. You are the only one left alive in my will." His voice grew hard. "However, my money is tied up in investments. I've moved more to cash over the last week, but that's all still in banks and financial institutions. Physical money is harder to amass without drawing attention. The police always assume you are using it for some criminal enterprise when you have even a few hundred dollars on you, and we'd need a lot more than that. Those kind of withdrawals are tracked."

"What's your point?" She demanded.

"I have a few thousand on me and a few thousand more elsewhere, but that won't make a lasting difference. I can't write you a check, because you'd need a bank account to cash it and a government ID to access it, which I know your aunt has been dragging her feet on getting for you." He sighed. "Kyrie, your best chance to get safely away from this is if you let me take you out of the country. I can get you away next weekend. Perhaps sooner. But I can't see any way that I can manage to get your friends out of the country as well. Heck, do they even want to run away from their families?"

Kyrie's lip curled with anger. "Mom and dad always said you'd come up with the best ways to thwart their D&D campaigns and make things a challenge for them. I'll explain everything to you in person, but you have to find a way to save my friends." She hung up the phone. Her heart raced. *Practice forcing Kim to do your bidding, then get Lars to do what you want.* She closed her eyes, not wanting to resort to the manipulations her parents always rewarded. *If you force your friends to run away, will they forgive you?* She hung her head. *You can't do it, even to save them, because then they are just puppets.*

Chapter 5

Dennis Hurlington sat in the office chair in front of the metal desk bolted to the painted steel wall and brought the computer back to life. The forced air blowing from the vents in the metal ceiling smelled of machine oil, but years of exposure had removed his ability to notice it. After entering his user ID and password, the lock screen disappeared, showing the existing video feed of a man sitting in a large living room filled with decorative trim, statues, and paintings. The warm natural glow of the sunset illuminating the room curled Dennis' lips, even though he could not see the wall of windows off to the other man's left.

"Your Holiness," the brown-haired man in the video said, bowing his head in deference. "I'll join you in the bunker after my meetings are complete."

"Leonard, I saw the reports of the Bruce family," Dennis demanded, his frustration pushing aside the annoyance of seeing the thirty-six-year-old sitting in his lavish living room.

Leonard nodded reflexively. "Yes. And the therapist appears to have died in an unrelated house fire ... that also consumed all of her records." The younger man lifted a coffee cup and sipped from the steaming mug. "As far as I've been able to see from the reports we have access to, the police have not connected the two events. But Bishop is definitely covering up."

Dennis leaned forward. "It means Satan is preparing to act. He's eliminating witnesses, including killing the last of the Epsilon cell while they were incarcerated."

Leonard nodded his head slowly. "Bishop has always cleaned up witnesses. However, I agree, there are other factors at play that indicate something significant is underway." Leonard set the mug down and leaned toward the camera. "The Heth Cell is fairly certain they know where at least three of Bishop's demons are staying in Olathe. Unfortunately, despite my attempts, our informants on the inside remain reluctant to share too many details. Michael Rodgers' death has shaken up Bishop's criminal organization, and that appears to have generated more internal scrutiny. They're looking for spies and might have taken out Sarah, the woman who handled Rodgers' travel arrangements." He added for clarity. "However, I am certain there is continued interest in the Landvik girl and her friends. The three demons in Olathe are likely there to clean up the mess and collect the girl. The last indication remains that they still want her alive."

Dennis mulled over the confirmation of his suspicions.

"However," Leonard continued, "even though I spent the entire afternoon probing, we still have no additional details on the vast majority of his other demons. They've simply gone dark over the last five months and have remained so. And that doesn't count the hundreds of others we suspect he's created but never had any intel on. Bishop is planning something, but what ..." He shrugged. "We just don't know."

"We need to eliminate the girl," Dennis felt the voice of God in his mind agree with the statement. "If the Devil wants her for some reason, we can't let her fall into his hands."

"Your Holiness," Leonard said patiently, "we know Rodgers had been looking for her for years, but why?" The younger man hesitated. "Could Satan have failed to bind her to him? We know she has power, and I hate to admit it, but she used us to fight Rodgers and his demons. The details are fuzzy, but the reports imply that some of Rodgers' own demons turned against him and killed him. Bishop's people are doing a good job of attributing Rodgers and his demons to the Church, making it seem as if we had an internal conflict, but we know that is a lie." Leonard shrugged. "Could it have been her doing? Did she free them from Satan's control?"

"She must die," Dennis repeated, even more certain of God's conviction.

Leonard nodded his head. "I understand. However, between the demons and the police, we lost both Zeta and Epsilon cells ... thankfully Heth was on the west coast at the time." The unspoken implication that they could have lost a third cell hung in the air.

"What is your point?" Dennis asked. Leonard had earned the right to question him from a decade of service, but the voice in Dennis' head wanted the Devil to suffer, and anything that thwarted the Devil's plans always seemed the correct choice.

"My concern is that this girl first took out the Zayin cell by herself. She didn't kill them, but they are no longer combat ready, and perhaps they will never be again. We lost Zeta and Epsilon at the farm. Heth is the only combat cell we have left that we can count on. Omega and Gimel cells are reluctant to kill, Taw is too new, and everyone else is either spread out, focused on identity theft to generate funding, or is just there to spread God's message." He pushed his coffee cup further away and out of frame. "You know that I would sacrifice myself to return Satan to hell, but we don't want to continue to crash the Church against the rocks if there is a better way."

Dennis frowned. "Leonard, I know the challenges." He looked around the underground room, with rust showing through the peeling paint on the metal walls. "I've been trapped here for years because Satan continues to hunt me. We are on a precipice; ruin lies on all sides. If the Devil wants this girl, we cannot risk allowing her to fall into his hands."

"Even though she seems to be fighting him?" Leonard crossed his arms. "We've always understood each battle before joining the fight. We don't know why Bishop has not sent more of his demons after her. It's been two weeks, and they have neither captured nor killed her. Perhaps the Bruce girl is the start of the cleanup, but if the Landvik girl is an angel sent to help—"

"No." Dennis clenched his hands and light radiated from the surface of his skin until he pushed down his anger, though not fast enough to avoid bleaching the edges of his shirt. "God speaks to me. He fears what will happen if she falls under the Devil's control.

Regardless of who she is, she needs to die to prevent Satan from getting her. The risk is too great."

Leonard nodded his head. "Your Holiness, I will do as you command."

"Send the Heth cell to eliminate her. They are our most heavily armed cell and have never failed to eliminate a target."

"And the demons that killed the therapist and Bruce family?"

Dennis considered the question. "Once the girl is dead, if the demons are still present, then eliminate them, but have Heth be cautious. As you've said, we've lost track of too many other demons. We don't want Heth to fall into a trap."

Leonard bowed his head.

Dennis exhaled. "I am sorry, Leonard, for losing my temper. I know you've spent a great deal of your inheritance on God's cause." He forced a smile to his face. "I will return to working on the recording for tomorrow morning's broadcast."

Leonard smiled. "Your Grace, one day you will once again walk in the sun. I promise you that."

Chapter 6

Becca looked over her shoulder and down the stairs to the first floor. She still wore the sweatpants she had gone to sleep in last night. She had no access to any electronics, which meant she had almost no motivation to even get out of bed. Her father's grounding had truly damaged her hygiene routine. However, she wanted to check her phone, and that required her father to retreat to the basement. This morning, he played on a handheld console in the kitchen for over an hour. *Almost nine and I've not washed my hair.* Before Kyrie, on a Saturday morning, she would have been at Michelle's house already. *Or if I still had a job, I'd have been at work by six.*

Becca breathed deeply to avoid allowing her emotions to surface. *Tina ...* She never considered the blonde a close friend, but Michelle had collected Tina, not unlike she had collected Kyrie, Aki, and Jake. *Why did they have to kill her? Why'd they have to make it look like a suicide?* Becca pushed the spiraling thoughts from her. *I don't want to be the next one.*

She returned her attention to listening for her father's activities, and she heard music playing from the basement. Her father spent most of his time in his darkened man cave, which she expected would give her a chance to do what she needed. She slipped into the bathroom and turned on the shower for cover. The old hot water heater needed time to push the water up to the second floor, so she hurried from the bathroom to the master bedroom. She pushed open the door and crept inside her father's private space. Her eyes passed over the neatly made bed and clean surfaces. She peeked around the doorway into the master bathroom, hoping she would not walk in on her father. She neither wanted to be caught nor to see him undressed. *If only I could sense people like Kyrie.* Her fists clenched. *Why the fuck did I agree to get involved with her?*

She swallowed and buried the anger. A sigh of relief escaped her lips as she confirmed her father was not present. "At least I won't have traumatic images burned into my mind."

Her phone sat facedown on the bedside table, and she crossed the room to her device. A charging cord kept it alive as though her father wanted to taunt her. She bent down and put her face near the phone to search for any string, dirt, or other markers her father might have left to indicate tampering, but she found nothing. Unable to contain her need to connect with the outside world, she snatched the phone from the table, flipped it over, and pressed the power button to wake the screen. Multiple notifications popped up. She scrolled through the list looking for any indication anyone else in their group had managed to send a message out of their home confinement.

Nothing. Becca shook her head, uncertain if she should consider that good news or bad. Confirmation of Tina's death had appeared on the local news the prior night. The report focused on the trauma Tina had experienced at the hands of the Church of the Righteous Revenge and how she had spent two weeks in therapy. Becca sneered at the tarnishing of Tina's name and then calmed herself. She would try to use one of the TVs without her father knowing to check if the news had any other updates. Her fingers automatically scrolled back up to the top of the notifications to double-check she had not missed anything. *I need the Internet to truly search for details,* but she dared not unlock the phone, which might alert her father to a violation of her punishment. *Assuming he hasn't changed the password like he did with the computers.*

Becca put the phone back on the table, shifting it slightly to match what she remembered of its original placement, and then left her father's bedroom. She lifted the bottom of the t-shirt she had worn to bed and had almost removed it when the sound of a large truck in front of her house stopped her. Her hands pulled down the shirt, and she continued past the bathroom to stop at the edge of her bedroom doorway. From where she stood, she could not see the vehicle through the window, but the revving of a motor definitely did not come from a car. She took a tentative step into her room just as a man in a bucket lift rose into her view. The white articulating arm jerked from side to side and up and down as it rose higher into the air, as if the operator stumbled over the controls.

Shit! Becca crouched down and moved further into her room to change the angle of her view, but she remained as far from the window as she could. The hydraulic motor continued to whine as the bucket approached the streetlight at the edge of the property line.

The pounding of her heart slowed. *Just workers.* She hated the streetlight ever since the city had trimmed the trees two years earlier. The nighttime annoyance always shone through the blinds and disturbed her sleep. Her father continued to refuse her requests for blackout curtains, claiming she exaggerated the impact of the light.

She watched the skinny man in the bright orange safety vest bring the bucket up next to the top of the light that hung over the street. The man glanced quickly toward her house and then looked away, as though checking to see if anyone was watching him.

Her skin prickled. *Why are they working on a Saturday? And the light wasn't out last night.* Becca's frown deepened as the man in the bucket glanced twice more at her house. She carefully crouched lower to conceal her form with her bed, hoping that would make it harder for the man to see her.

Her father's work included both digital and physical security penetration testing, and she knew from him that the man outside in the bright light would not easily see through the glare on the window of her darkened room. She would remain unseen unless she stood next to the glass. However, instinct insisted that if she could see the man, the man could see her.

Apparently satisfied no one watched him, the man quickly used a battery-powered drill to unscrew a metal plate on the light. He dropped the plate and drill into the bucket, then immediately fished wires out of the streetlight. She focused on his activities, but she found it hard to see exactly what he did with her distance from him. After several minutes, she thought that he had tapped into the electric wires and had new leads running to a small grey box. "I need my damn phone," she muttered, wishing again that she had thought through the trip she had allowed Kyrie and Michelle to talk her into. *I'd have come up with a better cover story if we had more time.*

"Stupid." She grabbed a notebook from her nearby desk and started writing down a description of the man. *Brown hair to his shoulders. White man,* her words barely legible in her haste. *Dark blue ball cap with red circle.* The man's sunglasses, oversized safety vest, and thick gloves hid most of his distinguishing features. *Not to mention the bucket hiding everything chest down.*

The man held the grey box against the top of the light, twisted it to point toward her house, then he called down to someone out of Becca's sight. The man in the bucket shifted the angle and then firmly pressed it against the top of the light, sending both the pole and bucket swinging slightly. He then pulled off a glove and drew out what looked like large zip ties from within the bucket.

Becca's dark skin froze. *The bastard is setting up something to spy on me. Shit. Fuck, I'm next.* Her mind raced, trying to think of anything she could use as a weapon. *Not that anything would do any good if they used their powers to crush me.* She would not entertain the idea of killing her own father, even if they tortured her.

She watched the man shove the loose wires back into the light and then run duct tape over the aluminum surface to hide the missing plate and to secure the leads to the grey box. He dropped the roll of tape into the bucket and immediately started to descend out of her view as though he had a date to get to.

Becca wanted to rush to the window to get a view of who else might be outside, but she did not want them to know that she had seen them, and the glare would not hide someone next to the glass. "Why did I ever let myself get involved in this?" She sighed, knowing the reasons. They had all witnessed Kyrie use her powers and knew that the risks extended beyond the new girl from Colorado.

Becca waited until the truck outside sped off and then she went to the window. A car down the street backed out of a neighbor's driveway, but no other indication of what just occurred stood out to her.

She avoided looking at the modified streetlight and instead looked across the street at the next closest light to her house. That one did not appear to have any modifications. *Shitheads.* She moved away from the window, left her bedroom, and rushed across the hall to her father's old office. Since her mother divorced her father ten years ago, and then moved across the country, the five-bedroom house only contained her and her father. His old office on the second floor became a room for expensive toys and old computer parts. The remaining second-floor bedroom held boxes of things her mother had left behind that neither of them considered throwing out. Her father's actual office had moved to the family room in the basement, next to the fifth bedroom and the storage area that acted as a computer and network server room.

She turned the handle and pushed open the door. Her father's business had grown significantly over the years, which allowed him to have shelves of gadgets, including collectible figures, multiple drones, and two shelves of DSLR cameras with countless lenses. Becca grabbed the closest camera body, a memory card, a three-hundred-millimeter lens, and a battery off a charger. She inserted the card and battery and then attached the lens as she went back to her bedroom. From the corner of her room, she took more than a dozen images of the box taped and zip-tied to the top of the streetlight. A six-inch antenna poked out the side of the box and pointed into the air. She focused on the clear piece of plastic on the side facing her, but the dark interior of the box concealed whatever mechanisms hid inside the device.

"Damn them," she muttered before she lowered the camera. The urgency of the man's actions worried her. *I sure as hell won't let them make me the next victim.* She removed the memory card, then went back into the office to put the camera, lens, and battery back where she found them. *Black girls don't survive the shoot-outs.* Kyrie's offer to ask Lars to take them all away no longer sounded frightening. *I could live on some beach and learn to drink vodka and flirt with hot guys.* The thought made her snort. Then she grew cold again. *Would they still kill my dad?*

With the memory card in her hand, she rushed into the bathroom and considered taking a shower, but the water had already run a long time, and her father would come upstairs to yell at her if she allowed it to continue running. *I'll just have to be stank,* she decided. She went back into her room, moved to her window along a path that avoided the box, and then pulled her blinds closed. "Pedos can get their kicks off someone else," she mumbled as she shed her outer clothes, changed her underwear, and pulled on a clean pair of jeans and a purple top that she had bought a month earlier. She picked up a pair of socks discarded on the floor and slid them on before grabbing her shoes. She snatched a knit hat from the top of her dresser as she left her bedroom. *It might be the end of April and too hot, but I'm not going out with my hair a mess.*

She listened to the sounds of the house as she descended the stairs, trying to confirm her father's activities. The low rumble of nineties rock continued to emanate from the basement. She pursed her lips. A glance at the clock sitting on the mantel let her know it was ten minutes to nine. The Red Hot Chili Peppers' song that had been playing started again, and Becca nodded her head. "On repeat, he'll be deep in whatever research he's doing for hours."

Her father had long ago covered the inside of all the basement egress windows with sheets of plywood to keep out light and prying eyes, so she had no fear of being seen outside. She grabbed her small purse with her keys and sunglasses from the kitchen counter and exited through the sliding patio door. None of their immediate neighbors had dogs or fences, so she cut through their backyards to access the next street. She examined the lights on this street for tampering before leaving the cover of a bush.

Fifteen minutes later, she slowed as she neared Michelle's house. She lifted her sunglasses and focused on the streetlight in front of her friend's light blue house. "Damn it." *Then I'm not the only one.* A bit of relief spread through her with the idea that perhaps they had more time before anything happened.

Becca looked at the yards around Michelle's house and frowned. She did not know any of Michelle's neighbors personally, and she heard kids playing behind the house immediately to her right. She cursed, backtracked three houses, and then cut through an overgrown yard to get to the next street.

Once she reached the house directly behind Michelle's, she turned off the sidewalk, ducked low as she passed someone's living room windows, and rushed over to Michelle's backyard. The windows in the back of Michelle's house did not reveal the presence of anyone, but from years of playing D&D at the Windall residence, she knew Michelle's father golfed nearly every Saturday and her mother would disappear with friends. *Michelle, you better not have mouthed off and made your parental units decide you can't be trusted home alone.*

The memory of Kyrie killing two men in front of her just two weeks ago surfaced, casting doubt on the idea of running away. Revulsion at the concept of death filled her, but she could not feel sorry for the two men who had tried to kill them. She had not seen the men on the Kansas farm die, but knew Tina and Michelle had. *More will die in my presence if I leave with Kyrie.* Her skin grew cold at the thought.

It's not like I pulled the trigger on any of them. And we all swore to never mention it to anyone. She forced a laugh, trying to banish the memory of death. *I sound f'ing ghetto.* However, thoughts of countless movies promising some supernatural revenge awaiting her pushed their way into her head. She shivered. *I need to stop watching horror movies. Though in this case, it's the f'ing truth.*

Becca breathed deeply, the smell of fresh cut grass blew in from the north, She squatted down and picked up a small stick that had fallen from the oak tree in Michelle's backyard. The fact that she recognized the tree as an oak from the leaves, combined with the knowledge that she had spent many of her younger years climbing in the branches, reminded her that she had more in common with white suburban girls than any black woman. The reality of her life left a taste of fraud in her mouth. She hated not fully belonging to any group.

A tear threatened to emerge. *Focus, Bitch,* she swore at herself. She pushed down the emotions, snapped the stick in half, and then approached the back of the house. "Two weeks without my phone and I'm reduced to being a barbarian." She threw the smaller piece, but the wind blew the shorter stick wide of the window, and it struck the side of the house without any noticeable sound. She threw the larger piece at Michelle's window, and it bounced off with a satisfying thud, but Michelle did not appear. "You better not be in the toilet."

She went back to the tree, grabbed half a dozen more sticks, threw three of them in rapid succession, and then waited. A moment later,

Michelle's face filled the window. Michelle's eyes grew wide, and then she waved to her to remain.

Becca dropped the rest of the sticks and wiped the dirt from her hands onto her pants. She crossed her arms, moved back under the tree, and leaned against the trunk to wait. Two minutes later, Michelle emerged from the sliding patio door and crossed the yard.

"What are you doing here?" the brown-haired girl asked.

Becca shifted her weight off the tree. "People are trying to kill us and you ask me that?"

Michelle frowned. Her eyes were red and puffy. "I don't blame Kyrie. She didn't ask for any of this. She didn't even know she was still in danger when her aunt brought her here."

"Yeah, I know." Becca dropped her arms to her sides. "Sorry about that. The thing with Tina has me scared. But it's worse. Now we have people putting up what I'm pretty sure are cameras to monitor our houses." At Michelle's raised eyebrows, Becca continued. "There's a box on the streetlight in front of your house. Some white asshole just put one up at my house. I got lucky and saw him wiring it up to point at my window." She bit her lip and shifted her feet. "I probably wouldn't have noticed it if I hadn't seen it happen."

"Shit." Michelle slid her right arm from the sling. "Shit. They are coming for us, like they did Tina."

"Probably," Becca agreed. "I'd guess Bishop, or Nalitran, or whatever his f'ing name is. But hell, it could be that damn church. Either would kill us without hesitation." Becca scratched her head through the hat covering her unwashed hair. She could feel the sweat making her scalp itch. "I didn't want to admit it, but Kyrie is right; we can't stay in our houses." A tear surfaced on Becca's cheek, and she wiped it away. "I don't want to die. I don't want my dad to die." She sniffed back more tears. "But if we run, they might kill him anyway."

Michelle turned back to Becca, her lower lip between her teeth. "My parents are out as normal, and the asshole is out with Sam. I heard them planning to go to a movie, so I've got probably three or four hours before there is even a chance anyone comes home." She rubbed her eyes. "Do you think Kyrie knows about these cameras? I told her I'd run off with her, but we need to let her know the rest of us absolutely need to come too."

Becca frowned. "That troglodyte barely knows how to use a phone; I doubt she'd recognize anything wrong with the light. If they put one on each of our houses, they probably have one or more on hers." She started to move away from the tree the two of them climbed when growing up. "My dad's analyzing some software for security holes. I doubt he'll leave the basement until late. But we need to see if Kyrie's aunt is home before we approach her house. Kyrie's bedroom faces the street, and I don't want to be seen by whoever is watching."

"What about Jake and Aki? Have you heard from them?"

Becca shook her head. "I glanced at my phone. My father leaves it on his nightstand to taunt me. No notices that I saw, but I didn't dare unlock it."

"My mom has my phone in her purse." Michelle slid her arm back into the sling.

Becca motioned with her head to the neighbor's yard. "You need anything, or can we go?"

"I ain't got nothing to take."

"Good." Becca retraced her route back toward the other street.

Michelle followed. She continued to whisper as they moved through the neighbor's yard. "They thought it was funny to leave me with my computer, but my parents changed the Wi-Fi password, so I can't get online. I've got a couple of decent single-player games, but with what happened to Tina … I just can't bring myself to play anything."

Becca shook her head. "My dad doesn't believe in Wi-Fi. Everything's hard-wired. He locked my network user ID and froze me out of everything." She grew quiet as they ducked low to pass under the neighbor's windows and then continued toward the sidewalk. "Come on, if I remember correctly, one of Kyrie's neighbors has a dog that we'll have to sneak past."

Chapter 7

Kyrie stifled a yawn and rolled her head from side to side. Her aunt had stolen her morning, forcing her to start cleaning at six. A terrible night of sleep, filled with dreams she could not remember, had left Kyrie awake when her aunt got up. The simmering anger her aunt continued to express forced her into servitude instead of allowing her the time to review her mother's documents.

Kim grunted a noise, and Kyrie returned her attention to the baseboard in front of her, the smell of dust filling her nose. *I doubt she's ever cleaned these. Sam definitely doesn't do any cleaning.* Frustration filled her face, and she shook the rag out and let the dust fall to the floor. Between Lars' reluctance to help her friends and the home confinement preventing her from expelling her pent-up frustrations, she doubted she could remain in the house for three more weeks without breaking something.

"Did I tell you to stop?"

Kyrie rolled her eyes and sat back on her heels. She slowly turned her head to face her aunt. "I've been cleaning since six. I should be studying for my finals," she offered as an excuse, though she could not see a future where she would still be in Olathe to sit for them.

Kim laughed and shook her head. "We've been through that. You have no chance of passing your classes, so there's no point in studying. Had my sister had a brain, she'd have left your no-good father before the two of them ruined your life." Kim walked from the open living room to the kitchen. "You know nothing of history,

English, government—you have no chance of catching up at this point."

Kyrie stopped herself from drawing in more energy. *Keep your powers secret,* she reminded herself, but did not reject the idea of causing her aunt physical pain in a way that would not reveal her abilities. "My parents taught me plenty," Kyrie snapped. *They drilled us in math, physics, chemistry. Not to mention blades, rifles, hand-to-hand fighting, our powers ... You don't want to see what we know how to do.* Kyrie circled her thoughts back to the implied deficiency. "Memorizing a bunch of names and dates is less useful than knowing where to find the information. Anyone with a rational mind would see that."

Kim turned back to face Kyrie. "Are you getting an attitude with me? I took you in out of the goodness of my heart. Kept you out of the system. And as a result, I've had to pay lawyers, deal with criminals breaking in and robbing my house, and then your total disrespect by running off to get involved in a gunfight where people died. Don't get me started on what I'm sure will be enormous hospital bills. You'll show me some respect." Her aunt sneered. "I guess that's just something else your mother failed to teach you."

Kyrie rose to her feet. Her six-inch height advantage over her aunt was evident even from halfway across the room. "My mother was a brilliant woman, and my father knew far more than you." Demand entered her voice. "Never call them stupid again."

Kim hesitated a moment before growing louder. "They involved themselves with something criminal. Why else run off and hide?" She lifted her hands toward Kyrie. "Your gang war with these cult members is proof of that." Kim turned toward the refrigerator and opened the door. "You've cost me a lot of money."

Kyrie sensed her aunt's frustrations, which added to her own. *Careful. Are you sure you want to manipulate her for something so petty? Focus on what you really need.* Kyrie push deeper into her aunt's mind, feeling the older woman's memories drift to an earlier conversation with her lawyer and the vindictive need to file a grievance against Lars for misconduct, motivated purely out of revenge and spite for having properly secured the trust.

Kyrie pulled back on the connection, not wanting to internalize her aunt's hate as her own. She shook her head and returned to the conversation. "You shouldn't have come after me. Lars would have taken me, and then you'd not be put out." *Let Lars take me away,* she sent to her aunt, not sure if she had performed the manipulation correctly.

Her aunt removed a can of soda and slammed the refrigerator door shut. "Oh, quit with your nonsense already. I'm not after the money. I'm trying to protect you from yourself—and that man. He's a predator, and once he has your money, he'll sell you off to the first human trafficker he can find."

Kyrie frowned. Her new friends used the word pedo enough that she knew what her aunt implied. While she did not trust Lars, she reminded herself that her parents had. "You're wrong. And you're the fool. The people who are after me won't have stopped just because some of them got arrested—"

"The cowards committed suicide while in jail," Kim interrupted. "The rest dead on a farm. Unless you've forgotten the dead bodies the police found you in the middle of! Stupid g—"

Shut up!

Her aunt twitched, as though bugs buzzed her ears. After a moment, clarity returned to her face. "I'm sick of discussing this with you. Go to your room and get out of my face." Her aunt waved her away.

Kyrie took a deep breath, uncertain why her attempts to silence her aunt did not fully work. She dropped the rag on the table and headed toward the stairs. *You need to figure this out. You will make her do what you want.*

She sighed as she started up the stairs. The implications of controlling other people's thoughts suddenly made her uncomfortable as the realization that in Colorado, while her parents had appeared to give her the freedom to roam and hunt—implying trust—they had controlled her, keeping her on a short leash. *You always behaved and did as they said.* She closed her eyes and clenched her hands. *But they commanded that obedience. Forced their will on us and … and made us forget.* Her mother's face surfaced unbidden in her mind, the binding stone hanging from her shawl in the worn filigree brooch. The command to forget her other self, lingered in the air. *How could she?*

Kyrie rushed up the stairs trying to block out the violation. Until she came to Olathe, she had no idea of the power the green stone had over her. She simply thought all adults could exert their will on children. *They used it as a means to make us avoid everyone.* Her eyes blurred with moisture. Without the daily reinforcement blocking her memories, her idyllic vision of her childhood began to fray.

Kyrie swallowed and suppressed the need to check on her binding stone. *They only wanted to protect you,* she told herself, willfully ignoring the evidence to the contrary in a desperate hope that she could go back to the happy days of living on the mountain.

She breathed deeply and forced herself to push the feelings down. Her thoughts and emotions had become too volatile in the last three weeks, and she just wanted to return to normal. *Spock kept his emotions suppressed,* she reminded herself, thinking of the Star Trek novels her father shared with her. *You can do it. Logic is the key.*

She continued to breathe, taking long and slow breaths as she walked to her bedroom, her right hand automatically making the Vulcan hand gesture her father had shown her before she had turned four. Of all the characters in Star Trek, she idolized Spock the most. *Logic and reason,* she reminded herself.

Our outburst at Kim must have come from the fact she spoke truth to me. You have no chance of passing the finals. She smiled at the self-reflection and felt more reasonable already. Her parents had not intended for her to ever attend a public school and so they had not prepared her for that. Instead, they wanted her to live and defend herself, from—at that time—unknown people. *You were never meant to pass these high school tests.*

She leaned against the door frame and stared at nothing in particular in her room. *But you're not going to run away and hide. You need to stop Nalitran. Perhaps there is a way to send him back to the other world.*

Kyrie moved deeper into the room, then bent down and slid the duffel bags out from under the bed. She opened the lighter one and took out one of her mother's most recent journals. A bookmark with bent corners and a faded image of a dragon marked the place she had stopped taking pictures. She opened the glue-bound volume. Her mother's writing filled the page, a mix of symbols neatly written across the grid-lined surface, with additional marks annotating new thoughts about the original text. None of the symbols represented any known language. When Kyrie turned five, she helped her mother develop a new alphabet and syntax to conceal her mother's ideas, a feat she knew her friends would tell her did not conform to normal human development. Even the revised math symbols they created, which would at least confuse any mathematician until they reverse engineer the meanings, made sense to her at that early age.

Kyrie narrowed her eyes. A sudden recognition of the form and style of the marks snapped into her mind, going beyond the memories of developing the language with her mother. A truth that had always hung just out of her grasp swung into her reach. As if stepping out of the fog of a dream, she could see the words written by a different hand. She swallowed. *We were so young when Awan dragged our soul away. How could we have known so much?* She froze. *If one of the Bound—or worse, Nalitran—got their hands on these ...*

She stood up, the panic drying her mouth. *Could Nalitran want them? Is that why he's after me?* She paced to the end of her bed and shook her head. "Mom didn't start working on them until after she went to Colorado. She couldn't even have known of the other world before then, could she? No." Kyrie nodded her head, adding physical confirmation to her belief. *There's no way he'd know about them. He must just want to control us. Prevent us from revealing his existence.*

She continued around the bed and stopped at the window. A silver car drove past the house heading north, but it did not slow down. She pressed her forehead against the cool glass as her attention slid to an old truck parked south of her house and on the other side of the street. The dull and faded green of the cab showed large patches of rust on the roof. The sides sported dents and scratches. Long wooden boards extended out over the end of the tailgate at an angle pointed into the road and toward her house. Cardboard boxes, rags, and assorted rubbish filled the bed of the truck, threatening to spill over the sidewalls and onto the ground.

Kyrie narrowed her focus. She detected the presence of two men in or around the truck. One man was in the cab, and the second one seemed to be in the middle of the overflowing bed. A moment later she felt the mental activity change and saw what looked like a pipe rising slightly off the boards to point directly at her window.

Instinct took over and power poured through her body. The gravitational field her mind created flung her backwards just as the window exploded. She felt a mass over an inch long deflect slightly as it skidded over the strong gravitational field pushing her body away from the window. The boom of a rifle firing reached her ears well after the bullet sped past her and through the wall behind her.

Drywall exploded into the room as a new hole opened in the wall inches to the left of the window. Kyrie's momentum carried her backwards over the bed as the second bullet sped past her and through the wall opposite the shattered window. Her momentum slammed her shoulder into the painted surface two feet below the pair of bullet holes, the force of her impact cracking the drywall. The sound of the second bullet firing reached her ears moments before a third hole opened in the wall under the window. Bedding flew into the room as the projectile's trajectory deflected upward into the edge of the ceiling.

Kyrie bounced off her desk and rolled into a flat position on the floor, her arms covering her head as five more shots exploded through the exterior wall and the empty window frame. She heard the truck's engine come to life and wheels squeal, the vehicle's sounds fading as her assailants sped away. One last sonic boom echoed through the neighborhood. Kyrie did not know where that projectile went, but it mercifully did not pass through her room.

A deafening silence filled the neighborhood. Then startled dogs voiced their concerns with a cacophony of barking. It took several moments more before she exhaled a sob. Her back hurt from where she had hit the wall and then the edge of her desk. *No more,* she swore. Rage pumped blood through her body as fear that her friends might be dead filled her.

Her senses opened back up and she recognized screaming coming from the first floor. Aside from her aunt, she felt no one else near or in the house. She extended her awareness until her head throbbed, but no immediate threats appeared to her.

Kyrie closed her eyes and directed a fraction of the excess energy she had pulled into her body to heal her bruised ribs and shoulder. With the pain subsiding, she moved into a crouched position behind the bed and peeked over the top of her covers. Her hands trembled slightly as she surveyed the damage. Fragments of glass hung from the edges of the window sash, while pointed shards covered her bed. Bedding and foam erupted from at least three spots in the mattress. The outside wall had two large holes, with drywall and insulation exploding into the room. She suspected the bed hid at least three more holes in the exterior wall from her view. She glanced at the ceiling and the interior wall behind her and saw smaller openings where the projectiles had exited her room. *Mom and Dad never had rifles that powerful.* Her mind tried to recall the length of the delay between when the bullets passed and her ears hearing the sound of the weapon fire. The rifles she used in the mountains had always fired subsonic ammunition.

Her aunt's wails of anguish brought her back to the immediate concern. She sensed panic coming from the older woman downstairs, but not at the level of distress that would indicate injuries. Her mind told her that some of the neighbors had emerged from their homes, but the sudden spike of energy she pulled through her body left her exhausted, and with the distance, she could not sense the neighbors clearly. *You need to limit the rate of power draw,* she chastised herself.

Her aunt's crying pushed Kyrie into action. *There could be more coming.* She moved the journal, still on the bed, back to the duffel bag and then opened the top drawer of the small desk. She removed the box of minis and her dice, and then tossed them in the nearest bag along with her sketchbook from the top of the desk. Those small items represented the only items of sentimental value she still possessed.

With a fifty-pound duffel bag in each hand, she stayed low and exited her bedroom, hoping to avoid anyone seeing her through the destroyed window. She descended the stairs quickly, cognizant of her vulnerability from the windows in the formal dining room, and those around the front door.

Despite the risk, she moved through the dining room to reach the stairs to the basement without her aunt seeing her. She raced down the stairs while her aunt's panicked wails of terror continued to come from the kitchen. *They shot at you. Why's she the one sobbing?*

Kyrie made her way through the basement family room, ignoring the large TV, coffee table, sofa, and multiple game consoles. Toys, clothes, dirty dishes, and a dozen cups covered the flat surfaces. Her cousin and his friends never picked up their messes, and she refused to do the work for them.

With her mind slowly recovering from the energy draw, she reached out to ensure no one waited outside the walkout basement. Not feeling any threats, she jogged two steps to the door leading to the large unfinished part of the basement. She used a gravity field to turn the handle and then pushed the door open with one of the bags.

The open area contained all the mechanical equipment, as well as piles of boxes and belongings. Narrow paths existed between the stacked items, allowing someone to navigate a maze of clutter that rose over four-feet high in some places.

Kyrie walked through a spiderweb on her way down a seldom-used path. Three weeks ago, she had to move dozens of boxes from what became her bedroom to the basement. At that time, she noted many gaps between the randomly sized boxes, discarded furniture, and dust-covered things. She pushed both of her bags into one of the gaps and then slid two boxes forward to conceal them. *If someone searches the house, hopefully they won't notice these here.*

The sounds of distant sirens became audible. Kyrie looked at the furnace. The ductwork extended upward through the ceiling and an interior wall to the attic. Her binding stone rested on a ledge high up in the stack, well beyond the ability of a human to reach it. Only someone else who could manipulate gravity and knew its location could find or retrieve it. *Unless they tear the house down.*

The idea of leaving the stone made her hands tremble, but when the police had come to the farm out in the county, they had stripped her of all her clothing at some point. *Most of it was covered in blood, and you were unconscious,* she admitted. However, she did not want them searching her again and inadvertently gaining control over her mind. *And without them even realizing it.* She hated the stone because of the power it had over her.

Based on the sirens' changing tones, Kyrie suspected two vehicles had arrived outside the house. She bit her lip and rushed back upstairs, leaving the means to control her in its hiding place. Her aunt had stopped sobbing, but the middle-aged woman remained huddled against the lower cabinets, cramming herself into the corner between the stove and the refrigerator. A large, jagged hole in the cabinet door near the microwave indicated the path of the last bullet through the side of the house.

"They shot at my house," Kim whined when she noticed Kyrie approach.

"There are police outside," Kyrie said, uncertain of the protocol. Her parents reinforced a distrust of authority throughout her life. Her experiences over the last three weeks had not changed that opinion.

Kim sneered. "This is all about you. I just know it. That Robert Landvik was always a no-good criminal. I just knew it."

Kyrie held her tongue. *We just got through telling you they would continue to come for us. Stupid woman.*

"Criminal. Just criminal."

Kyrie crossed her arms. While she might have lost some faith in her parents, they only did what they believed would protect her. *They weren't criminals.*

Kyrie sensed a man in the front yard and another near the garage. Someone on an electronic speaker demanded everyone in the house to come out with their hands in the air. Had Kyrie still thought adults could control her, the command in the man's voice would have had her running to the front door to avoid the expected compulsion.

Kyrie wrinkled her brow. The arrogant tone raised her pent-up desire to disobey, but then a nagging chill filled her mind. *Nalitran or Hurlington could always have a cop kill us.* A policeman trying to kidnap her was the catalyst that had driven her parents to leave society.

"Whoever is inside the house, put down any weapons and exit immediately with your hands in the air!"

More sirens approached the area.

Kyrie looked down at her aunt.

Kim's expression turned from fear to anger. "Why are they yelling at us? We were the ones shot at."

Kyrie did not answer her aunt. Despite the pain, she extended her senses and felt the man near the garage move to the far side of the bump-out for the dining-room windows. The gap between the garage and windows would conceal him from physical sight, but not her mind. The second man she believed likely hid behind the large maple tree in the front yard. *Is it safe for you to do as they say?* She contemplated rushing to the basement to grab her binding stone and then run out the back door.

"We will not repeat the request! Exit now!"

Kim got to her feet and pushed Kyrie toward the front door. "What is the meaning of this?" Kim shouted as they neared the door. "We were the ones shot at!"

"Don't make this harder than it has to be!" came the voice over the speaker. "We'll break the door down and take you out if you don't comply!"

"Don't you dare." Her aunt kept Kyrie in front of her. "There's a child in here."

Through the windows in the front door, Kyrie could see the edge of the man behind the tree and another man hiding behind one of the two black and white SUVs that sat at angles in the middle of the street. The man near the dining-room window remained out of physical sight.

"Exit now!"

"The alarm will go off if I open the door," Kyrie shouted back.

"Exit the house slowly with your hands in the air! Do it now!"

"Open the door," Kim finally snarled.

Kyrie unlocked the door and pulled it open.

"Hands in the air! One step forward!" shouted the man behind the tree.

Kyrie raised her hands and stepped outside the house as the warning beeping of the alarm panel near the garage door demanded the code.

"Move slowly to the edge of the porch and take one step off!"

Kyrie watched as two more black and white SUVs screeched to a stop next to the first two. The drivers' doors opened, and officers jumped out with their weapons drawn and pointed in her direction.

She could tell the officer hiding out of view on the front porch kept his weapon pointed at her as she stepped down to the walkway. The one who knelt behind the tree felt eager, but she could not tell what he wanted to do. "I've not done anything," Kyrie demanded, the frustration of having so many weapons pointed in her direction evident in her tone. *Does Nalitran control any of them?* The memories of the pain of being shot in Arkansas came unbidden, and she did not know if she had the self-control not to fight back with her powers if one of these officers attempted to kill her.

"Move forward and lay face down on the ground with your hands in front of you! We won't ask again," the man behind the tree shouted at her.

"You inside the house, take one step outside," shouted the man still near the vehicles over the speaker.

Kyrie moved forward. The beeping of the alarm sped up, signaling it would not wait much longer for the code.

"This is ridiculous," her aunt shouted as she stepped onto the porch. "Someone shot at me! Why are you pointing your guns at us?"

Kyrie's shoes touched the grass as the alarm started its earsplitting wailing. The officer behind the tree partially moved out from behind the tree; his finger shifted from the trigger guard to the trigger. Power flooded into her, knowing the man either lacked the safety discipline her father instilled in her, or actually planned to shoot her. "Don't point your weapons at me," she growled just above a whisper. "I've done nothing wrong. Point them elsewhere." Her eyes did not hide her anger as power radiated from her.

Kyrie stared down the man behind the tree, her head throbbing. A moment later, the pistol barrel lowered slightly. The two most recent arrivals, a man and a woman, lowered their weapons to point them at the ground. The officer behind the tree blinked his eyes and shook his head. His weapon rose back to point at her chest.

Don't point it at us again, she directed specifically at the man.

The officer rose to his feet and stumbled to the side, but he avoided falling to the ground. His pistol now in one hand, but still pointed at her.

"Get down on your knees!" The man demanded.

Kyrie's head throbbed and she broke her mental connection to the man. *Almost,* she told herself, surrendering the last of her discomfort at manipulating minds for the practical hope of any tool she could leverage to protect herself. She slowly dropped to her knees. Power burned her insides as she prepared herself mentally for someone to shoot her.

"Sarge, I was here a couple of weeks ago responding to a B and E," said the female officer, her weapon still pointed at the ground. "And you're the girl whose friend was kidnapped by those men on the farm southwest of Stilwell, aren't you?"

"Conley?" the officer behind the tree questioned without shifting his gaze from Kyrie.

"Look at the window," Officer Conley replied. "The latest caller to 911 reported shots were fired from the street instead of from inside the house."

"Yes," her aunt replied verbally, still on the porch with her hands in the air. "We were shot at. The girl's a bit slow. Why are you threatening us?"

The officer, who had been hiding near the dining-room windows, came up behind Kyrie's aunt and directed her to move forward, away from the house and the loud alarm. The other officer pointed his weapon down now that a colleague had entered the target zone. "Anyone else in the house?" came the forceful demand.

Kim shook her head. "No, just me and my miserable niece. This must all be her fault. Someone shot at us!"

Kyrie rose to her feet as Officer Conley motioned her forward. Once her aunt moved out of the line of fire, the man behind the tree, and the two closest male officers, readied their sidearms again and cautiously approached the front door.

The officer who had used the speaker motioned them back toward the other side of his SUV. "Remain here while Sergeant Klein and the others clear the house. We need to make sure no one else is inside."

Kyrie watched as the three officers slipped in through the front door. She eased up on the energy she held within herself. *Don't burn yourself out; you might need to defend yourself.*

"Can you tell me what happened?" Officer Conley asked, leaving the other four officers to focus on the house.

"Someone shot at my house," Kim whined. "I could have been killed." Her aunt looked up at the broken window and damaged exterior wall. "My house," she almost sobbed.

Kyrie felt her hands tremble from the excess energy she held within herself and allowed more of it to slowly dissipate into the ground. She saw a multitude of neighbors on their front porches and driveways watching. "I need to warn my friends," Kyrie said, the urgency of her fear driving her to leave a trace of command in her voice.

Conley nodded her head. "But first, what happened?"

"Tell her," Kim said. "I don't know why you always need to be difficult." Kim's eyes widened. "I need to find my son. Where's Sam?" She turned around and then looked at her hands. "My phone's in the house. He's out with Mike. I need to warn him."

Conley held up a hand, but she kept her focus on Kyrie. "Do you know who shot at you and why? Was it that church group that attacked you on the farm?"

"My parents never told me who was after us. But someone in the back of an old green truck shot at me through the window." Kyrie heard additional sirens in the distance. "They were parked over there," she pointed to the spot where the truck had waited for her. *Probably Hurlington,* she decided, still believing Nalitran wanted to capture her.

"There's some stupid cult after her." Kim paced back and forth. "Church of the Righteous Revenge." She stopped and looked at the officer. "I need to call my son to make sure he's safe!"

Kyrie turned her head toward the south. Her eyes grew wide as Becca and Michelle rushed down the sidewalk in her direction.

Officer Conley noticed their approach and raised a hand. "Stay back. This is a crime scene!"

"They're my friends," Kyrie said, moving in their direction until Conley grabbed her upper arm. Kyrie turned to face the officer who had helped her record what had been stolen when Michael Rodgers' Bound had broken in and stolen all of her aunt's jewelry looking for her binding stone. "They are in danger and need to come here." Her statement left no room for discussion.

Conley nodded her head, though her eyes did not appear to see. A moment later, the female officer waved Michelle and Becca toward them. "Come here."

"My son," Kim protested.

Conley's voice grew hard again. "As soon as the house is cleared, we can get that alarm turned off, and let you get your phone."

Kyrie pulled her burner phone from her rear pocket. While she did not consider Sam a friend, she had no ill will toward her younger cousin, and her aunt's panic filled the air, impacting Kyrie's own emotions. "You can use my phone." Kyrie unlocked it and held it out, hoping to keep her aunt distracted.

Kim glared at her for having the phone that had been confiscated from her, then took it and started dialing.

"Kyrie, are you hurt? Say no!" Michelle pleaded, coming up and giving her a one-armed hug.

"Just tired of being shot at."

Conley cleared her throat. "We need the details of who shot at you. What happened? Tell me again."

Kyrie wanted to ask Michelle and Becca why they had come to her house, but she turned to the officer. "There was an old green truck parked over there," frustration leaked into her voice as she pointed to where the truck had sat. "The back was full of boxes and junk. When I was at the window, I noticed a pipe rising up off some boards. When I realized it was a rifle barrel, I jumped backwards away from the window and over my bed."

"Oh my God," Michelle said. "Shit. They almost killed you."

Becca growled, "Michelle, let Kyrie tell the officer what happened."

Kyrie sensed a great deal of concern from both of her friends, but it seemed less about her almost getting shot than something else.

Conley leaned her head close to the microphone at her shoulder and pressed a button on the side. "Dispatch, this is Conley responding to shots fired. I need a BOLO on a green pickup truck with trash in the bed. Unknown occupants, potentially signal seven. Shooter might be hiding in the bed."

"Lots of rust and dents," Kyrie added.

"The vehicle is rusted and dented," Conley added.

"Ten-four," Kyrie heard over the radio. "All officers be on the lookout for an old green pickup. Bed filled with trash. Suspects armed and dangerous and possibly hiding in the bed."

Officer Conley turned down her radio as more instructions came out over the device. "Did you see the people who shot at you?"

Kyrie shook her head. "It happened too fast. I never even saw a person, only the rifle barrel move."

Conley nodded her head. "Okay. Can you tell us why someone would be shooting at you? This is the second time I've been to your house in a month, and I know you were involved with another event on a farm where several people died. At least four police officers were hurt out on that farm, so this is serious."

Kyrie felt Kim pacing in a circle as she again tried to call her son on the phone. "No," Kyrie said to the officer, her voice taking on a slight whine.

"Your parents never told you what trouble they were in? Nothing?"

Kyrie allowed her eyes to moisten, hoping that an attempt to look pathetic might stop the line of questioning sooner. "They never told me anything. I truly don't know. I was just a baby when they took me away." The officer frowned, and Kyrie suspected she did not believe her.

"You need to be truthful with us." Conley shook her head and allowed anger to reach her eyes. "There were more than fifty people murdered across a dozen states last night and this morning. We have important things to take care of, and if this is somehow related, we need to know." The officer crossed her arms. "So, tell us what you know."

"What?" Becca asked, stepping closer.

The officer hesitated, and after her face tightened, turned to Becca. "Haven't you seen the news? There were terrorist attacks overnight targeting business leaders, politicians, and random people." The officer shifted her focus back to Kyrie. "There is tentative evidence that points back to that extremist group that attacked you. So, you need to help us."

Kyrie probed into the woman's thoughts and knew the officer believed what she said. *How do we stop her questions?* Kyrie adjusted her posture, dropped her shoulders and slouched. "Do you think I want to be shot at?" She shook her head, allowing tears to slide down her cheeks. "I don't know anything. I promise. I just want my mom and dad back. I miss my mommy."

Conley sighed. "Okay. Fine. I had to ask." The officer turned her head as a van pulled up just beyond the police cars. A retracted telescoping pole with a satellite dish stood out as the most prominent feature on the vehicle. "Wait here."

"Sam, where are you? Answer your phone!" Kim hung up again. "Damn him."

"Ms. Leighton," Michelle said. "I believe he and Mike were planning to go to a movie."

Kim frowned and turned on Kyrie. "Why'd you have your phone?"

Please work this time, she begged of herself and then focused her will on Kim, diving deeper into her aunt's mind than she wanted. "You gave it back to me because you were worried something like this might happen and wanted me to be able to warn you."

Kim looked into the distance and nodded. "Yeah."

"I need to call my dad," Becca said. "Right now!"

Give me back the phone. Her aunt held out her hand. Kyrie took the phone from Kim's limp fingers and gave it to Becca before reducing her concentration on her aunt.

"Ms. Leighton," Michelle said, poking Kim's arm. "I think that cop wants you."

Kyrie completely broke her mental connection with Kim, and her aunt turned like a zombie toward the house, where the two officers stood by the front door. They continued to motion for her to approach, and Kim's mind snapped back to her. The older woman sped across her yard toward the men.

Becca spoke as she focused on typing on Kyrie's phone. "Don't react, and don't look, but someone put a camera on top of the streetlight in front of your house."

Kyrie kept her face neutral, despite the anger that boiled up within her. More than a dozen of their neighbors had approached the area, but they remained out of hearing as groups of them formed to watch and talk with each other. "When was it added?" She demanded.

Becca shrugged. "Some asshats put one up in front of my house this morning. I don't think it covers the street, but I don't know for certain." She looked up from the phone, her own eyes moist. "I have to warn my dad. I don't want them to do to him what they did to Tina's family." She sniffed back her tears. "I was wrong. We can't just stay and wait it out."

"What really happened?" Michelle whispered.

Kyrie looked at the front of her aunt's house, her vision passing over the streetlight, briefly recognizing a difference that existed between that one and the other lights on the street. Her attention fell on the broken window and damaged side of the house. "Someone shot at me at least eight times. The ninth bullet went through the kitchen."

"Shit." Michelle glanced at the first floor of the house as the alarm klaxon turned off. "What was that officer going on about? Fifty people dead?" She hugged herself. "Could it have been Hurlington that did all that?"

Kyrie weighed the options. *Would Nalitran have that many Bound scattered about that Hurlington would target?* She had no idea what the man did with his Bound or how effectively Hurlington tracked them. She put her hand on Michelle's good arm to stop her friend's trembling. "I don't know, but we have to do something. You've both made it clear we need an adult's help. I'm not certain I can force Lars to take everyone. When I spoke with him last night, he was reluctant to take any of you." She looked at the phone Becca continued to type into. "But I need to call him as soon as you're done."

"My dad finally responded," Becca interjected. "He's pissed, but he's on his way." She looked up. "I don't want him dead. We have to make sure we protect him as well."

Kyrie nodded her head to Becca, but she sensed Officer Conley returning to them. Kyrie's expression lost the hard edge, and she turned around with a lowered chin and raised eyes, hoping to appear timid. However, one neighbor, a middle-aged man with speckled brown hair moved out of his yard and into the street, distracting the policewoman.

"Sir?" Conley questioned his actions. "It'd be better if you stayed back."

"Understood, Officer," he said, stopping. "I just wanted to tell you I'm pretty certain that whoever was shooting was using a fifty-cal." The neighbor continued to approach after Conley waved him forward. "I'm Jess Simpson. A former army sergeant, and a regular at the local range. I didn't see it happen, but I definitely heard the shots."

"I'll need to get your information and a statement," Conley said.

"This related to the shootings and explosions this morning?" He asked.

Conley hesitated and her radio buzzed with various people reporting activities. "Hang on." She turned her attention to the house as Kim and two officers emerged from the front door. The three of them hurried in their direction with Kim on her phone.

Kyrie longed to find a forest to hide within. The open exposure and stares of the neighbors made her skin crawl. *And these adults will prevent us from getting somewhere safe regardless of what we say.*

"Sam, you stay there. I'll come and get you shortly." Kim hung up her phone. "I need to go get my son. He's in danger."

The male officer that had hid behind the tree ignored Kim and glared at Kyrie. "I'm Sergeant Klein." He glanced at the others. "Who are these girls, and who are you?" The sergeant's expression held no warmth as he turned to the neighbor.

"They are my friends," Kyrie said softly, probing the man's mind to judge how she should respond to him. This man seemed eager for a fight, and she doubted she would come out ahead in any physical conflict, though she wanted to punch him. "They ..." She glanced at Becca.

"We were just on our way over to visit when we heard all the sirens," Becca said with a trace of defiance and snark in her voice.

"I'm a neighbor that heard the shots," the middle-aged man said. "Former sergeant in the First Infantry out of Riley. Someone unloaded a fifty-cal into that house. I counted nine distinct shots."

The police sergeant frowned at the older man. Considered saying something, then turned to Kyrie. "Your aunt says this is all something to do with your father."

Kyrie shrugged, ignoring the desire to punch her aunt as well. "I have no idea. My father's been dead for almost a year, and he never told me anything." She let a tear fall. "I miss him, but he never told me anything." She looked away and slouched further, reducing her apparent height. Anger fed her energy draw, and she forcefully projected her thoughts. *You are done talking to us. Let us go now.* She could not hide the contempt she picked up from the officer from reflecting in her own face.

"I need to go get my son," Kim protested.

"Ma'am," Sergeant Klein said, "I told you, once we are done."

Kim glared. "I don't know any more. Why don't you go find the people that shot up my house?" She stomped her foot. "You said they're the ones that killed dozens of people this morning. I was almost one of the people killed!"

"Ma'am, we don't know that yet." Sergeant Klein turned back to Kyrie. "Tell me everything you know about what happened and who did this."

The fourth officer that had been in the house rushed over. "Sarge, they just said over the radio that they located a rusted out green F250 filled with debris near 154th and Ridgeview. Plates came back to a ninety-three-year-old in Atchinson County who no longer has a driver's license." The man shrugged. "Might have been stolen."

"Conley?" The Sergeant lifted an eyebrow.

Let us go, Kyrie swore each word at them. *You're done with us! Done with us. Go away!*

Conley shuddered and after a moment barely found her voice. "The girl didn't know anything a couple weeks back when this house was robbed, and she didn't see anything aside from the truck and a rifle barrel today."

Klein shifted uncomfortably on his feet, his eyes glazed. "I've got to deal with the reporters." He swallowed, then turned his body. "Conley, go investigate the truck, the rest of you secure the scene until we can collect whatever evidence we need." He glared at Kim. "Go get your son, but we'll have more questions later."

Kyrie tasted blood in the back of her throat. *We're not going with you, Kim,* she projected each word as though it was a threat.

Kim unlocked her phone and her lip curled when she looked at Kyrie. "You're not coming. You've caused enough problems and I'm not going to have you endanger Sam more by having you in my car with him." She stomped off to her SUV as she dialed her son again.

Kyrie exhaled. Her head throbbed from pushing energy through her body. Her emotions felt raw from having touched so many minds. She looked at Michelle and Becca, both of them stood silently watching, uncertain of what happened. Her chest expanded as she took a deep breath and then she wiped her sweaty hands on her jeans. The adults had left them standing alone in the road. "Can we trust your dad?" She finally asked Becca, knowing her father meant everything to her.

Becca questioned her with a glance.

"With everything," Kyrie responded.

"Everything but what we swore not to share?" Becca asked.

Kyrie nodded her head, knowing the others did not want to reveal having concealed her killing the men in Arkansas and then disposing of the bodies in a hole in the woods. "Everything but that."

After a moment, Becca nodded her head. "He's going to lose his shit, but yeah, I think so."

Kyrie's head throbbed. *Please,* she wished of the universe. *We need to get out of here before they kill one—or all—of us.* "Can I have my phone back? I need to call Lars."

Chapter 8

Kyrie watched the tall black man get out of a hastily parked car and approach them. His wide shoulders and shaved head made him imposing; his speed, concerning; his glare, menacing. The tension in his muscles and movement radiated his anger.

"Becca, you weren't to leave the house." He shook his head. "And to come here? Around her?" His deep voice vibrated the air. "How could you betray me like this?"

"Dad—"

"Don't dad me; get in the car now. We're going home." He looked around at the police, reporters, neighbors, and the broken window. A curse escaped his lips, too quiet to be heard. Then he turned his gaze on Kyrie, but he continued to speak to his daughter. "You'll end up dead if you continue to associate with her."

"Mr. Williams," Michelle said softly, looking up at the tall man. "It's not Kyrie's fault."

"Watch yourself, Michelle," he snapped. "You've been a close friend of Becca's for years, but I'll ban her from seeing you as well." He pointed at her shoulder. "You're still wearing a sling from getting shot. You're lucky to even be alive. I don't need my Becca to take a bullet." He looked back at the damaged house and shook his head. "Now they're doing drive-by shootings. Someone's going to get killed." He turned around and started walking toward his car. "Come."

"Dad," Becca said firmly with her feet planted, but kept her voice low. "The shit's already going down. It's too late to get out. I don't want you to die."

Kyrie spread her feet to keep from wobbling as she pulled herself out of Mr. Williams' mind, sensing little beyond the boiling rage. She opened her mouth to start talking but could not summon the courage to vocalize her words. *You need to calm down,* she tried to mentally project through her headache, knowing she had almost no likelihood of convincing him to help in his current state.

Mr. Williams spun around to face his daughter. "We're leaving."

"Dad, we can't talk here," Becca pleaded, "but we need to tell you something. I need you to listen to me. Please!" He offered no reaction to her pleading. "Please," she repeated.

"Fine."

Becca tensed. "I need you to take Michelle and Kyrie with us. We can tell you everything when we're away from here."

He crossed his arms. "You're going to tell me the truth now? After all this?" He lifted a hand toward Kyrie's house. "Two weeks since you ran off to Arkansas, now you want to come clean all of a sudden? The bullet-riddled house finally getting through to you?" His head shifted from side to side very slowly. "I've known you've been lying to me the whole time, but for the life of me, I've not been able to figure out why the hell you'd do it. I've always trusted you."

Becca moved closer to her father and lowered her voice. "Yes, this shit is scaring me. Tina didn't kill herself. She didn't kill her parents. I don't want them to kill you. To make me kill you."

He continued to growl his words, but with less venom. "Stop associating with her is the first step."

Becca's fists closed. "Someone put up what I'm pretty sure is a f'ing camera in front of our house this morning. There's one in front of Michelle's and one in front of Kyrie's. I'm certain we'll all be dead soon because of what we know. Especially if Kyrie is not with us. The people involved don't want the truth getting out. I'm sure that's why Tina was killed."

Mr. Williams cursed under his breath and turned away before coming back to face his daughter. "Everything? The truth this time?" He continued to stare at her. "Where's this camera?"

Becca nodded, but did not look away from him. "On top the streetlight. I'm guessing Aki's and Jake's houses will have them too."

They all turned as Kyrie's aunt backed her SUV out of her driveway, cutting across her yard and dropping off the curb to avoid the police cruisers. The determination on her face forced the four of them to move out of her way. She shook her head at them as she backed into a neighbor's driveway so she could turn south down the street. The northern route remained blocked by the police and the news crew.

"Where's she going?" Mr. Williams asked, his eyes narrowing.

"To get Kyrie's cousin and Michelle's brother," Becca said, starting to walk toward her father's silver four-door sedan parked thirty-feet away.

"She's just leaving … her here?" Mr. Williams' emotions shifted slightly, adding disbelief to his anger. "Are the cops allowing them to leave?"

Hopefully, what you did to the cops will work. The limited success with the pistols caused doubt, but all the officers had left them standing alone and had not returned.

"Kyrie didn't do anything but get shot at," Michelle said, following right behind Becca and her father. "Some cops already left because they might have found the truck the shooter used."

"Dad," Becca pleaded, "the police said a lot of people were murdered this morning. We need your help."

He looked over his shoulder at Kyrie. "Who's after you?" He lifted a hand. "Wait, any phones, smartwatches, or other trackers? Take them off." He frowned at their expressions. "Don't bullshit me by saying you girls don't have any. I'm not stupid enough to think you wouldn't have found a way to get a phone. You texted me, Becca."

Michelle removed her watch and Kyrie pulled her phone from her rear pocket.

Becca shook her head. "You have my phone. The only thing I have is this old watch Mom gave me."

He frowned, took Kyrie's phone and Michelle's watch, and then hurried to his car. He opened the trunk and put them into a metal ammo case that contained a copper-mesh basket that fit snugly inside the box. Next to the ammo case sat a large tool bag that appeared to store electronics, including a laptop, instead of wrenches. He removed his own phone, sports watch, and put them into the box before he latched it closed.

"Get in." He moved to the driver's door, opened it and climbed inside. Michelle got in behind him, and Becca slid into the passenger seat. Kyrie sat behind Becca. The old tan leather seats looked well cared for, though the color had faded in places, and a defined wear pattern revealed their age.

Mr. Williams started the car, turned his upper body to look out the rear window, and reversed so that he could turn around in the street. Kyrie felt his gaze rake over her in the process. She finally found her voice. "I promise, I never intended for anyone to get harmed and never wanted to put anyone in danger."

"Becca's told me that several times." He put the car into drive and accelerated, though he kept his speed low enough to avoid drawing the attention of the police. "Now, tell me who the hell is after you and don't ramble. I want you to get to the damn point."

Kyrie took a deep breath. *He's calmer, but not calm.* "There are things that probably shouldn't be said while you're driving." She sensed him about to object, so she hurried to offer something. "But on the trip to Arkansas, we learned about two groups that are after me."

"You have the gall to imply that you didn't know what was going on before you ran off with my daughter to who knows where and almost got her killed?" Mr. Williams turned his attention back to the road as he braked hard to avoid blowing through a stop sign.

Kyrie allowed some edge to return to her voice. *This is not the time to play timid.* "I've never lied." *Liar.* "My parents never explained anything to me. I don't think they actually knew much themselves. What I've learned has been in the last three weeks." Her nostrils flared. "All I've ever known is to avoid people, especially those in authority, and to hide. My parents' friend—who was supposed to come and get me—let my aunt take me back to Olathe against my wishes. Had ..." She wanted to blame Lars, but her decision to go to her nearest neighbor in the hopes of helping her mother had triggered everything. "Had I gone with him instead of coming to Olathe, I probably still wouldn't know who was after me." *Unless Lars is now working for Nalitran or Hurlington.*

"Dad," Becca said, placing one hand on the dashboard, "don't go directly home. The camera is watching the front of the house."

He turned his attention back to her. "I wasn't planning to." He navigated around a parked car as he picked up speed. "You have proof there's a camera at everyone's houses or just a theory?"

Becca tensed as the morning's fear returned. "I looked out the window just as some white dude in a bucket truck moved a lift up, popped a plate off the light to get to the wires, then stuck a box with an antenna on top the light. The guy, nervous as a brother pulled over by the cops, took off like white crackers in the hood as soon as they were done."

Her father frowned. "You've never lived in the hood. Don't let TV stereotypes warp your brain. I don't make money and live in a good neighborhood so you can pretend to be a thug. Have some self-respect."

Becca looked away for several moments. "I took pictures of the box through my window. Hopefully, the glare prevented the camera from seeing me." She pulled a memory card from her pocket and held it up.

Mr. Williams said nothing as the car sped down the street. He finally slowed as they approached a line of cars parked in front of a group of houses. "Who are these people?" he demanded of Kyrie. "Who shot up your house? Give me a f'ing name! Is it that church?"

Kyrie kept her voice hard and nodded her head. "They are one of the two groups. The Church of the Righteous Revenge. The leader, Dennis Hurlington, wants me dead."

"They are the ones that took Tina and shot Michelle," Becca's father stated.

"Partially true," Kyrie immediately corrected, her instinct for accuracy coloring her tone. She sensed Mr. Williams' irritation and softened her clarification. "His people came to the farm, but it was another group that took Tina and shot Michelle. That group wants me alive and used Tina as leverage. Hurlington wants to kill them as well, which is why the two groups willingly killed each other. That conflict allowed us to get Tina out." *Only to let her die later.*

Becca's father considered the statement for a moment. "I found old reports that Hurlington did some time for petty crimes thirty years back. Then he completely disappeared, only to show up leading that church ten years ago, but no indication of where he is today. Who's this other group and why do they want to kill each other?"

"You've been researching him?" Becca asked.

Mr. Williams glanced at his daughter and then back to the road, hitting the brakes as he drove up on a slow minivan. "Move your ass," he muttered, then turned his focus back to Becca. "Someone tries to kill you, you're damn right I'm going to look into it." He looked in the mirror at Kyrie after turning eastbound at the first side road to get away from the van. "Who is this other group?"

Kyrie sensed a nuance to his anger. *Protectiveness.* "The other man is Steven Bishop," she said, using his assumed name. "He wants to capture me."

"Who's that?"

"He's a rich bastard that owns Nalitran Enterprises," Michelle offered.

Mr. Williams glanced at her in the mirror as he blew through a stop sign and turned onto a primary street. The engine revved as he pushed the car to match the speed of traffic and prevented the minivan from pulling out from the next side road. "Why the hell would he care about some girl who spent her life on a mountain in Colorado. Even if she's some affair baby, that shit don't mean anything these days."

Kyrie's fists tightened at the slight against her mother, but she did not look away from his gaze. "That would best wait until you're not driving."

"Where are we going?" Becca asked, looking around quickly to gauge their destination and to change the topic.

He switched lanes and sped past a green SUV. Another glance in the mirror softened his expression, and he turned his attention to his daughter while shifting lanes again. "I really wish you'd have come clean sooner. We could have reported this to the cops and done something before things got this far out of hand."

"You can't trust the cops," Kyrie snapped.

Mr. Williams frowned. "Normally, I might agree with that, but this is different."

"Trust me," Becca said. "We can't go to the cops."

"Trust you? Even with all the lies?" He sped through a yellow light and continued heading east.

Kyrie watched as Becca shifted so she could look at her; Becca's eyes questioning. Kyrie swallowed and nodded her head. *Worst case if this goes wrong is you'll have to run on your own. And your friends die.* She pushed harder on projecting a sense of calmness, hoping it would help to prevent him from reacting badly.

Becca turned back to her dad. "Once we show you, you'll understand. But aside from that, the police might have covered up Tina's death. Most likely, Bishop's people killed her to keep his secrets."

"You think some dirty cops are involved?" He shook his head. "I hate to be the person that says it, but Tina was traumatized after what happened. It can make people snap. Do things you don't expect them to do. Do you have proof of your claims?"

"She wouldn't have done it," Michelle repeated, her cheeks wet.

Kyrie caught the street sign as Mr. Williams turned onto Pflumm Road and headed south. With the emotional pain from Michelle, the fear from Becca, and the anger from Becca's father, Kyrie felt her own turmoil building and had to block out the surrounding emotions.

They passed housing developments on both sides of the road as Kyrie tried to memorize their route in case she needed to get back to her aunt's house on her own. The landscape changed as they passed through an intersection. Tree-lined fields occupied the right side of the view, but a small regional airport on the left caught her attention. She understood the concept of planes, and had seen many flying over the city, but she had never had a chance to see a plane close up before. *They're smaller than I expected. How hard are they to drive?* She considered the possibility of stealing one to escape. *Or just use it to get back to Kim's house,* she added, realizing the distance to her binding stone only kept increasing.

"What were you all saying about murders earlier?" Mr. Williams asked, breaking the silence, his voice more even and less panicked.

"Not sure," Becca said, her tone projecting a subtle anger. "The cops and a neighbor mentioned something. I've not had my phone to keep up with things."

Kyrie shifted in her seat again, hoping Becca had not irritated her father with her attitude. "The officer didn't say much, but she appeared to think the killings had something to do with Hurlington. She mentioned terrorist attacks across a dozen states, but gave no details."

Becca's father shook his head as his breathing sped up. He kept his eyes on her in the mirror. "This cult you're somehow connected to— they're killing people across the country?"

Kyrie wanted to protest her involvement, but she held her tongue and raised a concern she had with the assumption. "I'm not sure Hurlington's church had anything to do with it. He wants to kill Bishop … and certain other people." Kyrie looked out the window as they passed a sign for Heritage Park with a small lake visible in the distance. She turned back to Becca's father. "Perhaps he targeted a number of people Bishop controls, but I don't think he attacks random people."

"Just people like you," Mr. Williams said. "What's the motive? I know his people said something about you being a demon to the police before they hung themselves." He raised a hand in surrender. "Or were killed. Either way, they're dead."

Kyrie shook her head and turned her attention to what was outside the car as they sped south. The lake had given way to sporting fields, but she did not have time to study the groups of people milling about before they crossed over a bridge and the landscape changed into woods on both sides of the road.

"Nothing?" he demanded.

Becca spoke. "Before Bishop founded Nalitran Enterprises, he ran a criminal organization. One of the men that died at the farm— Michael Rodgers—ran it. Rodgers didn't secretly work for Hurlington, as reporters are saying. Rodgers, we were told, had done things to Hurlington."

"I want answers," growled Becca's father.

"It should wait until you're not driving," Kyrie emphasized as the car continued up a hill. *We'll show you when we stop,* she projected and then pushed her hands into her lap to steady them. *It's just a campaign objective. Get the reluctant ... person ... to believe you and help.* She could not start thinking of her allies as NPCs, but thinking in terms of the game helped her to focus.

"Fine," he snapped. "We're almost there, and then I want no more evasions."

They crested the hill, and a large house appeared on the left side of the road. "Where are we going?" Becca repeated.

Her father shook his head and continued to drive. The trees on the left changed to fields and then back into a housing development, while the woods continued on the right. The sound of tires on blacktop filled the silence until he hit the brakes and turned right onto a side road leading into the southern entrance to Heritage Park.

Kyrie's eyes shifted between the windows on each side of the car. What she had thought to be a dense forest only amounted to less than a hundred feet of trees before opening into a large rolling grassland. The hills had a scattering of trees dotting the landscape, but the open space disappointed her more than she expected.

Mr. Williams turned into a small parking lot at the edge of the tree line and shut off the car. A small shelter covered a single picnic table with benches on all four sides. He glanced around and then opened his door. "We'll talk over there."

Kyrie opened her door and got out of the car with Becca and Michelle exiting right after her. She could not see or sense anyone near them. Mr. Williams walked ahead of them, already halfway down the concrete path to the shelter. Becca's hands shook, and Kyrie sensed all of their hearts racing. "We don't have a choice," she said more to herself than to them. *Could you steal the car to get back to your aunt's? The distance would take too long to run there.* With the shelter only fifty feet away, Kyrie did not have the time to address that question or to change her mind.

"Well?" he demanded when he stopped next to the table, his muscular arms crossed.

Kyrie took a deep breath and opened her worn-out mind. Energy swirled around and through her, burning her nerve endings as she pulled it from the ground to craft a gravitational field around Becca's father. Her eyes closed and she focused on visualizing the effect she wanted without harming him.

"Shit!" he cried as he tried to flail about. His voice rose two octaves as he continued to curse worse than Becca.

Kyrie's field held him tight as she continued to adjust the pressure, hoping to not squeeze him too tightly. The energy wrapped his whole body, forcing him to remain upright as she slowly lifted him into the air and shifted him sideways. Blood pounded in her ears, blotting out his demands for help. Sweat formed on her forehead as the power coursed through her body. She opened her eyes as her field held him a foot above the small picnic table. It had taken only a moment to move him, but that felt like a glacial pace compared to how fast she had flung herself away from the bullet that destroyed her bedroom window.

Her breathing turned to panting as the energy passing through her body spiked her internal temperature, threatening to cook her flesh and internal organs. Becca shifted uncomfortably next to her, and Kyrie dropped the large man onto the top of the table with less grace than she had intended.

Mr. Williams continued to cry out with inarticulate sounds as he scrambled down to the ground, putting the table between him and Kyrie.

"Dad," Becca cried, rushing to his side, her voice pleading. "That's why we couldn't tell anyone." She reached out and touched his arm to calm him.

Kyrie felt his heart racing as his panic shifted to terror.

"What the hell was that? Are you a demon?" His eyes never left Kyrie as he pulled his daughter behind him.

"No," Kyrie responded evenly.

"Did you drug me? What'd you do to me?"

"Mr. Williams," Kyrie said, command in her voice, masking the agony that made her want to sit. The sharp pain ignored, she stood at her full height and stepped closer, bringing herself under the small shelter's roof. "I am not a demon. We did not drug you. I didn't mean to scare you, but showing you was more likely to convince you than telling you."

His large eyes did not leave her. "If not a demon, then what are you? Some alien? How'd you do that? Are you messing with my mind?"

"You're hurting my arm," Becca said as she tried to pull her wrist free of her father's grasp. "She's not done anything to your mind. She bends gravity."

"A spellcaster, but with science magic," Michelle said, moving to stand beside Kyrie, her right hand out of the sling, offering physical support.

"This isn't some game," Mr. Williams snapped. "You some kind of space alien?" he demanded.

Kyrie shook her head. "I was born on Earth to human parents. I'm human." She swallowed. "At least most of me." *You can do this.* "You're the first adult—outside my parents—I have revealed myself to. Becca, Michelle, and the others only saw what I could do because some of Hurlington's men tried to kill me while we walked home that first week of school." She swallowed blood that drained down the back of her throat. "For my whole life, I simply thought of everyone who wasn't my parents as a threat. What we know only came out over the last three weeks." She glanced at Becca. "Much of it only because your daughter helped me." Kyrie immediately felt a sense of pride come from the older man, even with the continued fear. *We're safe. We won't hurt you,* she projected, knowing the additional damage using her powers did to her body.

"Kyrie saved our lives," Becca whispered. "She's not going to hurt us." Becca extracted her wrist from her father's grasp and then placed her hand on his arm. "We're telling you what's going on because we need help. Bishop doesn't want others to know there are people with powers." Becca swallowed. "And that means you're in danger and why we're certain Tina didn't kill herself or her parents."

Mr. Williams nodded his head to his daughter and then turned back to Kyrie. "So, you're human, but you can move me. How's this even possible?"

Kyrie sensed an intrinsic curiosity in him, but she could only shrug. "My mother was a physics professor at MIT. My dad was a programmer. Neither of them knew exactly why I'm like I am, though my mother spent the sixteen years we lived in Colorado working on the math to support her theories about transference between different universes." She took a deep breath. "We've learned that part of me came from a different world. A different universe. When I was born, apparently there was something wrong with me, and my mother and father explored any options to fix me. My aunt said that eventually it didn't matter how crazy the idea. That led them to a man living in Arkansas advertising natural healing. One Awan Brown."

"He's an older cousin of Steven Bishop," Michelle offered. "That's where the connection to Bishop comes from."

Kyrie's mind automatically probed the surrounding area, and she still sensed no one else within her range. She sat down at the picnic table, knowing it would make her less threatening and help keep her from appearing unsteady on her feet, prompting Michelle to sit down next to her. "Awan is the owner of land that had been in his family for generations. It happens to contain what might be a rip in the fabric of the universe," she said, recalling how her mother had described a similar concept in some of their D&D sessions. "A thin spot in the veil between worlds where energy, and what one might call a soul, could pass through."

Her mouth had grown dry. *You can say it.* "Awan pulled the soul of someone from this other world and forced it into my body."

"Shit," Mr. Williams mumbled and then stepped back. "You're a pod person. Your body was snatched. You are an alien!"

Kyrie glanced at Michelle and Becca; they both shared a questioning expression, uncertain of what Becca's father referenced, but just as interested in her response as he was. "I don't know exactly what a pod person is, but I've always had a sense there was another part of me, but which one is which, I have no idea." She forced her hands to remain at her sides. "I've asked myself many times, but I get no reply."

Becca rubbed her father's forearm. "Bishop wants to control her, and Hurlington wants everyone like her dead. Both will kill us because of what we know. Kyrie can protect us from others that have powers like hers."

Mr. Williams bit his lower lip. "So, this Bishop person is like you." He nodded his head as he considered his words. "Now Hurlington calling you a demon makes sense. He thinks Satan sent you."

Kyrie frowned, but she had to agree with their understanding of the other man's beliefs. *Even if you're no demon.* Aloud, she answered the question. "That's the short version. Whatever took over Bishop's body came over on its own and has been building an empire for decades. The man that was Steven Bishop was replaced by a being called Nalitran. This other being used Awan to pull souls from the other world and forcefully bind them to many other humans, making an army. Perhaps five hundred of them, based on Awan's count."

Her heart raced as she prepared herself to reveal her biggest weakness. "Sixteen years ago, Awan was still using the excess energy bleeding between universes to heal people. He didn't bind people unless Nalitran forced him. However, he decided the only way to heal me was to bind another soul to my body."

"What do you mean by binding?" Mr. Williams asked.

She bit her lip. *Mother, we know you would kill us for this, but this secret is ours to share.* She could only sense curiosity and fear. Becca's father still remained a mystery, but an undercurrent of honor seemed to exist in him. She exhaled. "The binding process includes a stone where part of the soul is locked, which allows someone holding it to exert control over the bound person. Dennis Hurlington—we were told—was a failed binding. They thought he'd die, but he escaped."

"Then he found God," Becca snipped.

Kyrie continued. "We don't know if any stone exists for him, but one that can control me does exist."

Mr. Williams continued to watch her. "And what would Bishop—Nalitran—do to you if he captured you?"

Kyrie shrugged. "Awan didn't say, but we know Nalitran wants to protect his empire. I assume he'd turn me into a slave, forcing me to do his bidding because he could control my mind." Kyrie probed the emotions coming from the others. Her head hurt too much to dive into their thoughts. All three of them had calmed.

"Shit, I need to think." Mr. Williams dropped onto the bench on the other side of the picnic table. "We're exposed with vulnerabilities all around us." He continued to stare at the wooden surface for almost half a minute.

Kyrie leaned forward, drawing his attention. "My parents' friend—"

"The lawyer," Mr. Williams interrupted.

Kyrie nodded. "I called him right before you arrived. He's been hiding because people were after him. He said he'd be here in a couple of hours. He was going to get me out of the country, but I refused to go unless he can take everyone with us. However, he still said it wouldn't be possible because his contacts didn't want State Department problems." Her shoulders tightened. "Do you have any way that you can get us out of the country?"

"Or to anyplace safe?" Michelle added. "We need to get Jake and Aki as well. We need somewhere to hide."

"But we can't reveal Kyrie's power to their parents," Becca said. "They'd freak. I told Kyrie you'd be able to handle the truth. Love you, Dad."

Mr. Williams tried to smile but ended up shaking his head. "You've not drugged me? Right?"

"No drugs," Becca said. "She flew you onto the picnic table."

"Drugs would've been better," he mumbled and then looked at his wrist before shaking his head, remembering he had taken off his watch.

Becca saw the motion and looked at her old Cartier. "Not yet ten."

He got up from the bench. "You're right; we need a defensive position so we can think. We're too exposed right now." He moved toward his car, still talking, more to himself than anyone else. "We need to hit the banks before they close. I expect I'll be limited to withdrawing a few thousand in cash from each one. I don't remember the limit, but I know that without advanced notice, they don't tend to keep that much cash on hand."

"What are we going to do?" Becca asked, following behind him, giving Kyrie and Michelle a quick, but hopeful, glance.

Kyrie suffered the pain and probed deeper into his thoughts. He still radiated fear, but she felt a strong sense of resolve. She stumbled after them with Michelle beside her. Her friend's expression was one of worry. 'I need rest,' Kyrie mouthed.

"We need cash to disappear," Mr. Williams said. "I'm just worried we might not get enough. Then we need information. Without information, we are blind."

"Can you get us out of the country?" Kyrie asked again.

Mr. Williams shrugged. He looked over his shoulder at her. "Possibly, but that would be risky. Immediate security first, then long-term plans later."

"Lars might have a few thousand dollars on him," Kyrie offered. "And I know where we can get almost thirty thousand."

He nodded, mentally recording the information, but he continued his verbal thoughts. "We also need to get in contact with everyone's parents." He glanced at Kyrie as he stopped at the back of the car. "But we need to do it so that anyone listening won't intercept what we have to say."

"I don't feel safe in exposing myself to the other parents," Kyrie said, waiting for his next move.

"Agreed." He swallowed again. "Still think drugs would be easier to process than this." He waved away her protest and then opened the trunk of his car to grab the laptop and another small box that he handed to Becca. "I want to see the pictures you took of the camera watching the house. Then you need to look up anything you can find on the terrorist attacks the police mentioned." He pulled another small box with a screen and an assortment of antennas from the tool bag. "Don't turn on the hotspot yet; I want to check if any active RF transmitters are on or in the car." He connected an antenna to the clear plastic device with black and white swirls printed on an interior board. He powered it up. "Time's not on our side. If the car's clean, I'll drop the three of you by the house while I go to the banks. Becca, I'll give you a list of things to grab. Then we need to find a vehicle these people won't know is attached to us."

"One of the red teaming vans?" Becca asked.

He nodded his head as he used the large dial to control the Portapack device.

Chapter 9

"Oh my God," Becca said as she scrolled through the results on her father's laptop. "CEOs, VPs of research, board members, politicians ... shit, so many."

Kyrie and Michelle both leaned forward, stretching their seat belts as far as they could so they could peek between the front seats at the laptop in Becca's lap. "Did that say Bishop?" Michelle asked.

Becca scrolled back up and stared at the screen. "Could this have been Hurlington? Could his people have done all that?"

Mr. Williams glanced at the screen as he finished the turn onto a side street. "I didn't find anything in my prior research that would make me think he had enough people to carry out mass assassinations. He seemed like a kook with a handful of extremists, not hundreds."

Becca performed another search. "There are so many people dead, though many have their names redacted," she mumbled as she scanned through the resulting pages before selecting one from a major site. "This just updated. Steven Bishop survived an attempt on his life at Perez University during a press conference. Two members of the Perez family, Melissa Rivera and her nephew, Diego Perez, suffered fatal gunshot wounds from a sniper on an adjacent building. Mr. Bishop, owner and CEO of Nalitran—fucking asshole," Becca injected into her reading before skipping forward. "The rest says one of his guards pushed him out of the way before the third shot, which injured the guard and would likely have killed Bishop. The shooter wasn't caught. The fucking guard should've let him die."

"Language!" her father demanded.

Becca rolled her eyes. "Is this really the time to worry about my cursing? You curse more than me."

"I'm an adult," he said slowly.

Kyrie swallowed, ignoring the bickering. *Who is more dangerous? Hurlington or Nalitran?* She bit her lip. *Depends on who you consider they are dangerous to. You, your friends, or everyone else?*

"Anyone caught?" Michelle asked.

Becca's father glanced at the laptop and then back to the road as some kids ran along the sidewalk. "Those killings are scattered over a dozen states. Whoever arranged it had to have a lot of people coordinating these things. It was a highly planned op. Especially if they are getting away without getting caught. For there to not have been leaks … the opsec on that …"

Becca continued to type. "So far nothing about the perps. Lots about the victims. Some were shot, others poisoned, and there were at least three explosions, killing an estimated twenty people. The reporters fear there could be many more not yet discovered. Death toll now estimated over a hundred." She scrolled through more links, and her voice rose. "At least one shooter is dead. Looks like an executive that killed three other executives at a company I never heard of. The shooter died after a gunfight with private security." She leaned forward, and her voice rose. "We might have proof it was Hurlington. This says the woman had links to the Church of the Righteous Revenge on her phone." Becca looked up. "Not seeing much else other than suspects unknown or police are investigating." Becca swallowed. "If they all got away, Hurlington could send even more people after us."

Kyrie watched Mr. Williams think as he drove. His constant glancing in the mirror at her echoed the anxiety she felt coming from his mind. She cleared her throat. "My parents always taught me that when all else was equal, eliminate the easiest targets first to keep them from causing trouble so when you turn your focus on the more powerful enemy you are not distracted."

"What are you suggesting?" Becca's father asked.

She kept his gaze through the mirror. "We have to figure out if Hurlington or Nalitran is the more vulnerable and then eliminate that one before shifting our focus to the next threat."

"You mean kill them?" His question was almost a statement.

"They won't hesitate to kill any of us," she responded.

Becca's father took a deep breath. "I test people's security, find weaknesses and exploit them. The people Becca read off as killed are high profile. You don't do that and not get caught without planning this for months, if not years. We don't have the resources to replicate that even for a single person, and Bishop—or this Nalitran—will only increase security after getting shot at."

"If we don't try, we might as well give up now," Kyrie snapped. "My parents didn't hesitate to kill my characters when I tried and failed, but they were brutal to me when I didn't even try. I can't see this as any different." Kyrie ignored Michelle's fidgeting. "Success is life; failure is death." *It has to be said.*

Mr. Williams accelerated the car as a decision solidified within him. "I was originally thinking of dropping the three of you at the house so you could pack some supplies while I got the cash." He shook his head. "I worry that will be too risky to go home at all. Even though the car doesn't appear to have any trackers or listening devices broadcasting, someone might have put more than one camera on the house." He turned back onto a primary street. "Becca, I'll need you to do some typing for me. Then, we need to use the computer to call everyone's parents. There is a call center app that can spoof numbers and make VoIP calls. Since we don't know if there are any listening devices around the others, I want to get them to meet us in person where we can hopefully avoid notice. But we have to assume one—or both—groups have tagged any car they had access to, which means we won't have a lot of time once everyone's in the same place. Whoever's watching is definitely going to notice if everyone is in one place."

Becca swallowed, and some strength returned to her voice. "Sure, Dad. Just tell me what to do."

Kyrie and Michelle remained hidden in the rear of the car, their heads below the level of the windows to keep from being seen. Kyrie felt the weight of her eyelids, and if her physical position in the footwell had any comfort, she would have fallen asleep. However, even with Becca having moved the seat forward, the back seat had minimal room, and the cramped space squished her sides.

She looked between the front seats at the dashboard, but the car's clock had turned off with the vehicle. So far, Mr. Williams had managed to get five thousand dollars from his first two banks, and he expressed hope his business bank would allow a slightly larger daily cash withdrawal. Neither stop felt quick to her.

"Aki is freaking out," Becca said as she continued to chat with their Japanese friend using the computer. Mr. Williams' call with their parents had resulted in the return of Jake and Aki's phones, while Michelle's mother used Michelle's phone. All details of their plans went through the encrypted messaging app, with the explicit instruction to not say anything communicated aloud. "At least Aki's parents agreed to close the shop early. They will be there at noon. Michelle, your mom is royally pissed at you."

"Great," Michelle moaned. "Add it to the list of reasons I'm worthless."

Kyrie glanced at the laptop screen and saw the small clock tick over to five after eleven. "We need weapons. My aunt kept my swords and daggers because I convinced her they had value, but she didn't let me keep my dad's rifle." She tried to breathe deeply, but her knees pressed against her chest. "The rifle the man in the green truck used was far more powerful than anything I'd seen before. I wish I had seen it clearer."

"I don't even have a pocketknife," Michelle said, her legs bent behind her as she lay across two-thirds of the seat to protect her shoulder. "But Jake's father often has a pistol on his side." She frowned. "He's a gun nut. We might be able to convince him to give us some guns."

"I swear he's a cracker," Becca said. "Hides it well enough around me, but I doubt he'd blink if someone put a collar around my neck." She frowned. "And my dad doesn't like guns. He always said a black man with a gun is a white man's target."

Kyrie narrowed her eyes. "I still don't get all the hate."

Becca shrugged. "Different is bad. Black is different from most people." She sighed. "It's not that bad here. Mostly I get side-eye. But my mom used to live in a small town in Alabama. Five years ago, she wanted to play mom again, and she took me to visit one of her cousins in what was a fully racist town. I'll never forget the hateful glares from the white people who assumed an eleven-year-old girl must be up to no good. If they could've stepped on me and squished me like a bug, they would've."

Kyrie looked up as Becca's father came out of the bank and rushed to the car. The door flew open, and he dropped into the driver's seat. The glance and then immediate shifting of his gaze away from her spoke to his discomfort.

"Managed to get them to give me three, which gives us a total of eight. Not as much as I wanted." He turned to Becca as he started the car. "Has Dylan confirmed he can get the van to us?"

Becca nodded. "He said it would take an hour to load the gear and drive it to the drop-off."

Mr. Williams' hand shook slightly as he backed out of the parking spot, catching Kyrie's eyes as he looked between the seats before lifting his head to look out the rear window. "We need to get your aunt on board with this. We don't need cops chasing us across the country. But like your lawyer friend, she didn't answer her phone on either attempt."

Michelle sat upright, and Kyrie climbed out of the space between the seats so she could sit normally again. "She doesn't have the messaging app on her phone, and my phone's in your trunk. Which is all the more reason we need to go by the house. I need my things, and if she's there, I can get her to go to the meeting spot."

Mr. Williams shook his head. "Your house is being watched. Anything we need we'll have to buy later. Becca, try calling again."

"No," Kyrie demanded. "This isn't something you can buy. I need my mother's papers and ..." She steeled herself. "I need my binding stone. If someone else has it, then I'm lost and you're all dead."

He glanced at the car's clock. "Fine. But if the police are there, they might not let you leave again. Plus, there might be other cameras and audio transmitters in the house."

Kyrie nodded. "I can sense when other people are about. I'll avoid getting caught."

He sighed and shook his head. "Becca, try the lawyer again."

"Do you want me to come with you?" Michelle asked as the car slowed one street over from Kyrie's aunt's house.

Kyrie did not shake her aching head. "The time in the car had helped immensely." *But you're not back to normal at all.* "It'll be faster if I do it on my own." She sensed both disappointment and relief from Michelle. As the car slowed to a stop, she pushed open the door, jumped out, and then sprinted into the yard of the house behind her aunt's, each footfall pounding in her head. She slowed only enough to put her hands on the top of the three-foot high black metal fence so that she could more easily vault over it.

Her mind fought through the pain as she probed for people nearby. "This house's empty," she mumbled, sensing no one in the house that owned the yard she raced through. *Three people in the house on your left,* she told herself, thankful that the tall wooden privacy fence around that house's yard shielded her from the dog and people who were on the first floor.

Kyrie leaped over the rear part of the metal fence and into Kim's yard. She felt her aunt, Sam, and Mike on the first floor of the house. No other minds registered to her tired senses. The trees in Kim's backyard provided cover for her, and she quickly reached the exposed basement walkout of the tan building.

She forced her breathing to slow and examined the windows leading into the unfinished part of the basement. A mental nudge with a gravity field unlatched the locks, and she slid the window up with her mind. No longer caring about visible damage, she pressed her shoulder into the screen, ripping the mesh free of the frame.

Kyrie paused, listening for a change in the conversation upstairs as well as expanding her mental search for any threats. She picked up her name being said, but she could not hear the substance of the conversation. *We'll be out of your hair shortly, Kim.*

With no sign of immediate threats, Kyrie continued through the low window and took in the clutter. It did not appear to her that anyone had searched through the basement. Conscious of the time, she made her way to the duffel bags and pulled them out of hiding. With them in hand, she moved to the furnace, set down the bags, and closed her eyes. Her awareness narrowed. While she could sense the world around her, even through walls, distinguishing between stone, wood, and air took more effort. Living things stood out much easier because they radiated energy, but the limited electromagnetic emissions coming off the passive structures concealed inside walls always seemed to feel like one homogenous mass.

However, the specific piece of wood where she put the binding stone haunted her and when she explicitly focused her mind, she could sense a connection to the stone. It took her only a moment to locate it. She created a gravity field high up in the stack and pushed the green stone off the two-by-four ledge. Wrapped in gravitational energy, she directed the stone down the narrow path around the vertical duct and wires. It flew out of the narrow gap into her waiting hand.

Kyrie looked at the oval stone adorned with facets. The green gem had no inner glow and resembled little more than colored glass. *But mother wore it every day in that filigree brooch. You saw it constantly. Once you loved seeing it. Now you despise it for what she did to you.* Kyrie exhaled slowly, knowing Awan had said destroying it might kill her. *If they try to take it from us, could you destroy it to protect everyone else?*

Kyrie didn't answer. She slipped the stone into her right pocket, picked up the duffels, and carried them into the finished part of the basement before setting them down again. *We're going out the back,* she reminded herself.

She took the stairs to the first floor two at a time. Mike's voice clearly rang out. "My mom's lost it. She keeps saying I need to come home immediately."

"It's not safe for you to walk home alone." Kim's footsteps echoed hard on the wooden floor as she paced. "I can't believe the police have left. Who's going to protect us if the murderers come back again?"

Kyrie exited the stairs and cleared her throat, drawing a startled jump from all three of them. They stood deep in the kitchen, perhaps subconsciously hiding in a place with fewer windows.

"Where have you been?" Kim demanded.

"We don't have time." Kyrie projected a desire for obedience and mentally assumed the role of party leader. "It's not safe here." She walked toward the counter, opened a drawer where Kim kept loose pens and note pads. She grabbed a marker and a pad advertising a plumber from the top of a pile of old papers in the drawer. "If you want to know what to do," she said as she wrote the address that Mr. Williams had passed to everyone else, "be at this place, at this time, and we'll tell you." She ripped the top page off the pad and handed it to her aunt. "Don't say it aloud. Someone might have bugged the house, your phone, or something else you carry with you. In fact, you should probably leave any phones and smartwatches here."

"What the F?" Sam demanded. "This is crazy."

Kyrie looked at her cousin and nodded her head in agreement. Then she turned and hastened toward the stairs to the second floor.

"Where are you going?" Kim demanded. "Get back here."

Do as you're told, Kyrie thought, her mind focused firmly on her aunt as pain laced through her. *Shut up and go to that address at noon.* When her aunt said nothing. "I'm getting my weapons," Kyrie responded. "People are trying to kill me, and they'll kill all of you in the process. Sam, convince your mom to do as that note says. They shot up the house this morning. They'll do it again."

Kyrie rubbed the green stone in her pocket. *You need to find a safe place to keep it.* The idea of throwing it into a river or burying it in a hole in a forest kept surfacing in her thoughts. *But can Nalitran sense the binding stones from afar and find them?* She pursed her lips. *He never found us on the mountain, so perhaps he can't sense them from that far away. What if someone else stumbles across it?* Mr. Williams' stare drew her attention, and she removed her hand from her pocket and placed it on the handle of the dagger she wore on her belt. Her other weapons remained in his car.

"You okay?" Michelle asked from where she sat at the picnic table next to Becca, who continued to keep her attention on the laptop. They had arrived only minutes before, but she had not paused in her Internet searches.

Kyrie considered the question. *You need to sleep.* She still felt overheated, even in the cool air. *Too much energy used.* "Reasonable." She decided to lie as the sound of a vehicle on the main street slowing shifted her focus. Less than a minute later, a silver car made a hesitant turn into the parking lot and selected the farthest spot.

"That's Aki," Michelle said, rising off the bench. Mr. Williams stopped his pacing and started walking toward the vehicle, his RF hacking device in his hand.

Mr. Daido Hino exited his vehicle first. The diminutive man wore a grey three-piece suit. He wore black-framed glasses that matched his short black hair. Aki and an older woman got out of the back of the car. Aki's bright t-shirt offered a sharp contrast to the tan pantsuit of her mother, Mei.

As Becca's father closed in on the three of them, Mr. Hino bowed his head and then cleared his throat, but Mr. Williams raised his hand to silence them. The smaller man straightened, but he accepted the paper that instructed them not to speak and to remove any watches, phones, or smart devices and leave them in the car.

Kyrie watched Mr. Williams proceed to walk around the exterior of the vehicle while watching the screen on the Portapack. He moved around it twice more after Aki and her parents dropped their devices into the front passenger seat. Becca's father then nodded his head toward the shelter. *You need to learn about technology,* she reminded herself. *Your enemies know how to use it, and that gives them an advantage over you.* While the cabin she grew up in had electricity, they did not have any phones or electronic devices. A CD and cassette player had been the most advanced machine her parents had owned.

Mr. Williams and the three Hinos walked in silence to the shelter. "Aki," Kyrie said, and her friend nodded her head in response. The other girl reached up, grabbed the end of her long black hair, and bundled it together in her hands. Her parents remained stoic and stood just in front of her, trying to hide their irritation and anger, but Kyrie sensed it clearly.

"Williams-san, if you will please explain what is going on," Aki's father said in perfect English with no trace of any accent.

Becca's father, standing seven inches over the smaller man, bowed his head. "I'd rather wait to explain the full situation when the others arrive. But the short version is, we are all in danger. Assassins shot up Kyrie's house this morning, and we know people are watching our homes." He used his head to gesture to the car. "Is it normally kept in the garage?"

Mr. Hino nodded his head. "Yes. I drive my MX-5 to our store. We only take the Camry when all of us need to go somewhere together." He glanced at his wife. "The Mazda only seats two."

Mr. Williams set the Portapack on the table. "My car stays in the garage as well. So far, I've not found a tracker on it. Even when I crawled under it. But your house likely has a camera watching your comings and goings. Perhaps your business as well. If your other car stays outside for any period of time, it might have a GPS monitor on it."

Mr. Hino considered the statement and then spoke. "I heard reports on the news that these mass killings might be related to that church that harmed our children. I had hoped that the troubles were behind us after the farm. However, the sad news of the Bruce family has left our daughter in pain and, obviously, the events of this morning are frightening."

"The girls don't believe Tina killed herself or her parents," Mr. Williams said softly. "And given the evidence I've seen, and what I've been told this morning, I'm taking the kids out of town. I asked you here because Aki and the both of you are all at risk. If you are willing, I want to take her with me as well. I think it is the best way to keep them safe."

Mrs. Hino spoke with urgency in a language Kyrie did not understand. Her husband responded curtly. Before they could continue, three vehicles turned into the parking lot. Kim's SUV sped to the nearest spot. A red four-door sedan that contained Michelle's parents parked between Kim and Mr. Williams' car. The last, a large dark-blue vehicle much longer than Kim's SUV, parked on the side of the lot, ignoring the two free parking spots. The position and length of the vehicle effectively blocked Kim and Michelle's parents in their spots.

Kyrie extended her already open mind in the search for threats, but she only sensed the people she could see. Waves of anger coming from the new arrivals did not ease her exhausted mind.

"Give me a moment," Mr. Williams said, picking up his Portapack and the paper with the written instructions.

Kyrie followed after Becca's father, sensing the man who drove the large dark-blue vehicle radiating an emotion that she considered threatening. She kept her hand off the handle of her dagger, but she readied herself to protect Mr. Williams from the man she presumed was Jake's father.

The door to the large vehicle opened and a blond man slid out. "What's the meaning of this?" Anger radiated from the older man's eyes. His thin hair with stringy ends blew freely in the wind. Kyrie noted the pistol in a holster on the man's belt.

Becca's father shook his head and held out the piece of paper as he continued to close the distance. The shorter man, about as tall as Mr. Hino, stormed forward and snatched the paper. "Be plain and … what in the hell is the meaning of—"

Kyrie had kept pace with Becca's father. *Please be calm,* she tried to project.

"Kyrie, you disgraceful little bitch, you do not get to simply demand my—"

"Quiet," Mr. Williams growled, his deep voice menacing, and pointed to the paper Jake's father read.

Kyrie glanced at the spikes of color changing on the screen on the Portapack, then turned her attention to Jake. The lanky boy from school looked broken, and her anger grew. *No one harms my friends.*

"Christian, what nonsense is this?" demanded Jake's mother as she came around from the passenger side of the vehicle.

Silence! Kyrie screamed mentally. Everyone hesitated, including Michelle's parents, who had gathered their son from the back of Kim's SUV.

"Please," Mr. Williams said, "wait to ask questions."

He looked down at the screen in his gloved hands and shook his head. Kyrie no longer saw the spikes of color on the device. As Becca's father moved around the vehicles, she followed after him. He crouched down, then dropped to the ground around the rear of the dark-blue vehicle. Kyrie watched him scoot under the vehicle with Expedition written across the rear hatch.

A moment later he pulled off a black box and purposely shook his head to warn Jake's father into silence. He looked at the device that just fit into his large, gloved hand and then set it on the ground. He went to each of the other vehicles and removed one from Kim's SUV and a third one from Michelle's parents' sedan.

The others stood in quiet stupor. *This is your campaign.* Kyrie stopped following after Becca's father, took the paper from Jake's father and walked around to show everyone what it said. She pointed to their wrists, purses, and pockets and then towards their vehicles. Slowly they all obeyed, then they all followed her toward the shelter.

Once they reached the picnic table, Kim moved to the far side to get out of the sun, pushing her son behind her. "Do you want to explain yourself now?" Kim demanded, though her voice barely broke a whisper.

Kim's question sparked Peggy Windall, an older version of Michelle with greying hair. "What are you doing out of the house, Michelle Jane Windall? You're already grounded until you're eighteen. Where is your sling? You'll tear the stitches!" The older woman kept a hand on her son's shoulder and stood next to her husband.

Michelle did not move to join them on the other side of the table. "I don't need it," Michelle replied.

"You endangered Mike by hanging out with her," Michelle's father shouted.

"Me?" Michelle snapped back. "Mike is Sam's friend! He'd have been there regardless of who my friends are!"

"Quiet!" Kyrie snarled, the charged emotions weighing on her, but she refused to close down her mind in case a threat emerged. She exhaled slowly. *Don't roll a one.* "Your lives are all in danger—"

"Because of you," snapped Jake's short father, followed by Jake's mother agreeing.

Kyrie tilted her head and glared before she remembered she needed to keep everyone calm. She took a moment to steady her emotions. "Your kids know things that people will kill to keep quiet," Kyrie answered, pushing more energy through herself in the hope that projecting a desire for everyone to remain calm would be worth the physical cost to her body. "Tina didn't kill herself, and she didn't kill her parents. And a lot of people were executed overnight. The people after us won't stop. They tried to kill me this morning, and they will come for my friends, either to eliminate them, or to use them as leverage against me." She widened her stance and forced herself to shift her gaze between the people in front of her. *Just like when you had to convince the royal council not to execute you in your dad's last campaign.* "There is something big going on." *Project confidence, even if you're not certain. You need them to allow the others to come with us.* "Those of us who know the truth need to go into hiding. We have to leave now. Otherwise, it is only a matter of time before they are dead, and you with them."

"We need to go to the police!" Jake's mother shouted.

"We're leaving," Jake's father yelled. "Boy, get in the car!"

"Michelle, come here!" Her mother pleaded.

"Stop!" Mr. Williams roared, using his size to his advantage. "We are beyond all of that. It is too late to go back to the way things were." He used his head to indicate the parking lot. "What I took off your vehicles are GPS trackers. They radio home their position at least every minute when moving. The people after our kids already know we are all together right now. We don't have a lot of time to bicker and argue." When everyone held their tongue, he continued. "Some of you already know it, but in case you don't, I specialize in security penetration testing. While those trackers are not expensive, renting a bucket truck and putting cameras on the streetlights in front of all our houses is. If it was me, I'd already have hacked your computers, perhaps your cell phones, and planted other recording devices in and around your houses." He softened his tone. "Our meeting right now is a triggering event. It will force them to act. They now know for certain that we know things and their actions are to eliminate people that know things."

Mr. Ottiman sneered, putting a hand on the pistol at his side. "I'll shoot anyone who threatens my family."

Kyrie sensed the fear he intended his bravado to mask. "You can't be everywhere at once. They shot up my aunt's house. The bullets ripped through multiple walls."

"They said it was a fifty-cal," Michelle mumbled. "That'll go through walls and rip a person apart." She looked around at the stunned expressions from the adults. "What? I use them in first-person shooters all the time."

Mr. Ottiman swallowed. "Someone was shooting a Barrett?"

Kyrie moved a step closer to everyone, her head again throbbing from the forced concentration and energy usage. "The only option is to go into hiding." She looked at Michelle, Becca, Jack, and Aki. "The five of us need to disappear. I know how to hide. My parents taught me throughout my whole life."

"You'll not be taking my son anywhere," Mrs. Ottiman screeched. She grabbed his wrist and pulled Jake closer to her.

Kyrie glanced at her aunt, whose face had paled. Sam and Mike stood next to each other; their frequent glances showed confusion and fear. Aki and her parents, on the far side of Kim and Michelle's parents, had not moved or spoken aloud. She looked at Michelle and Becca, who stood on her left. Her heart raced as she pushed a sense of calmness into the air, but she had no idea if it made any difference.

Mr. Williams continued speaking. "As Kyrie said, none of you are in a position to protect your kids and the rest of your family at the same time." He cleared his throat. "Based on what I learned this morning, I truly believe this is the best option. I can take all five of the kids and disappear. Between my cyber skills and Kyrie's living in the wild for more than a decade, I think we can keep them safe." He raised a hand to silence the others. "My hope is that if I take them away, the people coming after them will see less value in all of you." His volume increased. "I would still highly suggest you all go on immediate vacations. Go somewhere you've never wanted to go before. Use cash and not credit cards. Leave your phones and anything that could track you behind."

"That's impossible," Kim said. "I'd lose my job, and I'm already strapped for cash."

"The alternative is being dead," Kyrie snapped. "Don't forget what happened this morning." Kim paled again.

"We need to go to the police," Jake's mother demanded. "And the church will help."

Mr. Williams looked at his bare wrist and frowned. "We don't have time to argue. I'm leaving and taking as many of the kids as you'll allow." He looked at each parent. "I don't believe anyone who keeps their kid with them will live to see Monday."

Mr. Hino spoke, cutting off Michelle's father. "Williams-san, how would this actually help my girl? How would we even find you later? How will we know they are safe?"

Aki leaned against her mother, allowing the older woman to wrap a protective arm around her. Kyrie held back the tears of knowing her presence had forever upended these people's lives. *And any that refuse will die.*

Mr. Williams continued. "I won't share any of my plans. I can't risk anyone saying something later to compromise the op. However, we will stay out of sight until we can figure out a way to deal with the issues. And before anyone suggests we all go together, having the five kids with me will already draw more attention than I like, but I can manage that. However, I can't hide all of you."

"Mom," Michelle pleaded. "If I stay with you, then Mike is in more danger, and so are you and Dad. You need to let me go with them."

Kyrie looked at Kim. "I'll ask Lars to give you some of the money when I talk to him. You never wanted this mess. You need to let me go. If you don't, what happened this morning is only the beginning."

Kim's pallor turned to indignation. "It's not about the money!"

Kyrie ignored the lie; a car just passed the tree line and slowly approached the parking lot a hundred feet away. The arguing had distracted her, and she only now noticed it. The passenger, a black man with cropped hair, met her eyes just before the car sped up. She lost sight of them briefly as the Expedition blocked her view. The two people barely registered in her mind, as if something muted them, but the oddness of their mental presence stood out like a beacon in the night. *Bound.* "Everyone get down," she ordered as she pulled her dagger from its sheath.

"What?" several parents exclaimed. Her friends instantly obeyed.

Jake's father strode forward, coming between her and Mr. Williams. "This is ridiculous."

Kyrie continued to watch as the car headed west, away from the shelter. The road climbed a gentle hill, and the trees around the shelter blocked her view of the car. She turned to Becca's father. "They're like me," she offered, maintaining the security they had agreed upon.

"Shit! Decisions now," Mr. Williams snapped, wrapping the cord for the antenna around his Portapack. "Becca, laptop."

"We're leaving," Jake's father demanded.

Kyrie moved past the shorter man and headed toward Mr. Williams' car and her swords. She had just reached the parking lot when a white panel van sped past the trees. Instinct pulled power into her. The sharp pain of the heat made her stumble. She sensed three determined men in the vehicle.

"Down!" she cried as the van screeched to a stop at the other end of the lot, the door already open.

The first man leaped out, a rifle against his shoulder. Dressed in black with a helmet and a hard face mask, he looked physically massive. He had waited to fire until he had steadied himself on the ground.

Power rushed from Kyrie. At seventy feet, she struggled to push the front of the barrel into the air as bullets erupted from the weapon. She managed to lift it just high enough that the burst of rounds flew over her head and ripped through the trees behind her.

Jake's father stood paralyzed next to her. She ripped the pistol from the man's holster, thankful that nothing snagged the weapon's removal. Anger at the man's attitude caused her to use more force than necessary to shove him to the side, physically throwing him to the ground in front of his vehicle.

A second man jumped out of the van as Kyrie leaped behind Kim's SUV. Glass shattered and bullets ripped through thin sheet metal and into the vehicle's interior and out the other side as the first man fired another burst as he tracked her movement.

Damn it! Kyrie continued to the front of the SUV as she examined the pistol for a safety. On the mountain, she had learned to shoot the rifle, and her father had at one time brought a pistol home. However, her parents had usually preferred the use of the bow to avoid attracting attention with the noise.

Another hole blew through the passenger door just behind her. A moment later, she heard the sound of the larger rifle firing. *The bastard from earlier,* she swore.

Sensing the two men moving to go around both sides of the parked vehicles, Kyrie winced as more energy flowed into her body. She felt their positions, and with the two men now only thirty feet away, she concentrated on lifting both barrels at the same time just as she rose above the hood of the SUV. Both men fired again, but their shots went high. Kyrie gripped her weapon with two hands and squeezed off two shots at the man with the rapid-fire weapon.

The man grunted as both rounds struck him center of mass, but Kyrie could see the impacts did not significantly affect him. *Armor.* She pulled more energy through herself, feeling blood run from her nose. She continued her mental fight with the men to keep their barrels elevated as she scanned the area for another weapon.

"Give up, or we'll kill your friends," the second man shouted, shooting a round toward the shelter, again going high.

Kyrie rose back over the hood of the SUV and fired two shots at the face of the second man. The first shot went wide, striking the side of the white van. The second shot splattered against the edge of the thick mask and slid off over the man's shoulder. *Shit.*

The first man unloaded another burst of rounds, pelting the front of the SUV before Kyrie could mentally push the weapon away. She fired again, aiming for the man's trigger hand, hoping the gloves he wore did not offer as much protection. The shot missed his hand and hit him in the chest again.

The sounds of a car racing in their direction held her second shot. She spared a moment to glance into the park and see the two Bound men speeding toward them. The black man hung out the passenger window, a rifle in hand. A long burst of shots flew in the direction of the van. She heard the pinking of bullets through sheet metal and the cracking of glass, but most of those rounds missed their target.

The second man pivoted quickly, took aim and fired into the oncoming car. He recovered from the recoil and fired again.

Kyrie narrowed her focus on the first man, and she opened fire again, squeezing off three shots aimed for the man's trigger hand. The first struck the rifle body and fragmented. The second flew over the rifle and hit the man's shoulder, but the third sprayed blood against the rifle and the man's face mask. The bullet entered just under his index finger and ripped through the man's hand, sending fragments of bullet and bone all the way into his forearm.

He screamed in pain and dropped the rifle, though the sling kept the rifle from dropping to the ground. He grabbed his bleeding right hand with his left and stood upright.

No mercy. Kyrie knew she had fired eight times, but she did not know how many bullets the pistol held. No longer under immediate threat, she took longer to aim, firing a single shot toward his neck, which he had exposed as he turned toward the van, reeling from the pain of the wound to his hand.

The second man had fired twice more before his companion stumbled to the ground. The car with the Bound drove off the road and bounced into the grass. Kyrie turned the pistol on the man with the large rifle. She aimed for his exposed neck, but she struck him in his armored shoulder.

He staggered to the side, the impact causing obvious pain. He dropped low, using Becca's father's car as cover to reach his fallen companion. The first man, which Kyrie knew was not dead, struggled to his feet, and with the help of the second man, they rushed toward the van, which had driven into the grass to rescue them.

Kyrie looked into the eyes of the van's driver through a half-dozen holes in the cracked windshield. She fired the pistol a tenth time, striking the driver in the shoulder, but he also wore armor and merely reversed as soon as the first man landed in the van. Kyrie hoped the wounded man would bleed out before help could save him. She tried to fire again as the van spun around to rush for the exit, but the weapon merely clicked with the slide locked back.

As if waking from a fugue, she shook her head and used her senses to take in the situation. Blood ran from her nose, her ears rang, and while she thought someone was shouting something, she could not hear their voices. *Heal,* she demanded, redirecting the energy burning her insides to fix the damage to her ears while she examined herself for any other physical injuries. Her overheated brain throbbed, and more blood oozed from her nose.

She wiped at her face with her hand, smearing the red fluid that had reached her chin as she turned to face everyone else. Becca's father stood first. "The time for thinking is over, I'm leaving! Any of the kids coming get in my car now!" He stared at Kyrie's face. "Are you hit?"

Kyrie shook her head. "I'm fine." She rushed to Jake's father and held out the pistol to him. He stared at her and the blood again dripping down to her mouth. A moment later, he carefully took the weapon from her hands.

Aki's parents hugged their daughter and pushed her forward. "Protect her," Mr. Hino demanded.

Michelle nodded to her parents, who stood a dozen feet away. "I have to go." She rushed after Becca, racing to the sedan.

"Get away from me," Kim said. "I want nothing of this." She looked at the destroyed rear windows of her SUV. "I still have three years left on the loan."

Mr. Williams stopped next to Jake's father. "I can keep your boy alive. If he's coming, we are leaving now." The shorter man hesitated and finally nodded his head, but said nothing aloud. "Good. Now, I suggest all of you leave immediately, get the rest of your families and get out of town." He continued toward his car and shouted over his shoulder. "On Monday, call the school and tell them you're pulling your kids from class for the rest of the year because of the risk to their lives. Say nothing more. We don't need the police looking for us. It'll put everyone's life at risk."

Chapter 10

Nalitran glared at the state police captain. "What do you mean the man escaped? Do you not have competent people on the force? It's been hours since this happened."

The man with hints of Native heritage cleared his throat. "Mr. Bishop, it is understandable that you are angry. Had your bodyguard not reacted as quickly as he did, you would likely have suffered Ms. Rivera's and Mr. Perez's fate. I understand how that is impacting you. However, we didn't know about the impromptu press conference, and the university manages its own security team."

"Is Oscar okay?" Nalitran asked, knowing multiple news teams congregated in the neighboring community room of the library. After the shooting, the police rushed many of the gathered people into the nearest building that appeared secure. He doubted the reporters could hear him, but the captain seemed to respond favorably to the expression of concern for others, and he would repeat whatever he heard. *Weak man.*

The officer moistened his lips. "Your bodyguard is still being treated, but I believe the wound is not life-threatening."

Nalitran nodded knowingly. *As a dolunar, the man's life is mine.* He always carried the binding stones of his guards and continued to order his injured soldier not to heal himself. He could not risk the doctors asking why no bullet hole existed in the man's shoulder, so his selected guard would need to suffer in pain for a while.

"The feds will be here soon, and they will have a number of questions. However, and I'm sure your assistant has briefed you already, there have been multiple terrorist attacks last night and this morning." The officer shifted his weight to the other foot. "While it is too soon to rule out someone having a specific issue with you, it appears possible that you might have simply been targeted in a larger effort to assassinate business leaders."

Nalitran frowned. "I'm certain someone will eventually work out the details."

Yrginda cleared her throat. "Mr. Bishop, I need to speak with you. Geduvar."

Nalitran narrowed his eyes. The dolunar general had uttered a bastardization of the word for a critical issue, but neither human ears nor human throats could actually form the sounds needed to speak their native language. He turned back to the officer. "Can you excuse us? It has been a couple of hours since I was shot at, and I'm certain there are people who need me to respond to the event so others do not lose faith in my businesses."

The police captain nodded his head and then motioned to the two other officers who had stood by as silent observers. "We'll be waiting outside the door until the feds clear us to remove the lockdown."

Nalitran waited for the police to exit the community room. The only people who remained were six of his bodyguards and Yrginda. He dropped his voice and spoke in his native tongue, butchering the words with his human limitations. "What is so critical it could not wait?"

"It appears Hurlington had a cell of operatives arrive in Olathe. They shot at the girl around the time you were shot at. She appeared to have left the house, and our watchers lost contact until several of the parents started to gather at a local park. Two of the warriors went to observe. The third has lost contact with the observers."

Nalitran growled and balled his hands. "Was she injured?"

Yrginda held her ground and eventually shook her head. "No. She walked out of the house when the police arrived. It appears the cell missed her, despite shooting directly at her through the side of the house."

"Execute Hurlington."

Yrginda raised an eyebrow. "The operation was not as successful as we had expected. While all the primary targets we expected to kill are dead, the success rate of the secondary and tertiary targets was eleven percent lower than expected."

Nalitran spoke slowly, further distorting the dolunarian words. "Hurlington cannot be allowed to kill the girl. We can pin the blame for the next round of murders on one of his generals." *I need to hunt,* he swore silently. "We'll release more intel that an internal fight for control led to the mass murders and can account for the future waves." Yrginda nodded, and Nalitran continued. "Take the plane and get to Olathe. Your only task at this point is to bring her in. Do not fail me in this." *If only I didn't need to be seen and manage all the stock transfers and purchases.* He longed for the days when he personally led warriors into battle. However, his role now prevented direct involvement.

"Take Ontrc and Zvnic," he commanded.

"Yes, warlord."

Nalitran unbuttoned his dress shirt and lifted a white t-shirt, revealing muscular abs and a strap around his chest. He selected two small stones, a red one and a green one, from the twenty-two he carried and unclasped them from the leather strap. He handed the binding stones to Yrginda. Yrginda bowed her head and immediately left the room as Nalitran fixed his clothing.

Yrginda sat in the back seat of the SUV as one of the corvlian Bound drove. A task fitting for the mentally damaged slave. Ontrc, a tall, green-eyed dolunar Bound, sat beside Yrginda with Zvnic, another dolunar Bound, in the front seat. The four of them said nothing as they headed for the airport.

Yrginda adjusted the skirt he wore, irritated at the limited mobility the tight garment provided. He hated the body Nalitran had put him into. The female lacked the strength and resilience of his natural form, even with all the physical training he forced it to endure. His twelve years in the body taught him that most humans saw their females only as objects, something only a foolish dolunar would do with their females.

The phone in his hand vibrated, and Yrginda unlocked the device. The pilot's message indicated the flight plan to New Century

AirCenter between Gardner and Olathe had been successfully filed. *Not that it will do any good for me to go to Olathe.* Yrginda's jaw clenched. Nalitran's obsession with the girl risked destroying years of planning. *It would have been better if the girl had died.* Moving up the attack on Hurlington risks adding plausible deniability to the narrative that the reclusive man had orchestrated all the killings.

And the team is not ready. My very involvement risks more scrutiny on Michael Rodgers and that ill-planned operation. That was only two weeks ago; the police haven't remotely concluded their investigation. Yrginda's head shifted from side to side as he stared at the back of the driver's seat. *All my planning could be wasted because of his ego.*

Yrginda mentally ran through the implications of who he could pull from their tasks to deal with Hurlington. The original assault team members currently had other assignments, and only some of them could reach the target in time. He would use the privacy of the plane and flight time to Kansas to issue orders to mobilize those available to him.

"General, do you know what happened to those in Olathe?" Ontrc asked in their native language.

Yrginda looked over at the dolunar occupying the body of a thirty-two-year-old man. *Why did Nalitran put me into a woman's body when he put so many others into males?* Yrginda put the phone into his large bag, which contained a sealed case with twenty binding stones. "Urdner and Libcr are dead," he responded coldly, having checked the stones earlier.

"General, what is our objective?"

Yrginda wondered the same thing. He had spent a decade carefully guiding Nalitran. Their legendary warlord had done well enough for himself in the nineteen years before Yrginda had been ripped from their world, building a small fortune, but Nalitran had lacked long-term focus and had only flirted with taking advantage of the rules of this world. *It was me that helped truly grow his fortune and understand how to leverage all the human weaknesses.* Project Kvotar and all the current operations came from him, fed to Nalitran in a way the Warlord would consider them his own. *And now, instead of staying to plan, he becomes reckless, focused only on his living forever.*

Yrginda wanted to snarl. With his tugmor, or soul, broken, he could not move to another body. When he died, he would cease to exist, and Povnrcac, their creator, would not facilitate his rebirth, for their god could not reach into this universe. *Nalitran should not have bound dolunar, only corvlians. He should not have bound me.*

Yrginda looked at Ontrc, a man he personally bound on Nalitran's orders. *Destroying tugmors should only be done to the enemy, not to our own people.* As a former member of the priest caste, he knew the disgrace of the action. *And so does Nalitran.* Aloud, he answered the question. "We locate the girl and track her until we have sufficient operatives to collect her."

Chapter 11

M r. Williams sped down 175th Street toward Kansas Highway 7, but he quickly slowed and moved toward the shoulder. Police cruisers, with their lights and sirens blaring, barreled into the oncoming lane from Mur-Len and headed toward Heritage Park.

Jake's knee vibrated against the center console with his anxious energy. His fingers played with the bowstring of Kyrie's longbow, which rested on the dash, ran between the front seats, and poked Becca in the side. "Do you think the others will get away before the police arrive?" Jake's voice broke as his head followed the movement of each police car.

Mr. Williams punched the gas as soon as the patrol cars passed. His own hands shook on the wheel. Kyrie's muscles ached as if she had run up a mountain five times in a row. She had used half the box of tissues Mr. Williams had in the glove box to stop the flow of blood from her nose. The energy she had pulled through her flesh had cooked her insides, and she could not bring herself to pull in more to piece together the emotions of everyone in the car. However, crammed into the back seat with Michelle, Aki, and Becca, the four of them had no room for comfort, and because of the physical contact with Michelle, she could not help but pick up some of her friend's emotions. Mixed with the trepidation of uncertainty and fear, remained a desire for affection and acceptance. Michelle desperately wanted Kyrie's approval. While Kyrie knew of Michelle's attraction to her, the prolonged contact amplified the awareness.

"What's happening?" Aki asked, her cheeks damp from tears. "Where are we going?"

"I'm sorry, girls, but you're going to be uncomfortable for a while," Becca's dad responded. "We need to swap out this car for something no one will connect to us. Then we need to find someplace safe to hide for a while."

"How much does he know?" Jake asked, turning his head, but unable to see Kyrie, who sat behind him and against the door.

"You all better have told me everything," Mr. Williams snapped. "You promised, Becca. Surprises could kill us."

No one ever knows everything, Kyrie told herself. "He knows of my powers," she said aloud. "And who is after us and the thin spot between the universes."

"Did you kill that man?" Aki whispered. "There was so much blood on the ground. So much blood." Aki shifted her gaze. "So much blood on you."

Kyrie could not miss the tremble in Aki's voice. She tried to shrug, but with Michelle leaning against her, she had limited movement. "He wasn't dead when they got him into the van," she offered, hoping to appease Aki. *Though we hope he's dead by now.*

Becca's father cleared his throat. "I'm asking again, because it could mean life or death, but any of you still have a phone, smartwatch, or something else that tracks what you do?"

"No, Mr. Williams," Michelle and Jake said immediately. Aki shook her head after a moment.

"I need to call Lars," Kyrie said. "He never answered, and he should know not to come to Olathe to look for me."

Mr. Williams glanced at the car's dash. "I'll need to stop for some gas before too long. You can use the computer to call again when we do."

Becca leaned forward. "That was both Nalitran's and Hurlington's men, wasn't it?"

Kyrie nodded her head. "I felt the two Bound in the car when they paused at the parking lot entrance." She swallowed, feeling uncomfortable at the memory of the mental impression she had picked up from the men in the van. "The ones that shot at us were not Bound. I believe they were Hurlington's soldiers. They had a very strong conviction in what they did."

"I can still hear the bullets," Aki said, squeezed between Michelle and Becca. "The guns were so loud. In the chat, Becca said they used a rifle on your aunt's house. Was it the loud one?"

Kyrie glanced at her hands. An acrid scent with a hint of sulfur clung to her, strong enough to break through the iron smell of her blood. "Yes. I've not seen one that powerful before." She looked across the back seat at Becca. "We need to decide who to take out first. Nalitran or Hurlington. If we can eliminate one of them, it will make it easier to deal with the remaining one."

"You mean kill them," Aki's voice rose. "Murder them."

"Both of them are a danger to all of us," Kyrie tried to state evenly, wanting to avoid agitating Aki further, but struggled with her own frustration of everyone not seeing the obvious. "To your families. To a lot of other people."

"Yeah," Michelle agreed. "All those people Hurlington killed overnight and this morning. Just wish the bastard had taken out Nalitran. That would have made our lives easier."

"I hope my dad won't be stubborn," Jake muttered. "I think he was in shock. He's always talked big, but I saw him just standing there when those men jumped out of the van." He twisted in the seat so he could see Kyrie. "Thanks for taking his pistol and pushing him to the ground. He'll hate you for eternity for doing it, but you saved his life." Jake frowned. "My mom's going to freak, though. She'll be screaming at my dad for allowing me to go with all of you."

"Let's hope they don't decide to report you as kidnapped," Becca's father said. "But I'm glad you decided to come."

Kyrie felt the pause and the unstated certainty of Jake's death had the decision gone differently. "We'll need ranged weapons at some point." She glanced at the bow. "Ones that don't take a long time to build up skill and accuracy to use."

Becca's father frowned. "Before we start down that road, let's first find a safe place to hide, learn more about these people, and identify their weaknesses." He shook his head. "Guns just incite others to shoot at you first."

Aki wrung her hands together. "I just want my parents to be safe."

"They seemed like they understood the risks," Michelle said. "I don't think they'll stay home."

Aki sniffled back tears. "My dad said to go. He'd keep my mom safe." She let out a deep breath as tears again slid down her face. "Everything just got so real so fast."

The others stopped talking, and Kyrie let her eyes sag a little. *You need some time to recover your strength,* she told herself as her exhaustion crashed against her ability to stay awake.

Almost an hour and a half later, Mr. Williams turned down a long dirt driveway past a cattle pen. Kyrie woke to see weeds filling the space between where the cows could reach their heads through the fence and the potholed road. A faded white metal barn in the distance had one of the large sliding doors off its rails and leaning against the side of the building. The house that sat on the property looked abandoned with boards over several windows and the peeling, pale blue paint showing multiple layers of other colors and exposed wood beneath it. The only indication of regular activity was a bare spot in the lawn created by someone parking a vehicle that leaked fluids.

"Where are we, Dad?" Becca asked, shifting position to avoid her ribs grinding into the door's armrest as the car bounced down the driveway.

"This place belongs to one of Dylan's uncles." He said as he drove into the barn that contained a metallic blue work van with an enlarged boxy backend. The rear split doors of the van had no windows and was covered with a large electrician's logo advertising 'Powerful Quality and Low Resistance Pricing' with a plug snaking around the words.

"Who's Peter's Electric?" Jake asked as they pulled alongside the extended-length Ford Transit van.

Becca's father turned off the car and opened the driver's door, letting the stink of cow manure in. "It's a front. There's a website and lots of fake reviews going back half a dozen years. I've got magnetic signage for three other services stuck to the inside of the roof of the van. Can swap things out in just a few minutes when needed."

Kyrie opened the door and stumbled out of the car until she regained her balance, relieving the pressure of four people being crammed into a space made for two and a half. She had already extended her worn senses to look for threats, but she only felt animals in the area. The draw of power hurt more than normal, like hot water on a sunburn. She reined in her powers and turned her focus to the larger vehicle. The solid sides and tinted driver's window hid the interior from inspection, but the physical size implied everyone would have enough space to stretch out.

Becca's father tossed his car keys onto his seat and closed the door. "This vehicle, and two others, are registered at a strip mall in Sheridan, Wyoming. They belong to a bland entity with a name that could apply to any of the businesses. That way, if someone looks up the plates, they won't track it back to my red teaming business. They don't require the names of the owners there. Great way to hide illicit businesses and foreign capital."

Aki nodded her head. "I've been reading about those lax laws." Unlike normal, she offered no additional commentary.

Kyrie stretched her shoulders and scratched the backs of her hands. She had not had a chance to wash them when Mr. Williams had stopped at the gas station, and the gunpowder smell and residue of blood now annoyed her. *Not as bad as the stink left over from butchering a deer, but you're ready for a shower.*

Becca came around the rear of the car and handed Kyrie her unstrung bow. "This is a pain in the ass to ride with."

Kyrie took the weapon. "We'll need to get some arrows."

"Yeah, I'm sure we can find a general store in the next town across from a pub. Buy a score of arrows, a suit of armor, and some healing potions while you're at it." Becca shook her head and turned toward her dad. "I don't suppose there's a place to pee anywhere nearby. You only let Jake go into the gas station when we stopped."

"Cameras, Becca. We don't want to leave a trail, and if everyone went in, someone might have noticed and then they might decide to review the recordings." Her father opened the trunk and pulled out the ammo case with their phones. "Jake, take this. Becca, keep the laptop. You can plug it in once we're on the road, and then we can try Lars once again." He pulled out Kyrie's two swords and handed them to Michelle. He grunted as he lifted the two duffel bags of books and papers and set them on the ground.

Kyrie handed Aki the bow and picked up both bags, one in each hand. She acutely felt the automatic draw of power that augmented her strength, but she could not resist showing off. *These are your companions. You need to protect them, not brag.*

Mr. Williams grabbed his own utility bag of electronics. "I think the house is unlocked. There should be a bathroom on the first floor. Everyone be quick about it. I want to be on the road as soon as possible." He walked to the back of the van and opened the doors. A curtain, with magnetic connectors down the center holding the two halves together, concealed the interior from view. He pulled it apart and stuck the magnets to the open doors, revealing a long galley with desks, bins, and electronics on both sides.

Kyrie saw four swivel chairs bolted to the floor, each alternately offset to utilize both sides of the van. *Not as much room to spread out as you thought.* Nets and cages contained a multitude of electronic devices and boxes, preventing them from falling to the floor as the van moved. Currently, the dozen monitors that filled the walls of the van between the desk and the overhead bins remained dark.

Mr. Williams climbed into the back. "Technically, you're not supposed to sit in these while we are moving. No seat belts and such, but we don't have a lot of options."

"This is amazing," Jake said, stepping in front of Kyrie to climb in next. "What is all this for? And how much did all this cost?"

You don't know how any of those things work. The nagging doubt rose up in her gut. She hated the idea of being weak and lacking.

Becca inclined her head and Kyrie stepped in next. "It's a mobile hacker space," Becca replied to Jake, following after Kyrie. "Dad's made a lot of money testing other people's security."

Mr. Williams took the ammo case with their electronics from Jake. "Okay, everyone, drop your things. Go find a bathroom in the house. We can't stay here long." His tone left no room for discussion. He raised a hand as Kyrie started to drop the duffel bags to the floor. "Kyrie, let's store those bags up near the front."

Kyrie stood straighter, giving Jake enough room to move around her and exit the rear of the van. The lanky boy moved to Aki's side, and with Michelle and Becca, the four of them glanced into the van before obeying the implied request for privacy.

Mr. Williams cleared his throat and stood upright, his more than six-foot stature having room in this oversized space. "I'm putting a lot on the line in trusting you. The most important thing to me is Becca's life." He shifted his feet, but kept his attention on her face. "I don't know what you are, what your goals are, or how you do what you can do. I honestly didn't see everything you did at Heritage." He swallowed. "I was on the ground, covering my little girl. But I heard the guns. I saw the blood that disturbed Aki. I see the unease in Jake, Michelle, and Becca." He paused to breathe. "You don't seem phased by it. I don't know how that makes me feel. Happy that you'd run at someone shooting at us or scared shitless that you'd kill any of us in our sleep if we pissed you off."

His last statement startled Kyrie, and she almost dropped the heavy bags. *Do the others fear you that much? Are they scared you'd hurt them?* She felt her eyes moisten, but then forced her emotions down. The bags hurt her hands, so she took only a moment more to set them on the floor. "I would never hurt you or any of my friends." She glanced around the van's interior before returning her attention to Mr. Williams. "I don't know what I am. Not truly, but despite what my parents tried to instill in me, I know I can't do this on my own." She pointed at the monitors and the things in the bins. "And not just because I don't know how to use these things, but because deep down I know I don't want to be alone in the world."

Mr. Williams nodded his head slowly. "I have to admit that you scare me a lot." He hesitated. "I still don't know that you're even human. However, Becca and Michelle trust you, and no matter how stupid I think some of their decisions are, I do trust their judge of character." He breathed heavily and then offered a tentative smile. "I'll let you put those bags here in this space under the desk. Then go use the bathroom. I'll finish putting the other things away."

Kyrie returned his smile, moved around him to store her mother's papers and D&D books, and then exited the van. *We won't harm our own party*, she told herself, ignoring her memories of when her parents had NPCs turn on her and how she reacted to their betrayals.

Kyrie sat in the swivel seat closest to the front of the van. The curtains that separated the cab from the back were open, with the powerful magnets holding the center edges against the side of the van. However, the rest of the material swayed back and forth as they barreled down the road. Becca sat in the front with the laptop plugged into a 120-volt outlet and charging as she followed her father's instructions.

"We need to find a sporting goods store somewhere in Topeka," her father said. "Then we need to pick up some toothbrushes and basic items. Last, we need to find somewhere to camp for a few days. I don't want to risk a hotel."

"There's not much camping in Kansas," Jake said from the far back. "At least nothing good." He leaned forward in his seat to hold Aki's hand.

"I'm planning to leave Kansas," Mr. Williams replied. "I want something remote, but not too remote. Somewhere we can get to today and has cell coverage."

Becca's eyes rolled, and Kyrie heard her mumble to herself. "Great. Camping."

"East?" Jake asked, and Mr. Williams shrugged in response. "Hawn State Park is not a bad place." Jake glanced at Kyrie. "Lots of hiking and wooded trails. Even a ten-mile loop. I've seen people jogging on it before. I think it's about a five-or six-hour drive. But you'll need a credit card to reserve a spot." He frowned. "We had to deal with that problem when we went to Arkansas. I don't think my parents got the bill yet. Otherwise, I would have heard about it already."

Kyrie's shoulders lifted at the thought of being able to burn off some energy. *Woods and running. Please, let's go there.*

Mr. Williams nodded his head. "Becca, pull up the directions. When we stop for supplies, I'll pull up one of my aliased crypto cards."

Kyrie examined the contents of the van in more detail as they drove down a highway in Topeka. The back had no windows, just walls of equipment on both sides. The narrow desk space had two keyboards and two mice for each of the four chairs and six monitors mounted above each desk, three per chair. Two large computer tower cases separated the space under each desk between the chairs. The four powered-down computers were fixed to the floor with heavy straps. Numerous colored cables and other boxes of varying size clung to the walls, the underside of the desks, and fixed to the floor in neat bundles with straps. Labels described things as switches, UPSs, and PIs.

Above the monitors, the bins with netting held various cases. She read labels for cameras, drones, antennas, and tools. The other cubbies further to the back of the van remained too far away for her to read the contents. On the ceiling, she saw several layers of signs. A green and brown sign advertising Jim's Plumbing covered several behind it.

Everything kept in its place. The order felt good after what otherwise had been a chaotic day. *And you might get to sleep outside in the woods tonight.* She closed her eyes, her anticipation driving her to imagine the sound of birds and the smell of leaf litter on the ground. *Perhaps a fire.*

The van changing direction roused her from her reverie, and she turned her focus to the road ahead of them. They turned off the highway. From where she sat, she could not see much, but multiple signs lined the street advertising a multitude of stores.

"The good thing is there are two sporting goods stores here," Mr. Williams said. "We should be able to get everything we need. And there's also a Wally-world to get the other things."

"I'm getting hungry," Becca said as she looked up from the computer.

Mr. Williams pulled into a parking lot. "Becca, I'm going to need your help getting what we need." With no windows in the back, the van lacked a rearview mirror for him to catch anyone's eye, so he shouted over his shoulder. "The rest of you need to stay in the van. Pull the curtain closed now, so any cameras or someone walking by can't see you."

Kyrie, closest to the front, got out of her seat, pulled the magnets from the metal walls and slid the curtain closed. The six magnets snapped the heavy material together automatically, closing the seam.

The back of the van darkened considerably. While she could see well enough, she felt Aki's anxiety increase. The van stopped moments after she returned to her seat.

"Hey, Becca, that laptop have any games on it?" Michelle asked through the curtain.

"No games, work tools," Mr. Williams said as he opened his door. "We won't be gone too long."

"Do you know what to get?" Jake asked, getting up from his seat so he could stand next to Aki.

"I've been camping before," Mr. Williams said as his door closed.

"We'll be back shortly," Becca offered, following after her father.

Kyrie breathed deeply, processing her memory of Mr. Williams' emotions to look for signs of betrayal. *He's scared, but won't turn us in.* She stood up and pulled the top of the heavy curtain open just a bit so that some light made its way into the back of the van. The friction of the slides kept the magnets from pulling the top of the curtain back together. *Keep the party's spirits up.* "How is everyone doing?"

Michelle sighed and then shuddered. "They weren't shooting directly at me, but I thought I was going to die out there."

"Me too," Aki said, leaning forward to rest against Jake's side. "And will I ever get to see my parents again? I hardly got to say goodbye before we drove off." Jake squeezed her closer to him.

Kyrie bit her lower lip. "I don't know," she admitted.

"My parents have Mike." Michelle could not hide all of her pain. "They don't need me." She looked up to meet Kyrie's gaze. "And I think you're right; our leaving will hopefully take the heat off them."

Kyrie looked at Jake. His emotions rolled around, shifting from extremes. "We didn't give you much time to consider things."

He shrugged. "I'm still dealing with Tina being gone." He sagged. "That was only yesterday."

No one had a response, and the others stared at various items in the back of the van. Then Michelle lifted her head. "You know, we're all together. We could play some D&D to take our minds off what happened." She shrugged. "But only if you're all up for it. I don't want to press it if you're not."

Kyrie perked up at the suggestion. The games with her parents, despite the lessons they tried to teach her through the sessions, still remained a fond memory. "I have my books and my mother's adventure notes."

Jake nudged Aki, and she nodded her head. "It would be good to get my mind off things."

Michelle let out the breath she held. "I think Tina would want us to play. She loved the world-building. I'll think of a way to include her memory somehow."

"Becca, get some of those camp utensils."

Becca sighed and grabbed six sets of silverware off the shelf as well as six sets of stacking bowls. She dropped the items into the third cart. "Dad, it will be okay."

Her father turned to face her, and she saw the slight tremor in his hands. The normally unflappable man could barely keep the terror from his face. She moved to his side and wrapped her arms around him. "I don't know why, but I trust Kyrie, even if she's a damn troglodyte. She can't even use a phone, but … she's got other skills."

He wrapped an arm around her. "You even know what she is? I keep thinking I must have watched some horror movie and am having a shit dream." He hyperventilated. "I felt what happened earlier. The pressure wrapping around me. When I look at her, I just know there is more going on in her head. It creeps me out. Knowing what I know, I can't help but see the alien in her."

Becca continued to lean against her father's side, enjoying the safety of his presence. "She can feel emotions," she whispered, "so she knows what you're feeling about her. She's probably just trying to avoid you hating her. I think she's scared, but too stubborn to admit it."

"It's not hate, it's goddamn terror," he admitted. "She's not …" He squeezed her again. "I keep telling myself she protected you, but then I look at you, and you seem like what happened today is just a minor thing. How is that?"

Becca swallowed and pulled herself away from her father. *I don't know what the fuck I'm feeling,* she admitted to herself. *I'm becoming gangsta with all the bullets flying about.* "It's all the active shooter drills at school," she joked, then grew serious. "I trust her to keep me safe."

He narrowed his eyes and considered her for a moment. "You didn't go with her and Michelle on the farm. But you saw her do what she did today somewhere else first, didn't you? In Arkansas?"

Becca nodded. "She dealt with a couple men when we met Awan, but she didn't have ..." Becca searched for a word that would not incriminate them if anyone should be listening. "What she borrowed from Jake's dad." *I'm not supposed to tell, but he needs to know.* "She did something like what she did to you, just pushing down. The guy looked like a car dropped on him when she was done. A second guy, she used a bunch of rocks from the ground instead of lead. They got her twice first, but she healed the wounds in minutes." Becca lifted her eyes to look into her father's face. "I don't know why, but what happened hasn't bothered me as much as I thought it should. Perhaps because they were trying to off me," she added as much for herself as him.

He moved forward and squeezed her again. "We shouldn't talk about this here. I'm glad you're okay, but we need to get going."

"I'm glad you're here with me," she admitted. "I wouldn't want to do it without you. You're all I have."

Chapter 12

Dennis Hurlington sat next to his brown-haired benefactor. The office chair creaked from extended usage, but the mesh back, swivel arms, and lumbar support reflected the expensive nature of the original purchase. Like the rest of the bunker, the conference room had steel walls and ceilings, but a layer of industrial carpet tiles covered the floor, deadening the sound of the chair sliding under the long table. An additional ten chairs sat around the table, with only Leonard occupying the nearest one.

No one beyond himself and Leonard ever entered the underground fortifications. Originally built in secret by Leonard's father from an ancient cave system on the vast Minnesotan property near the Canadian border that had been in the Beirtal family for generations, Leonard had upgraded the accommodation's security after his father died. Dennis spent the last five years upgrading it further, as it provided an outlet for his extended idle time.

"Leonard," Dennis said, using the mouse to pause the video feed they watched on the large monitor mounted to the far wall, his distress waking the voice of God in his mind.

"Her powers are formidable." The younger man pulled up the chat on the laptop in front of him. "Jacob has been called home by our father. Ron said he succumbed to shock and blood loss."

Dennis replayed the four feeds again. Leonard had synchronized the recordings from the four cameras, three of them worn by the members of the Heth cell, and one mounted on the dash of the van they had driven. When they had watched the events live, the anticipation of success had been high. Heth had followed two of Satan's demons right to where the girl had gathered with her friends. *I should have known things would have gone wrong after she survived the first attack with the fifty-cal.*

Dennis focused on the girl's face, memorizing each detail. She carried a cold detachment. A brutality of action. He saw a trained soldier on the other end of the camera lens. The shifting of tactics, aiming for the vulnerable hands of his loyal soldiers, once she realized the body armor protected his followers. *She must not be underestimated.*

"At least we killed two demons," Leonard said as he lifted his gaze to the large screen to see Luke firing the Barrett rifle through the windshield of the oncoming car.

"The demons tried to protect her. We can't allow her to live." Dennis turned away from the replay to look at his most loyal follower and financial benefactor. "Did Ron and Luke ditch the van successfully?" *The flock must be protected,* he admitted, agreeing with the voice of God.

Leonard nodded his head. "They did, but now they are questioning the news. The reports of the killings overnight are spreading." Leonard pulled up one of the message boards they maintained on secure servers across the dark web. "A lot of news outlets have run with the sparse evidence released by the police and are saying we assassinated all those people. Several members of Iota and Kappa cells have reached out to ask if we performed the strikes." Leonard turned to face Dennis. "At least five people have said they are leaving the church as a result, even though I've denied it."

"Satan undermines us again." Dennis released the mouse, fearing he might crush the plastic device in his hand. *Satan is winning,* he growled, echoing the anger of God. "Tell them that the Devil clouds the minds of the innocent to turn them away from the righteous path."

Dennis turned his attention back to the screen, where the recording relived Luke trying to apply pressure to Jacob's neck wound. Blood covered the floor of the van and both men's bodies. "We don't have a clear feed for when Heth took their initial shots at her. How'd they even miss?"

Leonard hesitated. "They initially believed they had succeeded until they listened to the police radio. I'm not sure how she survived a direct hit." Leonard swallowed. "On the other topic, based on the reports, it is likely that whatever Bishop has been planning started last night. And he means to destroy us at the same time. The handful of killers that were caught—or should I say were killed—had things on their phones that apparently indicated they are associated with us, but I've seen no activity on any of our actual servers, so whatever they pointed to must be a false flag. But now many of the news programs are replaying a local KC channel's footage of the Landvik girl's house and the farm from two weeks ago, further implicating us."

"This is all bullshit," Dennis demanded, turning the laptop so he could see it better. "We've only just started hunting her. Bishop's man pursued her for sixteen years. We weren't even organized back then. How did Satan manage to spin Michael Rodgers as being a member of our church?"

Leonard shrugged. "Satan has many people working for him. It is not that hard to fabricate evidence and use a few dirty cops." The younger man swallowed. "But our biggest weakness is Kappa cell. If any of the people threatening to leave reveal the details of the others in the cell, it could impact all thirteen members. That's almost twenty-five percent of our remaining followers." He bowed his head. "Forgive me. This attack on the girl today looks too much like the other executions. I should have been aware of them and halted the op so it wouldn't draw more attention to us."

"Satan knew when to strike us." Dennis scanned the messages and pushed the laptop away from him. "He's undermining us. Destroying our credibility and poisoning the faithful. No one will believe the warning we are trying to bring to the world. He even faked an attempt on his own life."

"Forgive me, Your Holiness."

Dennis exhaled slowly. "You are not to blame. We are fighting the Devil, not a corrupt businessman. He has supernatural powers. We need to make sure our people do not lose hope."

Leonard put his hand on Dennis' arm. "Your Grace, there are still those of us who know the truth. I've been posting evidence to Kappa and the others. I've told them it is a false-flag campaign."

"Do they believe you?"

Leonard's shoulders sank. "It's too early to tell."

Dennis nodded. "I'll make a broadcast. We don't want to lose our supporters." He hit the table with his fist. "Damn it. This will make it a lot harder to recruit new followers."

"We will find a way." Leonard turned the laptop back to himself. "Perhaps more will see through the lies and join us. If not, each cell is limited to its own servers now that we have the general recruiting server offline. Any damage is, by design, contained."

Dennis felt the anguished frustration of God in his mind. *You're right,* he told the voice, *I've spent too many years hiding away.* He turned to Leonard. "It's time I went back into the world and dealt with her directly."

"No!" Leonard's animated denial almost knocked over a water glass. "Satan just wants to draw you out to make it easier to kill you. It is too risky for you to leave. We can rebuild from this."

Dennis took a deep breath. The prospect of leaving the bunker frightened him. The last attempt on his life involved half a dozen of Satan's demons, and even with God's blessings, his recovery required weeks of healing to regrow the muscles of his left leg, not to mention the pain from the burns that blackened the flesh of his abdomen and chest. *I am strong enough. God protects me.*

He swallowed the emotions he felt. "Leonard, only when people experience the miracles firsthand do they become true followers. The videos and broadcasts help keep those in the fold inspired, but we've seen how hesitant the new cells are." He knew what God required of him. The video loop repeated, and he lifted a hand. "We've seen firsthand that our best soldiers can't stop this girl. It will take someone God has anointed with holy powers to actually return her to the underworld."

"Your Holiness," Leonard said softly. "I understand." His most devout follower lowered his head. "Please allow me the time to ensure you have the support and protection you need. I do not want to see you come to harm. I'll recall Heth to protect you."

Dennis smiled and placed his hand on Leonard's head. A decision fifteen years earlier to rescue a then twenty-one-year-old boy from being taken by Bishop's demons had changed his fate. At the time, he had no concept of Leonard's wealth and resources, only the knowledge that he did not want more demons implanted into humans. The formation of an official church and the recruiting of followers had all come from Leonard. "Of course, my son. We will not throw away what has been built."

A loud beep echoed through multiple rooms of the bunker, and a red light above the door flashed. Dennis pulled the keyboard closer, closed the recording of the failed attack at Heritage Park, and pulled up the live camera feeds from the Beirtal family estate. He cycled through two screens with four rows of five cameras each before stopping on the third screen.

"Shit," Leonard said as they watched five heavily armed men rushing into the rear door of Leonard's family house. Covered with helmets, body armor, and tactical gear, their identities could not be determined, but their purpose was unmistakable. "At least there are no servants on the property right now," Leonard mumbled, having always sent everyone home each afternoon so that he could walk the path to the bunker undetected.

Dennis shifted to the next set of cameras and then to the fifth screen that showed the cave entrance and the interior of the cave. The infrared light and sensor captured the dark cave interior just outside the concealed bunker door. He shifted to the next set of cameras that showed several of the passages and rooms in the bunker as well as the rear exit at the end of a quarter mile long tunnel.

"Are they police or feds?" Leonard wondered. "Perhaps they fear I was a victim of the assassinations as well? But then, the police would have rung at the gate, and there are no vehicles in the view of any of the cameras. They had to come onto the grounds over a fence somewhere."

Another alarm flashed internally, changing the slow flashing of the red light to a rapid flashing. The control module Dennis wore at his waist vibrated, and he backed up to the prior group of cameras. A dozen armed men just appeared at the cave entrance and headed inside. They moved quickly, checking different branches of the natural cave with lights mounted on the ends of their AR-rifles.

Dennis felt Leonard's shock and terror. The honest emotion kept him from doubting the man who had devoted so much time and money to the Church. "Go to the armory and grab a pair of go-bags. Put on some hearing protection. We won't have much time." Dennis removed the control module from his waist and activated the small tablet. The customized device pulled up the status of the bunker, from power, lighting, air handling, and water filtration to security and defense. Dennis turned off the lights in the main hallway and the rooms closest to the main entrance. The armory was a floor above them, near the middle of the facility, to allow for a rapid response at either entrance.

Leonard grabbed his laptop, slammed it closed, and rushed quickly from the room. Dennis trusted the thirty-six-year-old to know what to grab. The man had not trained directly with any of the cells to avoid exposing his identity, but he used his private range at least once a week.

Dennis continued to navigate the bunker control module, setting a thirty minute timer for the oxyhydrogen tanks to release their contents into the server room; the nozzles aimed directly at the computer hardware. Combined with the thermite packs, he did not expect any data would survive the self-destruct protocol.

He then pulled up the camera for the primary entrance. Three men had already deployed shaped breaching charges around the reinforced bunker door and were now backing away. With time running out, he left the conference room and made his way down the twisting corridors to the metal stairs where Leonard would return from the armory. The only long straight passages in the bunker were those just on the other side of the primary entrance and the back door.

A loud explosion compressed the air inside the bunker, making his ears pop. Dennis winced and then felt God pull power into him to heal the damage. *Thank you,* he told his protector. He turned his attention back to the handheld control module and shifted to a four-camera display showing the cave exterior with most of the invaders. The ruined bunker door could no longer be seen because of the smoke from the explosion. The two feeds of the interior stairs and the long passage leading into the complex remained dark due to the lack of light.

He sensed Leonard coming before hearing the younger man's leather-soled shoes on the steps. *Come in as a group,* he commanded the invaders. He watched as the first half of the dozen men passed into the smoky passage, the lights on their rifles showing their movement in the camera feeds. The other half held back and waited. Dennis frowned at the screen, which showed the first six men quickly descending the stairs just inside the entrance.

"I've grabbed two go-bags and a third ammo pack," the heavily laden Leonard said. He unwound one AR-15 from around his neck and held it out. Dennis nodded his head toward the floor, and Leonard set down the rifle, a pistol, a backpack, and an ammo bag.

"Come on," Dennis grumbled at the men in the video. The second set of three moved through the ruined door as the first six left the stairs and rushed down the long passage. "I want to get you all at once," he swore. He swiped the tablet to shift to a view of the rear exit and passage. So far, that part of the compound remained quiet.

"Do you think the police have managed to connect me to the Church?" Leonard asked. "I know we've talked about contingency plans, but ..."

Dennis flipped back to the concealed cameras monitoring the front entrance. The men in the passage had slowed their advance, and now the last three men rushed down the front stairs. *Finally,* he told God, knowing his protector would not give him more than he could handle. He swiped to the defense menu, which had automatically activated because of the alarm. He pressed the button to ignite the first set of Claymore mine-inspired explosives.

Pressure waves ripped through the bunker as C-4 devices hidden in the passage light housings exploded from the ceiling above the stairs and the long passage. Each one broadcast an arc of seven hundred soft steel balls at over three times the speed of sound. Because of the low ceiling height limiting the spread of the projectiles, Dennis installed the devices every three feet. His initial firing triggered every other device, giving him a second chance if needed.

Dennis swiped back to the camera feed, and he activated the emergency lights. One camera appeared to no longer function as ricocheting projectiles must have taken out something critical. Smoke filled the view, but the ventilation system quickly cleared the air in the corridor, revealing the image at the end of the long passage. Six vaguely humanoid masses lay on the floor, the more durable parts of the tactical gear still discernible, but the rest had no clear indication of their original purpose. Blood and gore covered the walls.

Leonard looked at the dim screen from where he stood and paled. "I ..."

God's approval kept Dennis from feeling any unease in his stomach. When it came to death, he allowed the Almighty to control his actions, knowing that if God chose to act, the results carried the weight of divine righteousness.

A moment later, he found his voice. "We will be careful. We no longer have video of the stairs, but we can hope that it was equally effective."

"And there are the five men, possibly demons, in my house."

Dennis nodded his head. "We will leave them for now. I don't want you to come to harm. Let's go out the back."

Chapter 13

They left Topeka and headed towards Kansas City on the back roads to avoid the cameras and tolls on I-70. The four seats in the back of the van lacked armrests and seat belts and swiveled smoothly on their central posts. The four of them fought to keep from spinning as Mr. Williams zoomed around the many curves in the road. The support pole bolted to the floor transmitted every bump into their bodies, making the ride quickly shift from the relief of escape to an irritation that would, over time, turn into torture.

Kyrie, using her feet on the floor and a hand on the narrow desk to keep steady, leaned forward so she could better see Becca's laptop screen. A grainy and intentionally blurred video of the attempt on Bishop's life was playing on a news site. The title above the video said, 'Steven Bishop spared a horrific fate by the heroics of a young guard.' The zoomed-in video showed a muscular man tackling Nalitran to the ground. *Was that man a Bound? Did he even have a choice?* She wished the shooter had not missed their mark.

Behind her, Jake had left his seat to sit on the floor next to Aki, helping to steady her seat and offer comfort. *Their panic is subsiding,* she told herself as worry about Lars continued to build in her gut. "Can we try calling Lars again?" Kyrie asked.

Mr. Williams shook his head. "When we stop. I don't want to give away that we are in a vehicle in case anyone is listening."

"We don't know if he's tried to call me back. Can the laptop receive calls?"

"Not with the setup I have," Becca's father said.

"Is there anything we can do to be productive?" Michelle asked, eyeing the powered-off monitors and keyboards on her left. "I could look up things on the computer."

"I'd need to power up the network and other devices," Mr. Williams said. "Perhaps when we stop. The van has some large batteries that driving will help recharge, but we really need shore power to run things for an extended time. Dylan forgot to keep the van plugged in, and they are not fully re—"

"I've found a video that hasn't been taken down yet," Becca interrupted.

Kyrie saw the shudder that ran through Becca's upper body as the wide shot still had the fidelity to capture the spray of blood exiting the back of a woman's head. *Based on the sound of the gunshot, it wasn't like that big rifle,* she decided.

Becca swallowed. "Let me download it before it's pulled."

"So …" Michelle started, now kneeling on the floor next to Kyrie so she could see the screen. "How can we kill someone whose guard is that fast?"

Kyrie allowed the silence to hang in the air for only a moment. *This is your fault. You're responsible.*

"You still want to kill them?" Aki demanded from the back.

Kyrie and Michelle nodded their heads.

"I don't like the idea of murder," Mr. Williams said loudly without turning his head to face them. "I'm barely recovering from the shoot-out at the park. Premeditated murder will get us locked up for life, or put on death row if you're like me and Becca."

Kyrie frowned. "If we don't stop them, it's likely they will end up killing us."

"I know," Mr. Williams replied. "But it doesn't mean I have to like it. We need to do more research. Perhaps we can surface things that the police can use. They aren't all corrupt. If we expose Bishop's—or Nalitran's—crimes. If we reveal Hurlington's location … especially after all the murders that seem to point to him. They'd remove him from the field, and we'd not have to risk killing people."

"There is something to be said for not going to jail," Jake added, his left hand holding Aki's tightly.

Could it work? Kyrie asked herself. *Trying to kill them will be risky, but perhaps we can get others to kill them for us.* "I'm fine with allowing others to deal with them, as long as it will stop their people from coming for us." Her voice grew harder. "But until then, we need weapons for protection from anyone else who might come at us."

"Yeah," Michelle agreed. "Hurlington might have a lot of people free to come get us after all those purges."

"I don't think it was Hurlington," Becca said, her face still focused on the laptop.

"Reasons?" Her father prompted.

"I just found yet another video that someone who'd been in the audience posted. Bishop's guard started moving before the first shot."

"Let me see," her father demanded. The vehicle slowed as his attention shifted from the road to the laptop.

Kyrie leaned forward as Becca replayed the video taken from the lower edge of the steps in front of a building with a dozen glass doors. The man she had seen in the earlier video stood on the far side of the open area, his attention fixed on Nalitran. He started moving quickly, passing behind a man with dark curly hair just before the bullet passed through the man's skull. He cleared the back side of the woman before her fatal shot was fired. The third shot, delayed a fraction longer than the gap between the first two, only came after the man had pushed Bishop out of the way.

The van lurched slightly as Mr. Williams corrected the direction and accelerated back up to the speed limit. "I didn't see an earpiece on the guard's left side. Did you see one in the other videos?"

Becca hesitated and then shook her head. "I don't think so. Let me check." She pulled up the video of the woman's murder and went back in time before the shooting. After scanning through a dozen seconds of footage, she paused the image and shuddered. "I can't unsee that." She swallowed. "Nothing in his other ear."

Mr. Williams nodded his head. "Limit what you watch. You shouldn't be seeing things like that." He took two long breaths. "But from what you saw, he probably acted without a warning someone sent. At least not an obvious one." His voice rose in pitch. "Is it possible that Bishop had all those people killed and blamed it on Hurlington? But why? What does he get?"

Jake readjusted his position on the floor. "He's rich, but could he get away with that?"

Kyrie did not turn away from the image of the guard's face frozen on the screen. *The eyes seem dead. Definitely a Bound.* She contemplated the open questions. "Mr. Williams, you already thought Hurlington didn't have the people to pull off the murders. Could this be a way for Nalitran to eliminate Hurlington? Especially if Nalitran wants me alive and Hurlington wants to kill me. The Bound at the park appeared to try to stop Hurlington."

Jake nodded his head. "Yeah, that would be a way for Nalitran to flush Hurlington out. It'd get a lot of cops looking for him and would make it easier for Nalitran to collect you."

Michelle agreed. "As a DM, that makes sense to me."

Mr. Williams continued to focus on the road. "Perhaps, but there is likely something more motivating it. Those kinds of ops are expensive and take a lot of effort. It would have started long before you resurfaced. So, I can't see it being related to you. I'm still struggling with so many people being able to successfully keep it secret."

Kyrie tried to consider the motivations, but she did not have enough information. "Nalitran can force the Bound to do things and keep them from talking. That adds weight to the theory it was Nalitran and not Hurlington."

Mr. Williams sighed. "We can't do anything until we can stop." He looked at the clock on the dash. "We've still got hours to go. Now why don't you all tell the damn truth this time? Start from the very beginning and leave nothing out."

Kyrie, Becca, and Michelle recounted the events of the last three weeks, including explaining how Kyrie killed the two men in Arkansas. Aki and Jake remained huddled together, sitting on the rubber floor mat instead of the rotating seats. Jake's presence helped to tamp down the anxiety Aki emitted at the retelling of the events they had all promised not to share with anyone else.

The miles rolled by as Kyrie went through the details of the conflict on the Kansas farm. She described using her powers to find, and then remove, the binding stone from Michael Rodgers so that she could order the Bound to protect her as simple fact. She had not fully reconciled how she felt about ordering someone to die versus killing them in the heat of battle. *It shouldn't be different, but it feels different.*

"And if someone uses their powers to take your binding stone from you ..." Mr. Williams left the unfinished statement hanging.

"It's like a massive weight on me," Kyrie acknowledged, her hand consciously not touching the visible lump in her pocket. "I'd have a strong desire to comply with what they want. I might not even realize I was doing it. If I resist, the pain can cause me to collapse." She pushed some loose strands of her long hair behind her ear. "I used to think all adults could compel kids using mental pain. Since my mother died, I've started to realize my ability to resist is likely related to how focused the person holding the stone is." She glanced at Jake and then back to Mr. Williams. "When a couple of people have possessed my stone, I found I had difficulty not doing what they wanted, but I had different levels of awareness of the control."

Michelle reached out and put a hand on her forearm.

Kyrie allowed the contact and turned her focus to the duffel bags. "With my mother, I never realized how much control she had over me until the reinforcement stopped."

"Where are you keeping this binding stone?" Becca's father asked. "Not that I'm wanting to take it from you, but I don't want others to rip it from you either."

Kyrie moved her hand to cover her jeans pocket. "I need to find a safe place for it." *But where?*

"Somewhere those after you won't know to look." Mr. Williams changed lanes and sped up to pass a truck. "You said Nalitran's people already tried to steal it. Do we know if Hurlington is aware of these stones? You didn't seem to know of its power until recently, and you've said he's a failed binding. Would his people try to take it as well? And you said that guy, Awan, said destroying it would kill you."

All of her friends had possessed the stone for periods of time; only Aki had carried it without knowing how it could control her. Jake had tested the control with her permission, though his test had been a poor choice. Michelle and Becca had helped get it off the farm in Kansas, and they had plenty of opportunity to use it against her. *But that doesn't mean they will always respect you.* She banished the doubt within her. "I really don't like others knowing about the stone."

"We definitely can't risk destroying it," Michelle pleaded. "Even if Awan lied or was wrong, the risk that something would happen to her is too much!"

Could you just bury it in a random location? She bit her lower lip. *No, you know you'd never let it out of your sight again.*

"Can we stop for some food and a bathroom break?" Becca asked, changing the subject. "We've been driving for several hours."

Mr. Williams noted the sign for the rest stop that had prompted Becca's question. "We'll stop at the rest stop just ahead. We can all move about and pee. Then we can call Lars again."

They all used the facilities and even bought some snacks from the overpriced vending machines. The six of them gathered around the farthest of the multiple covered picnic tables, the laptop and cellular hotspot powered up with the VoIP software ready to place a call.

"Remember, no one talk, except for Kyrie," Mr. Williams said, handing her a second wired headset, the first already on his head. He looked out at the highway and shook his head. "The noise cancellation should remove most of the wind and vehicle noise, but it will pick up other voices."

Kyrie put the headset on and nodded. He tapped the trackpad to start the recording and made the call. She heard the sound of the ringing three times, and then the line went quiet. Kyrie shifted her focus back to the screen and saw the status showed a green box with 'Active' next to the numbers.

"Hello," came a female voice. "I believe the color I'm supposed to say is red. You can give me the code for the day and month, but there's really no point. I don't have a good understanding of the formula. However, we do need to talk."

Kyrie went cold. *He's betrayed me! Or they captured him.* The options spun around in her head.

"Are you there? We've been trying for over an hour to get you to answer."

"Where is Lars?" Kyrie asked, her voice even despite the numerous scenarios playing out in her head. *Is he dead? What have we revealed to him? Where is he?*

"He's indisposed for the moment," came the female voice. A callousness not quite hidden under the projected sweetness. "But it is important that I speak with you. You are in danger from Dennis Hurlington and his church. I can help protect you. Where are you? We can get you to safety tonight."

Kyrie's mind raced. *You need to rescue Lars!* However, the reality that it could be nothing like rescuing Tina weighed on her. *They'd expect you to try. Mother would ensure you couldn't repeat the same tactics twice.* Her heart raced as multiple ideas quickly led to logically fatal outcomes. *If he's not already dead, they'd kill him to keep their powers secret.* She bit her lip. *Is he even in danger? Could he be helping them?*

"Kyrie?" came the voice.

Mr. Williams motioned for her to continue speaking.

"Michael Rodgers was not interested in protecting me. Why would I assume you are?"

The woman sighed. "I'm truly sorry for what that man did. I read about it in the news. He was a pathetic man who secretly aligned himself with Hurlington." The woman paused. "I, on the other hand, want to help you. I'm glad you managed to avoid falling victim to Hurlington's murder spree. So many people died. And he even tried to kill you twice today. Going into hiding with Jason Williams and your friends was a smart idea. However, we are better equipped to protect you. We can even protect them as well. Tell us where you are and we can ensure everyone is safe. Even the rest of your friends' families. We can track them down and bring them in as well."

Kyrie glanced at Mr. Williams, who looked at her with an expression of concern. *He thinks you might believe this woman.* She turned back to the laptop. *Mother would expect you to play along, even if it costs Lars his life. Survive at all costs.* She wanted to disagree, but she would not risk the others to save someone she did not actually know.

You can still try to save him. Get information. "How do I know you are not one of Hurlington's people pretending to work for Bishop?

You haven't even given me your name. I don't even know if Lars is alive."

"You can call me Inda," the woman said. "We can meet face to face, and you should be able to tell I'm not one of Hurlington's killers." The woman's tone shifted, revealing a trace of annoyance. "I can have Lars brought to you as well. People were hunting him, and he suffered an injury, but nothing life-threatening."

Kyrie felt the woman hang on the last two words, offering a veiled threat. "And just where would you want to meet?" She needed to buy enough time to develop a plan. *If it is even possible. The woman is saying nothing.*

"Wherever is convenient for you?" The woman said, her voice revealing an increase in excitement. "Are you still in Olathe?"

Kyrie saw Mr. Williams' hand hovering over the mouse, with the pointer on the disconnect button. *Get information.* "Why does Bishop want me?"

"What does Bishop have to do with this? It is I reaching out to you. I want to protect you. You don't deserve to become a victim of Dennis Hurlington. That man is evil." The woman's sweet voice continued. "I only want to make sure you and your friends are safe."

Kyrie shook her head, remembering how just talking to smart NPCs seldom extracted data, but often had her reveal things she wanted to conceal. *Mother, would you want us to provoke her or not?* The gamification of her life told her what her parents would want of her. *You know you can't save Lars if they have him. Not this time.*

Kyrie made her decision. "You've provided nothing of value to me, and I have no reason to believe you. This conversation is a waste of time."

The woman's tone grew hard. "Lars might fall victim to Hurlington if he decides not to remain with me because you refuse to trust me. Hurlington's church will kill your friends' families without my protection. Eventually, they will find you and your friends, and then your friends will suffer as well."

Kyrie felt her protectiveness stir, and her hands tightened into fists, but she pushed it down. *If they don't think you care, they might leave them alone.* She swallowed. *Lars, we're sorry you were caught in this.* Aloud, she kept her voice even. "Veiled threats require that I care. So far, you've offered me nothing of interest. You have Lars' phone and a basic understanding of the code, so you already have Lars. Which means you know that we've never met and have only spoken a few times. Likely, you've already killed him because he knows nothing about me and my plans." *Don't pretend to not care about your friends; the woman will have learned how important they are from Lars. But perhaps the others …* "If you could find me and actually threaten my friends, you'd not be trying to get me to reveal myself to you. I'm done."

"Wait," the woman said, a slight growl coming through the connection. She uttered some phrases in a language Kyrie initially did not recognize, but memories of the otherworld broke free and crashed into her conscious thoughts. Images of bipedal forms with leathery skin, the color and texture of yellow limestone, filled her mind. Their solid black eyes, elongated muzzle, pointed teeth, and the sharp bony protrusion that extended from the end of their upper limbs caused her to wobble on her feet.

The woman continued in the language, the words muddled by mouths and ears not capable of replicating the full range of sound. "I can see you are practical. You're dolunar, aren't you? I can see the hunter's instincts in you. How you defeated Rodgers using Hurlington. How you tracked down Awan. You're a warrior. The real Nalitran is here. It is not just someone using his name. Your leader and master wasn't destroyed. He lives. He is calling all his faithful followers to him. He will rule this world and you are being called to service. His name is not being used by another pretending to greatness. I know Rodgers screwed up and allowed Awan to pull you here. You didn't have a chance to learn the truth of things, then those humans," the word a slur, "isolated you on a mountain and prevented you from being welcomed into the pack. We can fix that. Allow you a chance to serve our Warlord in this world. We will rule the humans and dominate the planet."

Kyrie struggled to keep up with the woman's quick speech, her mind translating a language she had learned, but not heard or used in her human form. While she understood the words after a moment of thought, she could not bring herself to vocalize a response.

"Come back to the pack," the woman commanded. "That is an order from your master."

"No," Kyrie managed in the foreign tongue, struggling to formulate even the single concept in the language. She pointed at the laptop, and Becca's father tapped on the trackpad, ending the call.

"What was that at the end?" He asked.

Kyrie staggered backward as she pulled the headset off, dropping it to the ground. Her mind struggled with childhood memories of another existence that seemed out of place in her head. *Yours or mine?* She begged, and as always, no reply came.

"Kyrie?" Michelle cried, grabbing her arms to help keep her standing.

"Are you okay? Who was that woman? What did she say at the end?" Mr. Williams asked.

"What's going on?" Becca demanded, followed by the others repeating the same.

Kyrie swallowed, forcing the long-suppressed memories away. "The woman thinks I'm one of them, but I'm not." Kyrie sank to the ground. *You're not one of those things,* the word a curse, not even wanting to assign it the same consideration as a rabid animal.

Eventually she looked up and breathed. The fear in the others had multiplied, and she sensed their doubt. *Why didn't you remember his name before now? Why didn't you remember what those beasts are?* She looked down at her hands, her dull nails at the end of her fingers. "Nalitran was a warlord that for a time ruled a nation in the other world. I learned about him growing up. He was defeated before I was born. He's not like my people. He ... My people tore his soul from him and cast it into the void. They caused this." Tears rolled down her face. "They cause all of this."

Michelle knelt next to her and wrapped her good arm around her. "It's not your fault."

Kyrie forced herself to breathe. *Of course, it's not our fault! You weren't even a child! But our people ...* She pushed down her rage, knowing Michelle did not deserve it. "The woman thinks I'm a dolunar, like Nalitran and her. She's wrong." Kyrie looked at each of them in turn. Kyrie let out a long breath. "I'm not one of them. I'm corvlian. I'm a corvlian."

Becca's father wrapped the cord around the headset in his hand. "Not to sound cold, but is that something we can use to our advantage?"

Focus. Use logic. Bury your emotions. Kyrie breathed and then pondered the idea for a moment. She shrugged. "I don't know yet." She shook her head to clear her thoughts. "Sorry. My mother forced me to repress the memories of the other world. They're starting to come back, and that overwhelmed me."

Mr. Williams nodded. "That woman was being careful not to say anything that tied her to Bishop. She pushed hard on the idea that everything is Hurlington's doing. I'd say she protested too much and said nothing. At least until she started in on that weird language. Did she say anything more about Lars?"

Kyrie shook her head as she stood up, trying to remember the words the woman used. "He might already be dead. I don't know. I don't even know if he was loyal to my parents or working for Nalitran or Hurlington. This is not like when they took Tina. I don't think there is any way we'd be able to rescue him, even if we had a way to find out where they have him. They won't fall for the same gambit twice."

Becca frowned. "With a nationwide manhunt for Hurlington, he's definitely not going to send people to us like he did last time."

"Will they go after our parents?" Jake asked, his arms around Aki.

Kyrie started to shake her head and then shrugged again. "I hope my indifference will keep them safe. If it had been my mother, then the woman was casting out threats to see what might generate a reaction in me. I ignored what she said about your parents and just focused on you."

Mr. Williams picked up the laptop. "It felt reasonable to me as well. But we should go. I want to listen to the recording again, and you can translate the last part for me." He did not wait for an agreement and headed for the van. "It'll be after dark before we get to the campsite at this rate."

Chapter 14

Kyrie felt the hot wind blowing across her fur as she sat in the clearing. Her mother lounged under the blue-green leaves of a cluster of trees with an older female elder. The two of them chatted quietly while another girl from their community practiced a rolling tumble in front of her.

"Have you started your warrior training?" the older girl with tawny fur asked.

Kyrie shook her head. "Mother says I'm not old enough. But one day I will fight like my brothers and sisters have."

The other girl moved closer, grabbed the glass bottle from the ground and whispered in her ear. "Have you felt the power? Have you tasted it yet?"

Kyrie swallowed. Instinct told her to lie, as children with early abilities ended up being treated differently, but she trusted her friend and they were both part of the divine caste.

"It changes you," the other girl said before taking a drink. "The power changes you. I always want to feel it in me."

"How does it feel when you use it?" Kyrie allowed her teeth to show her eagerness. She then moved closer to her friend's ear, hoping her mother would not hear what she said. "I've also felt the power flowing through me, but Mother won't let me use it."

"It feels wonderful."

Kyrie nodded her head knowingly. "How many others can touch the power?"

The other girl twitched her ears, showing her uncertainty. "I've been told six in six four times, though in our colony it might be twice six times more."

Kyrie's mind instantly converted the first numbers to one in two hundred and sixteen and the second to mean one in three. She opened her mouth, but then she could not remember what she wanted to ask the other girl as her memory shifted. The hair on her neck stood on end as the sky seemed to burn her human eyes with its violet hues.

"Girls, to me now!" Kyrie's mother shouted as the other corvlian charged forward on all fours.

Kyrie's focus snapped back into her feline body, and the world returned to normal. Panic built in her as she struggled to orient her memory. With painful slowness, she turned her head in the direction in which her mother's companion ran. Two forms emerged into the clearing, their thick sandy-yellow skin glistening in the bright sun. Their black eyes centered in their long angular faces, showing no compassion. The two naked males charged forward on only their rear legs with projectile weapons in their small hands. Their long, razor-sharp claw that extended from the tips of their upper limbs remained folded back against their forearms to allow their fingers to work the weapons.

"Come!" demanded Kyrie's mother.

Kyrie leaped into motion, sprinting on all fours away from the dolunar fighters, her slightly older friend already four leaps ahead of her. Kyrie's heart raced. The dolunar seldom attacked their community, but the afternoon exploration had taken the four of them further afield than normal.

The crackle of energy buzzed Kyrie's ears and flew past her to strike her friend's rear leg just before the older girl reached the trees, sending her friend tumbling into the dirt. Kyrie's mother bounded forward, grabbed the girl in one arm and held out her other arm for Kyrie. The distance felt like it continued to grow no matter how fast she ran.

Behind her, Kyrie heard the snarls of an angry corvlian. When she reached her mother, Kyrie leaped up and into a protective embrace, her own claws digging into her mother's flesh so nothing could shake her loose. Her mother turned and ran into the woods. Kyrie looked over her mother's shoulder. The older corvlian, her friends guardian, had fallen to the ground. One of the dolunar lie beside her, its head removed from its body. The other dolunar held his hands against a deep gash in his left leg that bled profusely. The hole in that dolunar's chest appeared to only hit one of its three hearts.

Kyrie lost sight of the clearing as the jungle closed around them. She looked at the other girl her mother carried and could see no light left in her friend's eyes. *No!*

Kyrie sat up panting as though she had sprinted three miles all out. The tent remained dark with Michelle, Becca, and Aki crammed into the shelter with her. Her mind immediately located Jake and Mr. Williams in the smaller tent ten feet away. A handful of other people slept at the neighboring campsites, but she sensed no immediate threats.

She wiped the sweat from her face. *Zvarncr,* she thought, knowing her human throat and mouth could never replicate the proper sounds to speak her friend's name. A deep longing and regret filled her. She knew her friend had died that day. *Death follows you,* she complained, certain she would never meet Lars and know if he had remained loyal.

Kyrie quietly unzipped her sleeping bag and slipped out. She had picked the spot closest to the tent flap in case she needed to defend the others. Still fully dressed because she had no other clothes, she grabbed her shoes and pulled them on. Sensing the noise had already disturbed Michelle's sleep, she quickly unzipped the flap and stepped out of the tent into the cool night. The smell of pine, walnut, and soil filled the air, tainted by the remnants of smoke from campfires that had burned down during the night. Thankfully, the odor did not contain hints of burning flesh from funeral pyres.

The rectangular metal firepit sat cold on the ground in front of the tents. Mr. Williams' large van occupied part of the long cement pad twenty feet beyond the firepit, a power cord running from a hidden connection in front of the rear wheel to the campsite's outlet. They had arrived after sunset, and Jake had managed to direct them in setting up the tents using the van's headlights.

Kyrie looked up at the tall trees above her. The lower branches had long ago been removed, preventing her from being able to touch any of the leaves. In the other world, her claws would have allowed her easy access to the topmost branches without effort. *Six fingers,* she remembered, *though our feet would have had five.*

Tears moistened her eyes, and she started walking, stopping only long enough to tie the laces of her shoes. Despite the location being wooded, she sensed the multitude of campers around them. Tents predominantly filled the southern loop, but a few of the sites had trailers.

She continued along the paved road that ran through the campground, taking in the smell of fire and forest. The surface road created a couple of loops, making something of a squished figure eight. A smattering of lights provided just enough illumination for her to navigate the road toward the bathhouse they had used the previous night.

Everyone you let get close dies. Her feet moved on their own, converting her fast walk into a sprint. Her eyes burned as she raced around the larger loop, her shoes on the pavement causing more noise than what others would consider polite, and she felt a few people stir. She ran faster, trying to outrun the sounds and her memories. However, the circular route brought her to the toilets even before she felt the need to breathe heavily from the exercise.

"Zvarncr," she whispered, her vision still smeared from tears, knowing the sounds did not feel correct in her mouth. More memories of running through the jungle with her neighbor filled her mind. Her older friend liked to wrestle. "And bite," Kyrie mumbled as she looked down at her furless left arm and knew her human skin lacked the toughness of her other self. A longing to tumble and pin someone to the ground filled her.

Kyrie considered resuming her run, but she recalled Becca's complaints about the lack of fresh underwear, and as a result, she did not want to work up a sweat. While she had always hand-washed her limited clothing when living on the mountain, she did not relish the idea of doing it naked, and then having to stand around bare-assed until her only clothing dried. *It'd make Jake blush.* She smirked at the thought.

She entered the breezeway of the bathhouse, passing the four private showers on her left, and went through the pair of doors into the women's toilet. She used the facilities and then washed her face and hands in the sink. *We don't even have towels,* she complained as water dripped from her chin. *Taking a shower will be a problem. But you still stink of gunpowder.*

Kyrie looked at herself in the mirror and did not recognize the changes. The hardness of her features and the shadows under her eyes spoke of a person she did not want to see. Her blonde hair seemed thinner and unkempt. When she left the tent, she had not grabbed the hair tie she normally used to pull her hair into a tight ponytail. *This is the person your parents wanted you to become. Cold and hateful.*

Kyrie sensed someone approaching the bathrooms, and she wiped away the excess water from her face with her hands. She turned her head in the direction of the other person's approach, using her still-tired mind to look through the wood and cinder block wall. Her hand moved to protectively cover the bulge her binding stone made in her pants. *A woman,* she finally decided. The lady continued to move with slow purpose. A frown crossed Kyrie's lips, the pain of loss still too fresh in her mind. *You just want to be alone.*

The wall limited how deeply she could probe the woman's thoughts, but she did not believe the other person presented a threat. The idea that not everything required a designation of friend or foe lingered in the back of her mind, but it had not yet materialized in her conscious thoughts.

Her nostrils flared, and she forced her hands to her sides. *You failed both Zvarncr and Lars,* though she could not claim to truly remember either. She marched out through the set of doors. The older woman, having just entered the breezeway, jumped at the sudden movement.

"Oh," the silver-haired person exclaimed after a moment. "You're up quite early."

Kyrie softened her expression. *Don't be hateful. She's not a dolunar.* "I had to go to the bathroom," Kyrie eventually mumbled.

The older woman chuckled. "Same, though I imagine I have to make the trip more often than you. Like me, the water tank in The

Old Girl keeps leaking, so we don't have a working toilet in the trailer."

Kyrie gave the woman a closer examination. Dressed in what appeared to be a robe, she carried an oversized bag on one arm and had curlers in her hair. A strong, flowery perfume emanated from the woman and polluted the air that moved through the open area between the showers and toilets.

"Rupert, my husband, scheduled a repair weeks ago." The woman shrugged. "But getting The Old Girl in for repairs hasn't been quick. So, I've got to make the long walk two or three times a night, or I'll pee the bed." She smiled. "I'm not old enough for diapers yet." The woman winked knowingly.

Diapers? Kyrie tried to form a response, but the odd conversation left her without a solid frame of reference, and the woman's thoughts seemed to ramble as much as her speech. "I …" she started and then hesitated when she sensed Michelle, Becca, and Aki approaching from the direction of the tents.

"It's a bit early in the year for school to be out, unless you're home schooled, I guess. Am I really off with the months?" The old woman shrugged. "Which isn't out of the question. When you retire, it's hard to keep track of the days. Are you home schooled, or is it already the end of May?"

"It's the end of April," Kyrie offered as an answer, knowing a lie about the calendar would not last scrutiny. "I should probably get back to my tent."

The older woman nodded. "Even in my day, talking to silly old ladies next to the bathroom wasn't groovy. Hope your camping …"

Kyrie felt something spark in the woman's mind. *What are you thinking?*

"You remind me of someone," the woman said as Kyrie's friends approached the woman from behind. Her eyes lit up. "Now I remember. I saw you on the news. Rupert had been complaining about the potato salad. We had the volume down on the TV. It was too much listening to all that happened." The woman shook her head, and her free arm moved to touch her forehead, chest, and then shoulders. "All those poor souls." She lifted her gaze back to Kyrie's face. "But I saw your picture. Someone shot at your house in Kansas."

Kyrie's heart raced. *You've not been here even for one night, and you've been recognized.* She forced herself deeper into the woman's mind, looking to see what else the woman knew, and felt a sudden snap as the connection solidified. The taste of dry chicken filled her mouth as she sat across from a balding, hunched over man who ignored her in favor of a book of crossword puzzles. A sneer reached Kyrie's lips as the news with a picture of her face played in the background, the volume turned down so that she could have a conversation that the man refused to participate in. *I hope you like your potato salad without salt,* she heard the other woman think, before her attention turned to images of her aunt's house on the TV.

"Kyrie?" Michelle asked.

Kyrie shook her head, pulling back slightly before the memory of the earlier argument that required the salt-free retribution played out in the woman's memories. *Breathe,* she told herself, hoping she could make the woman forget. "You never saw me," Kyrie growled at the woman, the irritation the woman felt for her husband still too fresh in their now shared thoughts. Memories of her own mother telling her to forget that she once had claws surfaced, building her rage.

Kyrie forced her fingers straight. "You never saw the news," each word spoken separately. A vague memory of a movie lingered in the background of the woman's thoughts as the other person's mind invented ways to comply with what Kyrie told her. "You watched that movie," Kyrie agreed. "You don't know me. You don't recognize me. You don't want to even look at me. You'll look away anytime you see me."

The oversized bag slipped to the ground as the woman's arms went slack, and her eyes turned toward the wall on her right. "I never saw you," the woman repeated mechanically.

"Kyrie?" Michelle questioned again, but Becca smacked her good shoulder softly to keep her quiet.

"Go to the bathroom and then go back to sleep," Kyrie demanded, hoping her mental pressure on the woman would hold. *And without destroying her mind, like Nalitran does to his Bound.* She did not know the impact of her actions, and the clinical side of her reminded her, *the only way to learn is to experiment.*

Kyrie stepped out of the woman's path and motioned with her head for her friends to step back. She moistened her lips and pulled herself the rest of the way out of the woman's head. The old lady stood motionless for a moment, then shook herself, looked down at the ground, picked up her bag with a muttered question, then continued into the bathroom.

Kyrie turned to see her friends' jaws hanging open. *Damn, the fear and anger they are feeling.*

"What was that?" Michelle whispered.

Becca's hesitation lingered in the air. *She definitely understands.* "I'm starting to remember things." Kyrie looked at the ground. "Things my mother forced me to forget." She swallowed. "That woman recognized me."

"You messed with her mind," Becca demanded. "She's not one of them, is she? She's just a person. No binding stone." There were no actual questions in the statements. "You do something like that to our parents? To us?"

Kyrie quickly shook her head. "Never to you." She motioned for everyone to follow her away from the toilets.

"I have to go," Aki said.

"Hold it until the old woman's done," Becca snapped, moving to follow Kyrie. "I want to hear what justification she has. And we don't need the old woman seeing any of us if she recognized Kyrie."

They deserve to be angry. Kyrie walked around to the other side of the bathhouse, away from the tents, and into the cover of the trees. Even she found the darkness hard to see through, but it provided enough distance that, hopefully, their voices would not carry.

"Why are you out here by yourself?" Michelle asked, barely above a whisper.

"I had a bad dream," Kyrie replied automatically.

"Enough, Michelle. I saw her control that woman." Becca turned her ire to Kyrie. "You told us that you can't read minds, just emotions. You implied that it requires a binding stone to control someone. You ever plan to tell us the truth?"

"I'm only now discovering the truth myself." Kyrie wanted the others to believe her, but she closed down her senses, trying to avoid any risk that some manipulation might slip through her conscious control. "I didn't even know I had been doing anything until you all asked about my phone. I just knew I needed it, so I took it back. It's not clear to me, yet, but I'm now wondering if I started doing similar things with my parents when I was very young. Was that when they made me start to forget things?"

"That would make sense," Michelle offered. "Mike has my parents wrapped around his finger. I watched him take advantage of it all the time, but they brushed off my complaints. With your powers, you'd have turned them into even bigger slaves than my golden-child brother has with my parents."

Becca scoffed. "You should have told us the truth."

"Did you manipulate us?" Aki asked quietly. "Our parents?"

"Not any of you," Kyrie responded immediately. "I ... I don't know how to describe it. But I think you are the first real people I've ever had in my life, and I don't want anything to change that." She turned and paced a few steps in the dark. "My parents pretended to be so many different people, I'm no longer sure who they were. Were they ever any of the different personalities?" She blinked back her tears. "They made me forget." Kyrie looked down at her hands. "Made me forget I once had claws. Told me the other world didn't exist. That it was all part of playing games." She tried to clear her vision and stopped moving. "Yes, I tried to calm all your parents' emotions and make them agreeable to allow you all to come. It doesn't always work. I think it depends on how strong-willed the other person is. But I don't really know. I've not had a chance to learn my true powers yet."

Michelle stepped forward. "Well, in terms of game, I'd say you're not at geas level of spells yet, but perhaps suggestion or command."

Becca turned toward the bathhouse, one hand on her hip and one pointed at the building thirty feet away. "Really, Michelle? I saw it. She definitely put a geas on that woman." Becca turned her focus on Kyrie. "You dominated her. You controlled her. Awan said the minds of the Bound in Arkansas were damaged as a result. Is that what will happen to her?"

"Truth?" Kyrie asked.

"Yes," Becca snarled.

"I have no idea." *You hope not, but you had to act quickly.* "I'm realizing that while my parents let me use my physical powers, they blocked me from any mental ones."

"And you're just now getting your memories back," Michelle offered. "It may take time."

Aki exhaled; her voice clinical. "I can see a parent doing that. You'd have been a child forcing the adults to do anything you wanted. Ice cream, toys, really anything that you might want without any self-control. And with your knowledge and power from the other world …"

"I was a child there too." Kyrie sniffled back the mucus filling her sinuses. "I was young when Awan snatched me away from my other mother. I dreamed—or remembered it—clearly for the first time Friday morning. Everything before that was always just fog and vague ideas."

Michelle stepped forward. "That drawing you said you did overnight of …"

"A corvlian," Kyrie completed. "That's the closest I can vocalize the word. She's what I remember of my other mother. I can still hear her voice calling for me, pleading for me to come back. To not leave." Kyrie shook her head.

Michelle stepped closer, and Becca grabbed her good shoulder to hold her back. "I'm sorry you're feeling sorry for yourself, but what have you done to my dad? You changing him?"

Kyrie took in a sharp breath. *They're right; you're not acting like a warrior.* She centered herself. "At most, I tried to calm his emotions, so he'd be willing to listen and believe us. Nothing else."

Becca said nothing in response, and Kyrie almost felt relief that it was too dark to see her expression.

Michelle turned toward her longtime friend. "Becca, I believe her."

Aki spoke before Becca could respond. "The problem, Michelle, is that Becca doesn't know if any of us can trust what we believe. If Kyrie could be made to forget everything about the other world, and if she has mental powers that impact us as if we were Bound like her, then she could make us believe anything she wanted."

Kyrie wanted to protest, but the words would not come. *You've destroyed the party, just like Mother always said. This must be why she said you always had to be alone.*

"However," Aki continued. "I'm inclined to trust her." The other girl breathed deeply. "I heard the fear and pain in her voice. And while this shit that's going down has me scared beyond words, I know she wants to protect us."

"Damn it," Becca said. Silence hung in the air until they all became uncomfortable. "Kyrie, be up front with us from now on. Please."

"I promise," Kyrie replied, double-checking that she maintained her clamp on her mind. "I'm still learning what is happening to me. I'm scared as well," she admitted. "I've never had friends before, and I don't want to lose any of you. And changing who you are would mean you'd just be more NPCs like my parents threw at me."

Michelle stepped forward and hugged her. "We'll get through this."

"Can I go pee now?" Aki asked.

Kyrie opened her mind and searched the bathhouse. "Yeah, the woman's gone."

"Good," Aki said, hurrying out of the trees.

Chapter 15

N alitran ignored the background noise of his private jet, which had returned from Kansas to pick him up in Tucson. They had reached forty-five thousand feet and were about two and a half hours from Northwest Washington. Two Bound guards sat silently in their seats, taking up a fourth of the space in the aircraft. The dolunar warriors he forced into human bodies had retained their absolute loyalty to him and never complained about performing their duty. Later, he would allow them time to rest, as even his most ardent supporters needed some personal time, especially when human hormones and physical limitations wore at their minds.

The dolunar Bound he ordered to take the bullet for him would remain with the three corvlian Bound at his rented penthouse in Tucson, once released from the hospital. The corvlian slaves received only as much consideration as the value they provided. The more cooperative ones, he allowed them to keep their mental capacity so that he could enjoy their torment. The difficult ones he broke and they served him in the form of expendable robots.

Nalitran had not bound the two pilots in the cockpit. However, the two men each enjoyed a large salary, and he monitored their private communications to ensure they did not reveal anything that might occur on the plane. He did not restrict them from talking about where they flew, as the required ADS-B transmissions coming from his aircraft publicly revealed all those details to anyone listening on the correct channel. However, the flight logs did not always report all the passengers, and he would not risk a pilot revealing those details.

Nalitran glanced at his watch. It just turned two AM in Kansas. He woke the laptop sitting on the desk in front of his leather seat and started the secure video conference. The news reports he had seen about the Landvik girl had not pleased him, and being trapped in Tucson without a secure location to conduct his business had only stoked his anger.

A minute later, Yrginda joined the meeting. The normally well-kept woman looked haggard, with loose hairs poking out from her head. "What is your status?" he demanded in their native tongue in case someone had managed to sneak a listening device aboard his jet.

"Two of our warriors watching the girl were killed by the same Hurlington cell that we believe shot at her in the morning. Our third warrior had remained at the safe-house monitoring the trackers, cameras, and listening devices on the friends and families." Yrginda continued, her tone emotionless. "It is likely one of Hurlington's people somehow identified our Bound and put a tracker on their vehicle. The police have recovered our GPS trackers, which someone removed from the targets' vehicles. They also have the bodies of our warriors and another tracker from our car."

Nalitran's face contorted, and he leaned closer to the laptop. "I would not call them warriors if they were so incompetent that Hurlington's men so easily tagged them. Was it the Williams man who found our trackers? What have the police said?"

Yrginda's jaw tightened. "We are aware of several spies Hurlington installed in our organization. We used the ones we knew of to feed him the intelligence we wanted him to act upon. When his people acted on the surfacing of the Landvik girl before Rodgers did, we discussed the fact that other spies had gone undetected. It is likely the leak of their location came from at least one spy."

Nalitran stared at his general through the video feed. The unspoken challenge from Yrginda, that he had argued against an immediate purge, hung in the silence. "And this cell—which one was it? Are they as dead as Hurlington or are they still pursuing the girl?"

"We do not have complete access to the Olathe police files, and with Project Kvotar having activated almost every law enforcement agent in the country, our operatives are limited in their ability to gather intel. Regarding the cell, I'm certain this was Heth. They used a Barrett, or equivalent, which would make it Hurlington's heaviest armed team." Yrginda's eyes radiated anger, though her voice remained even. "Additionally, Hurlington escaped the assault team, killing all but five."

Nalitran smashed his fist into the desk. "How did you fail?"

"Our focus has been Project Kvotar. Hurlington wasn't supposed to be eliminated this soon, which means the kill team was not fully assembled."

"I don't need excuses," Nalitran snapped.

"I offer no excuses to justify failures in my judgement. I merely state facts for what occurred. These operations contain variables that we cannot fully know or predict, and when the timing is adjusted to be outside any planned window of engagement, you have to anticipate less than perfect execution. Only with additional resources can additional contingencies be covered."

Nalitran reined in his anger. Yelling at his general for things outside Yrginda's control would not change the outcome. "Please continue with the sitrep."

Yrginda's voice remained mechanical, as if Nalitran had not just expressed any emotion. "Hurlington likely had a secondary exit in the bunker that we were not aware of. He also had what appears to be modified Claymore mines in the ceiling along the main entrance. The infiltration team advanced all three groups into a very long kill zone due to the length of the passage. They were obliterated instantly. He also triggered a self-destruct protocol in the server room. The team that entered the Beirtal home found no one and went to the cave, where they found the remains of the bunker team, but they had to retreat from a full search due to smoke and fire filling the passages."

"And you don't know where Hurlington is now," Nalitran stated, knowing Yrginda would have led with that information if she had it available.

"We do not. It is assumed he used a watercraft to escape onto the nearby lakes. He could use the waterways to land almost anywhere. Northern Minnesota is covered in lakes and rivers."

Yrginda softened her expression, though anger still shone in her eyes. "The Landvik girl appears to have fled with her friends and Jason Williams. The other families are scattering. The Hino parents returned to their house and left again after only a few minutes. Same with the girl's aunt and the Windall family. Only the boy's parents have remained in their home. As I mentioned, the GPS trackers were removed from the vehicles, though we expect we can still track the families' locations through other means."

Nalitran saw his general hesitate. "Tell me."

"I'm not certain there is any value in pursuing the parents. While I'm certain it would put leverage on her friends, I spoke with the girl on the lawyer's phone. She is a warrior. She expressed no compassion for Lars. We know for some reason she likes those that are of her age. The rescuing of the Bruce girl demonstrated that. However, I believe she is dolunar and will calculate the tactical value of the others and not surrender to save them. Additionally, the Bruce girl could also be explained by the fact that she had the advantage over Rodgers. I personally believe that is why she pursued that avenue at all."

"If she's dolunar, why is she not submitting herself to my rule?"

Yrginda shrugged. "Perhaps she is one of the traitors who let the enemy capture you. Perhaps she does not believe you are truly our warlord. I do not know. I only spoke to her on the phone briefly. She did not succumb to my entreaties."

Nalitran frowned. He knew that just because he had ruled the dolunar empire, it did not make all of his people loyal. *Some are cowards. Some were traitors.* However, most of the ones that he brought to this world and survived the binding to human bodies offered their fealty. *It is the corvlians I brought over that I have to break.*

Yrginda continued. "I do not have the people available to search for Hurlington, the girl, and to deal with their families. On the positive side, the lawyer is secured, and a sighting of Awan was reported."

Nalitran paused to consider his options. "Pull the operatives from Kvotar who have executed their targets. Bringing in the girl alive is the most important task, then Hurlington and the rest of his people."

"Warlord, we cannot do that."

"I gave you an order!"

The expression on Yrginda's face made Nalitran wish he had his general's binding stone on him.

Yrginda's voice remained cold. "Anyone we pull from those who successfully eliminated their targets will draw suspicion for their disappearances. Most of them are likely under surveillance right now, and any that are not, will draw the attention of law enforcement if they walk away from their supposed lives. This will make them hunted, and then they will be of no use to us in a covert capacity. They will only draw more attention to the girl."

Nalitran hated having the obvious pointed out to him. "Then, pull some of those from the targets that were not in position and have not acted."

"If we do that, we will likely never get them back into position in time to eliminate the targets in mass."

"Select those assigned to the least valuable targets until you get sufficient numbers. I want her brought in alive."

Yrginda reluctantly nodded her head. "And Lars, Awan, and the families?"

"Bring the lawyer to the northern site when you can. Have Awan eliminated with someone from the shadow org. The families are the least valuable; eliminate them if you have time and resources. But we don't want it tracked back to us, especially since Rodgers' connection to us became unfortunately very public."

Yrginda nodded her head. "My next report will be at seventeen hundred UTC."

Nalitran nodded his head. "Thank you. I know this is not your fault." He ended the call and breathed deeply. His guards heard every word of the conversation, as they all understood the language. While he could control them with their stones, he wanted them to act willingly, and so he had to show reason despite his rage.

Yrginda ended the call on the laptop. The dolunar warrior focused on keeping the emotions of the weak human flesh in check. The last twelve years of living in the female shell had only increased the rage he felt. Had he been on Nalitran's estate, he would have tempered his anger with a couple of hours in the gym to strengthen the body he had been forced into. In a hotel room in Olathe, dealing with the fallout of Nalitran making sudden changes to the plans because of a girl, he did not have the time to spare for exercise.

The least valuable targets have the least effective operatives, he complained to himself. *This is a foolish enterprise.*

"General?" Ontrc asked.

Yrginda turned to face the three Bound he had with him in the room. Two had come with him from Tucson; the third had been assigned to watch Kyrie and her friends. The tall, green-eyed man almost revealed a level of concern in his expression. "It is after zero two hundred now. These bodies need sleep," Yrginda stated.

"General, is there something we can assist with?" Ontrc continued.

Yrginda sat back in the chair. "If you want to be of use, you will rest your bodies. Tomorrow will be very busy. We need to refresh our intelligence on the families and see if there is any indication of where Jason Williams might have gone with the Landvik girl." He pondered the question of his own next steps. Project Kvotar had taken years of planning. Now he needed to start fresh with new targets and new objectives. "If the Ottiman family is still in location, perhaps we can find a use for them. The girl may not care if they die, but perhaps we can leverage them to get others looking for the girl."

"And Hurlington and Awan?" the Bound questioned.

Yrginda pursed his lips. "If you can arrange for Awan to disappear completely, that will save me time. Remember, he's Bishop's cousin, so all traces of him need to be removed without anyone being aware." Yrginda rose from the chair. "Hurlington is a greater problem. We know he has abilities. His failed binding was twenty-two years ago, and even if the human is in control, he's managed to accumulate powers. Given the fact that we don't know where he's gone, I will call Nalitran's friend in the FBI in the morning to quietly have them look for both the girl and Hurlington."

Yrginda crossed his arms. "Now, the three of you return to the other room and rest. I want you functional at zero seven hundred."

The three Bound bowed their heads and left his room. Yrginda turned back to the laptop to evaluate who he could pull from Kvotar. *Nalitran's obsession will destroy all my work. The least valuable assets have the least capable operatives assigned.* Yrginda knew all of his choices were dolunar Bound and would have been in body for perhaps a year or less. *Or simply lack any real power because they didn't come from the priest caste.* He hated the idea of using dolunar as fodder to wear down the Landvik girl until he and the more capable Bound could contain her. The corvlian Bound lacked the reliability to operate effectively without constant controls so they had only minimal roles in Project Kvotar. *One does not throw away their own pack. A true warlord would understand this.*

Chapter 16

Becca stood with Michelle, Aki, and Jake near a set of boulders overlooking the creek. The morning dew made the stones too wet to sit on. "We have a problem," she said, keeping her attention on Michelle, who she expected would object.

"Kyrie is just learning what she can do," Michelle said almost on cue.

"And can you be certain she didn't make you say that?" Becca demanded.

"I'm still trying to digest it," Jake admitted. "I wish the three of you would have woke me as well. I miss out on too much because I have to sleep with your dad."

"Ew," Becca said, "don't say it like that."

"Hey," Jake raised his hands, "that's not what I meant."

Aki crossed her arms and kept her attention on Becca. "And what do you want us to do about it? She can read our minds and, based on last night, make us believe anything she wants. You have a way to stop her?"

"She's not going to do that to us," Michelle insisted. "I trust her. She's scared and alone with people trying to kill her."

Becca put her hands on her hips. "And what if she's backed into a corner? Two campaigns ago, Aki betrayed the group when you pressed her with the choice of dying or saving herself."

"That was just in-game," Aki complained. "I'd not do that in real life."

"And Kyrie was raised on D&D by her parents. Is this all just a game to her?" Becca shook her head. "I ..." She frowned. "I'm not saying she's going to do anything to us, but I'm worried that it's possible."

Michelle looked each of them in the eye. "Kyrie ran at the men in Arkansas and got shot twice. She went to save Tina. She charged at the men in the van that tried to kill us yesterday." Michelle chuffed and stared at the ground. "I can't believe that was just yesterday." She looked up again. "The point is, she's risked herself to protect us. I'd say she's been backed into a corner several times already."

Aki swallowed. "But what if the corner is different? What if she does something we can't accept and we decide to leave? Would she let us go, or would she force us to say?"

Jake put his arm around Aki, but he said nothing. A look of indecision on his face.

How'd you let yourself get mixed up in this? Becca sighed. "Look, I'm not saying we do anything. I'm not even saying she'll do anything. But we should be prepared to look for any signs one of us is getting manipulated and bring it up to the others."

Michelle shook her head. "She doesn't want NPCs. She wants friends, and I'm confident she won't betray us."

Becca glared at her friend.

"But," Michelle said, "I'll say something if I ever suspect something."

Aki patted Jake's hand and then held it in her own. "And what can we do if something happens? She can stop men with rifles and survive getting hit with bullets. What can we do to her?" She turned to Michelle. "Not that I would do anything to harm her. But if she does something, am I supposed to play lawyer and argue for her to undo it?"

Becca considered the question. "Yeah, I think that is all we can do. Unless any of you have any better ideas. I mean, we're dead without her. Nalitran and Hurlington will kill us if we're on our own, so I'm not about to block her and boot her from the server. I just want to know that if I'm not acting right, one of you will say something and help me take back control of my own head."

Aki and Jake nodded. "Definitely."

Michelle forced a smile. "Of course I will. And since you put it like that, I'd want all of you to do the same. I guess I'm overly protective of her. Perhaps she's already messed with my head."

Becca snorted. "No, Michelle, you've always collected broken people. Which I guess says something about me as well."

Michelle moved closer and gave Becca a hug. "Friends."

"Friends," Becca agreed.

Kyrie had allowed the others to sneak away without her, knowing they all felt uneasy around her. She had managed to actually fall asleep again and had remained so until well after sunrise. When she fully awoke, she expanded her senses and found Mr. Williams alone in the van. A vague memory of him rising early lingered in her thoughts, but it had not fully woken her at the time.

The fact that the others had not returned worried her, but she hesitated to do anything. *Please don't hate us? Though it's not like you can fix it if they do.* She tried to slow her racing heart, not wanting to feel the fear of more potential loss. *You won't harm them, no matter what they do.* The statement did nothing to make her feel better or calm her anxiety.

No longer able to benefit from more rest, Kyrie climbed out of the sleeping bag, grabbed her shoes, and left the tent. The campground had numerous other people milling about. Trails of smoke rose from various firepits, and the smell of cooking meat wafted to her nose, triggering a growl of complaint from her empty stomach. They had only grabbed absolute necessities from the stores on the way to the state park, and that had not included a fully stocked fridge.

She moved to the van and noticed a drop cloth covering the rear door. She hesitated a moment before opening the back of the van and climbing in through the curtain. The monitors and various LEDs provided the extent of the interior lighting.

"Make sure the work mat stays in place. I'm hiding the license plate," Mr. Williams said.

Kyrie pulled the tarp down to re-center it before she shut the door behind her. He held out one of the bags of beef jerky that they had purchased from a gas station the evening before while he continued to use the mouse with his right hand. She walked over, took the half-eaten pouch, and pulled out a sizeable chunk of food. The dried meat, salt, and spices tasted wonderful to her empty stomach. She dropped into the nearest chair and swiveled it to face the three active monitors in front of Becca's father. "Thank you again for not believing the worst of me."

He shook his head, but he did not turn his attention away from the screens. "Brutal honesty. I don't know you. Or even what you are. Perhaps human. Perhaps not. I'm protecting Becca, and you seem like the best option. However …" He pulled up a webpage and played a video, the muffled sound going to the headphones he had slipped down to his neck. The images flashed between her aunt's house, the barn in Kansas where she had used Hurlington's men to defeat Michael Rodgers, and then pictures of herself and Tina Bruce. After a bit, the video switched to a reporter talking from behind a desk. Mr. Williams paused the playback. "It's just KC news, but it's on the Internet, and it could spread. The other big networks are running stories on what is being called a tsunami of terrorist attacks targeting our economy. They've been using lots of water symbolism, each graphics department trying to outdo their competitors."

You have to tell him. "Brutal honesty," she repeated back to him, her heart racing. He continued to work without looking at her. *Use your mouth.* "An old woman stopped me at the bathrooms overnight. She'd seen a report like that video last night when eating dinner." Kyrie took a deep breath. "I did something to her that I hope will make her forget about the story and seeing me."

He swiveled to face her. "You didn't kill her, did you?"

That might have been an easier option than admitting this. She shook her head. "I'm just becoming aware of some of my powers, like in the last day or so. I seem to be able to influence other people's thoughts and memories." She felt Mr. Williams' spike of fear. "It's not the same as if someone held my binding stone, but it seems some people are susceptible to what I can do." She breathed deeply, fully conscious of the stone in her pocket. "I commanded the woman to forget me. I don't know for certain it worked. But if she recognized me, other people might as well. I don't think I can do what I did to her to everyone that might see me."

Becca's father sat without saying anything. His imposing form remained still as he wrestled with what he wanted to say and do. Eventually, he spoke. "You do anything to my Becca?"

"No," Kyrie replied, holding his gaze.

"There's a lot in what you didn't just say."

"I've not forced you to do anything, aside from perhaps calming down when we first told you what was going on."

He turned back to the computer screens, and Kyrie felt his multi-layered terror. "I'll have to figure out how I feel about that. But that can wait. We need to do something about your appearance. We can't be running around the country trying to avoid people if any random person will recognize you. I need time to work without interruptions." He glanced at her. "I had hoped to stay here at least until the end of the week, when we lose this camping spot. My hope was we might then grab one of the dive-up spots they don't allow people to reserve online."

Kyrie nodded her head. In-game, she often used spells to disguise herself. In real life, her powers did not work that way. "I was thinking of cutting my hair. Not sure what else I can do to change my appearance."

"Cut and dye it," he agreed. "As a blonde, I could see people recognizing you even with shorter hair." He swiveled back and typed on the keyboard. "Perhaps colored contacts, but we need to watch how much we spend. I already used more cash than I wanted, and I need to save the crypto I've got. Just burned some this morning paying a hacking group to find more details on Hurlington's servers. I expect there will be a lot of people looking for them, so we won't have much time to act. We're not broke, but it cost me more for the haste I requested."

"There's the thirty thousand in Colorado," Kyrie offered.

"Too risky. At least one of our two friend groups are watching your old place, and I'd put down money that both are."

Kyrie nodded her head and wanted to change the topic, but they had more needs. "Last night I realized we don't have any towels. We also don't have any ranged weapons to defend ourselves."

He rubbed the stubble on his chin. "Realized the same lack of towels this morning. No razor, no change of clothes, no cooler with food. I wasn't thinking of all the things we needed yesterday. I just wanted enough supplies to get us here so we could work in peace." He turned his head toward her. "The weapons I'm a bit more concerned about. They tend to make people want to use them." He turned back to the screen and continued scrolling through sites.

Kyrie nodded her understanding of his concern. *But if you don't have weapons when you need them, you die.* She leaned forward as a headline on the screen caught her attention. "That says some church people were arrested?"

Mr. Williams stopped scrolling and clicked on the link. "I'm only partially caught up on the news from overnight, but I read this one earlier. Apparently, one of Hurlington's cultists turned themselves in and then dropped a dime on twelve others." Kyrie wrinkled her nose at the comment about dropping money, but she chose not to ask for clarification. "They claimed they were only spreading the word of God and had nothing to do with the killings. Ten of the other twelve were arrested overnight. What I saw earlier said the remaining two are on the run, but the news story is three hours old." He checked another window, where text scrolled by in bursts of activity. Not seeing what he wanted, he turned back to the browser window. "Another site compiling data on the killings said that the five suspects identified as either having taken part in—or supported—the terrorist attacks are dead. Each killed in a shoot-out. If the feds have anyone under surveillance, or kept someone alive to arrest them, they haven't told the reporters."

Kyrie considered the updates as her senses alerted her to the approach of the others. "With Hurlington's people getting arrested, Nalitran's shifting of blame appears to be taking that threat out for us."

Mr. Williams nodded, but hesitated in showing full agreement. "After the attack at the farm, the church took down the public messaging server Becca used to lure Hurlington's people to you. I'm pretty certain each individual cell has its own private server to limit risk, so not everyone might be taken down easily. But there will be a lot of people watching. I'd like to get access before all the servers are shut down or filled with feds. I don't want to risk hacking things the feds are tracking. Even with my protections, they might have methods of locating us."

Kyrie did not react to the van door opening. "But there is still a chance that Nalitran's framing of Hurlington will eliminate him for us, which will allow us to just focus on Nalitran himself."

"Keep the work mat over the license plate," Mr. Williams called out to Becca as she entered the van. Jake fixed the mat after Michelle and Aki entered.

Becca grabbed the pouch of beef jerky from Kyrie on her way to the front of the van. "God, I need some coffee. And a real f'ing bed, but I'm happy to have the guy shooting at us eliminated."

Michelle moved to join Becca to make room for Jake and Aki. "But why kill so many people to frame Hurlington? And why risk someone shooting at him? He could have been killed if the guy missed."

Mr. Williams typed on the keyboard, and a table of numbers rolled across the screen. "I spent part of last night before going to bed working on that very question and finished the script to gather the data this morning." He looked at the numbers that had stopped at the bottom of the screen. "I'm using various data sources, but from what I found, of the eighteen public companies impacted by the attacks, Bishop owns short positions in seventy-two percent of them, and for the last year, he has been stockpiling cash. Lots of cash."

Aki raised her eyebrows. "They always say to follow the money."

Mr. Williams tapped his fingers on the narrow desk. "I can't be certain, but it appears he's got short positions in another twenty companies not directly impacted by the murders, but I'm guessing the market is going to react badly when it opens tomorrow. And the two political targets killed had a reputation for being anti-business. I have no way of knowing what, if any, stake he has in the handful of private companies that lost senior leaders."

"So, he's going to make a lot more money," Jake said, standing next to Aki. "This is all about money?"

Mr. Williams shrugged. "Or at least reduce the cost of the short positions. The market's been up over the last year, and if the positions are coming due, he might have had to buy high to cover the positions. The killings were too well planned and coordinated to be a last-minute operation. This was all in motion well before Kyrie surfaced." He turned his chair to face his daughter and took the pouch of jerky from her. "Hurlington was likely intended to be the fall guy for a while. My guess is the creature calling himself Bishop might even know where Hurlington's located. Probably will use someone to kill him so the man can't talk, then claim whatever reward there is, saying the killing was in self-defense. But regardless, I have hard money on Hurlington being dead before the cops find him."

"Then Kyrie's right; we only need to focus on one bastard," Becca said.

Aki cleared her throat. "What if we find Hurlington first and warn him? Perhaps we can use the video and any evidence Hurlington has to get Bishop arrested. Surely someone else will see through the fraud. It would keep us from … going to jail for …" Aki wrung her hands.

Kyrie blocked out the fear coming from Aki to avoid internalizing it. "Hurlington sent men to kill me twice yesterday and three times before that. He can't be trusted, even if Nalitran is trying to kill him."

"It could have been Bishop using people to frame Hurlington," Aki pleaded.

Kyrie shook her head. "The people in the van were not Bound. However, the two in the car that shot at the van were. And I'm pretty sure the guy with the big rifle killed both of the Bound."

"But—" Aki continued.

Mr. Williams cleared his throat. "Killing someone will be our last option. If the feds can arrest Hurlington before Bishop—Nalitran, kills him, then perhaps he'll live long enough to be able to tell the cops what he knows. But I agree with Kyrie; he's not someone I would trust. I'm still going to try to track him down so that we can avoid him, and hopefully raid his servers for data. He's been operating for more than a decade, so hopefully he's amassed a lot of dirt on Bishop."

Michelle crossed her arms. "I agree with Kyrie that we need some way to protect ourselves. What happens if some more people show up with guns? We don't have Jake's father's gun for Kyrie to use."

Mr. Williams' jaw tightened. "Guns draw attention."

"What about something less lethal?" Jake asked. He glanced at the floor. "My father is a bit nuts about having weapons around the house. But he also had things like Tasers and stun guns. Perhaps we can get some of those."

Becca considered the idea. "We saw the Bound in Arkansas deflect the rocks Kyrie launched at him. They'd just block something like that."

"What if we built it into a glove?" Jake asked. "I've built all kinds of props for theater, and I remember some videos I watched a while back where people concealed the electrodes in a glove."

Aki nodded her head. "It might save us if someone did grab us. You wanted ideas, Becca."

Kyrie sensed a silent message between the others, but locked down her mind to prevent intruding on her friends. *You need them to trust you.*

Mr. Williams nodded his head. "If you can make it so it's not obvious and won't shock the person using it, it might be worthwhile. Probably be good for all of us to start wearing gloves anyway to reduce fingerprints."

Michelle moved a step closer to everyone. "And I went down a chemical weapons black hole when I was researching poisons for the campaign where you all went into that underground city. There are some cleaners we can buy almost anywhere that can make gas bombs that would make it hard for someone attacking us to breathe."

"Making chemical weapons is a crime," Mr. Williams said. "Plus, gas can be blown back into your face."

Kyrie quickly considered delivery methods for mixing separate liquids, such as having a small glass jar inside a larger one. *But there is no guarantee the inside jar will break in the pool of liquid from the outer one. Though a gravity burst could break it.* Before the conversation could move on, she blurted, "I like the idea. Maybe not for everyone, but I think I could make it work."

"I'm sure I can find videos on anything we need," Becca offered.

Her father cleared his throat. "We can look at all of that, and even figure out how to have things we can't buy locally shipped to a drop location. But first, I want you all to recall everything you know about Michael Rodgers."

Becca narrowed her eyes. "Rodgers? Why him? He's dead."

"Yesterday, you said he was in charge of Bishop's criminal empire. He tried to locate Kyrie for years and knows about the Bound, even controlled several." Mr. Williams stood up. "Criminal empires are just like corporations. They have accounts receivable, invoices, payroll, even HR. Bad guys who are not getting paid are not going to keep working for the crime boss. The bosses want to make sure they get every penny they are owed. They even have auditors to make sure the people keeping the books aren't stealing too much. They will have computer systems with copies of standard corporate software to track everything and IT guys to run them. We find where these servers are located, perhaps we can get even stronger evidence against Bishop. Coupled with anything we can steal from Hurlington, if we can find his servers, and add in the circumstantial facts we're putting together, we just might be able to bury Bishop and have the feds do the hard work."

Kyrie nodded her head, though she doubted it would resolve the threat. *A dolunar won't be stopped by cops and prison.* However, she understood everyone else's need not to be arrested. *For now, his suggestion is probably the best option.*

Mr. Williams looked at Jake. "Can we leave the tents up, or do we need to take them down?" At Jake's questioning expression, the older man clarified. "We need to go to the store. Another set of clothes for all of us, towels, a cooler, food, ... lots of things. Perhaps stun guns and soldering irons." His stomach growled. "If we need to take it all down, I want to get started now so we can get some food, supplies, and come back here to continue my research."

Jack nodded his head knowingly. "We can leave them up. It's not like there is anything of value in them."

"Good. Go unplug us." Mr. Williams got up from the computer and made his way up to the driver's seat. "Becca, I want you to work while I drive. It's at least twenty minutes to Farmington, and the batteries have enough charge. I want you to dig up anything you can on Rodgers. We need to find out who reported to him and start building a target list."

Becca sat down in the vacated chair. "Sure. I'd already gathered things on him a couple weeks ago, like a Chicago address. I can get more."

After a drive-through breakfast, they divided into pairs to get the items on their lists from multiple stores, including scissors, hair color, and shampoo from a beauty supply shop for Kyrie. The shopping trip drained a sizable amount of their cash reserves, but it filled the back of the van with plastic bags and a pair of large ice chests stocked with food.

They returned to the campground before noon and again divided their efforts. Jake and Aki took all the new clothing to the laundry room to wash and dry the gigantic pile of garments. Becca and her father worked on researching Michael Rodgers to see what traces of Bishop's criminal organization the dead man might have left behind. Michelle took Kyrie to the showers to cut and dye her hair.

Kyrie sat on the small bench while Michelle pulled different things from the bags, occasionally stopping to rotate her shoulder.

"Let me finish healing you," Kyrie insisted. After a moment, Michelle stopped moving and allowed Kyrie to put her hands over the wound. Kyrie connected with her friend's mind and directed Michelle's body's natural processes to work faster as she pushed energy into the other girl. Ten seconds later, Kyrie stepped back. "That should help."

Michelle pulled on the collar of her shirt and then removed the bandage taped over the bullet wound to reveal a pink scar. "It feels so much better." The brunette smiled. "I guess this means I really can't go back home for a while, otherwise the doctors will get suspicious. Not that I want to go home," she added quickly.

"Probably," Kyrie agreed.

Michelle tossed the unneeded bandage on the edge of the small bench and finished organizing the bottles of hair color. "You should probably take off your shirt. This will get messy, and we'll need to get your hair wet."

"Do we really need all these colors?" Kyrie asked. "Can't we just cut it and turn it brown?"

Michelle kept her voice from breaking as she sorted through the supplies. "I helped Tina go from blonde to brunette a couple years ago. Unless you want your hair to look like a terrible dye job, we need to do a fill color and step you down from blonde to brown. You can't go in one step."

Kyrie nodded, trusting that Michelle knew what she said, but not relishing the amount of time she would have to commit to the process. "Hopefully, once you chop back my hair, it will go faster."

Michelle frowned at her. "You've got lovely hair. I really don't want to cut it that short. We've got enough dye that we can keep your hair long."

Kyrie shook her head. "I agreed with Becca's dad. The more drastic the change, the fewer people will recognize me. The pictures of the pixie cut looked good to me. Anything short, like that singer Becca's father mentioned. The one named after the berries."

Michelle shook her head. "O'Riordan from the Cranberries? You need to update your playlist to something this century." She stared at Kyrie's hair. "I'm not a stylist. I'll probably butcher your hair."

Kyrie crossed her arms. Michelle radiated less a sense of uncertainty and more a desire to preserve the current state of her appearance. "I'm not concerned. You said the trimmers we got for Jake would work on me as well."

"Fine." Michelle took a deep breath. "Sorry, I …"

Kyrie put a hand on her friend's shoulder. "We'll get through this. I'll protect you."

Michelle shook her head. "No. It's not that. I miss Tina. I can't believe she's gone." She looked up, and Kyrie held her gaze. "Aki and Jake are upset about leaving their families. They aren't saying much to the rest of us, but Aki cried several times last night, and they keep talking to each other about it."

Kyrie nodded, well aware of the anguish the two shared.

Michelle continued. "Becca has her father with her, so she's not lost her family and doesn't have reasons to be sad, other than that we lost Tina." Michelle compressed her lips as she considered her words. "I think there's something wrong with me. I don't really feel anything being away from my parents and my brother. It's like I've always been waiting to leave. But while I don't care about leaving them, I still feel so alone and don't want to feel that way. Is there something wrong with me?" She wiped at her eyes. "How are you so calm with the death of your own mom? And now Lars being taken? It feels like we're both alone in the world. I guess I'm pulled to you because I like the different. And now that I might never see my parents again, I feel more like you than I originally thought. Not that my problems are anywhere near yours," she added hastily. "It's just …"

Kyrie pondered the primary question in Michelle's rant for a moment. Various hypotheses presented themselves as she considered her own emotions. *You're like Spock,* she told herself and then mentally laughed at her inability to pinpoint what emotions she actually felt. "Michelle, I simply have no choice but to keep moving. My feelings change daily as the memories I was forced to suppress come back." She shrugged. "And perhaps it is something of my other self that influences me. I don't want to come off as cold, but my whole life was in preparation for being alone." *Unless you're also here talking to me.* She received no response from her supposed other self. "Just having someone else I can trust with me is not something I ever expected."

Michelle nodded. "Well, those are all things that will definitely mess you up."

"I am so sorry for not warning all of you about what I discovered with my abilities." Kyrie felt her eyes burn and blinked away the pain before tears could fall. "I don't want any of you to hate me. I promise I will never mess with any of your minds."

Michelle moved close and wrapped her arms around Kyrie. "I know. The others are just scared. They'll come around. They don't think you are a bad person."

Kyrie smiled, sensing Michelle's acceptance of her through their physical contact. "Thank you."

Michelle stepped back and wiped her eyes. "Are you sure you want me to cut your hair?"

Kyrie nodded her head. "Yes, please, let's cut and dye it. I'm going crazy being kept closed up, and I want to get in some exercise. Plus I have a lot of reading to do."

"Fine. It's your head. Just don't get mad when I make it look like a five-year-old butchered your hair."

Chapter 17

Dennis Hurlington sat at the kitchen table in a rundown cabin two miles from the lakeshore. One of the shell companies Leonard's father created to hide the family wealth owned the land and building. Leonard's estate included many esoteric properties, most of which were leased to other businesses and people to generate income. This rustic cabin lacked the proximity to marketable activities, as it had been purchased when Leonard's father had felt nostalgic about embracing nature. Its current state reflected the difference between intention and action. A caretaker came out monthly to tend to the property, but no regular guests had lived in the single-story building for twenty years.

"Not having access to high-speed internet is a pain," Leonard said from the other side of the table. The half-eaten remains of his evening's freeze-dried rations congealed inside the pouch in front of his laptop. The burner phone next to it provided the connectivity. "Things are pretty bad out there. Based on the news reports, a few more CEOs were found dead." He forced a laugh. "I'm not in that report yet, but there are at least two dozen names of people being withheld until families are notified. I think most of them are secondary casualties from the explosions that took out groups of people. Several companies have released press statements ahead of the police officially releasing names."

Dennis tried to focus on the voice of God, but his rage at the collapse of his church and his efforts to warn the people of this world that Satan and his devils lived among them would not allow him to concentrate. "Any news on the girl? What of the Heth cell?"

Leonard frowned. "No news on the girl, but someone in Kappa turned themselves in to the police. I've stayed off their message server as I expect the FBI is all over it, and I don't want to risk leading someone back to our location." He looked up from the laptop. "The new dark web recruiting server is definitely compromised since Theta, Iota, and Kappa all directed people to those message boards."

Dennis agreed with Leonard's wariness. The servers he destroyed in the bunker contained primary copies of data and raw video, but the servers used by the cells, and those that represented the public face of The Church, were hosted outside the Beirtal estate to avoid data breaches that could trace back to the compound. *Security through layers.*

"I suspect Theta and Iota might break given the news. They seem to be thinking it's better to turn yourself in than look worse by trying to hide."

Dennis frowned, but he could not fault the logic. The cells were limited in size for protection, but each was only as strong as its weakest member. "We need to reassure those at risk of breaking that it wasn't us. However, you are correct; it is likely those cells will collapse anyway. Perhaps it's prudent to even avoid engaging with the larger ones if it could risk revealing our location."

Leonard nodded his head. "Agreed. I'm confident Heth will remain faithful and hopeful Daleth will as well. But the ones that had not committed to actually killing the demons are probably going to collapse. We can monitor for a while, then re-engage with any who stay faithful.

"Fortunately, I regularly shift the crypto that Mu and Rho gather to wallets we control," Leonard continued, "so we will not be short of funds for a while. I'm not sure how much I can take from my estate without drawing attention. There are systematic transfers to crypto I have in place, but we'd have to re-disperse those funds to avoid someone tracking it through the ledger."

Dennis drank from the glass of water that had warmed from sitting on the table for hours. "Do we have any leads on the girl?"

Leonard shook his head, and Denis realized he had asked the same question at least half a dozen times.

"Let me ping those servers for new messages." The room fell silent as the techno-savvy heir typed away on the laptop. After a few minutes, he looked up. "I'm not sure we should trust this or not, but we got an unexpected update from Sarah, our spy who arranged travel for Rodgers. She had been dark for the last two weeks. Her explanation is that with Rodgers gone, things have been in chaos, and priorities have kept changing. She added that she no longer can see the special orders to leadership, but because of what she knows, she managed to briefly see instructions to silently destroy any data on the Landvik girl, Lars Solberg, Kimberly Leighton, Awan Brown, you, and The Church. She said the memo indicated Rodgers had ..." Leonard looked up and used air quotes, "'acted as an agent of The Church, which undermined the Durten Industrial Complex and did not represent the values or morals of the organization.' The message goes on to say she only had a chance to see some recent orders briefly and there appear to be plans to move IT to a different location. She did not get to read the other details."

Dennis frowned as he considered the validity of the message. Then a memory sparked, and God demanded more. "Who was on the list?"

"The Landvik girl, the lawyer—"

"No, the odd name. Awan ..."

Leonard looked back at the monitor. "Awan Brown."

Dennis felt a stirring of memories. A dark forest. His hands were zip-tied. His heart racing. The voice of God purred in his mind as a memory of warmth and blue-green vegetation filled his vision. *The doorway to heaven!*

Dennis flung his arms wide as he lurched forward, knocking his glass off the table. The thick vessel bounced across the linoleum floor, leaving a trail of water. "Awan Brown! That is the servant of Satan who brings demons into our world." Dennis nearly wept; he had only heard the muffled first name once and had never been able to remember it since. "He's the one who tried to bind me to Satan, but God came to protect me instead. We need to find everything we can about him. If we kill him, we'll stop the Devil from bringing across more demons. We can stop Satan's blasphemy!" *And the gateway back to heaven. We can access it.*

Leonard quickly typed on the keyboard. "I'll get started looking for information right away. Plus, I'll try to get us some transportation. Ron and Luke from the Heth cell should be able to come here in a day or two. I want them around to offer you protection."

Dennis tuned out Leonard. God wanted him to see heaven. That was the answer. The gateway would solve his problems.

Chapter 18

"Wow! You look good," Jake said as he and Aki came back to the campsite with bags of washed clothing. Aki slowed her pace, and he blushed. "I mean, Michelle did a great job with the trimmers."

Aki narrowed her eyes at Jake, but then she softened her expression. "It does look good."

Kyrie looked up from the journal in her lap, smiled, and nodded her head. The lack of weight and cool air reaching her scalp felt odd, but it also reminded her of her younger self when her parents had chosen practicality over vanity. *A new beginning or a return to the past? Beginning,* she decided after a moment of thought. "Agreed," she said, knowing Michelle still preferred her hair long.

Michelle shrugged as she poked at the fire growing in the firepit. They had buried the hair in the trash instead of burning it because of how far the smell would carry. "Still think keeping it long would have been better, but it doesn't look bad." She stood up. "Since the both of you are back, I'll get the burgers started for dinner. Then we can finish rolling up our new characters," Michelle added as she started for the van. "I'm anxious to try some AD&D, since we only have Kyrie's parents' old books."

Jake and Aki looked at each other and nodded, then followed Michelle to store everything the two of them carried in the tent.

"Do you want to play as your other self?" Michelle paused in her movement to ask Kyrie. "You said your parents had made up rules to cover the differences. With the dreams you are having, you might remember some other powers we could work into the campaign."

Kyrie considered the question and shook her head. "Not sure I'm ready for that yet."

Michelle offered a smile. "If you want to talk more about your dreams, just let me know."

Kyrie nodded, but she returned her attention to her mother's writing about how higher-dimensional structures might interact with each other. She wanted to focus on the theories and tried to push aside the uncomfortable question of knowing which part of her is which. She did not want to consider how much of a killer might exist within her.

The others continued to talk around her, and she took a long breath. The marks on the page, now a familiar memory, pulled her in, though the occasional inconsistencies in the lettering and word choices fought to distract her. *Concentrate,* she chastised herself, as she reread her mother's writing that centered on mathematical pressure points created when the higher dimensions of each universe collided. The theory devolved into speculation about how the universe they lived in contained far more matter than anti-matter, and a curiosity about whether the other universe might be the opposite. *We do need a way to explain why there is so little antimatter here, since theoretically it should have been balanced with matter after the Big Bang,* Kyrie thought, remembering some of the fun speculation she performed with her mother. *Focus!*

Kyrie continued to study her mother's writings while the others moved around her. Their activities faded into the background until Michelle shook her shoulder.

"Food?" her friend asked, a plate with a burger in her hand.

Kyrie took the offered food. "Thank you."

"Becca and her dad are going on about work permits and building power needs." Michelle shrugged. "I thought her dad was a hacker, but it seems they are doing less breaking into systems and more searching through public sites for random data and stalking people on social media."

"Not like the movies at all," Jake agreed as he continued to devour the burger in his hands. "I was hoping for something more thrilling."

Michelle grabbed the last burger and sat down next to Kyrie at the picnic table. "I hope you don't mind, but I've been flipping through the D&D folders. Your mom created so much backstory for some of the NPCs." Michelle bit into the burger, chewed, and quickly swallowed before letting out a small burp. "She's even recorded notes about conversations you had with different people. I'm assuming Lana might have been one of your characters. I read about a merchant who lied to you so you'd kill someone named Dolfer, but you refused to believe the merchant. That seems messed up, trying to get you to kill when you were so young."

Kyrie tried to recall the campaign, but a decade of almost daily playing blurred her recollection of specific interactions. "I'm not surprised. She did that a lot ... had people lie to me." *Don't ever trust anyone,* her mother's voice came to her. She frowned at the memory. *You're wrong.*

Michelle wiped some grease from her mouth. "Do you mind if I use some of the notes to run the campaign? Mostly the maps and world-building pieces," Michelle added quickly. "I wouldn't want to steal the characters, as you probably have specific memories of them. But I didn't take any of my own maps, and it'd be easier if we had something to go on."

Kyrie shook her head. "Just keep things in order. My mother play-tested her theories, and I might need to cross-reference the journals to the sessions."

Becca and her father climbed out of the back of the van with their used paper plates and empty soda cans. "Any more to eat?" Becca asked after she saw the empty grill.

Michelle nodded with a full mouth. "I can put more burgers on," she mumbled around the food.

"What do you hope to achieve with those papers?" Mr. Williams asked as he fetched another can of soda from the ice chest.

Kyrie considered the question and opened her mind to sense if their neighbors might have moved within hearing distance. She doubted it, but she lowered her voice anyway. "I'm looking for a way to stop more people from becoming Bound. If I understand the math, then perhaps I can prevent anyone else from being ripped from the other world. That would prevent him from continuing to build his army. Maybe I could even find a way to seal the path between worlds."

Jake and Aki stopped their quiet conversation and looked over at Kyrie. "I know you've had recent dreams, but do you remember the other world? What it felt like to cross over?" Jake asked.

Kyrie swallowed. She felt the pressure of the binding stone in her pocket against her thigh. The seemingly inert green crystal had no reaction to her thinking about it, but she felt a physical connection to it. *You need to hide that somewhere.* "I'm remembering fragments. There were so many plants. The aroma of the flowers drifting through the air was constant." She looked into the middle distance, trying to recall parts of her dreams. "I lived in a jungle with lots of trees and large leaves on the vegetation." She moved her focus back to the others. "But I can't say the whole world was like that." She nodded her head as thoughts of a different life came to her. "I'm pretty sure my eyes could see a wider spectrum of light. I'm not sure, but I think my human mind translated my memories into seeing more blue and violet colors."

"That's wild," Michelle said. "I'd never have considered the light might be different. That'd be great to add to a campaign world."

"And the people looked like the cats you've drawn?" Aki asked.

Kyrie turned her head to face the smaller girl. "Some of the people. Others were very different." *Your friend died instantly,* she reminded herself, not wanting to think about the thick yellowish skin of the dolunar as her eyes lost focus. "Without my mother using the stone to make me forget, I'm remembering more. My people lived in close communities. We were hunters." *Killers really,* she admitted to herself. "But we honored nature and loved the plants." She brought her attention back to Aki. "And I might have even have had a pet," she added, her eyebrows narrowing as a memory of a pearlescent, lizard-like creature surfaced.

"Would you go back?"

Kyrie heard the worry in Michelle's voice. "I don't believe that's possible. I don't know what part of me belongs there, or if it's even still whole." She sighed. "Plus, my body is likely gone." The memory of watching funeral pyres burn away the dead surfaced in her thoughts. Her other nose had been sensitive enough to easily separate out the burning flesh from different corvlians. "And I'm not sure the overlap between the universes would even allow it. When we were in the grove in Arkansas, I felt a push of energy into this universe. Kind of like a river dragging everything downstream." She shrugged. "There is definitely some ability for my awareness to reach into the other world. Perhaps it's like an electric current, nature pressing for the flow to go in one direction, but it can be forced the other way as well. I just don't know for certain. I'd suggest going back to investigate further, aside from the fact I'm sure it's watched."

Becca swatted at something unseen near her face. "Damn bugs."

Mr. Williams remained standing near the table. "The journals and notes from your mother will tell you how you might close the hole in the worlds?"

Kyrie shook her head. "More to let me know if it's even possible or not. My mother could not feel the energy or the other world. She spent years speculating about what the mechanisms might be and trying to use math to prove or disprove those theories."

Mr. Williams nodded his head. "I don't know how long we'll be able to hide successfully. If your mother worked on it for more than a decade and still didn't get an answer, do you really think you can complete it in a matter of days or perhaps weeks?" He kept his attention on her. "The math might not be the way to go. Instead, just figuring out how to close the hole is likely more important than making the math work."

Kyrie nodded her head, though she did not fully agree. *You could waste time trying to figure out how to do something that's not possible instead of changing direction to focus on something else that is. The math lets you avoid dead-end paths. But he's not wrong about the time it might take.*

Mr. Williams turned his attention to Aki and Jake. He hesitated and then swallowed. "Look, this ain't any more comfortable for me than you, but it needs to be said. Your parents aren't here, and I'm sure they would object to the two of you getting busy, if you know what I mean."

Jake paled and tried to say something. Aki looked down at the table.

"Dad," Becca complained.

"Don't, Dad, me," he snapped. "I'm not stupid. I know all of you are old enough to understand how things work, as well as feel the urge to make it work. If you don't know the how, ask Becca; we've had the talk."

Becca turned and moved several steps away.

"If you can't avoid it, then cover it." Silence filled the air as Aki and Jake tried to find somewhere to look. Mr. Williams lifted his hands in surrender. "To spare my daughter—and the rest of you— from dying of embarrassment, that's all I'll say on the matter." He sighed and then sat down at the table. Everyone except Kyrie remained quiet and continued to search for an excuse to be somewhere else. Eventually, he spoke. "With that out of the way, how is everyone doing? I'm supposed to be the adult here, so I probably should act it."

"I'm doing okay, Mr. Williams," Michelle said, her voice initially a bit higher than normal. "I know it's stupid, but I feel like I'm finally no longer in my younger brother's shadow."

The tall man nodded. "I'm sure your parents care about you. They came to the park when we asked them to."

Michelle shrugged. "Kyrie's aunt had Mike with her." She forced a smile. "I'm okay, really. I've always been independent."

He lacked a response and turned his focus to Jake and Aki. "How about the two of you? I know this has turned your lives upside down."

Aki exhaled. "I'm worried about my parents. They've always been good to me. But I'm pretty sure they probably already left town. They've always been pretty private people. I just don't want Heritage Park to be the last time I ever see them again."

Kyrie sensed Aki's distress and fear. A conflict raged within her younger friend. *Your own fear of change made you disobey. Your determination is what keeps you going.*

"I can't say it will get better," Mr. Williams said. "But time numbs all things. I'm hoping we can find a way to get back to normal."

A fire simmered in the back of Aki's eyes. "The world is changing faster than I ever expected." She forced a laugh through moist eyes. "I've always wanted to stand against the oppressors and make things better. I just never thought it would happen overnight, and before I even graduated high school." Aki played with the plate in front of her and then pushed it away. "I talked tough for years. I never imagined society might collapse around us so fast. How a tyrant might undermine everything, and so few would stand up or even know what's happening. That I'd be this scared."

Kyrie closed the journal sitting on the table. "My parents always told me fear lets you know something is wrong. Don't ignore the warning, but don't let it consume you. Instead, overcome the cause."

Aki bit her lip. "I'm trying. I'll get there. We'll change the world. Take it back before it's too late." She did not vocalize that she might die trying, but the realization forced her to lean further into Jake. "I just need time."

Jake pulled her closer and squeezed her tight.

Everyone remained silent for several moments, then Mr. Williams turned to Jake. "Your parents appeared angry. Do you think they will accept your leaving, or will they call the police to report you missing?"

Jake chuffed. "My dad's got a temper, and my mom clings to me. I didn't give them time to object to my going, and she'll be driving him mad by now." He picked up the empty can of soda from the table and finished the warm remnants. He put the can back down and looked at Mr. Williams. "I hope they stay safe and get my younger brothers and sister out of town, but I'm not sure they will leave. They're so damn stubborn." He breathed deeply. "I have no idea if they will call the cops and report me missing or not."

Becca's father sighed. "Then we need to shave your head." Jake's eyes grew wide. "A buzz cut if not shaved, but we need to change your appearance." Mr. Williams looked back at the van. "The cell signal here isn't the greatest, but if we can keep a low profile, I want to stay here for at least the week I reserved. Longer if we can. I expect all campsites will get a lot busier once school is out, and I don't want to have to sleep in a parking lot. There's not even enough room in the back for the four of you, let alone for six of us, given that the front seats don't recline."

Jake ran his hand through his hair and consciously moved it back to the table. He turned his attention to Kyrie to change the subject away from his thick hair. "What about you? Any thoughts on rescuing Lars? You've not brought it up."

Kyrie shook her head. *If only there were a way to know for certain.* "We don't know anything about the woman who has him or where they might have taken him. It's not like it was with Tina." She detected emotional pain from the others when she mentioned their friend's name. "I don't like abandoning him, but I can't see a path toward freeing him either. I have my doubts that he's even still alive. I definitely don't trust the woman." *Damn dolunar.* "I wish it was different, but I believe he's lost to us."

Jake nodded and Aki looked away.

"We'll figure something out," Michelle said.

Kyrie stood up, knowing the others did not like her calculated evaluation of the situation. She softened her voice and allowed some emotion to leak from her. "Adaptation is what my parents taught me. Don't die from a lack of reason." She looked through the trees toward Pickle Creek, only about a hundred feet away. While a run through the woods would feel refreshing, she did not want to risk being too far from the others to protect them. Instead, she turned her attention to the paved road that ran through the campground. "I know it's getting late, but we should start some training. I need to run to deal with my feelings, or I'm going to go crazy. The rest of you should come with me."

Becca rolled her eyes. "That again." She put up a hand to stop her father from speaking. "Yeah, yeah, I know. Sitting in front of the computer will make me fat."

Mr. Williams also stood up. "That's why I had weights in the basement. But you ain't fat. None of you girls are."

"Does that mean I'm fat?" Jake asked, his tone playful for once.

Becca's father glared at him. "You're a damn beanstalk. You should eat more and work out." He sighed. "But seriously, Kyrie's right about exercise." He looked behind himself at the van. "Anyway, I need to get back to work."

Kyrie ran back and forth around the campground and along Park Drive to the parking lot for the park office for another forty minutes after the others gave in to exhaustion. She let her mind wander as her feet hit the ground. This simple route did not tax her like running in the mountains, but simply getting her blood moving offered relief to her pent-up energy.

She stopped her exercise when the lights around the campground started to come on. The others, aside from Becca's father, had nearly finished creating characters using her parents' old D&D rule books and blank sheets of paper. A slew of questions assaulted her as the others struggled to understand the differences in the game mechanics.

"This stupid THAC0 thing," Becca complained. "It's f'd up math is all it is."

Kyrie lifted an eyebrow as she took a hot dog from Michelle. "It's not like you're using a Laplace transform to solve second-order differential equations. It's just the number you need to hit armor class zero."

Becca glared. "And just why is a lower armor class better than a higher one? Makes no sense."

Jake ran his hand over his recently buzzed head and forced a change of the subject. "Becca, what did your dad find earlier?"

Becca shoved some chips into her mouth and chewed before answering. "The Durten Industrial Complex that asshole Rodgers managed, five years ago, they had extra fiber runs to the building. My dad said you don't have two separate fiber runs unless you are concerned about maintaining redundancy." She drank from the soda can in front of her. "The company is likely a front. On paper, it manages the building and rents warehouse and shop space to other businesses like plumbers, machine shops, and people fabricating things. He said, all the power coming into the complex for all that would easily mask any power needed to support a small data center, so the only thing we have to go on is the extra fiber. The only problem is they have more than a dozen locations around the country. We've not researched all of them, but of the three we've looked at so far, the one outside Chicago is the only one with any fiber connections." Becca grinned. "And that's the one closest to where Rodgers lived, and his online profiles indicated he worked."

Becca's father stepped out of the van. "I thought someone was going to bring me something to drink."

"Sorry, Mr. Williams," Michelle said. "Kyrie stopped running, and I forgot."

He sighed as he opened the cooler and frowned. "I forget how fast food disappears with teenagers." He shook the water from the can and opened it. "I'm not complaining. I'd rather you girls eat than starve yourselves."

"Thanks, Dad," Becca complained. "You still trying to give us body image issues? Telling us to run wasn't enough? Now we need to eat more?"

He crossed his arms. "At least I know your snark isn't damaged."

Aki shifted the conversation. "Sounds like you and Becca might have found where the criminal empire is run from?"

He sat down at the table and pulled the bag of chips away from Becca and reached inside to grab a handful just before she snatched it back. He glanced at the campsites on either side of them. One had a speaker going, and the campers at the other site had gone somewhere else. "Don't know, but that industrial complex is a likely spot. Most of those kinds of places are built on reinforced slabs so heavy machinery won't fall through the floor. Any expansion of offices is normally just expanding outward or upward. Ten years ago, when that Durten Industrial Complex bought the existing site, they dug out a basement under part of the building. It's just another question on a growing list. Right now, I'm searching for anyone who might be employed in an IT or executive role. If I can phish them, we might gain access to the network and learn more."

Kyrie swallowed the food in her mouth. "Can criminals operate in the open that easily?"

Mr. Williams laughed. "They operate in the open all the time. They just mask their illicit activity with mundane things."

He leaned forward. "The street view of the complex shows a ten-foot-tall chain-link fence with razor wire. There's a large electric gate with a keypad for entry at the end of an isolated road that only goes to the complex. A dozen businesses are there based on the maps app. Most of them are likely legit and probably don't know anything about any criminal activity. The genuine trucks delivering parts and workers coming and going all day and night offers cover for anyone tied to crime." He put some chips from his hand into his mouth. "Who's going to notice another box truck with drugs or stolen computers when a dozen other box trucks come and go all the time?"

"I want to help do some hacking," Becca said. "You never let me do more than practice on things you have in our basement." She pulled out some chips and shifted the bag back to him.

"Cus I don't want you committing crimes. Jeez, girl. I've told you that before." He turned his focus to the others. "All the red teaming my company does is with express written permission of the companies that hire me."

"Not when you're hunting bug bounties," Becca shot back.

"Yeah, well, that's different. I still follow good ethical practices."

Becca crossed her arms. "These bastards are criminals who've tried to kill us. Ethics don't apply."

His shoulders slumped. "Fine. But I will supervise what you're doing. I don't want you to reveal anything about us." He lifted a finger and pointed it at her. "And you can't start using what I teach you to mess with the kids at school that piss you off."

Kyrie chuckled. "That's what I'm for. I can mess with them in ways they can't trace back to us."

Mr. Williams looked a little uncomfortable. "Regardless, until I get someone to fall for a phishing campaign, or find an exposed server with a vulnerability, we're not going to get access to their computers. So, you'll all need to find something to keep you busy. Pretend you're all still in school and study for your finals."

"With what books or devices?" Becca shook her head. "No phones, remember. And you're using all the network bandwidth on the hotspot, so it's not like we can get online."

He shook his head. "Do some PE."

Becca glared at him.

"D&D," Michelle countered. "We're playing D&D and that's final."

Chapter 19

Nalitran sat behind his mahogany desk in his palatial office and reviewed the coded report from Yrginda. The list of people she planned to pull from their targets had the potential to keep him from acquiring a key technology company building robotic drones for mining. *Perhaps it's acceptable. I could simply let others take the risk of fully developing the technology. Then force my way into the company later.* His long-term plans for taking over the country still had a lot of potential scenarios that would converge over time.

He jotted a note of approval into the application, knowing that Yrginda had already started informing the Bound of the change in their priority. He would pull the binding stones from the vault and put them on his plane for delivery later today in case any of the soldiers needed stronger compulsion to perform their duties. Seven of the ten selected for reassignment functioned in menial roles, such as cleaner or maintenance staff that wealthy people always overlooked. As such, their value and loyalty moved in similar ratios.

The light on his desk phone illuminated, and he pressed the intercom button. A female voice on the other side spoke without his prompting. "Mr. Bishop, Albert Geral is here for your appointment."

Nalitran locked the tablet with Yrginda's report, removed it from the desk, and placed it in a drawer. He looked across the wide room at the ten-foot-tall pair of oak doors forty feet away. The stained glass above the carved wooden doors depicted a mountain rising above a jungle. "Send him in."

Half a minute later, an aging man with grey hair and a three-piece suit pushed his way through the heavy doors. The man stood upright, but the office's circular vaulted ceiling with five large triangular windows spread equally around the room made Geral seem diminutive. Undaunted by the impossibly large white fur rug that occupied the center of the radial parquet floor, the man crossed the room and approached Nalitran's desk.

"Albert," Nalitran said when the man came to a stop just on the other side of the three seventeenth-century rosewood armchairs in front of his ten-foot-wide desk. "I am pleased you could visit me on such short notice."

The greying man inclined his head and lifted his briefcase. "I am always at your service, Mr. Bishop." The man grew serious. "I was mortified to learn of the assassination attempt on you on Saturday. I am thankful that the bastard missed. I hope they catch the men responsible for all this chaos."

"Thank you for your kind words, Albert. I will say the attempt on my life definitely makes me angry. Angry enough that I am willing to be ruthless in the market."

Albert grinned. "More ruthless than normal?" The older man glanced at the center chair. "May I?"

"Please," Nalitran said, using his hand to highlight the offer. "The Asian exchanges showed a lot of uncertainty in how to react, but Euronext fell immediately on opening and pretty much everything in the Americas is down this morning. Asia did slip once Europe opened. It's still early here, so I expect the Americas will continue down even more sharply."

Albert took the offered chair and placed his briefcase on his lap. "I knew all the major indexes would collapse when I saw the pre-market trading this morning. There is turmoil in too many important corporations with … the loss of so many senior leaders."

Nalitran kept the grin from his face. Albert had no problem destroying lives by maximizing financial returns for the wealthy, but he lacked the stomach for actual killing. *Weak in real convictions, but effective at what he does.* "As you know, I've been concerned about the short positions I have. Most are not due for a number of months, but—"

Albert nodded his head. "Despite the cause, this downturn in the market can help you realize significant savings and avoid losses where some investments have outperformed expectations." The old man moistened his lips, not mentioning that he had argued against Nalitran taking short positions in some of the companies. "Not all of the names of the people killed have been released. The market will probably fall further as additional names become public knowledge later in the week."

Nalitran leaned forward. *If the girl had not been in play, I would have waited.* "It is hard to predict the market. While I might get more profit in holding out, I want to clear the liabilities." Nalitran lifted a document from the side of the desk. "I also want to execute a number of purchases at the same time. Some are in the market; most are private holdings." He slid the papers to the edge of his desk. His financial fixer reached forward and grabbed the bundle. The list of companies included a mix of ones directly impacted by the assassinations and others to provide cover. "The timing of some of these may seem cruel, so I will need you to be discreet with the offers. You might even need to wait until issues of succession are resolved."

Albert scanned down the list. "You can count on my discretion. I see you've included your target ranges and source accounts." The old man nodded. "Good. I can work with this." He looked up. "What is the timeframe these need to be completed by?"

Nalitran smiled. "I would say by the end of the summer, but definitely when the prices are down." The deals Albert held in his hands represented his public actions. He had a separate list of companies that would soon have his most loyal Bound acting in leadership roles. *And those partnerships with Nalitran Enterprises will not cost me anything.*

Albert smiled back. "Of course. Anything else you need me to address?"

Nalitran shook his head. "No. I thank you for coming on such short notice. I know this accelerates some of the things we had been discussing," Nalitran smiled, "but one must take advantage of opportunities when they present themselves. Even if the circumstances are tragic."

"Of course," Albert replied as he stood. "I will review the details, and if I can improve your position even further, I will do so." With a bow of his head, the old man turned and headed toward the doors.

Nalitran remained seated as his financial agent left his office, the oak doors audibly closing shut. *Timing is everything,* he admitted. Moving up activities that most of the media widely anticipated would not draw suspicion, but many of his planned actions pushed the boundary of even the most aggressive businessman. *I will have to space out the other actions. It would raise too many questions otherwise.*

He removed the secure tablet from the drawer and entered the long passphrase. *Now where did the girl go, and how quickly can Yrginda get my agents reallocated?*

Chapter 20

After staying up too late, Kyrie did not remember any of her dreams, but she knew memories troubled her rest. Aside from Becca's father, she rose before the others and spent the time studying the journals. The smell of the trees, campfires, and earth centered her and allowed her mind to focus. Eventually, the others emerged slowly, and one by one, each complained about not having coffee. The clock hit ten before everyone had eaten, showered, and gathered together at the picnic table where Kyrie worked.

"You all still have to figure out how to get past the orcs to rescue Aki," Michelle said. "I don't plan to make it easy on your first-level meat puppets."

"I'm already out of spells," Jake complained. "Not having cantrips to spam really reduces old-school wizards to nothing."

Aki looked at Jake. "You need to free me before they decide I'm dinner."

Becca rolled her eyes. "We could shove a file up his ass and let him get captured as well, for all he's worth now. Then you'd at least have a chance of escape."

Kyrie wrinkled her brow. "I don't get it."

Becca turned to Michelle. "Do you want me to explain to the troglodyte, or do you want to do it?"

Michelle glared at Becca. "Be nice." She turned to Kyrie. "People sneak things into prison by putting things up ... well, any opening available, so the guards won't find it."

Kyrie raised an eyebrow. "That doesn't sound wise."

"Agreed," Jake said. "I'm not shoving anything up my ass."

The group remained silent until Becca sighed and pulled a foot up onto the bench so she could lean against her leg. "I missed calc this morning and would be in gym right now. It feels weird to be skipping school. I mean really weird."

Aki nodded as she leaned forward to put her head on the table. "I dreamt I overslept my finals and failed."

"You're all f'ing nerds," Michelle griped. "We always complain about having to go to school, and now you're unhappy we have parental approval not to go?"

Becca rolled her eyes. "Because people are trying to kill us. Don't forget that part. Puts a damper on things."

Kyrie closed the journal. Part of her wanted to game, *but we have to be responsible first.* "I can show you all some survival skills." She looked at Becca. "Plus, get a workout in."

"I'm not made for running," Becca complained.

Kyrie nodded her head toward the rocky creek only a hundred feet away. "I grabbed a trail map from the check-in booth yesterday. The whole of the Whispering Pine Trail is ten miles." She saw the others raise their eyebrows. "We can cut that down to about six miles if we only do the north loop." Kyrie frowned at their expressions. "And if you are all that worn out, there is a connector trail that cuts the north loop in half. If you all can't walk three or four miles, you ain't going to survive long."

Michelle shrugged. "You all could be running from the orcs, and Kyrie can show us how to hide in the woods to escape them."

Becca shook her head. "Fine. But let's see what my dad says about it."

Kyrie grinned. "I already checked with him this morning before you all got up. He thought it might actually be good if we weren't all just hanging around the tents looking like vagrants and drawing attention to the fact we aren't in school. There are only a couple of others our age here."

"Of course you did," Becca said. "Bugs and sweat, here we come."

Escaping into the forest relaxed Kyrie, and she could tell it helped the others as well. For a good third of the loop, the trail followed along the creek. In some places, the water fought its way around rocks and boulders, other parts of the creek opened into wider flows, allowing for deeper pools to form near rocky cliffs and outcroppings. The earlier spring rains provided enough flow to ensure picturesque views along the path.

Away from the creek, the others complained about the changes in elevation, though Kyrie thought of the inclines as little more than lumps and bumps when compared to her mountain in Colorado. They spotted a group of three deer and a snake as they traipsed along the rocky trail. Bird songs and the wind rustling through the leaves provided the background melody to their quiet conversations. The others rejected Kyrie's suggestion that they actually hunt for food.

Michelle narrated scenarios for the campaign, and the others quickly opened up and participated in describing the heroics of their characters. Kyrie subtly pushed them along by leading the way, keeping them from meandering too slowly as they continued the hike. The pace still felt like crawling, but listening to the others unwind helped her.

They explored the five backwoods campsites along the northern loop, three of which had campers. While Kyrie considered the isolation of those sites a positive, the others objected to the idea that they would have to carry all their supplies miles into the woods. "And no power," Becca said, rejecting the possibility out of hand.

The trip took them just under five hours, and while Kyrie knew she could have easily run it in just over one, the fact the others finished it in good spirits left her satisfied. *More important that they enjoyed it than anyone got any exercise.*

"Kyrie, Becca," Mr. Williams called from the van when they started to tear into the food reserves back at the campsite. "Come here for a moment. I want to discuss something."

Kyrie left the last bag of chips, but Becca grabbed it as the five of them made their way to the van. They piled in, with Becca opening the bag on the way. Inside, Mr. Williams had at some point powered up a second computer, though a screensaver with three-dimensional bubbles merging and breaking hid the contents of that system's monitors.

"It appears the crypto I spent for someone to find me some of Hurlington's dark web messaging servers paid off faster than expected. It's using an open-source message board with an older version of Apache. Fortunately, whoever is running this thing isn't current on patching. I got in and have admin access."

"That was fast, Dad," Becca said. "Anything good on it? Can you find Hurlington from it?"

"Zero logging on the box," he admitted. "And even if there was, backtracking IPs on Tor to the prior node won't be useful. But from the application data, it appears there are a pair of people in a cell called Gimel. The users have names of Soldier One and Soldier Two, so nothing useful there. Those two have been questioning The Church and its leadership since Saturday's killing spree. Most of the early responses came from a user called Prelate. One came from a user called The Prophet. It's been quiet since."

"Any good intel in the messages?" Jake asked.

Mr. Williams shook his head. "Nothing much. It reinforces our belief that Hurlington wasn't behind the killings, but it might also be for show. Hard to tell if the two users believe the responses. Neither of those two have replied since the last message from The Prophet denied any involvement."

"Anything indicating where Hurlington is?" Kyrie asked, not understanding much of the technical items Becca's father had said.

"No." He swiveled his chair to face her. "But you and Becca managed to get a response from someone on the public board before they took it down. This message board seems to be dedicated to a single cell." He inclined his head toward the monitor beside him. "Good secops; really limits the blast radius. If most of the people involved don't know how many other cells or people are out there, then they can't betray any larger trusts." He brought the discussion back to the point. "I have admin access to the host and the application. I could create an account on the message board for us and see if that will draw Hurlington out before someone turns this server over to the feds."

"You think he's still a risk to us?" Aki asked. "With the news media and cops searching for him, and the arrest of that other cell, can he even send people to kill us anymore?"

"A wounded animal is the most dangerous," Kyrie responded automatically. "Until he's arrested," she refrained from saying killed, "there is still a risk."

Mr. Williams cleared his throat and said what she had held back. "Even locked up, he might have people on the outside still taking orders. However, there's nothing on the server to give away any other hosts, but perhaps we can taunt him into pwning himself and thereby leading us to his other servers." He put his hands on the keyboard. "The two of you got them talking the first time, so I thought that it might be best if the two of you wrote the messages. Especially, Kyrie, if you have a better understanding of him and what being bound might be like."

Becca set the bag of chips down and wiped her fingers on her jeans. "Let's mess with these f'ers." Her father started adding a user on the admin screen, and Becca put a hand on his arm. "Name the user 'The Girl You Couldn't Kill.' That'll piss them off."

He shook his head. "There is every chance the feds might end up on this server at some point. We don't want to leave blatant evidence we had communicated with him and then the feds sweep us up as well."

"Then why have us send the message?" Becca demanded. "If he doesn't know it's us, he might not respond. And if we make it obvious, you're saying people will think we were involved."

Her father sighed. "I believe there's a setting that can prevent messages from being written to disk and then automatically delete them after being read. Though that's not foolproof." He raised a hand. "But the username is likely to be externalized to disk so that it can survive a reboot." He entered a value of NotYourEnemy, set a password, saved the user, and then went to the config screens to adjust the application settings before returning to the message screen.

Kyrie leaned forward and considered how her parents might run Hurlington as an NPC. *What drives him? What does he know?*

She pursed her lips. "We don't know what went wrong with Hurlington's binding, but from what Awan said, sometimes the human overcomes the being brought over. But he must remember at least something of the other mind. Perhaps more than others might realize."

Mr. Williams slowly nodded his head. "Can you make use of that? We need to get access to his other servers. He might have them on the dark web or in a basement somewhere. If we can determine where he's at, that might lead us to the data. However, we have to be prepared to revert to other tactics."

"Are you wanting to make him mad?" Kyrie asked.

"No. At least not yet." He hesitated. "Unless you think that will help. We want to keep him coming back to talk with us. Depending on his browser, we might be able to inject some malware and install something on his device that would ping us his actual IP address, but we want to make sure it's not obvious." He frowned. "We have to watch for the same attacks that might come for us as well. So far, I've not seen anything on the server that would deliver malware."

Kyrie accepted the explanation without understanding. "Then let's see if we can make friends."

Becca crossed her arms. "Friends with the guy who's tried to kill you at least five times?"

Kyrie ignored the comment. "Tell him we know what they did to him in the forest. We know what he saw and felt. But he needs to focus on his true enemy. He needs to focus on Bishop. Who is really Nalitran, a dolunar, from another world."

"And how is that spelled?" Mr. Williams asked.

"With symbols not on your keyboard," Kyrie replied instantly with a smile.

Mr. Williams frowned. "I'll just type it as it sounds then." A moment later, he hit send on the message, and everyone held their breath in anticipation. Moments turned into a minute, and the clock continued to run without a response. "I don't think this thing is configured to send notifications out to anyone. Too risky. Too easy for someone to track those. Likely, they just check the server from time to time." He moved his mouse and shifted the window to the screen on the far right. "I'll keep working and let you know if we get a response."

Michelle eventually broke the silence. "The orc issue while we wait?"

Mr. Williams continued to stare at the screen. "Don't get too distracted. We'll be going out for dinner. The things we ordered yesterday, including the half-dozen stun guns, should arrive sometime today at a drop box in Bloomsdale, then we'll need to hit a hardware store for gloves. I think we can pick up some pizzas while we're out."

"Cheese only for me," Becca said.

"We'll plan on a couple of pizzas," her father responded with only a slight eye roll.

Chapter 21

Kyrie wiped the tears from her eyes with her fur-covered arm. Zvarncr's body burned on the pyre next to Zvarncr's guardian. Hundreds of other corvlians stood around the open circle, the sounds of the movements muted by the crackling of flames. "I will never see her play again," Kyrie moaned through her sharp teeth.

"Hush, little one," her mother whispered.

They remained standing around the fire until the smell of burning trees overwhelmed what remained of the burning bodies. Two of Zvarncr's older siblings remained to tend to rites in the grove while everyone else left the circle to return to their homes several miles away.

"Be strong," Kyrie's mother said. "Their essence will return in time, reborn into a new life. Those dolunar were not ones that could destroy them. They only killed their mortal bodies."

Kyrie looked up into her mother's green eyes. "But I want my friend now. How will I ever know when she returns?"

"Little one, the lines of our clans run strong. I have borne your older siblings more than once. One day you might bear them as well." Her mother looked around them. "You may not feel their essence yet, but those ready to return to their clans are always waiting to spark a new life."

Kyrie stopped walking. Her fur stood on end as coldness ran through her. "But the dolunar have captured essences before and destroyed them. They want to eliminate us. The warriors speak of it all the time."

Kyrie's mother offered a mournful smile. "Our two species have tried to destroy each other since before written records. They worship a god bent on domination, and their clerics can indeed rip one's essence from them and destroy it. But it is difficult to do that to a powerful mind, and the process requires time. Urdnin and Zvarncr died far too quickly for that to have happened. And those two dolunar that attacked us were no clerics." She crouched down. "Little one, be at peace; we are no strangers to the power the dolunar clerics wield. Our clan is filled with people who rival the strongest of any dolunar cleric. That is why they attack us so often. Like them, we can rip their essence from their bodies, trap it, and destroy it to prevent them from being reborn as well. It is a weighty burden to live with, but it is necessary. One day you will grow in power and be as strong as any other."

Kyrie swallowed and then extended her claws. "I want to destroy the dolunar now! If we destroy all of them, then they cannot be reborn, right?"

"Little one, it is not that easy." She lifted Kyrie's chin with her hand. "A mother determined enough can create new life from nothing, bringing a brand new essences into existence. While it is rare and much harder, it has prevented both our peoples from annihilating each other over the eons." Her mother stood. "While I find their god repugnant, and that those beasts have no value, only by finding peace will we ever truly be allowed to live."

Kyrie wiped away more tears. *I don't want peace; I want them to pay for hurting Zvarncr.*

Kyrie slowly opened her eyes and wiped away the tears she had shed during her dream. The darkness outside the tent told her it was still well before sunrise. While she knew she had not slept much since they had turned in after a late night of D&D; she knew sleep would not return easily. Instead of trying, she slipped from her sleeping bag and quietly left the tent so that she could patrol the campground.

The scattered lights allowed her to navigate along the road as the implications of continual rebirth weighed on her. *Is that how Nalitran knew to bind someone's soul to a crystal?* A memory of a corvlian talking about how someone with the ability and knowledge could use a prism to lock away a dolunar's soul, forcing it to live on while they butchered the body. The creature could then be tormented, never able to escape the mineralized confines. Death only came with the breaking of the prism.

Only he figured out how to do a partial binding of the soul, tearing it into parts, one in a human body, one in a binding stone. Her hand slid into her right pocket so that she could reassure herself she still had possession of her greatest weakness. *Did our binding hurt?* She could not remember anything after the icy darkness of transitioning between universes. *At least you can't until after Mother and Father took us to Colorado.*

The raw emotions of the memory hurt too much for her to continue thinking about anything related to her friend. Instead, she continued to walk and let her mind focus on the world she now existed within. Determined to remain undetected, she moved softly and used her mind to identify the various campers as they slept. The vast majority of the campsites had occupants, many of them in the second loop with RVs, trailers, or large vans like Mr. Williams'. *So many people.* The shock of realizing how many people existed after living her life on the mountain had not fully faded. *Mostly older people,* she decided after feeling many of the minds she passed.

Just to her right, she came upon the trailer with 'The Old Girl' in large letters on the side. It sat in the second loop of the figure eight and under some tall pine trees. A red pickup parked directly in front of the trailer looked new. She felt the old woman and the man she had seen from afar sleeping inside. Although the distance and the trailer's walls kept Kyrie out of the woman's thoughts, a sense of distrust and paranoia radiated from the woman. The power of the emotions overwhelmed Kyrie's sense of the man.

Kyrie shivered as though bugs crawled on her skin. The unsettling feeling made her hurry her pace, moving away from the trailer and the occupants. She tried to remember the woman's mind from her encounter early Sunday morning. Lingering irritation with the woman's husband bubbled up in her, and she pushed it away. *You hate being in other people's heads. Their thoughts linger.*

Kyrie resumed her walking, putting the old woman out of her mind and hoping that all the emotion that came from the high school students over the last three weeks had not drastically impacted her own personality and behavior. She had no answer to that question and shifted to her thoughts on her human mother's theories. As long as Nalitran could make more Bound, she knew she and her friends would have no choice but to fight an ever-replenishing army. *And souls pulled from our other world will never be reborn to their families.*

Despite her attempt to shift her focus to other things, the other world continued to intrude. *Can the breach in the universe even be healed?* Years of journals contained her mother's theories and failed attempts. Each new cycle started fresh, where her mother restated the problem and things she concluded might have merit and what could never work.

Mother wasn't trying to close the path between worlds, just prove that she wasn't mad, Kyrie realized as she once again passed the bathhouse. *Ideally, if everything exists in its own space, infinite universes could have superposition and overlap with no direct interaction. But perhaps once you reach a certain dimensional construct, they no longer overlap, but instead sit side by side, like atoms in a lattice.* The idea intrigued her. "Then us, living in a projection of three-dimensional space, might normally overlap without interaction with other three-dimensional projections. And if a higher dimensional representation of our existence somehow crashed into a neighbor, allowing the lower dimensional projections to slide between each other's existences, it might appear to us as moving between universes. Like moving a window from one computer monitor to the other," she added, thinking of Mr. Williams working in the van.

She pursed her lips. *Mother had considered something like that. The idea has merit, but how could we even prove it? Like the ball and circle issue moving down in dimensional space, we have no actual concept of higher dimensions.*

She kicked a rock off the road and into the grass. *And how would we impact a higher dimension to push them apart so they didn't crush each other? We've seen energy flowing through, so could enough energy going the other direction push them apart?* She frowned as her mind quickly calculated numbers that began to push into sums that would create a singularity. *A black hole would solve all our problems permanently.*

She stopped on the road. A trio of raccoons examined her in the darkness. The mental energy radiating from them did not resemble human thought, but deep down, she knew they felt the equivalent of confusion and annoyance at the presence of a human. "Don't worry, I won't harm you," she mumbled through a yawn. *You probably do need to get some sleep,* she told herself. *Perhaps near the creek so you can listen to the water.*

Becca opened her eyes. Her father had closed the van's rear door, and the noise roused her from an uncomfortable sleep. *Had you not joined in this insanity, you wouldn't be sleeping on the f'ing ground. You'd have your coffee and would be going to school like any normal teenager.* She sighed. *And wouldn't have a clue about anything going on in the world.*

She sat up. Kyrie's sleeping bag lay crumpled and empty near the tent flap. Michelle had also risen at some point and left the tent. That left just her and Aki. The girl they always decided would be a prominent lawyer looked at her with sad eyes. "What?" Becca asked, a frown already surfacing on her face.

Aki shook her head. "Nothing. I just couldn't sleep."

Becca groaned and sat up. The thin camp mat did not provide much in the way of cushioning. "Have I mentioned I hate camping? The bugs, the dirt, the lack of coffee."

"You need a tiny hut spell," Aki said. "Though this gives more perspective on adventuring parties getting a long rest."

"Yeah," Becca agreed. "Speaking of long rests, you and Jake taking things to the next level?"

Aki shrugged. "I don't know. Part of me says we're only together because the world fell apart around us. But part of me says we could be dead tomorrow, so why miss out today?" She sat up so she could face Becca at eye level. "But it's not like we really have any place with privacy where we could sneak off to if we wanted."

Becca snorted and then pointed in the direction of the creek. "There's a billion miles of trails Kyrie wants us to run around out there."

Aki frowned. "Sure, a bed of poison ivy is definitely romantic. No thanks."

"Showers?" Becca asked, a grin creeping onto her face.

"Those are disgusting." Aki grinned as well. "But you can do yourself there if you want."

Becca shook her head. "I barely want to go into them clothed. I can't imagine what other people have done in them." She pursed her lips. "Though they are not the worst showers I've had to use. At least they're private and don't have twenty other girls in there watching you."

"True that."

"I guess I should check on my dad. What about you?"

Aki looked at her knees and shook her head. "No idea. I feel pretty useless. Three weeks ago, I thought I knew what the future held. Now everything is different. I can't believe how fast things are falling apart, and it feels like there is nothing I can do about it. Kyrie is … well, Kyrie. You're helping your dad hack the world. Michelle's keeping everyone's spirits up and feeding us."

"I can't believe she's cooking," Becca mused. "Never stopped complaining about her mother asking her to cook at home."

Aki chuckled. "Yeah. I think she wants Kyrie to think she's useful." Aki looked up. "Heck, even Jake's studying designs for making the stun gloves with what we got. Everyone has a purpose except me."

Becca swallowed. She did not need Kyrie's abilities to tell Aki hurt inside. "My father says a lot of things. Most of them are cringe, but he's told me more than once that not everyone is needed in every situation, but everyone has a situation where they will be needed at some point. When you can sit one out, don't feel bad, just rest so that you can be ready for when you can offer something."

Aki nodded her head. "That makes sense."

"Usually he says it when he's kicked my ass at some game, so don't give him too much credit for wisdom."

"Your dad's pretty smart. Even if he scares the shit out of me most of the time."

Becca chuckled. "Just don't tell him that. He'd get an even bigger ego." She turned her head toward the van. "I should probably check on what's going on."

Aki stretched. "I need to shower, and then I'll see what help I can provide Jake."

Becca crawled to the tent flap and unzipped it. "Find a spot without poison ivy."

Aki threw a shoe at her as she scrambled out of the tent. Becca laughed as she zipped it back up, giving her time to escape, though Aki did not rush after her. With the mock conflict abated, she went to the van, opened the rear door, and crawled in through the curtain, closing the door quietly behind her. The glow of the monitors provided the only light, though the green on black terminal windows her father preferred cast little actual illumination. He glanced at her and resumed typing on the keyboard in front of him. His shoulders slumped with fatigue.

"Shit, Dad, you ever going to sleep?"

He frowned, but did not turn to face her. "This mess we're in doesn't give me time to sleep. I close my eyes and keep seeing you get shot by men jumping out of vans."

She moved to the seat on the same side of the van as him and sat down. "Yeah. I keep seeing all the blood on the ground." Her fingers touched the keyboard, waking the monitor, which requested a password. "Ya think that man Kyrie shot lived?"

"No idea, and I don't want to think about it. I know you said she's already … dealt with a couple of others, but I prefer not to look at her as though she's a cold-blooded killer." He looked at the floor of the van and shook his head. "I know she can read my mind, and I'm afraid she might take offense." He looked up. "What happens then?"

Becca shrugged. "Despite everything I've said, I don't think she would harm any of us."

"What about her messing with our thoughts?"

Becca turned to face her father. "I'm not defending her, and her not telling me she could do that shit pissed me off." She signed. "But I think she's terrified of being alone. She knows messing with your head will turn me against her, and likely the others. I think we're safe." *I hope we're safe.*

He turned back to his computer and continued working, ignoring the obvious gap in her logic. "How are you holding up?"

"I want some coffee, damn it."

He laughed. "Well, I'd say you're doing okay then."

"My back hurts. I want my bed. I don't like camping and bugs." She pulled up a browser window and began searching for recent news articles. "I found a damn spider on my sleeping bag last night. You know how hard it is to go to sleep thinking there are spiders in your sleeping bag?"

"Don't put thoughts into my head," he replied. "What about the others?"

Becca skimmed through an article reporting the names of fifteen more of Hurlington's people an anonymous source reported to the police. The people made up cells named Iota and Theta. *Fifteen more gone.* She frowned. *Only six arrested, but it's at least a start.* Aloud, she responded to her father's question. "Aki and Jake really miss their parents, and Aki, like me, is wondering how three weeks ago we didn't have a damn clue about how any of this was going on. Michelle's just happy to be away from her parents and the golden child brother."

"She really have it that rough?"

Becca considered her response as she moved to another news article talking about the global stock market fall on Monday and overnight trading in Asia and Europe continuing to see declines. "Probably not as bad as she makes it out to be, but the little bastard does get almost everything he wants. Michelle's been at odds with her mom for the last three years. If she was actually ghetto, she'd have moved out onto the streets a year ago. But where you gonna go in Kansas? Not like Olathe has a lot of places for you to disappear."

Her father grunted an agreement. "Warm bed and hot food will keep most people at home." He continued to run a search through public records for details on anyone who worked at the Durten Industrial Complex. "How are you doing?"

She turned to him. "Honestly, I'm freaked out. What if they decide I didn't have good enough grades so far to pass my junior year?

What if I have to redo a bunch of classes?" She tilted her head and looked up at him. "I could work for you. Be a hacker."

"Nope," he responded before she even finished. "You're finishing high school before I let you work for me. Then I want to see you go to college."

"You think college will teach me even half of what you know?" Becca shook her head. "You make good money. You always say so."

"Girl, college is about getting a well-rounded education; don't try to use logic to get out of it."

She grinned, knowing that each time she asked, she softened him up a little more. "I'll convince you yet. Just turn me loose and I'll show you what I already know."

He remained quiet for several minutes. "You know I'm proud of you, right?"

Becca stretched out and patted his arm. "Yeah, I know. Love you too, Dad." She turned her focus back to the computer and pulled up a fourth site that had an updated list of all the people missing or killed that had ties to the terrorist attack on twenty-nine April. "You didn't ask about Kyrie."

"Something I should worry about with her? Beyond the obvious?"

"I don't know. I give her a hard time all the time because she don't know shit about computers, but I think she feels a bit lost. Like, she was always the best at what she did, but she don't know anything about stuff outside her mountain." Becca shook her head. "I won't argue math and science with her. She's got that down better than any teacher in the school district. Maybe I shouldn't tease her so much."

"I couldn't say," her father responded. "Ever since you all said that she was once a cat, I can't get that out of my head. Sometimes I think she looks at me like a panther would, and I wonder what she's thinking. Is she planning to play with me as if I'm a mouse?" He paused in his work. "I'm certain she's the best thing to protect us against armed attacks, but she's got a lot more than just white-girl problems."

Becca grunted her agreement as she continued to look for details that might mention any of them. "Fuck."

"Language."

"Don't language me, Dad. Jake's mother and father were on TV last night." She clicked on the video and waited for the ad to finish playing before the image of Jake's parents returned, standing in front of their house, their Expedition parked in the driveway. She noticed that Jake's father at least did not have his pistol on his hip.

"I only want my boy to come home," Jake's mother said through the computer speakers. "I know he's scared. The violence that has come to Olathe is unprecedented. One friend killed herself; another's house was shot up. The whole sad event at the farm." She turned to face the camera and held up a picture of her oldest son. "Jake, if you are listening, please call. We want you home safe with us."

The video cut back to a studio with two reporters sitting behind a desk. "Several local teens and their families have fled the area, hoping to escape the violence that is somehow tied to the terrorist massacres that took place Friday night and into Saturday morning." A picture of Jake occupied half of the screen. "Christian and Oliva Ottiman refused to be chased from their home, though their son, just under seventeen, decided to leave with a family of one of the friends and has not been in contact since. They are asking for anyone who has seen him to get in contact through the tips line below."

Becca stopped the video playback and stared at the screen before slowly turning to face her father. Mr. Williams left his seat and exited the back of the van. Becca returned her attention to the screen. *The stupid bitch. What a Karen. What is she thinking?*

A couple of minutes later, Jake, Aki, and Michelle climbed into the back of the van. A towel around Michelle's head drying her hair. "Kyrie must be on a morning run," her father said. "Play the video again so everyone knows what's going on." He remained at the back of the van while the others gathered around Becca.

Kyrie really wanted to range farther, but guilt at being any more than ten or fifteen minutes away from the others kept her to a small section of the Whispering Pine trail just on the other side of Pickle Creek. The trail had some incline, which helped to increase her physical effort as she sprinted back and forth along the worn path.

Each time she turned around, she would come back, ford the creek, and check the campsite a hundred feet from the water.

As she ran, she practiced throwing small stones into the air and then launching them forward with a gravitational snap. Her targets were limited to dead trees, both still standing, and those that had already fallen. The accuracy of her improvised projectiles dropped off significantly with distance. The odd shapes and uneven masses of the stones fell victim to air resistance and chaos caused from tumbling. A long gravitational push reduced the drift, but that required much more effort and concentration.

At thirty feet, she seldom missed, and because of the large mass of the stone, the impact ripped through softer wood and shattered the stone into fragments when striking harder surfaces. *If you can't have a rifle, then the river rocks here will make a decent close-range weapon.*

She shifted the plastic cup she found discarded along the trail to her other hand as drops of rain landed on her head. She had already gathered nearly fifty water-smoothed stones in the cup and had worked out a mental design for a pouch to hold them if she could convince the others to take her to a store that carried material, needles, and thread.

A distant roll of thunder filled the air. *Better get back before you get soaked.* She covered the top of the cup with her hand to keep the stones from falling out as she jogged back to the campsite. *You also need to ask Becca about removing any fingerprints from these,* she added, realizing the police might track her involvement based on finding stones buried inside someone.

Kyrie approached the campsite as the dark cloud that had shed a few drops of water on her moved further east. However, the grey sky promised more rain would soon come. Her mind reached out to locate her friends, in case they had taken shelter from the approaching rain somewhere else. Their heightened emotions drew her to the van, and she broke into a sprint, her breathing heavy because of the prior hour of exercise. She quickly reached the back of the van, pulled open the doors, and climbed inside.

"You're here, good," Mr. Williams said to her. The laptop with the call center software sat in front of Jake. Everyone else gathered around him and Mr. Williams.

"What's happened?" Kyrie remained at the back of the van, with Michelle, Becca, and Aki between herself and the others. She kept the stones ready in case she needed a weapon.

"We're about to call Jake's mother," Mr. Williams said. "Apparently, they didn't listen and remained in their house. Not sure what they were thinking, but last night they went on the news asking for Jake to come home."

Why? Kyrie wanted to ask aloud, but her open mind picked up the distress and fear coming from all of them, and she hesitated.

Jake ran a hand over his buzzed head. "Why couldn't they have listened? I need them to listen this time."

Mr. Williams looked Jake in the face. "Again, assume this will be recorded and someone will try to trace the call." Becca's father's hand hovered over the mouse. "Are you ready?"

Jake nodded, and Mr. Williams pressed the button. The sound of ringing came from the laptop speakers. A woman with a rough voice answered.

"Mom," Jake said.

"Jake, is that you?" The woman spoke faster. "Where are you? We need you to come home right away."

"Mom, you were supposed to leave town! Staying puts Mary, Adam, and Ethan at risk."

"We are not being driven out of our home!" Jake's father snapped, making it obvious they were using a speakerphone. "Now tell us where you are."

Kyrie felt the rush of frustration from Jake. Aki kept her hand on his shoulder, offering support.

"I can't do that," he growled. "You know what happened. If I come back, it will happen again."

"You are my boy," his mother said. "I won't let you run off like this."

Mr. Williams motioned with his head. Jake nodded his own and then turned back to the laptop. "Is there someone who approached you? A woman?"

Mr. Ottiman spoke again after a moment of silence. "Jake, you need to come home. God will protect us from those cult members. The police are already making arrests. We promise it will be safe."

Jake leaned forward and closed his eyes. "Dad, you need to leave town and hide. This isn't over, and those being arrested likely had nothing to do with all the assassinations. You can't trust that woman."

"The woman's not your concern. I'm your father, and this is an order. Tell us where you are. These people can protect us. They will even protect your friends, including the girl that's caused all this trouble. They promised to help."

Tears fell from Jake's face. "I love you both," he choked out. "Keep the others safe." He looked up at Mr. Williams, and Becca's father terminated the call.

"I'm so sorry," Aki said as she leaned into him, pulling his head against her side as she stood next to him.

Becca crossed her arms. "It's probably that woman that has Lars. I'm sorry, Jake."

Her father sighed. "We knew it was a risk. Getting everyone to successfully disappear was always a long shot."

"I don't want anything to happen to them," Jake moaned. He wiped the tears from his eyes and looked up at Mr. Williams. "Is there anything we can do?"

"Destroy Bishop's empire," came the older man's reply. "We have to hope that will be enough." He stood straighter and grew serious. "Truth is, it's only a matter of time before they find all of your parents and us. Even if we got Kyrie's other money, it won't last forever." He looked down at Jake. "I'm also not sure just having buzzed your head will be enough. We already had a woman recognized Kyrie. The only thing that might be in our favor is the news is filled with more details on the assassinations, speculation on where Hurlington is, and what his motivation was in the attacks." He moved the laptop to the side and closed the lid. "But we'll likely need to disguise you more than we have."

"We could dye his hair as well," Michelle said.

"What's left of it?" Becca questioned and then shook her head. "Not much left to color. Dress him up as a girl," she decided. "You were mad last year that you didn't get the part in that play where some dude pretended to be a woman."

Jake went from confused to narrowing his eyes. "Bartholomew in Taming of the Shrew?" Becca nodded, and he blushed. "I was mostly joking. I thought you all might let me in on some girl secrets if I wore a dress around all of you."

Becca shook her head. "Girl secrets? Like how we know all you boys are stupid?"

Mr. Williams huffed as rain started to pelt the roof of the van. "We'll sort out a disguise later. Right now, we have work to do. I'll power up the other computers so you can finish figuring out your shock gloves. Just don't discharge anything inside the van. I don't want the static shock to fry any of the electronics."

Chapter 22

Yrginda ended the call on the cloned phone. *I knew the families were worthless.*

"General, do you want us to eliminate them?" Ontrc asked.

Yrginda turned to face the three Bound. The three men obviously had been chosen for their physical presence when Nalitran had them bound. He considered the question. "There is no point. I already read the minds of the whole family. They know nothing, and based on that call, the boy is aware of the danger his parents are in and is smart enough to know it is pointless to come home despite their pleas." Yrginda tugged at the tight top and adjusted the skirt he wore. The frumpy clothing and badly applied makeup he had used to meet the Ottiman family were already in a dumpster. "Killing them won't sate my urge for vengeance. It won't do anything but draw more attention to us since I had to meet with them in the first place."

The tall man nodded his understanding. "Do we track the other families?"

Yrginda shook his head; the once again tightly controlled hair remained in place during the movement. "Beyond the efforts already in place, we can only hope someone sees them and reports the boy's location to the tips line."

Yrginda considered his next move. Until they determined the girl's location, the other ten Bound he pulled from Project Kvotar would remain in three large cities where they could all quickly book a flight. Their continued separation provided operational security, as none of them had any apparent connections from the perspective of the outside world. *But staying in Olathe is pointless. The girl won't come back here.*

The three Bound glanced at each other, and Vridac, the shortest of the three, but still taller than Yrginda, cleared his throat. "General, I do not like the turn of events. Urdner and Libvr died at the hands of Hurlington's men because they had returned to protect the girl."

"I am aware," Yrginda said, allowing a subtle warning to surface in his tone.

"They will never be reborn." Vridac used his hands to call out their surroundings. "In this world, Povnrcac cannot reach us. The human gods are weak, if they even exist at all. None of us will live again because of our binding, and there is no hope our tugmor will return home to our own world."

"Your point?" Yrginda demanded.

Vridac lifted his chin. "You carry our binding stones. You could free us from our slavery, and we could live out what life remains to us." The other two nodded their heads in turn.

"You dare to speak treason to me? You think that Nalitran would allow your words to go unanswered?" Yrginda ground her teeth, power flowed into her body in case these three dolunar thought they could take him because of his female body.

"We speak truth," Ontrc said. "If you were to free us, we would swear loyalty to you. We know you were one of the warlords who took over after Nalitran had been defeated."

Yrginda swatted away the suggestion. "Nalitran holds my binding stone. I would not survive betraying him, and you should take care he never reads your mind to uncover this disloyalty."

"General, we are no fools," Vridac said. "Nalitran is not the noble warrior he claims. He fell at the hands of the corvlians. He only rules us here because he fractured our tugmor, destroying our ability to ever live again. He discards us easily, fully knowing we will never live again, only to replace us with more of our kind from home. If he limited the bindings to corvlians, that would be one thing, but he pulls more of us than our enemies. It is blasphemy what he does."

"The gods of this world are pathetic," Ontrc agreed. "They provide no power, and we could never appeal to them for help. Nalitran knew exactly what he did when he had us stolen from our own world. It was always a death sentence for us. But for him, he will continue to live forever, and he continues to discard us as if we are nothing."

Vridac nodded his head. "The damn corvlians should have simply destroyed his tugmor instead of trying to punish him further. By throwing him to the void, he became an enemy of dolunar and corvlian alike."

Yrginda expressed no emotion. These warriors spoke the truth. The fact that they felt comfortable vocalizing these sentiments to him meant he had not been careful enough with his own thoughts. As Nalitran's general, he had more freedom than any of the Bound and should be the last person they approached. *I'm not in a position to gain freedom yet. Their plotting puts me at risk.* He carried their stones, which meant he could eliminate them easily. *And they know that.* He pursed his lips. *Every asset contains some level of risk. Every gamble a potential win or loss.* "I will not release any of you. To do so would be treasonous." He turned away from them. "You will continue to do as I order."

"Yes, General," they each said. The unspoken truth that he had not executed them conveyed more than any words could.

Chapter 23

The rain started in earnest after they discussed the call with Jake's parents. This kept everyone crammed in the van to stay dry. After two hours, Mr. Williams gave up working because of the noise and spotty cell coverage. Instead, they went back to Farmington to resupply the coolers with food and to get some tacos for dinner. With the stronger cell coverage, they remained in a strip mall parking lot so Mr. Williams could work more efficiently.

"Can we check out some of the stores?" Becca asked. "Or just walk around to clear our heads? The rain's stopped."

Mr. Williams looked away from the monitors. "I still don't like the idea of you all being seen together. Especially with both Kyrie and Jake being in the news."

Becca persisted. "There's a number of stores here; we could pair up and go in different ones. Even get some makeup for Jake."

"Hey," Jake said. "No one's going to believe I'm a girl with my shaved head."

Becca rolled her eyes. "Fixed easily enough with a wig."

Kyrie closed the journal in her lap. She did not mind the closed space, but the length of time without moving did wear on her. "We could just walk around in one of those neighborhoods a few blocks away."

"No," Becca said. "I'm not walking miles through neighborhoods in some backwards town. You might be fine, but I look like the kind that'd be accused of robbing someone."

"We could play D&D quietly," Michelle offered, trying to provide a route for peace.

"Stop," Mr. Williams barked. "Everyone stay put and silent. We got a response on the message server." He dragged a browser window from the monitor on his right to the center one. "The Prelate starts by saying this is a private server and we have no business here. Then The Prophet—I'm assuming Hurlington—demands to know who we are and what we want."

Kyrie moved to the edge of her seat so she could see the monitor. "Tell him I'm not a demon. That we know Nalitran is behind all the assassinations and is blaming him. He needs to stop focusing on people who have done nothing to him. We want to stop Nalitran as well." Kyrie looked at Becca's father. "You want access to his servers, right?" She asked. He nodded. "Then just tell him we want access to the servers—"

"We don't want to be too greedy with our asks right from the start. We need to build trust first, or he might abandon this message server."

Kyrie bit her lower lip. "Okay, then ask him if he dreams of a jungle world with a violet sky."

Becca's father added the last and hit send. "That should be enough for now. I want to make sure he doesn't sign off and take hours to get back to us. Or worse, never check the server again."

They all sat silently waiting. Mr. Williams occasionally refreshed the browser, knowing each time would generate a new route through the Tor network to the server. A minute later, a new message appeared in their inbox. He opened it and quickly scanned the text. "This is from The Prophet. It says that Satan has seen beyond the gates of heaven and knows what exists there. Our words don't prove anything. God demands Satan is returned to hell, and he will not be dissuaded by the attacks against his church."

Kyrie stared at the keyboard. "If I could only see him, I might better understand what needs to be said to him." Her mind raced with potential solutions, but nothing stood out. *You don't know him well enough. He's a boss and we don't understand his motivation.*

Becca cleared her throat. "He's an ultra-religious nutjob. What if we tell him that Kyrie is an angel Satan tried to steal from God? She needs all of God's faithful to help her return Satan to hell. But she can't fight Satan when people are trying to kill her."

"That sounds pretty good," Michelle said. "Aki gave up arguing logic with the nutcases at school because they're too dumb to understand anything but their own rhetoric."

"They're all brain locked," Aki agreed from where she sat on the floor next to Jake. "It just pissed me off trying to convince them that grass is green and the sky is blue."

Mr. Williams considered the statements and glanced around the van. "Perhaps an encrypted call might help to convince him as well. I'll suggest that. And if he wants video, we've got the tarp that can hide the background so they won't get details on where we are." He quickly typed a reply and sent the message.

"I hate waiting," Becca said, dropping back into her seat.

Mr. Williams turned his to face Kyrie. "If we do a call, do you think you can play the role of an angel or divine being?"

Kyrie wanted to immediately answer yes, but she paused to consider her response. "I could probably do it. The only trouble is I know more about the Norse gods than Christianity."

"Just be arrogant," Aki quipped.

Mr. Williams remained serious. "If he starts quoting Bible verses, you'll have to try to redirect the conversation. I wouldn't recommend trying to make up things. Just remember, getting anything useful is a long shot. So don't feel pressured to be perfect."

Kyrie put the journal on the narrow desk across from her. "I grew up pretending to be other people and had to constantly adapt to my parents taking on different roles. Our goals are to get him to stop trying to kill us, get access to his servers, and remove him from the board. That's what I'll focus on."

"D&D for the win," Michelle said. "Those are clear campaign objectives."

Thirty minutes later, Mr. Williams had launched a private server on the dark web running encrypted video-conferencing software they controlled. Time ticked away as they waited silently for Hurlington to connect to the other end. Kyrie regulated her breathing, forcing herself to remain calm. *He's tried to kill your friends, but you need information,* she reminded herself. In the oddness of illogical human minds, she found the attacks on herself much easier to ignore than those on her friends.

The screen changed as another person joined the meeting with their camera also turned off. The designation for the other party simply stated unknown caller. Kyrie waited, her parents instilling in her the idea that she could gain power through silence.

"Demon," a male voice said through the computer speakers.

While the software had options to prevent recordings, Mr. Williams had launched the application in a virtual machine and so had full control of the output regardless of what the application wanted. Becca's father had described the idea of a software setting to block recordings as a feature designed to give the ignorant a false sense of security. As such, Kyrie knew she also needed to avoid incriminating herself in anything that she might say. "Mr. Hurlington, as I said before, I am not a demon."

"You claim to remember the lands of heaven. You must be a soul cast out of the land of promise. Someone unworthy of eternal peace."

Kyrie fought the urge to speak quickly. Without her ability to sense the man's emotions, she needed to listen to his words and tone. "Many have been stolen from heaven. They were not cast out, but enslaved. We have a common enemy. Nalitran seems bent on gaining money and power. He once ruled the dolunar, and I suspect he wants to take over America and perhaps more."

A huff came through the speaker. "We are not the same," snarled the man on the other end of the call. "Satan knows God speaks to me and wants me dead. You, he wants alive to use as a weapon. I've seen the orders. Demon or not, whatever power you have will be unleashed against the world like a plague of locusts." The man remained silent for a moment. "Against your friends. Against anyone you care about. Against Satan's enemies. You should have allowed me to eliminate you quickly to spare everyone the suffering that is to come."

Kyrie's heart sped up. She knew his statement contained truth. *You won't be used.* Her voice became hard. "I refuse to be someone's slave. If I'm to die, it will be fighting against whoever threatens my friends and not because someone thinks I might be captured in the future." She paused, sensing the concern about the direction of the conversation coming from Mr. Williams. *Change his mind,* the voice in her head said. *Find a connection. Is he part dolunar or corvlian? Pick.* "Do you remember the smell of the turri flowers? The sweet, yet slightly spicy taste of them on the wind just after they start to form seeds? Did the rain feel warm as it soaked through to your skin?"

The man on the other side remained silent, the noise suppression software removing any sounds of movement and breathing from the transmission. Eventually, he spoke. "The leaves tasted bitter, though the flowers were fragrant."

Kyrie released the breath she had unconsciously held. *A connection.* "I was stolen from my home just as you. I want to punish the man responsible—"

"Satan," Hurlington snapped. "He is no man! He is the Devil come to earth to herald the end of times. He replaces humans with demons, binding them to his will so that he can subvert our society, recreating hell on earth."

Kyrie nodded her head. "Indeed, Satan has come to this world. You've been fighting him for years." She searched her memories for anything her parents might have said about Christianity. *Narrate a story.* "I was sent here to defeat him. But I was too young and vulnerable. I needed to imbue the essence of earth to become its defender. I had to first become human so that I could defeat Satan on this plane of existence. He architected events so that he'd use you against me. He turned those who opposed him against each other so that he has no challengers."

Kyrie listened to the silence and let it hang in the air, hoping Hurlington would fill in his own truths to make her story complete in his mind. She felt Becca's father growing anxious for her to press their adversary to keep him engaged, but her father had taught her patience as a weapon.

"The voice of God acknowledges that you are a powerful force, but being young, you are vulnerable to Satan's will. He tempts people with terrible choices, making them think they must do his bidding. If you fall under his spell, nothing will stop the end of times from wiping life from this mortal plane. Hell will be unleashed, and everyone will burn for eternity."

Kyrie shook her head ever so slightly. "I will die before I allow anyone to control me." *Never again will we submit.*

"I want to see your face," Hurlington said. "Measure the truth of your words with my eyes." A moment later, the video feed activated, revealing a man with sandy brown hair and tired blue eyes. His features washed out as the remote camera tried to compensate for the lack of light in the dark room. The screen the man stared at was likely the only source of illumination.

Kyrie looked over at Mr. Williams and raised an eyebrow. The tarp behind and around them concealed the nature of the van, but it would allow him to see her new haircut and color. He hesitated only a moment before nodding his head and leaning forward to click on the control to activate the intentionally low-resolution webcam.

Hurlington inhaled as he watched her. "You are young of body, but ancient in your countenance. Even with this terrible connection, I see the age in your eyes." He looked upward, to the corner of the screen. "You must be the hacker parent."

"I am," Mr. Williams said coldly.

"Dennis," Kyrie said, drawing his attention back to her. "I will not tolerate any more attacks on me and those under my protection."

The man on the screen forced a chuckle born from despair. "The Church is destroyed. Those I thought were faithful are on their way to our heavenly father or have abandoned the mission in favor of worldly rewards, trading their eternal existence for more time on this mortal plane." The resignation in his eyes weighed down his shoulders. "There are but a handful left."

Kyrie felt her opening. "Then help us carry on the torch. We have evidence that Nalitran faked the assassination attempt on himself. We believe everything that happened on Saturday was an attempt for him to enrich himself and gain power. You've been fighting him for years; you must have records and information. Spies inside his organization. Share those details with us before someone destroys them."

The man on the screen shook his head and looked down. "Satan knew of my sanctuary. He sent his demons to take it. I had to destroy the servers and all the records."

Kyrie felt Mr. Williams' heart sink, and a frown rose unbidden to her lips.

"Your Grace," a voice outside of view came through the computer speakers. "We have the encrypted backups stored off-site. The primary records might be gone, but the backups still exist. Perhaps a computer specialist will make better use of them than we can until we find a new location to relaunch the servers."

Dennis nodded his head as he considered the statement. Then he turned to look at Mr. Williams. "Is that something that would be useful?"

Becca's father leaned closer to the camera. "I'd initially want to focus on records of Bishop's—or Satan's—criminal organization. But if you also have records of his demons and his other operations, I can use that." He hesitated for a moment. "I'm less interested in the videos you broadcast to your ... faithful," he added, looking for the proper word. "I'm sure there is value in those messages, but video files are large, and I need to quickly parse through the data and don't want to spend days downloading everything before I can start." Mr. Williams softened his gruff voice. "Though I will take anything I can get."

The man off-camera spoke. "The backups are mostly separated by category, but not fully. They are concealed on several servers not tied to The Church. I will work on gathering the encryption keys for the files and send you the details."

"The sooner I can get the data before the feds take over any of your servers, the better," Mr. Williams added.

"Do you know of a woman working for Satan?" Kyrie asked. "A demon. A dolunar who might have taken a friend of my parents, Lars Solberg."

"There were several women who lost their souls to Satan's demons. He has a powerful one always at his side. A woman that was once Elsa Donaldson. She seems to direct most of Satan's day-to-day activities." Hurlington shook his head. "We did not track your lawyer friend. We simply became aware of your existence when Michael Rodgers' search for you was reported to him. Since he was focused on you so strongly, we knew you were important to Satan. I knew Michael before he tried to have a demon possess me."

Mr. Williams asked his next question. "Is the headquarters of this criminal empire that Rodgers ran located at the Durten Industrial Complex outside of Chicago?"

Hurlington nodded his head. "Yes. Though they have several facilities across the country."

Mr. Williams' mouth tightened. "If you have so much information on them, why didn't you turn it over to the police, or even just do to them what you've been trying to do to these kids?"

Kyrie felt the anger boiling under the calm exterior of the large man beside her. The protective rage stemmed from the danger Becca faced.

Hurlington turned his attention back to Becca's father. "If we eliminated them, then we would have lost access to critical information." He turned his focus back to Kyrie. "As far as Satan's woman, the people we tried to get close to either of them simply disappeared, and like with you, our snipers have always missed." Hurlington leaned closer. "We've tried to send Satan back to hell, but until we break his control over those protecting him, we simply have not been able to do so."

The other voice cleared his throat. "I should warn you that we've received intelligence that they plan to shift their IT resources out of Chicago because of the scrutiny tied to Rodgers. I don't think they planned for him to be wrapped up in their attempt to pin the blame for the terrorist attacks on us."

"When?" Mr. Williams asked.

Dennis shrugged. "It is unclear. But I would expect soon. You won't have much time to hack their systems." He glanced away and then back toward the screen to stare at Kyrie. "God forgives you for any sins you have committed."

My sins? Take your religion and ... Kyrie calmed the outrage that flashed behind her eyes. "Do not send more people to kill me or my friends." Her voice lacked any trace of emotion, but the clinical tone and subconscious power draw chilled the air inside the van.

The man in the video feed nodded his head. "God trusts that you will do what is necessary if Satan captures you. Do not fail God and His mission. Remain faithful, and we can all gather together in heaven for our eternal rest." He sighed, looking off into a memory. "An existence filled with light and smells and warmth."

"Hang on the call," said the other man. "I'll provide a file with all the details in the chat." The video feed disappeared, and the screen showed the audio was muted.

Mr. Williams turned off the camera and muted their end of the connection while they waited for the information to be transmitted. "Smug, mother—" He looked abashed.

"Fucker," Becca finished from where she stood at the edge of the tarp and out of the camera view.

"Yeah," her father agreed. He took a deep breath. "If they are shutting down the servers in Chicago, we need to find a way in fast." He stood tall and calmed himself. "Hopefully, what Hurlington said is true, and they won't send any more people to kill us."

"Please be true," Aki said from the rear of the van. "I really don't like people trying to kill me."

Kyrie fought with the anger still in her. "Hurlington was really only trying to kill me. Nalitran is the bigger threat to all of you."

"Great way to lighten the mood," Becca said. "Have they sent the data?" She asked after an alert appeared on the screen.

Mr. Williams leaned over the keyboard. He ran a command to quickly scan the text file that the unknown man on the other end put into the chat. The command line that parsed the file returned with no warning messages, so he dumped the contents to the screen and then scrolled through the output. "Server addresses, user IDs, passwords, and what appears to be encryption keys." He continued scrolling. "Looks like they spread different data over a number of sites. Probably over a hundred keys listed here." He looked at Kyrie. "Let me sit and start copying these files to servers I control before something happens to them. Then we can download things that look interesting and see if we can build a case to bring down Bishop."

Chapter 24

They picked up additional supplies, such as epoxy, wire, and additional tools, at a home improvement store before returning to the campground. At the gate, they picked up more firewood so they could cook dinner, but the firepit and all the kindling they had previously collected still dripped with water. The interiors of the tents had survived the downpour, but humidity made everything damp, and their shoes tracked mud everywhere they went.

"I hate camping," Becca complained. "Every damn time we go, it rains."

"It didn't rain when we went to Arkansas," Michelle challenged.

"Yeah, but ..." Becca pointed to everything around them. "Things happened."

Kyrie noticed their neighbors watching as the other group sat next to their fire pit with a roaring fire. She took a few of the fresh pieces of split wood from the bundle and put them into their fire pit. "I can get this going in a little while if you want. It'll keep the bugs away."

"And you can sit on a bag," Michelle added. "We have enough left over from shopping."

Becca shook her head and then tossed her hands in the air. "Fine."

"I'll get enough for everyone," Aki said as she and Jake climbed back into the van and emerged a moment later with a handful of shopping bags. She handed one to everyone else and then to Kyrie. "You think we have a chance to put everything back to normal? Can we stop him? Can the tear be fixed?"

Kyrie crumpled up another piece of cardboard packaging to stuff under the tripod of firewood she created. She wanted to provide the appearance of using normal means to light the fire. "I won't stop until we stop Nalitran. For the other, I honestly don't know. I have thoughts about how to do it, but I don't know if it would work."

Aki's face fell, and she let out a slow breath. Kyrie could feel her hope slipping away. She glanced toward their neighbors, but the group of four people had shifted their focus to cooking some small white cylinders on metal sticks. "The problem is, we can't perceive dimensions outside the three we know, or four when you include time. Outside of thought experiments, I have no known way to interact with these other dimensions."

Michelle shifted the cut vegetables from one plate to another. "I just want to be able to teleport or banish someone to another plane of existence."

"I still don't get it," Aki said. "I've never been good at math."

Kyrie pushed some heat into the split logs as she used a lighter to set the cardboard on fire. "Imagine a two-dimensional world that just has length and width, no height. Now, take a sphere in our three dimensions and project it into two dimensions. The two-dimensional people could only see a circle. Just a single slice of the sphere."

"I didn't ask how many dimensions there are," Jake said as he removed screws from a second of the six stun guns they had. "I said I cast fireball."

Kyrie wrinkled her nose and looked at Jake.

"It's a joke," Becca said. "Jake, quit being stupid."

Kyrie turned her focus back to the explanation. "As the sphere passed through the world of those two-dimensional people, over time, they would only see the circle grow and then shrink. If a four-dimensional object passed through our world, we might see a cube, or a sphere, or any shape, but the actual object might be many more dimensions that we simply lack a way to interact with."

Becca adjusted the bag under her rear. "And you think there are higher dimensions at play?"

Kyrie nodded her head. "It's only speculation, but that's my thought." She sighed. "I haven't worked out a way to prove it or actually impact anything aside from an explosion so powerful it creates a black hole."

"See, fireball is the answer," Jake said as he tried to pull the two halves apart.

Kyrie continued to push energy into the wood, causing the fire to spread from the cardboard to the logs. "Only we'd need more energy than exists in the solar system. And everyone would be dead."

Becca huffed. "Yeah, let's not do that."

Jake tossed the glove he and Aki had worked on across the table and shook his head. "Damn thing's too tight if I put the rubber glove in it, and I could still feel the wires getting hot."

Aki picked it up and slid the glove onto her hand. "Fits me."

"But the wires were getting too hot," he complained.

Becca crossed her arms. "Do we even know it will work on one of them?"

Kyrie placed another log into the fire and stood up. "Only one way to know."

Michelle shook her head. "No. We're not going to do that."

Kyrie looked at them. "I'm more durable than most. If they don't impact me, then you might just make things worse for yourselves. We can still build some chemical bombs. Glass test tubes in a bottle."

Becca raised a hand to stop Michelle's protest. "I hate to agree with this, but Kyrie's right. I don't want to expect something will stop them and find them laughing at me." She turned to Michelle. "I'll put it into game terms, if they can only be hit by magical weapons and the gloves aren't magic."

Michelle moved closer to Becca and growled her reply. "Yeah, but you don't hit your party members with different swords to see who's resistant and which weapon is magic." She turned toward Kyrie. "We can go to the store and buy bleach. Mix it with almost anything, and you have poison gas and possible burns because the reaction generates heat."

Kyrie put a hand on Michelle's arm. "We need to know if the gloves will work. I can take it. They aren't supposed to kill, just hurt."

Becca looked a little less confident. "Not supposed to kill, no. Just hurt, perhaps leave you dizzy for a while."

Kyrie glanced around at them. "Let's take one off to the trails so we don't have an audience. Test it on me, and we'll know."

Michelle moved to stand in front of Kyrie. "I don't want you hurt."

Kyrie looked at Aki and Jake and raised an eyebrow. They looked at each other and slowly nodded their heads. "It would be good to know this isn't a waste of time," they finally said.

The emotions Michelle radiated moved Kyrie to reach out and hug her. "I'll be fine. Really." She stepped back, walked to the van to grab an unmodified stun gun, then headed toward the creek. "You all coming?"

The other four quickly caught up with her. They removed their shoes and followed Kyrie to the other side of the creek, before following her up the trail away from the campsites. Once they reached a spot where Kyrie could not feel anyone near them and the ground was mostly sandy without too much mud and rocks, she stopped.

"Who wants the honor?" She asked, holding out the black box with a pair of electrodes extruding from one end. She put a hand on her hip like Becca often did. "Really, no one wants to zap me?"

Jake shook his head. "I don't hurt women."

Aki and Michelle shook their heads.

Kyrie sighed. "You'll all need to practice how to use these things at some point. My father insisted that I learn to fight so I could do it without hesitat—"

Becca grabbed the stun gun from Kyrie. "I'll do it."

Kyrie turned her arm toward Becca. "Do it."

Becca frowned, looked at the device, and pressed the trigger. Crackling sparks jumped between the electrodes. Kyrie glared at her, daring her to press the device against her bare arm, while at the same time containing her instinct to use her powers to protect herself. *This is testing a surprise attack.*

Becca hesitated a moment more, then pressed the device into Kyrie's biceps.

Kyrie's arm cramped, and the muscles across her body spasmed. She crumpled to the ground as her legs no longer offered stability.

Becca did not maintain contact with Kyrie's arm, and the strain on her nervous system disappeared shortly after she hit the ground.

"I'm sorry," Becca cried, dropping to the ground next to her. "I ..."

Kyrie waved her left hand at Becca, her right arm still cramped and burned slightly. She slowly opened her eyes. "You'll need to keep it against a target for longer than that." She swallowed and pushed herself into a seated position.

Aki and Michelle knelt next to her, joining Becca. "Are you okay?" They both asked.

Kyrie took a couple of moments more, pushing the energy she had absorbed into the injury on her arm. She then turned to them. "When it first hit me, I couldn't react. But the moment the electrodes left my arm, I could've struck back."

Jake bit his lip. "The warnings in the instructions were that anything more than two or three seconds could cause a heart attack."

Kyrie stood up and wiped the damp sand from her pants. The others stood as well. "You'll have to surprise them, and I wouldn't stop shocking them until you know they won't be able to fight back. If they're that close, they could easily kill you."

Becca looked at the device in her hand. "At least we know it will work." She looked up. "Want to go again?"

Kyrie shook her head. "No."

After they returned to the campsite, they split off to work on different tasks. Michelle, still not happy with Becca, focused on cleaning up and organizing their food. Becca joined her father in the van to sort through the data and investigate other Durten sites where the servers might move. More confident in the solution, Jake and Aki returned to working on the gloves, looking for other ways to solve the problem of space and the wires heating up. Kyrie used some of the epoxy and a small tool bag they purchased to fashion her rock pouch. Then, she used isopropyl alcohol and a cloth to wipe down the stones. With her ammunition sanitized, she went back to the journals, sitting next to Michelle as her friend looked over the campaign notes.

The next morning, Michelle ran them through the next phase of her campaign while she fixed breakfast. She awarded everyone enough experience points to reach second level after they freed Aki from the prison cell. Kyrie noted several fudged dice rolls to prevent any of them from actually dying. She suspected none of the others had the stomach for one of the party to die, even in-game.

Once the morning routine started, Kyrie went for a high-intensity run, sprinting along the path, pushing her body as hard as she could. The exertion allowed her to drown out the resurfacing memories of times when her mother manipulated her, even at the protests of her father. The shattering of the perception of a unified home left her wondering what else of her past did not represent a truthful depiction.

Drenched in sweat, she finished the hour of exercise feeling both tired and yet relaxed. She gathered a towel and a change of clothes from the tent. With limited sets of clothing, she would need to do a batch of laundry later in the day.

"You're gonna look like a man working out like that," Becca quipped from the picnic table with a laptop in front of her.

Michelle frowned and smacked Becca on the shoulder. "She looks hot regardless."

"Hot, sweaty, and stinky," Becca joked. She turned to Kyrie. "I'm just messing with you, you know."

Kyrie smiled at Becca and tried to ignore the undercurrent of mixed emotions. She did not feel malice, but some amount of internal pain and confusion, though none of the physical attraction Michelle seemed to feel. "I'm just going to be more inflamed than the rest of you."

Becca narrowed her eyes and, after a moment, laughed. "Swole. The word's swole." Becca shook her head.

Kyrie shrugged. She knew that much of the current slang went over her head. "Inflamed? Swole? Whatever you want to call it, I can go all day." She grinned, knowing she got the sexual innuendo correct because Michelle choked on her drink. Kyrie turned and strutted off toward the bathhouse with a swagger, causing Jake to say, 'Damn.'

The hot shower helped to relax her muscles and made Kyrie feel human again. She finished drying her hair with the towel and once again wondered why she had not cut it short sooner. While still damp, the short hairs of the pixie cut would not remain wet for what always felt like hours. It made her hair care routine much simpler.

"What'd you do?" An old man's accusation carried through the shower door.

Kyrie had already registered the presence of the old woman and her husband, who camped in The Old Girl trailer. They had approached separately, the man a couple of minutes ahead of his wife. He had been in the toilet when his wife arrived and then she waited for him outside the door.

"The park rangers want us to meet with them at the main office," she whined. "I need you to drive the truck up there."

Kyrie froze. She opened her mind further and tried to push through the interference of the wall and metal door. The impatience the woman radiated felt more pronounced and not just residual annoyance for having to wait for her husband to finish in the toilets.

"Natalie, what did you do?" The man repeated. "I told you to leave things alone."

"That black man is suspicious," the woman snapped. "There is something wrong with him having those five kids. What if he's connected to all those killings that took place?"

"Natalie, he's just a guy with his daughter and her friends."

"They should still be in school. If nothing else, they are truant and need to be brought back to school."

Kyrie felt another woman and a young girl approaching, which silenced the old man and woman. Kyrie quietly pulled on her underwear and continued to dress as the little girl sang her way toward the women's bathroom.

"I've already called," the woman snapped. "They are waiting and will have backup. So quit your complaining and drive me up there."

Kyrie heard the man groan. "Fine," he said after a moment as he started to move away. "But this is on you. I want nothing to do with it."

Kyrie rushed to pull on her top and shoes. *Damn it, your meddling didn't fix the woman.* She tossed her dirty clothing, the shampoo, soap, and brush into the center of the towel and opened the door of the shower. *What to do? Michelle, Becca, we need you here.* She knew she could not project her thoughts very far, but she needed to stop the old man and woman. *Without killing them. But they already called. Is it too late?*

Kyrie ran around the back of the bathhouse and into the tree line northwest of the campground. The old woman's RV and truck were in the second loop and to the northeast. Her mind raced with things she might do to stop them, or at least slow them down.

The old woman continued to nag her husband as they traipsed east across the campground, heading toward the central playground. Kyrie assumed they would then head north on the other side of the loop, keeping on steady ground and staying away from the other tents and RVs.

Kyrie sprinted north on the west side of the loop, and then, using the cover of other trailers and tents, she turned to the east. *Please ignore us,* she tried to broadcast to anyone who might see her running past their campsite. She moved too fast to know if her mental commands worked, but no one shouted out at her as she dodged around trees, tents, and vehicles to keep the old couple from seeing her.

In total, she sprinted less than four hundred feet before coming to a stop behind an empty tent. The Old Girl trailer sat on the other side of the paved road. The red pickup the couple used to pull the trailer was less than thirty feet away from her. *Set the camper on fire? Break the windshield?* Her mind raced with ideas. She could not yet sense the old woman, but she knew they would soon be able to see their own site, and her, if she moved past the tent.

Damn it, you need more time. Kyrie looked around for something that might block the truck. *Break a limb from the tree over the truck?* She doubted she could generate the force needed at her distance to break a branch thick enough to block them. *Move the fire pit in front of the tires?*

Tires. She pulled in additional energy and aimed a narrow beam of gravitational energy into the front two tires. The vehicle lurched backwards slightly, but the engine kept it from rolling more than a little. Kyrie remained too far away to hear the escaping air, but she could see the tires deforming as the front of the vehicle gradually lowered itself closer to the ground. *Mental caltrops work as well as iron ones it seems. And if a young man struggles to replace tires, this old couple will have even more trouble,* she added, recalling the person her aunt almost hit.

Kyrie felt the old woman coming north along the road. Her husband lagged behind her. Kyrie backed up, keeping the tent between her and the two people. The trees offered some cover, and she raced back through the sites until the next RV blocked the view of the pair. Once she reached the paved road, she almost broke into a fast sprint, but then froze. *Mother would turn this into a trap.* Her mind ran through different possibilities, and she swallowed. *If it is just the old woman's vehicle, that will make the police believe her story even more.*

She drew in more power and resumed a fast-walking pace back toward the van and the others, hoping they would all be at the campsite. As she walked, she flung gravitational pulses at the tires of random vehicles. Sweat beaded on her forehead, and she struggled with the distance to some of the tires, aiming for a mix of front tires, rear tires, and those on trailers. She avoided attacking every campsite so that the van's unruptured tires would not create suspicion. To distract herself from the growing pain, she mentally performed the math to keep a running tally of the percentage of campsites she hit, keeping the number below twenty percent.

Her pace continued to increase as she grew closer to the van and her friends. Tired, but not exhausted, she searched for everyone and breathed a sigh of relief when she felt all five of them. *One last tire,* she mumbled silently, slashing the front tire of their neighbor's minivan forty feet away.

She moved around a clump of trees and saw Jake and Aki working on a second glove, with Aki using a screwdriver to poke pieces of rubber into the fingers. Michelle and Becca remained at the picnic table, Becca engrossed in the laptop, and Michelle in the D&D notes. Mr. Williams remained inside the van.

Michelle lifted her head. "All cleaned up?"

Kyrie shook her head. "We have to leave now! Start gathering everything up."

Michelle paled and then nodded her head. Becca, Jake, and Aki all looked at each other and then started moving.

Kyrie opened the back door of the van and climbed in through the curtain. She spoke before Becca's father could greet her. "I was in the shower when I heard the old woman demand her husband drive her up to the park office. She said the park rangers wanted to talk to her about us. Her husband was reluctant, but it sounded like she's already called them."

"Shit," Mr. Williams said. "There's only one road out of the campground. If they already have cops looking for us, they could block us from leaving." He rubbed his hand over the fuzz that had accumulated on the top of his head. He got up from his seat.

"I put holes in the truck tires. That will slow them down. They didn't see me." Kyrie moved to the side as Mr. Williams headed toward the back of the van. "I also punctured seventeen other tires on my way back so it wouldn't look like we targeted them."

He paused and looked at her. After a moment, he found what he wanted to say. "Anyone see you?"

"I did it from afar."

Kyrie felt Michelle and Becca at the rear door. They opened it and climbed in. Mr. Williams turned toward his daughter. "Becca, start getting everything into the van. Don't worry about packing it up neatly. Perhaps we can get out of the park before they decide to stop us."

Becca moved, heading for the tent as Michelle stood in the open doorway. "What's going on?" Michelle asked.

Mr. Williams stepped out of the van. "Gather everything up. We need to leave in the next five minutes."

Kyrie followed him out. She hesitated as Mr. Williams continued talking while he moved to the side of the van and unplugged the shore power from the hidden outlet in front of the rear wheel. "Hopefully, they won't have anyone at the check-in booth watching for us to leave. We can't beat a radio, and it's almost a mile to the park office."

Kyrie frowned, looking for options. "There will likely be someone there. Whenever I go for a run, there is. However, I could cause a distraction. Perhaps a fire in the woodshed. Or perhaps make whoever it is simply ignore us." *You made the woman paranoid. Do you want to damage someone's mind?* "I think I could make them fall asleep."

He nodded as he considered the suggestion. "Might work. But if the woman makes another call, the cops might just come down to the campsite anyway." He looked over at the tents as Aki and Jake emerged. Sleeping bags in their arms. "Just toss it all in; every minute counts."

Kyrie turned and moved to the larger tent. She grabbed an armful of pillows, clothes, and personal items from where Becca had piled them. Jake was already on the way back from the van and started pulling the tie-downs from the tents as the others continued to scurry around like an army of ants picking clean the carcass of the campsite.

Eleven minutes later, Mr. Williams drove them around the lower loop, which avoided driving past the old woman who had triggered their early exodus. Kyrie sat in the passenger seat, prepared to address any threats while the others attempted to consolidate the mound of camping gear that made moving between the seats impossible.

"If there are cops who have blockaded the road, we have to be careful," Mr. Williams told her. "They'll likely have body cameras that will record everything you do and say. Their cars often have cameras too. At a minimum, looking out the front and back, but possibly in all directions." He glanced at her as he shifted further right on the road to allow a car coming from the other direction to pass. "So if you do something with your powers, they might get a clear view of it."

"We don't want that," Kyrie said. She had become aware of body cameras from her prior interactions with the police, but she had not realized that their vehicles also recorded.

"Stop here," Kyrie commanded at fifty feet from the small booth on their left. A golf cart and the firewood shack sat in a gravel lot on the right side of the road, and Mr. Williams pulled into the grass just before the lot. The check-in booth did not have a gate, but it occupied the point separating traffic into the main campground and a small, paved loop with overflow campsites. She noted that about half the overflow spots had trailers and people moving about.

She opened her mind further, looking for points of high emotion. While distance limited her ability to perceive feelings, no one in her range emitted anything that drew her concern. One person occupied the booth, but the small building only had windows on two sides, and neither of them faced the van. She removed her seat belt and jumped out of the vehicle, closing the door behind her.

Kyrie moved with intent, her mind focused on the person inside the booth. *A woman. A slightly agitated woman.* The other campers did not appear to take any special notice of Kyrie as she approached the rear of the booth. A tack board contained pinned messages, and she made an effort to feign interest in the content. The closer she grew to her target, the more awareness Kyrie had of the woman. *She's waiting for something explicitly, though perhaps doesn't know what?*

Kyrie did not take the time to delve into the woman's thoughts, knowing they needed to act quickly before the old lady and her husband summoned the police. *Sleep,* she commanded as power flowed from her, pushing a desire for rest into the woman. *Sleep. You are so tired.* The woman's mind bent to her will almost instantly, and she felt and heard the young lady slip off the stool and crumple into a mass against the interior wall of the booth.

Kyrie breathed a sigh of relief. The woman had fallen into an immediate deep sleep. *Better than killing someone.* She looked back at the van and motioned for Mr. Williams to come forward as she crossed to the right side of the road to get back into the vehicle. "She's sleeping," Kyrie said, jumping in and fastening her seat belt as the van moved quickly along the park's main road.

"I guess Michelle's right; high-level mages are always good to have around," Becca said from the rear seat Kyrie normally used.

Kyrie nodded in agreement. *What would Mother do next?* The rules of the outside world did not align entirely with fantasy, but the more she interacted with people beyond the mountain valley where she grew up, the more she realized her parents had woven subtle details into their narratives.

"What about a drone, Dad?" Becca asked, her voice too soft. "We could fly it up and see if there's a group of cops there."

"It'd make too much noise and draw even more attention," her father responded as they made their way up the gentle ridge. "We'll have to hope for the best."

Kyrie undid her seat belt as they neared the top of a rise, but they had not finished rounding the last bend that would take them to the overlook parking lot. "Stop here. I'll scout on foot." Mr. Williams hesitated and then stopped the van. No shoulder existed, so the vehicle blocked one lane of the road. "I've been running up and down this hill for exercise. If there are watchers at the turnoff for the park office, they will see us enter the overlook or the dump station. I'll sneak closer and see if it's safe." She opened the door.

"Wait." Mr. Williams grabbed her wrist. "Becca, get a pair of walkies. You can signal us when it's safe."

Becca clambered around in the back and soon pushed one of a pair of small radios with short antennas toward Kyrie. "It's set to channel two. Just turn this knob to turn it on, then press this button to talk. Don't say much. Anyone listening on that channel will hear."

Kyrie took the device, nodded her head, and jumped out the door. She heard Michelle yell 'Be safe' as she shut the door and entered the woods on the right side of the road, opposite the overlook and park offices, as the trees and ground vegetation on the right side remained denser and offered more cover than the area around vista point.

She plunged through the undergrowth and forced her way up the ascent. Compared to the much steeper slopes in Colorado, the path she chose offered little physical challenge, aside from the vegetation. Once she felt insulated from view, she increased her pace and tried to follow a path that mirrored what she remembered of the direction the road took.

When the incline leveled off, she moved even faster, pushing her senses as wide as possible to search for people. Her head throbbed, but she needed enough time to reduce the noise she made before stumbling upon someone. She slowed as she neared the dump site on her side of the road. The entrances to the overlook and park offices sat just on the other side of the park road.

Damn, she swore, noting a person in a green and white patrol car near the driveway to the park offices. The officer sat at an angle, facing mostly into the park, watching for people leaving. She evaluated the different approaches and decided to continue carefully through the woods, passing the dump site so that she could approach the officer from the rear.

The sound of the idling vehicle covered the noise she made rushing through the dense ground cover. Fifty yards beyond the driveway, as the ground started to descend, she shifted her path closer to the main park road. She stayed low and looked for a place where she could cross the blacktop, hoping the officer would not look over his shoulder.

Go! She sprinted through the mowed area and across the park road back into the woods, where the land fell away quickly into a valley. Using the topology of the land, along with the trees, she moved uphill toward the vehicle and the occupant. She soon returned to the level of the road and driveway. *You can't just flatten his tires. He'd just radio for someone else to come.* While she wanted to experience the thrill of a high-speed car chase, she did not want to do it when so much was at risk.

Kyrie continued forward, trying to get close enough to connect with the man's mind. However, the plants under the pine trees on this side of the main road offered little cover. At sixty feet, she felt she could probably puncture the closest rear tire, but the man would still be alert. She needed to get much closer to impact his mind. *And then you'll likely be on video, and he'll see you.*

Kyrie looked over her shoulder at the driveway toward the park office, which continued further south with slightly denser ground cover. *You could loop south toward the buildings and come up on the passenger side of the car.* She breathed deeply as she looked for other options. Nothing came to her, so she backed off to head south, feeling the press of time weighing on her.

After she moved twenty yards toward the park offices, she sprinted across the driveway and then dropped low to use the limited vegetation for as much cover as possible. Movement always drew attention, so she waited for a count of ten before lifting her head to look at the car in case the officer had caught her in one of his mirrors.

The man did not appear to have changed his position, and she let out the breath she had held as she stretched her senses again to look for threats. She frowned. Three additional men on the other side of the nearest building registered in her mind. *Enemies on multiple flanks. If you don't deal with them, they'll likely come after you.* She weighed the options and turned toward the closest of the three buildings. The structure would cover her approach to the three men, and she expected the ground cover would protect her from the man in the car. *The dice always come up ones when you need a good roll the most.*

Kyrie moved around the far edge of the closest structure. She hugged the edge of a small garden running along the side of the building. A short wire fence with stakes separated the fresh plants from small animals. At the corner of the building, she leaned forward to watch the men that stood in a parking lot. Two work trucks and a pair of white SUVs with green stripes on the doors sat at odd angles. The three men stood near the SUVs, just twenty feet away from her.

"Repeat that," one officer said into a radio that was a bit larger than the one Kyrie carried in her hand.

Kyrie could not make out the response, but based on her view of the man's profile, she thought the park ranger's face puckered. *What's going on?*

The man with the radio repeated what he had heard. "The Martins claim someone slashed their tires, and now we're getting reports of several others with flat tires throughout the campground." The man pushed a button on the radio and spoke into it. "Is Sarah still at the booth, or is she investigating?"

Kyrie looked around for options. She did not think she could knock out the three people simultaneously, and even if she could, doing so would draw a lot of suspicion. Sweat rolled into her eyes, and she wiped it away. *You're holding too much power,* she reminded herself, knowing that she had subconsciously continued to absorb energy and had not released enough of it.

"I think this is more than what we want to address," said another ranger, the shortest of the three. "If this has anything to do with all the killings, these people will be heavily armed."

The third man shook his head; the eye-roll Kyrie couldn't see was evident in his tone. "It's an old white woman scared of a black man. That's why I initially told her to come up here. I ain't going to be accused of racial profiling because some old couple are upset Jim Crow is over."

"Someone slashed a bunch of tires in the park," the one with the radio said. "We should go check it out. Those five teenagers could definitely be involved. No one's said anything about the terrorist attacks, or that two of them are black, but slashed tires are reasonable suspicion. Let's go."

Shit, Kyrie swore.

The first man moved toward the driver's door of the far SUV. The short man shook his head. "This is a bad idea. We should wait for the feds or the staters."

Kyrie pulled in more energy to rupture the tires, but hesitated, knowing they would just use the radio. The short ranger emitted the most fear, giving her a target. She reached out mentally, making contact with his mind as the third man put a cigarette into his mouth. *Make him panic,* she told herself, wanting a distraction to buy more time. She pushed emotion into him, sourcing her own terror during the dolunar attack that took Zvarncr from her.

"Shit!" the short man cried and jumped up and down before slapping the lighter from the other man's hand. "There's a damn propane tank right there. You'll kill us all!"

Kyrie, still in the man's head, automatically turned her attention to the rusty white tank next to the third building. The cylinder sat forty feet from her. The mental feedback from the man reverberated through the connection, drawing her focus to the warning labels on the side of the tank and then immediately to the small line coming out of the bulge on the top. *Gas burns.*

She ripped the small metal pipe in two with a gravitational wave that also scarred the larger tank. Already bursting with energy, she concentrated on heating the area where the vapors escaped from the breach she had caused. Three seconds later, a roaring flame shot forth, burning the ground next to the tank and billowing out and up into the air with a deafening roar.

Her mental connection to the man sent panic through her, and she stumbled backwards as the three men jumped away from the ball of fire. The uneven concrete pavers under her feet tripped her, and she fell backwards. Her knees buckled further from the shock of one of the metal stakes holding up the fence piercing her lower back. She barely contained a cry of pain as she twisted away, ripping the rusty two-foot-long post from her, tearing a larger hole in her body. She collapsed onto her right side and slammed her binding stone against the concrete pavers.

White-hot pain cascaded through her, and she lost all connection with her powers and the man's mind. She spasmed on the ground.

Kyrie could not move for several moments. Her mind simply failed to work. The sounds of screaming and shouting eventually roused her consciousness. Not even the pain of translating between worlds compared to the sensation that had just paralyzed her.

Get up! She screamed at herself. Time stood still as she wrestled for control of the energy that had rampaged uncontained through her body. A gasp for air allowed her to regain enough awareness of her surroundings that she could struggle to her hands and knees. Her chest expanded and contracted, forcing air through her lungs. *Are you still there? Did I kill you?* The silence in her head was deafening. Her heart raced. *Please, I didn't mean to hurt us.* The moments passed with no response, and she tried to contemplate what it would mean to truly be alone. *I'd be dead too if the binding stone was destroyed.*

The voices of the men shouting forced her to focus. She could feel their presence again and relief that she did not appear to kill her other half eased her racing heart. The men had moved farther from the corner of the house and the flames shooting out of the propane tank. The warm blood running out of the hole in her back made her dizzy, but she pushed up from the ground, grabbed the radio, and staggered back toward the road. She saw and heard the watcher's car backing down the driveway toward the buildings.

"At least he's distracted," she mumbled. She shifted the radio to her left hand as she crashed through the woods. Her right hand shot into her pocket and pulled out her binding stone. It did not look cracked or broken to the naked eye, but the impact against the paver still lingered in her body.

Kyrie stored the stone back into her pocket and mentally kicked herself for not pulling away from the man's mind before triggering the propane fire. Her body subconsciously directed energy to heal her back, but the power moved slowly, and she only managed to reduce the external bleeding.

Every muscle ached. Raw determination forced her continued movement toward the road, panting through the labored breaths and damaged internal organs. She slowed enough to turn on the walkie-talkie and press the large button on the side. "Come now," she begged. Becca's curt affirmative let her know the message had been received.

She staggered from the tree cover and crossed the road well before Mr. Williams made it around the curve. Smoke became visible in the air as the van stopped for her. She climbed into the footwell and dropped to her knees so that she could put her chest against the bottom of the seat. A bloody hand barely pulled the door shut.

"What happened?" Mr. Williams demanded. "Are you shot?"

Kyrie shook her head, and Becca and Michelle moved forward to put their heads between the seats. "Landed on a stake ... and my stone."

"There's blood all over you," Michelle cried.

"I just need to rest," Kyrie said. *You need a safe place for our stone.* The conversation about how to sneak things into prison surfaced. *Would it be safe? You could always undo it,* she decided.

"Get one of my daggers," she mumbled, lifting her head from the seat and trying to not get blood all over the van's interior.

Mr. Williams looked down at her as he hit the gas and accelerated along the curving road. "Why do you need a dagger?"

She shook her head. "Michelle, get one of my daggers," she moaned. "I need to reopen the wound."

"Why?" Michelle, Becca, and her dad asked at once.

"I want to hide my binding stone," she replied, burying her face once again into the seat.

Chapter 25

Yrginda finished typing the research notes with his findings regarding Mr. Williams' business before he answered his phone. "Yes," he replied after hitting the speaker option.

"Elsa, this is Greg. Can you talk?"

Yrginda sat back and focused on the phone sitting next to the computer. He picked up the device and switched off the speakerphone. "Yes, Greg, I'm able to talk now." The anticipation of positive news sweetened his voice. *The human male is weak when it comes to their females.*

"You did not hear it from me, but a black man and five teenagers were reported by a couple staying at a campsite outside of St. Louis. The original complaint likely had no merit, but the police brought in the feds because of the potential tie-in to the assassination tsunami and the fact that numerous tires were punctured with no witnesses and a propane tank leak catching fire. One of the park police officers swears it was because another officer tried to light a cigarette, but the other two present swear that had no impact. To top it off, the black man, the kids, and the van they were in disappeared in the middle of the whole thing before their time was up at the campsite. They had to have left during the propane fire."

Yrginda shifted her focus back to the collection of notes on the tablet sitting behind her keyboard. "Really? That is an interesting story. When did this happen?"

"Five hours ago."

Yrginda put aside the lost time. He had no way of altering reality. *At least it puts them in a geographic zone and gives me another data point.* "Any information about the van?"

"Afraid not. No one saw the actual plate, and the information on the reservation appears to be fraudulent. The credit card used is a disposable one tied to a crypto account and an obvious alias. Crypto and the services that allow people to register one-time use credit cards are skirting the law.

"The van did advertise a Pete's Electric, but we don't even have a state for where that business might be registered, so we've not been able to track anything down."

"It'll be a front," Yrginda said. "Nothing else has been honest, so why would that be?"

Greg grunted affirmatively. "It was a metallic blue transit van. Some campers saw them leave, but none of the park police saw the van exit the park, despite them looking for it. Again, they left around the same time as all the slashed tires were discovered and the propane tank caught fire."

The girl is smart enough to know how to escape. She will not be easy to catch. "I'm assuming notices to local law enforcement were sent out."

"No one's reported seeing the van," Greg responded. "And rural areas don't have many cameras we can tap into. But if anything more comes in, I'll let you know."

"Thank you, Greg."

"Anytime. Next time you're in DC, let me take you out to dinner."

Yrginda kept the disgust out of his voice. "Of course, Greg. I would love that." Yrginda hung up the phone and put it on the table. He scrolled through the pages of notes he had already collected as well as the details the analysts had amassed.

"General?" Ontrc questioned.

"What do you want?"

"Is there something we can help with?"

Yrginda swallowed. He did not fully trust Ontrc or the other two, but they had been useful so far. Aloud he said, "We are dealing with intelligent people. The girl reportedly does not understand the modern world, so she aligns herself with a man who is an expert in security. He's built a career in penetration testing. Both physical and computer systems. They know we are after them. They do not appear to be afraid of Hurlington, at least not enough to come to us for security." Yrginda raised an eyebrow. "They knew about Rodgers and his attempt to kidnap her. They stole Rodgers' binding stones and used the Bound against Hurlington and then the police to clean everything up."

"You have said the girl is a warrior more than once," Ontrc said. "Could Awan have brought over another warlord like yourself?"

Yrginda had already pondered that question and felt it likely. *However, I am not fool enough to think that a free warlord would accept any of us as loyal servants. Not that I would become one.*

He stood up. "What is the girl's current objective? Simply disappear? Unseat Nalitran? Take over control?" Yrginda walked around the hotel suite, the high heels he normally wore making no sound on the carpet. "What do they know, or worse, think they know?"

"Not even Awan or Rodgers knew of the northern site," Ontrc said.

Yrginda glared at the green-eyed man. *But he is not wrong.* "To eliminate the threat, they need to unseat Nalitran. The Williams man will know that Nalitran's security is too tight for a direct approach. He might try to subvert his way in, but that will take time, and he would need to hire a new team. We already have dossiers on all of his employees, and we have them under surveillance. Which means Nalitran is not likely in direct physical danger." Yrginda picked up a bottle of water from the desk and took a drink. "So they would need to attack Nalitran indirectly. We just have to decide how they will do that." Yrginda pursed his lips, a human trait he hated, but could not dissuade the body from performing. A lingering quirk of the prior woman. *They know about Rodgers. Could they think of combating Nalitran through that connection? We've not yet replaced that human; therefore, there could be risk.*

"Do we just wait here in Olathe?"

Yrginda shook his head. "No, the plane is coming to pick us up. I think we should relocate to Chicago."

Nalitran activated the conference link and waited for Yrginda to pick up the other end. He did not like being without his general for this long. Yrginda took care of too many daily tasks, both tied to his legitimate businesses and to rebuilding the dolunar empire.

He looked at his watch and then crossed his arms. *A minute late. I do not like the disrespect.*

Two minutes later, Yrginda joined the conference call. "You are late," Nalitran demanded.

"Apologies, Warlord, the network on the plane did not want to connect." Yrginda sat near the front of the plane and faced the rear, leaving Nalitran only a webcam view of the closed cockpit door behind her.

"What is your status? I know you recalled the plane, but I have not heard any new updates since twelve hours ago."

Yrginda leaned forward ever so slightly. "There is no news on Hurlington. The members of the Heth cell have disappeared, but we have anonymously reported all the details we have on the other seven remaining cells. I expect most will be arrested soon."

Nalitran growled. "The girl. What of the girl?"

"We have no specific information about the girl. It is possible she might try to infiltrate the Durten servers. We've ordered a purge of data Rodgers kept on her, and are in the process of moving the rest of the data and applications because of the increased police scrutiny. Nothing in those systems can be traced directly back to you. The risk is minimal. The IT teams expect it will take at least two weeks to finish the transfer of the services and data once a new hosting location is finalized."

"And we don't have a self-destruct protocol like Hurlington used." Nalitran pulled up the quickly compiled report from the team members who survived Hurlington. It lacked a complete review as some parts of the cave system remained to be explored, with areas that had described something more sophisticated than Yrginda had ever planned for. "If we have to run clandestine operations on an ongoing basis, it might be worth investigating." *Though we should hopefully gain control of enough of the country in the next year, that it won't be necessary.*

Yrginda did not address the comments directly. "I'm assembling the girl's capture team in one location. If we get reliable intel on her location, we will move immediately. Until then, I want to avoid anything that could connect us to Project Kvotar or any other things that will draw police scrutiny. The project plan estimates another two years before we have critical mass and wealth that we can eliminate the effective government operations and instill our own."

Nalitran's lip curled. He knew the Kvotar timetables; he directed Yrginda to create the plans, but he felt they were too conservative. "I will remind you I need her alive. Make sure the entire team is committed to her capture and not her execution."

"I will reinforce that mandate personally," Yrginda said with no emotion.

"Good," Nalitran replied. "Once you are on the ground, send the plane back. I'll need to be in New York tomorrow."

Chapter 26

Kyrie rested her head on her rolled-up sleeping bag as she reclined on the floor of the van. She breathed slowly as the rhythmic sound of the wheels speeding over I-64 relaxed her. The wound in her back no longer bled, and she felt confident that her internal organs had regenerated. The muscles still needed more time to regrow strong connections, so she did not want to move.

"Are you certain you don't need any antibiotics?" Mr. Williams asked from the driver's seat. "We could see if a clinic might prescribe something. Perhaps a tetanus shot?"

Kyrie allowed some exasperation to enter her voice. "I should be able to heal without those things. My powers have kept me healthy all my life."

Michelle sat on the floor next to her. "I still can't believe you just shoved your stone into a hole in your back."

"I almost broke it," Kyrie demanded. "I can't risk that again."

Michelle patted her hand. "Just rest then."

"What if you are captured?" Mr. Williams asked. "You were concerned they'd take it from you. Now they have to cut you open to do that. If you're unconscious, you won't be able to stop them."

Kyrie tried to sense her stone, but lingering pain prevented her from having any awareness of it. "As long as no one says anything about it, hopefully no one else will know."

He remained silent for a while, then continued with his deep voice, revealing too much fear. "We'll need to get rid of all the blood-covered clothing and paper towels."

"Perhaps a dumpster at our next stop," Becca suggested from where she sat in front of a computer. The front seat needed a deeper cleaning to get rid of the residual blood.

"Possibly," her father answered. "Burning it might be safer, though. Hopefully, the cops won't find where Kyrie fell on the stake."

The conversation carried on for several minutes before Kyrie opened her eyes and looked up at the magnetic sign clinging to the underside of the roof. The one that had been there for Bob's Mechanical Service now graced the sides and back of the van. They had not gone more than ten minutes from Hawn before Mr. Williams had quickly changed the branding on the vehicle. Two hours later, they had stopped again, and he printed a fake Missouri temporary tag and used that in place of the license plate.

She turned her head to Michelle, who continued to radiate concern through their physical contact. "I'm okay, really."

Michelle tried to smile. "I know."

"When we get a chance, can we find a rest stop?" Jake asked from the back of the van.

"And dinner," Becca chimed in.

"We're just on this side of Louisville," Becca's father responded. "I'll find a place to stop, and then we can figure out our next steps."

"Do you think the changes to the van will work?" Jake asked from the back. "A lot of people at Hawn know what we all look like."

"I don't know," Mr. Williams said. "I really don't. I'm struggling to see a clear next step. Perhaps we can pay cash for a small RV and get them to leave their old plates on it for a while. But there's a lot of unknowns, and we're short on time. If Nalitran is cleaning house at Durten Industries, we don't have the time to do a full workup and slow burn the infiltration."

Becca shook her head as she continued to work from the seat near Kyrie. "Ain't no one falling for the phishing yet either. Could their systems be catching all the attempts? Do we try another campaign?"

"We need to watch how aggressive we are," Mr. Williams said. "Too many attempts and it might alert them to our target."

Kyrie tried not to yawn and gave up before asking her question. "You said the other day that the best way to hack a system is to have physical access. What if we go back to the break-in idea you mentioned?"

"Getting access requires a lot of planning and people," he said as he took an exit ramp. "Ideally, we'd get someone hired at one of the businesses. Perhaps even Durten. Let them scout for us, but not do anything to give themselves away. Then we'd figure out how to get someone with computer skills in to put a network tap, or other compromised device, on the network so that we can get remote access. But it won't take them long to move operations to a new location."

"Perhaps breaking in won't be that hard," Michelle said. "We've got a mage on our side. She could take out cameras and knock out guards. Perhaps even read their minds for access codes."

Kyrie smiled up at Michelle. *She's got more confidence in you than you do.*

Mr. Williams shook his head. "That's still very risky."

Becca swiveled her chair forward. "You said it already. We're running out of time. If we can't get in quickly from the outside, we have to do a burgle."

"I know," he muttered. "I've just been trying to come up with any other option that's a lot safer." He turned onto the crossroad, changing their direction from the east to the north. "What do you all want for dinner? We can look for a campsite near Chicago after we eat."

They pulled into a new campground northwest of Chicago just after ten in the morning. They had taken turns sleeping on the van's floor at a rest stop along the highway, and now all of them wanted nothing more than to crash in a tent.

This campground was located on private property with a small man-made lake that was encircled with a gravel road. Sixty campsites backed up onto the fishing lake, which also had canoes for kids to explore. A small section of beach with imported sand offered a place to swim, though with school not yet out, and the cool morning air, no one had decided to partake of the muddy water. The lack of any real tree cover made Kyrie long for their time at Hawn.

A bathhouse existed near the back of the property and close to the campsite Mr. Williams had reserved. Kyrie had already changed out of her ruined shirt and stained pants before leaving the van. She took the opportunity to get showered and wash away the dried blood that clung to her skin. Unlike Hawn, which had separate showers, the women's toilets also contained five stalls that separated the wet area from a semi-dry area with a curtain. The water only reached a warm temperature, but once Kyrie had cleaned away the remnants of the prior morning's events, she returned to the campsite and joined the others in the tents for some sleep.

By mid-afternoon, everyone had given up on getting more sleep, and they resumed their normal tasks. Jake and Aki continued to rework the glove design, using thicker wire and moving the battery pack and driver in the original housing to something they could strap around their chest and under their shirts. Another set of wires went to the trigger, which they operated from their left hand to make it easier to grab and hold someone with only one hand.

Michelle grilled some vegetables and hotdogs for dinner, and Kyrie watched the others as everyone ate. Her body still hurt, and a dull ache seemed to fill her soul. *You still here? I didn't hurt you, did I?* She looked at the ground, resolved to never getting a response. *Though what would you do if you ever did get a response? That would be weird.*

Mr. Williams tossed his dirty paper plate into the firepit. The spilled mustard and juices sizzled as flames curled the edges. "We learned as much as we can about the site from the internet. The satellite maps make it appear to be in the middle of a large section of woods and fields with sparsely populated rural roads around it. But they are more than a year old."

Kyrie tested her back by stretching to her left. The repaired muscles felt tight and still painful. *You need a little more time to heal. No time.* "I can try to get close. Perhaps even over the fence to see what things look like inside."

"I was thinking more about using a drone," Mr. Williams said. He looked up into the sky that was growing dark as the sun continued to set. The thin cloud cover moved slowly overhead, but nothing indicated rain would come overnight. "The main roads appeared to be on a mile-wide grid and the complex is in the middle of the land the company owns. They seemed to have kept a thick span of trees around it." He chuckled. "Great way to keep people from watching what you're doing. Also can provide cover for us."

"Can I fly the drone?" Becca asked. "You always say you'll let me, but then never do."

He shook his head. "Not this time. I'm hoping we can fly it at night. I have an infrared camera and a telephoto camera that we can mount to it. Not ideal for flight time, but I want to do a detailed analysis." He stood up. "Finish eating. I want to drive around the roads before it's totally dark so I can look for a place where we can park the van that won't be obvious."

Mr. Williams drove down the country roads lined with trees and fields. Farmhouses and barns dotted the landscape. He avoided driving along the road that led to the turnoff for Durten Industries, but traveled the three other sides of the property multiple times before pulling off the blacktop onto a field entrance. The gate, overgrown with grasses, had two ruts where a truck or tractor periodically entered the tree-lined field. However, given the time of night and lack of any lights in the field, he felt the position would not draw too much attention.

After pulling the front curtains to conceal the LEDs and monitors in the back of the van, he pulled a quadcopter drone from its case, installed an oversized battery, and connected two additional gimbal-mounted cameras to the underside.

"That's a sick drone, Mr. Williams," Jake said as Becca's father started a preflight check of the device. "I'd love to have one like that."

"Technically, you need a license to fly this one. And it's heavily modified, so you can't just buy one off the shelf."

"It drop bombs or have guns?" Michelle asked. "I love using them in first-person shooters to blow up tanks."

Mr. Williams rolled his eyes and used his head to motion for them to clear a way to the back door of the van. "They don't issue licenses for armed drones." He jumped out of the van, put the drone down on a clear spot near the road, then climbed back into the van. "Okay, let's do this carefully," he said more to himself than the others.

Kyrie moved to the front of the van so she could see over his shoulder as he sat at one of the computers. He pulled a wire harness out from behind the monitors and connected it to his controller. After powering it up, he activated a program on the computer and rearranged three windows with video feeds, none of which had a clear picture. He moved a fourth window with gauges and numeric displays off to one side.

"What's the range?" Jake asked. "Since we're in here, I'm assuming it's more than line of sight."

Mr. Williams smiled. "You've been looking at drones, have you?" He pressed a button on the controller and then moved the pair of sticks, generating a loud buzzing from outside the vehicle. The video feeds changed, one of which looked like a black and white view of the ground. The other two remained dark with vague shapes. "The antenna on the roof of the van should give me perhaps five miles of range."

The angle of view for the feeds shifted, showing more of the road and the trees on the other side in the black-and-white image. Mr. Williams then rotated the drone, panning over the van and catching the other direction of the empty road. Comfortable no vehicles approached, the drone quickly climbed above the height of the trees and turned east according to the gauges. The altimeter moved from seven hundred and fifteen feet when the drone was on the ground to almost eight hundred. In the distance, all three cameras displayed some faint lights. The trees and fields between them and the compound remained a dark and indistinct mass.

Kyrie watched intently as the drone approached the extensive building and fenced enclosure. Large lights illuminated the exterior, with black top and parking stretching around the two sides that she could see.

Mr. Williams brought the drone to a stop and hovered it a long distance from the building, where the primary color feed showed a wide-angle view of the entire building that they knew from the plans was two hundred feet wide and three thousand feet long. The long sides had multiple rolling doors and loading docks, but the details of the signs, smaller doors, and any windows remained fuzzy blurs on the screen. Two hundred feet from the building, near the back of the complex, a number of box trucks were parked against the fence.

He rotated a knob, and the second color view quickly zoomed in on the building. The vibration of the drone provided a hint of motion sickness, forcing Aki to look away. Kyrie fought the discomfort and watched as the details of the front of the building came into focus. A glass door closer to the left of the building than the center glowed with a light from inside. A large picture window next to the door appeared to have blinds covering it as the illumination there remained several orders of magnitude lower.

"Can't you get a better image?" Jake asked from where he crouched on the floor. "Is it windy or something?"

"Becca?" Mr. Williams asked.

Becca's voice became monotone. "As focal length increases, image stability decreases." She leaned closer and continued to speak to Jake, but used a more conversational tone. "It's dark, which means needing a lower shutter speed, which also makes for a worse image. Plus, Dad has it at max zoom to keep the sound of the drone as far from the target as possible."

"And it's windy," Mr. Williams added as his fingers continued to adjust the drone's position and move the telephoto camera back and forth to examine the tan-painted concrete block facade of the two-story part of the building. The upper-level windows remained dark with no indication of lights in the rooms. "The building is wide enough that there might be internal rooms with no windows."

"What does the gate look like?" Becca asked.

Her father rotated the drone slightly and pulled back on the zoom. The front gate came into view. A large wooden telephone pole just inside the fence line had an arm with a camera housing pointing at a keypad protected by three steel poles on the left side of the entrance. A light on a smaller pole near the keypad illuminated the area in front of the motorized chain-link gate.

"Great, a camera watching," Becca said. "We'd need to cut a hole in the fence along the sides, right?"

Her father nodded his head. "But there are likely other cameras, so it might not make any difference."

He moved the camera to examine the steel building behind the main offices. The advertisements online indicated the industrial spaces had twenty-five-foot ceilings with open girders. "I saw air conditioners and a satellite dish on the top of the main office roof, but it looks like most of the rest of the occupants aren't going to bother with cooling the spaces. There might be a way into the Durten part from the roof, but, if it was me, I'd have an alarm on the hatch."

Becca leaned closer to the monitor. "Can you fly over the roof and see?"

"In time," he replied. "First, I want to scout the edges. Look for dogs or people outside. Let's hope there are none and that these people don't bother with microphones on the building. I'd put some up and monitor for sounds of things like drones myself, but since it's an industrial complex, we can hope there's just normally too much noise."

Aki leaned against the desk, still avoiding looking too long at the shaky image. "I'd never think of using that for security."

Mr. Williams nodded his head as he stared at the changing video feeds. "That's why people hire me. Their blue teams install security controls; my red teams find holes." He flew around the building, keeping the drone several hundred feet away from the fence and over the trees. The telephoto lens covered eight businesses on the left side of the building and four on the right. Most of these locations had solid doors with externally mounted lights illuminating a sign and the entrance. A few had cameras that monitored the doors, but most did not.

He slowed the drone as they came upon another camera mounted on a wooden telephone pole at the fence line. He moved the drone back and forth, getting a view of most of the assembly despite remaining hundreds of feet from the complex.

"What am I not seeing?" Mr. Williams asked.

"People?" Michelle offered.

"Dogs?" Jack suggested.

"A way in," Becca said.

Kyrie shrugged, and Aki refused to watch the feed.

"What is it?" Becca finally asked.

"I don't see any power lines going to the camera housing. I don't see any data lines either. There is just an arm and a box on a wooden pole. If it was a metal pole, then sure, power would be inside, but a wooden pole needs conduit attached to the outside, and even though I can't see all the way around, I can tell from the profile that there's nothing on the interior side of the pole." He moved the drone toward the front of the fence line and focused on the camera at the gate.

"Wireless?" Jake asked.

"Mr. Williams hates wireless," Michelle quipped.

Becca's dad forced a laugh. "I do hate wireless. But a real security camera is going to send far too much data and use too much power to run off battery. Not to mention, I got a device in this van that can jam normal Wi-Fi radio frequencies, which would prevent a wireless camera from being able to send images." He nodded his head toward the screens. "Yeah, with the telephoto I've been able to look around all sides of that post; those cameras around the edge of the property are all fake boxes."

"So what does that mean?" Aki asked.

Becca's father rolled his shoulders and shook his head, but he kept his hands on the controls and his eyes on the monitor. "It's likely for show. Keeps the amateur criminals from messing with things, but avoids recording the professional criminals as they come and go. No one wants physical evidence that might put them at the scene of a crime with a timestamp."

"Then this might be doable?" Michelle asked.

Mr. Williams turned the drone away from the complex and back toward the darkness. Kyrie noted Becca's father shift his focus to the gauges showing altitude, speed, and coordinates. "I really don't like the idea of breaking into a place where we don't have a letter to hand to the cops to say it's all right. We'd end up doing real time if we're caught."

Kyrie shook her head. "I don't think they'd bother with the police."

Becca stood up and crossed her arms. "Stop lightening the mood like that."

Kyrie continued. "I can get us in. Cutting the fence should be fast. I can put any of the guards to sleep."

"We need them to not know we were there," Mr. Williams said. "If they see evidence someone broke in, they might look around. If they find a network tap, the gig's up."

Kyrie accepted the rebuke. "I can get over the fence and inside. My parents used sleeping guards as a trope in many of their games, and Michelle did it in our current campaign. Isn't that something that happens in the real world?"

Mr. Williams sighed. "It is."

"Then what I need to do is install your device, and you get remote access to search for user IDs and passwords." Kyrie looked at Becca. "That's what I've heard the two of you talking about."

"You can learn," Becca teased. "What you said is true."

"But," Mr. Williams challenged, "you need to know where to install it. Put it in the wrong place, and it's worthless. The network tap will only see data passing through it. You can't stick it between a PC browsing porn and the network and be of any use unless it's one that someone with decent credentials uses. You'd need to get me in with you." He froze. "Quiet, we've got a car coming." They all turned to the monitor that now showed lights strobing down the road as the vehicle continued behind the line of trees.

Kyrie moved a step to the front curtain and tugged the top closed to help reduce any light from escaping. She opened her mind to search for threats.

"Cop?" Jake asked.

Mr. Williams shook his head as the video image showed lights slowing down. He reversed the drone, but kept the cameras focused on them.

Kyrie pushed her senses further, trying to feel who might be in the car that slowed to a stop. "Damn," she swore, grabbed a sword, and pushed her way through the front curtain. Behind her, she heard the others' startled responses. "Bound," she replied as she threw open the driver's door and leaped out of the van. Her sneakers slipped on the tall grass as she sprinted toward the bright headlights behind them. The mental presence of the driver reacted to the emotions her friends unleashed in their fear.

Sleep! She screamed at the man. *You must sleep!* Energy ran through her body, which still had not fully recovered. *You are so tired,* she repeated as she forced her way into the man's mind, hoping her ability would affect a Bound as well as a human. If not, she needed to get within sword range.

The man's presence crashed into hers, and she stumbled from the mental impact, but she managed to keep her footing. She ignored the blinding light, using her powers to navigate to the door of the police car.

I will never submit, growled a furious presence in the man's head.

Kyrie pushed herself deeper into the man's mind. She felt like she had grabbed a rabid mountain lion with both hands as she fought to contain the dominant personality. *Silence,* she commanded using the dolunar language. While she had no frame of reference for how a dolunar mind felt, this being did not seem like the corvlians that Rodgers had controlled.

Never, came the sharp reply, but she sensed the personality had no motor control over the body it possessed. Some of that control appeared to fall to the subordinate presence that had fallen dormant.

Kyrie stopped at the open door with her sword raised. She continued to exert control over both personalities in the officer's body while examining the situation. The man had opened the door, his sidearm in his hand, and was about to step out of the vehicle when she repeated her command for him to sleep.

You can't control me! Our Warlord is my master!

Silence! she replied as she examined the two minds that had not fully integrated. The subordinate personality no longer felt whole, as if worms had eaten through its higher functions, leaving only what she might consider a zombie. The dolunar that occupied the rest of the mental presence seemed to inhabit the space that had been created. However, it also did not feel complete or even firmly fixed in the body.

Almost as if it were a bird stealing a nest, she decided.

I will destroy you! You will die! I don't know how you are free to act, but our Warlord will reward me for destroying a rogue traitor!

Kyrie kept her mental grasp on the dolunar. *Kind of like teeth around your neck,* she told it. A chill ran through her. *Awan held me like this when he ripped me from my body. But the dolunar is not integrated into the body, merely occupying it.*

Her eyes focused on the real world around her. She knew she had complete control, and so she reached into the vehicle, turned off the headlights, and then turned off the vehicle. With the darkness of the night returning, she stepped back and examined the two personalities. The hostile dolunar continued to snarl and curse at her, but he could not do anything. The subordinate man, once called Edward, seemed to lack the ability to express conscious thoughts, but retained memories of his past and recent events.

Kyrie lowered her sword as an image of a young woman tearfully demanding to know what was wrong with him forced its way into her head. She pushed back against the confusion the memory carried, knowing she could not allow it to overwhelm her.

Weak. Pathetic. You're corvlian, not dolunar, the creature that took over the man taunted.

Kyrie allowed more power to flow through her. Her will expressed more pressure, figuratively crushing the dolunar's essence. It screeched in her head as a fragment of what might be its soul broke off and dispersed into nothing, but the creature still lived.

"Are you okay?" Mr. Williams asked as he came up from behind her.

She spun around, her sword raised. With her mind connected to the officer's, she had not sensed Mr. Williams' approach. She lowered the weapon after a moment. "I'm dealing with a Bound," she intoned.

"Are the cameras running?"

A recent memory from Edward flowed into her mind, and Kyrie gasped from the sudden and unwanted intrusion into her own thoughts. After a moment, she realized what remained of the human had mechanically answered the question. "No," Kyrie responded to Mr. Williams. "The car's dashcam didn't automatically activate because the emergency lights were not turned on. And Gestr," she added, sensing the dolunar thrash even more at the mention of his name, "does not like turning on his bodycam."

Mr. Williams let out a long breath. "We still have to get away without him chasing us." He looked at the van and then back toward her. "What is one of the Bound doing here? Was he looking for us?"

Gestr continued to curse, and Kyrie tightened her grip on the dolunar's soul as a result, changing its mental bombardment into cries of anguish. At the same time, the human dumped multiple memories into her head, again ending with the young woman screaming, 'What is wrong with you!' and the man not able to reply.

Kyrie took a deep breath to sort through the chaos. *You have this,* she told herself. *Always be strong. Never give in.* The noise slowly abated, and she spoke to Mr. Williams. "I think he's just assigned to watch over the facility. To keep other cops from investigating anything going on." She stepped away from the open door. "He has a code to get through the gate. There is normally only one human guard watching at night."

She turned her attention to the human mind. "Have you seen the computers?"

Stop! Gestr screamed at her. *Nalitran will destroy you. You are a traitor. A parasite!*

Kyrie saw the memories of the first-floor conference room that led to a storage room behind the offices with large metal shelves. She saw the keypad and the ten-digit code that caused a hydraulic arm concealed in the wall to shift one set of shelves to the side, revealing stairs leading to the basement.

Gestr, you're our prey. You will not escape. Kyrie felt the creature's primal terror.

I don't want to die, it cried. *My tugmor was split. I can never be reborn!*

How many corvlians have you killed before being brought here? How many humans have you killed?

I will destroy you as my last act! Gestr snarled.

Kyrie felt the dolunar dump raw energy at her, and she fell to her knees. The heat from the power burned her. She pushed as much of the energy into the ground as she could and quickly regained control over the Bound. Relying upon instinct, she shredded the soul of the being occupying the body of the man who had once been known as Edward. The dolunar tried to fight back, but Kyrie already had the dominant position, and her attack took only moments.

"What's happening?" Mr. Williams demanded from three feet away, not daring to get any closer.

Kyrie allowed the shredded remnants of the dolunar's soul to disperse into the surroundings. The human body that remained merely existed, the mind no longer capable of conscious thoughts. She swallowed. "The Bound has been removed."

Mr. Williams hesitated for a moment. "Will the person recover? Will he remember anything?"

Kyrie shook her sweaty head. She could already feel the body dying and pulled away, closing off her mind. A moment later, the man started to convulse, shaking in the seat and sliding down. The sound of the drone's propellers increased as someone flew it closer to them. His body stopped moving just after the drone landed roughly on the road next to the van.

Mr. Williams stepped forward and around Kyrie. He reached in with his gloved hand and used the man's right fingers to turn the vehicle back on. Then, he used the man's left hand to turn back on the lights, ensuring he smeared any fingerprints that Kyrie might have left behind. Finally, he put the sidearm back in the officer's holster. "We want to leave it as he left it. When some other cops come by and find it, hopefully they'll think he had a heart attack and died trying to get out of the vehicle."

Kyrie nodded her head as she felt the last of the broken consciousness of the man fade away. *There was nothing you could do to save him,* she reminded herself. *Could someone break us apart as easily?* No answer came to her.

Mr. Williams moved. "Get the drone. Let's get out of here."

Chapter 27

Kyrie sat on the floor in the back of the van with Michelle next to her. They had parked in a busy mall parking lot. Jake and Aki had walked over to bring back several bags of Taco Bell food, which provided a three-AM snack.

"So you were able to break away the being that had taken over the human," Mr. Williams said. "Stopping it from using its powers and, if the human had not been so damaged, you might have freed him."

Kyrie nodded her head. "I'm speculating about the last part. This wasn't the first Bound I've communicated with telepathically, but it was the first one that I think was a dolunar. The others were under far stricter controls, and even their other minds seemed fractured because of Nalitran or people using their binding stones. But, like I said, there wasn't much left of Edward. However, a sample size of one is not conclusive."

"But," Aki said, "if you can free people from this, perhaps you might save some of them. Like you said, just because one of them is damaged doesn't mean others will be."

"We left a dead cop along the road," Becca said. "That's not good."

Mr. Williams put down the soda in his hand. "I'm more worried about Nalitran's people realizing it was us out here."

"He didn't know anything about me, or any of us. At least nothing that showed up in his memories. He didn't seem to have control over what I saw." Kyrie unwrapped another taco and started eating it while the others continued to talk. The use of her powers always made her hungry.

"Are we still going to try to break in?" Michelle finally asked, bringing the conversation back to the original topic. "Kyrie learned the access code and the secret entrance. That should make for a much easier dungeon crawl."

Mr. William sighed. "I'm not sure. It's really risky, given all the attention on us. I don't know how much longer we can stay in this van."

Kyrie felt him looking at her as if he wanted someone to provide a clear direction.

He continued. "I know we're fighting time, and I hear your arguments. If they purge data and move the operations, we'd have to start again and might not be able to recover the evidence we need. But, we might eventually get someone to fall for a phishing campaign, even if they move things." He ran a hand over his growing head of hair. "But again, we have no way of knowing when that will happen, and we can't be too aggressive. They seem to have decent security policies, and I'm not a nation-state that can order up a zero-day RCE. Physical access might be the only option."

Kyrie finished her taco and wiped her mouth with the back of her hand. "I should be able to do it," she repeated. "The cop remembered there being only a single night guard. You just need me to plug your device into a switch. The problem is we need to do it quickly before they change things."

Becca crossed her arms. "Like find out the cop is dead and remove his access?"

"Exactly," Kyrie said.

"Do you even know what a switch is?" Becca challenged.

Kyrie pointed to a box mounted under the narrow desk behind Becca.

"That's a small one. You need to find a trunk line that has important traffic." Becca shook her head. "Anyone of you know what a network closet looks like?"

Her father eventually broke the silence that had fallen. "Becca's not wrong. Each port of a switch only carries traffic to that one device. We need to get user IDs and passwords quickly, which means we need to insert the network tap between active devices. Something like a wireless access point and a switch or a trunk line between two switches."

Kyrie got up from the floor. "Then tell me what to look for."

Becca stared her down. "Not even you can learn that fast. Someone else will need to go with you."

Mr. Williams tossed the empty soda can into the garbage bag sitting next to his seat. "I f'ing hate this, but if we do this, it likely has to be tomorrow night, and I'll have to accompany you."

"Except you can't," Becca snapped. "I don't know enough about using the tap to see if there is unencrypted traffic or if we broke something that prevents you from being able to get access. That means I need to go."

"What?" Kyrie and Mr. Williams said at the same time.

"There is no way I'm letting you go, Becca." Her father shook his head vehemently. "It's not happening."

"I could go," Michelle offered.

"Do you even know the difference between a switch and a hub?" Becca demanded of Michelle. She turned back to her father. "You know I'm the only one who can do it."

"But it won't be safe."

"Is any of this safe?" Becca demanded. "I don't want to go, but you know it's the only way."

Kyrie crossed her arms. "I don't want to risk something happening to any of you. Let's do it now before anyone realizes the Bound is dead. I can figure it out if you tell me what to do."

Mr. Williams shook his head. "I need to activate the SIM card in the cellular modem on the tap. I'm not sending any of you in without a solid line of communication, which means picking up at least one burner phone. We need to get you masks and dark clothing." He grabbed a taco for himself and angrily unwrapped the food. "We don't even know how shielded the basement is. If a cell signal can't get out, then the tap will be useless. It doesn't have an IP address; it just copies traffic. So, we need something outside of their network to get the credentials we need out. If we can't access the server room or a network closet, then you have to find an access point that gets used as well as an outlet to supply power to the PI and modem."

"I can do it, Dad," Becca said.

Kyrie felt terror and pride from him as he angrily bit into the taco. She held back from easing his emotions, not wanting to risk affecting his decisions.

"We need to hope we can get back into the campground and get some sleep. Tomorrow afternoon we do some shopping, and tomorrow night we try this. If it doesn't work, we abort, and I continue working with Hurlington's data to see if there is enough proof there for the cops to do anything."

Chapter 28

Kyrie reached out with her mind yet again to confirm their surroundings. Becca had survived the half-mile trek from the van. Despite the overcast night, moving through an open field, and then a dense hundred feet of trees, neither of them had sustained any injuries.

"You weren't supposed to let me talk my dad into helping with this," Becca whispered as she rubbed her face under the ski mask. "They'll lock me up for life." She frowned. "Or more likely shoot me on sight. Black girl criminals don't live long."

Kyrie smiled, though the ski mask hid her expression. Despite Becca's complaint, she sensed excitement from her friend. "You've gone up at least one level. You'll make a good thief."

"Girls, focus," Mr. Williams said through the pair of Bluetooth earbuds they shared between the two of them. The open call on the prepaid phone Mr. Williams had picked up earlier in the afternoon remained a nonnegotiable requirement of Becca's involvement.

Kyrie moved toward the ten-foot-tall gate and the keypad that stood a dozen feet away from it on the left side of the pavement. She did not glance up at the camera on the wooden pole, just in case Mr. Williams had somehow missed a way for power to feed the device. A single light on a shorter pole illuminated the three reinforced pylons that protected the keypad from being hit by a vehicle. The harsh yellow of the light washed out the color of the faded paint on the keypad and the stains on the ground, but it did not mask the slight taste of the oil in the air.

"We are entering the code," Kyrie reported to those in the van. They had seen the news report of the cop who was believed to have died from natural causes, and hoped his six-digit code remained active in the system. If not, Kyrie planned to help Becca climb the chain-link gate.

"Well?" Becca asked, her hands moving up and down the strap of the tool bag she carried.

Five seconds later, the gate rattled and shifted to the right as an electric motor kicked into action. They moved through the opening as soon as enough space cleared for them to pass. "We're through the gate," Becca added as commentary, the two of them rushing toward the compound with Kyrie in the lead as the slow-moving obstacle continued to open.

Kyrie led them toward the corner of the building along an elliptical path that avoided directly approaching the glass front door. Becca kept pace right behind Kyrie. "What do you think the chances are that the guard is asleep?"

"Not high enough for my taste, Becca," her father said over the call. "Be careful."

You can do this, Kyrie reminded herself, conscious of the risk Becca took in coming with her. "Stay behind me."

At thirty feet from the building, she felt the diminished presence of one person deeper in the building. Even with the deceased cop's memories of the interior, she could not fix the precise location of the guard in her mind. *At least you know he's not at the security desk,* she thought. At fifteen feet, she decided the person must be patrolling the back offices on the left side of the building.

Kyrie adjusted her path and headed directly for the door. A quick visual inspection confirmed the lobby was empty. "I believe the guard is walking a security check or was using the better toilets," she said to Becca and those listening on the call. *And the guard feels like a woman,* Kyrie realized, as she felt the person moving.

Kyrie entered the same six-digit security code, and the door clicked as the magnetic lock released. She pulled the door open and focused on the mind of the guard, trying to push her awareness through the walls. "We are inside," Kyrie said softly. "I sense no one else."

Kyrie moved forward into the long lobby and paused in front of the security counter. Becca held the door, allowing it to close quietly behind them. Her original excitement had shifted to fear, and Kyrie gave her friend a thumbs up. Becca only nodded her head and then adjusted the bag that contained the network tap with a Raspberry Pi, patch cables, and a multitude of tools.

Kyrie took in the lobby. The memories she picked up from Edward remained incomplete, having only given her a vague sense of where she needed to go to access the server room that had been on her mind. Below her feet, the floor had dense industrial carpeting with a random pattern of organic shapes in various blue tones. Beige paint covered the walls, with multiple seats under the window. Half a dozen fake trees decorated the corners of the room with the company's name spelled out in large metal letters attached to the wall behind the counter. The far right wall had a single door with a small sign that indicated it led to a bathroom. Kyrie know the two additional doors, one on either side of the metal letters and behind the security desk, led to offices.

"Where to?" Becca asked. "That one looks like a bathroom." She used her head to motion to the door on the far right. "The other two appear to need badges."

Kyrie felt confident the door on her left included stairs to the second floor. The one on the right had the copier room and another hallway that led to the large conference room with access to the warehouse space behind all the offices.

Kyrie lifted a hand. "Stay here. The guard's coming from the left, and she'll be here momentarily." Kyrie rushed around the long counter and stood next to the door while Becca knelt down to use the security counter as cover.

Energy flowed into Kyrie as she readied herself to deal with the guard. While she could feel the woman and sense general moods, she could not read the woman's thoughts through the heavy door. The moment the door opened, the physical obstacle disappeared, and she slammed her consciousness into the woman's mind. The brutality of her mental attack stunned the guard, and a moment later, Kyrie felt the woman's defenses fall as her nervous system dumped hormones into her blood in response to the terror.

You are tired, Kyrie demanded of the woman. *Very tired,* she repeated, projecting her own exhaustion brought on from lack of sleep. Kyrie felt the security guard fight to stay awake, knowing her survival depended on it. *I'm a friend. There's nothing wrong. Just sleep. You're in your bed. Your dog is sleeping next to you. Sleep!* Kyrie commanded. The woman's instinct tried to resist and to fight the unknown. *There is nothing wrong. Sleep.*

Kyrie withdrew from the guard's mind and she immediately reached out to catch the woman as the guard collapsed to the floor, preventing the unconscious woman from hitting her head. The older woman wore a dark blue uniform and had a pistol on her hip and a photo badge on a retractable cord.

"Damn, that was fast," Becca said, slowly standing up. "Good thing the sleep spell doesn't have a saving throw. And her HP was low enough."

Michelle chuckled over the call. "I knew our mage would kick ass."

"Focus, girls," Mr. Williams demanded. "How long will she be out? Tying her up will reveal we were here. The goal is no one knows."

Kyrie shrugged. "I'd need to run experiments to know the impact. But I don't think any of you would appreciate me doing that to random people."

"Definitely not," Aki's faint voice filled the ear bud, hinting at her being a distance from the mic.

Kyrie smiled as she probed the woman's state. *She feels like she's in a deep sleep. You did well.* Kyrie pulled in more energy and added additional commands to the guard. *Sleep long and hard. You do not want to wake until the sun rises.* She looked at the woman's mental presence again as she crouched down. "Hopefully until morning," Kyrie told the others as she removed the badge from the woman's belt followed by the pistol from her holster.

"Do we need that?" Becca asked. She lifted the bulky shock glove on her right hand. "Nonlethal, remember."

Kyrie did not want to argue the point. She only wore thin leather gardening gloves to conceal her fingerprints as Jake only got three of the shock gloves working and Kyrie wanted the others to have them.

For a stronger defense, Kyrie carried her dagger and the pouch of stones in case they needed to deal with someone at range. "If the guard wakes up, I don't want her to have it. I'll put it back on our way out, and hopefully she will not notice." Becca nodded her head in understanding, but Kyrie knew her friend did not like the pistol.

Kyrie ignored Becca's fear in favor of her own sense of practicality. *If you need it, you don't want it to be on the woman.* She checked the safety and then slid the weapon into the back of her pants to keep her hands free.

"Let's go," Kyrie said as she used the ID badge to unlock the door on the right of the letters.

The door opened to reveal a long hallway with the same carpeting, but the beige walls had several paintings showing cityscapes hanging on both sides. The far end had a cream-colored ceramic sculpture that stood five feet tall and did not depict any specific object, but looked like several thick undulating blades of grass.

"Ignore the offices on the left," Kyrie said as she walked halfway down the hallway to a branching passage on the right. "We want the conference room down there." She turned into the second hallway and headed directly toward the door at the end. The guard's badge unlocked the door, and Kyrie stepped inside.

The lights in the conference room came on automatically, causing both of them to jump slightly. An oval table consumed the middle of the room with a dozen office chairs spread around the heavy wooden object. More paintings covered the walls, but left space for a large whiteboard on the other side of the table. The remnants of a discussion involving money covered the surface.

Kyrie noted the cabinets, sink, and coffee maker on the far-left wall. In the corner next to the cabinet was another door with a keycard reader. Kyrie moved around the table toward the door.

"Is this what corporate America looks like?" Becca asked as she followed Kyrie. "Sad carpets, worn chairs, and shitty artwork?"

"I can't see what you're seeing," Becca's father answered, "but if you're depressed already, then yes, that's living in a corporate office."

"Great, I can't wait to be an adult."

Kyrie smiled at Becca's joke, knowing her friend contained her fear with humor. She flashed the guard's ID and pulled open the door after it unlocked. The dark room on the other side of the door smelled of chlorine and oil. She stepped inside, found the light switch, and flipped five switches to turn on the industrial lights, revealing a large room with a twenty-five-foot ceiling supported by trusses covered in a white spray material.

The forty-five-foot-wide warehouse extended almost two hundred feet to her left and only ten to her right. Three rows of open industrial shelving, each five feet wide and twenty feet high, with four levels, filled most of the warehouse. The shelves closest to the door were bolted to the wall and went one hundred and fifty feet of the way toward a rolling door at the far left end. The middle shelves, separated from the others with a fifteen-foot-wide aisle, stood freely and covered the same length of flooring as the first shelves. The far shelves extended only twenty feet along the steel wall. Further down that wall was a scattering of machinery and tools, including a forklift.

Goods covered fifty percent of the first two sets of shelving, with many open sections. The heavy crossbeams and thick wire racks supported boxes, pallets of flooring, spools of industrial wire, fifty-gallon drums, metal paint cans, plastic bottles, and various loose construction materials. However, gaps between items could allow her to easily climb through the bottom section of the center shelves at several locations.

"Almost like IKEA," Becca said, stepping around Kyrie. She turned back to the shelves next to the door. "That's a lot of bleach. Guessing they have to erase a lot of blood stains." Becca stopped moving. "So, where's the entrance to the dragon's lair?"

"The far wall." Kyrie turned around and typed the ten-digit code into the keypad next to the door to the conference room. "Let's hope this code also works," she said as she pressed the last number. Immediately, the sound of a motor running filled the room as the shelving unit against the far wall moved eight feet to the left into the open space between the short shelves and the machinery.

"You be the spy," Becca quipped. "Just don't get the idea that I'm some Bond chick."

Jake let out a small laugh over the phone.

Kyrie narrowed her eyes. "What?"

Becca shook her head. "We should get moving."

Kyrie chalked the comment up to another set of references she might never understand and headed directly for the stairs the shelves had concealed. They went down into the floor and turned sharply to the left at the bottom.

The lower level of the complex, with five feet of concrete above it, had better carpeting and a more attractive blue color on the walls than the main offices above. The left-hand wall had six doors, each with its own keypad. Four doors and keypads were sunk into the right-hand wall. The paintings between the doors varied, but many had nautical themes with old sailing ships. Even the ceiling lighting that illuminated the space appeared less harsh.

"Dad, can you still hear us?" Becca asked.

Mr. Williams responded immediately. "You broke up a little, but yes, the call's not dropped. Hopefully, that means the cell signal on the tap will allow us to ex-filtrate the data. We'll have to see if they shielded the server room more than where you are. If so, you might have to fall back to putting the tap between an access point and whatever switch it is connected to. We can hope that will still capture enough traffic so we can get passwords and a partial map of servers. What are the ceilings made of?"

"Drop ceilings," Becca replied. "But we might find a network closet in one of the rooms." She turned to Kyrie as they crept down the hallway. "Do you know which one is the server room?"

Kyrie frowned. "I know the last one on the left is another larger conference room. The cop had been there before. He'd not been in any of the other rooms." She glanced at the first pair of doors on the right. "These look like bathrooms." She pursed her lips and closed her eyes, using her mind to feel her way through the surrounding walls. The empty spaces did not immediately register as having specific purposes to her. "I feel a lot of energy coming from behind the next door on the right."

"Like magic energy?" Becca questioned.

"Like electrical energy."

"That's probably it then," Becca said and moved to the door. The keypad on the wall looked like all the others. "Will the code work?"

Kyrie shrugged and entered the ten-digit code she learned from the Gestr. The back light behind the keys flashed red, and the door did not open. "Plan B," she said as she carefully used her mind to feel around the other side of the door to visualize the handle. She crafted a small gravitational field that pulled down on the door lever. Without a visual confirmation and no direct feedback, she continued to gradually increase the power of her field.

The handle on this side of the door moved slightly, but the door did not open. She stopped the flow of energy, fearing she might rip the handle off the door.

"Plan C." She closed her eyes as she searched for potential weak spots. *Feels like hollow walls with insulation,* she told herself. *You can knock a hole in that easily enough.* The door itself seemed solid with a metal door frame and a thick locking mechanism. She ran her gloved hands over the surface of the wall.

"Remember, we don't want anyone to know we were here," Becca said.

"Server rooms typically have a button on the inside for a door release," Mr. Williams said. "Normally, right next to the door. That might unlock it. People don't like to futz around with codes and badges if the gaseous fire suppression gets triggered."

Kyrie closed her eyes again and carefully felt her way around the other side of the wall. With additional focus, she felt the potential energy of wires standing out from the other wall filler. Using those clues to direct her search, she thought she might have identified something that felt like a button. *You don't have forever to do this,* she reminded herself just before she pressed the button.

Something clicked, and Becca immediately reached out and pulled down on the handle, releasing the latch and pushing open the door. "Got it!"

Noise greeted them as the roar of countless high-speed fans moved air through the servers. Flashing LEDs provided enough illumination to see five racks of servers standing in the middle of the room with large bundles of cables running from tracks on the ceiling into the cabinets.

Kyrie stepped into the room. Cold air blew down on her from the vents in the ceiling. She had not drawn a lot of power through herself yet, but the air-conditioning felt wonderful on her face. Becca shivered in the draft, and Kyrie wondered about anyone who might have to spend time at the desks with computer terminals that lined the walls. Both the noise and the temperature would become uncomfortable over time.

"The network runs are all dropping over there," Becca said, pointing to the center rack. "Dad, be glad these aren't like those pictures of cable hell you like to show me."

"Good," he responded. "Hopefully, someone labeled the runs as well. You need to have power for the pi. There should be power outlets you can plug into on the back of the racks. Though you'll need to conceal the tap and pi. I hate to say it, but if things were a mess, it would actually be easier to hide it."

Kyrie stood by the door. She opened her mind to search for threats as Becca examined all the devices with flashing LEDs and blue cables. *If you had the time, you could learn all that as well.* She let out the breath she held. *But that's why you have friends, so you don't need to know everything.*

Becca cursed. "Well, they're labeled, but with numbers and not words. This will take a moment." She looked over her shoulder. "Kyrie, can you look around and see if they have any medium-length patch cables? Three feet long or so. We don't have anything that matches the color of their cables."

Kyrie pushed off the wall and moved to the desks and storage cabinets against the walls. She pulled open a door to see a bunch of rectangular devices stacked in two piles with a label of 'bad drives' scribbled on some tape. Another stack of similar devices still in bags sat on another shelf.

"Shit. We have trouble; you need to get out now!" The panic in Mr. Williams' voice came through clearly on the phone.

"How many people is that?" Michelle asked. "I can't get a count."

"There are at least a dozen people who just ran out of a business further down the complex. They're sprinting toward the front of the complex. You must have somehow tripped an alarm."

"I've not installed the tap," Becca cried.

"Run!" Michelle and Aki cried. "Please get out of there!"

"It's too late; they are nearing the front of the building!" Mr. William demanded. "Hide. We'll try and come for you."

"How?" Jake asked. "We don't have weapons."

Mr. Williams swore. "Hide; we'll get to you! Jake, take the drone."

Damn it! Kyrie nodded her head to Becca. "Stay in here. I'll contain them in the warehouse and fall back here if needed." She pulled the pistol from her pants, ran to the door, pressed the button, and exited the server room into the hallway.

Chapter 29

Jason Williams threw aside the curtains and scurried to the driver's seat. He pressed the start button, but nothing happened. "Damn it! Damn it!" He looked around for the keys and then shouted over his shoulder. "Key fob's by the laptop!"

Outside light shone in his side mirrors. A moment later, the bright white lights were joined by red and blue flashing lights. "Motherfucker, not now!"

"Jake's struggling with the drone," Michelle said, bringing the key fob forward. "Shit."

"What's going on, Dad?" Becca's voice came over the speakers.

"Cops," Michelle cursed, then turned back to the computer.

"Bound?" was Becca's reply.

"Everyone quiet," Jason said and pulled the curtain closed. "Jake, just hover the drone; don't bring it closer. I'll try to talk our way out. God, please not a Bound."

Aki shook her head. "If it's a Bound, they'll kill us or use us against Kyrie."

Jason instinctively reached for the seat belt, then decided not to bother fastening it. *The van wasn't even running, so didn't break that law. Damn it, I need to get to Becca.* He glanced at the mirrors, but the blinding light kept him from seeing anything. *Come on. What's taking so long?*

He heard some quiet movement in the back and hoped the others would settle down and not draw attention. *If it's a Bound, we're dead.*

He clenched his fists and forced his eyes shut. *Not my Becca. Please, not my Becca.*

Nearly a minute later he caught movement outside the driver's side and a man tapped on his window with a long flashlight. Jason hit the button to lower the window.

"What are you doing out here in the middle of the night?" The officer asked. Light reflected off the side mirror made it hard for Jason to get a good look at the man's features.

"I had just stopped for a break. I didn't think it would be a problem. But I can move along if it is."

"Let me see your license and registration," the officer demanded coldly, his flashlight coming on and further blinding Jason.

Becca's father looked away from the light. "Sure, I've got it in the glove box."

"What's in the back of the van?" The office asked, his flashlight moving to the curtain. "I saw lights coming through that just a moment ago?"

Jason turned back to face the office. "Just tools and a speaker set that has RGB."

"Why don't you get out of the van?"

He hesitated. "Why? I've not done anything."

The officer squared his feet. "Get out of the van."

Jason put both of his hands in the air. "I'm not resisting, just asking questions."

"Out of the van!"

Mr. Williams nodded his head. "Just going to reach down and open the door with my left hand, okay?"

"Get out of the van."

Jason reached down slowly, unlatched the door, and gradually pushed it open. "I'm getting out." The officer backed up. The flashlight still held high so he could not see if the cop had his sidearm drawn or not. "I was just taking a break, not doing anything wrong."

"A cop died a mile from here last night, and you've got what looks like a fake temporary tag. I'll decide if you're doing anything wrong."

"I bought the van a week ago from a used lot outside Kansas City. The dealer put it on there. Perhaps it's just not in the system yet."

The officer laughed. "Is that the lame story you're going with? Turn around and put your hands against the van."

They both heard a click near the rear of the van and some sounds of movement over the engine of the police car.

"Who's in the van? Don't fuck with me."

Jason's mind raced. *I got to get to Becca, but can't do that locked up. Can't do it with a bullet in my back either. Doesn't seem like a Bound.* He tried to decide what to tell the officer regarding the others. The man would find that out soon enough.

"Identify yourself!" The officer shouted, fear and uncertainty in his voice.

"Just a couple friends of my daughter," he said. "They ain't a threat."

Jason felt the officer move up behind him and then grab his arm, twisting it behind his back. The first half of the cuffs slammed against his wrist, and he winced as the manacle closed too tightly. "Hey, I've been cooperating." He allowed his left arm to be pulled down and cuffed as well.

"Stay here," the officer demanded as he moved toward the back of the van. The man carefully peeked around the corner of the vehicle and then screamed in pain, collapsing to the ground in convulsions. The electrical clicking of the stun glove was audible.

Jason saw an arm reaching out from under the van behind the rear wheel. He moved in the officer's direction as the back door flew open and Michelle jumped out. Aki released her grip on the man's leg, and the officer began to move.

"Again!" Jason yelled, fearing one of the girls would get shot. Aki's hand grabbed his leg again, and the officer resumed the convulsions. "Get his weapons, radio, and find the cuff keys to get me out of these things!"

Aki released her grip on the trigger, and the man moaned on the ground. Michelle pulled his weapons free and tossed them to the side. She pulled off her right glove to start searching for his keys.

"No, get some plastic gloves before touching anything," Jason said as he moved to stand between the officer and the weapons. "Stay there to shock him again if he moves too much," he told Aki.

Michelle moved to get back in the van, but Jake jumped out as he pulled on some nitrile gloves. "I'll find his keys," he said as he quickly searched the cop's belt and pockets. A moment later, Jake held up the small handcuff keys.

"Quick, get these damn things off me. The asshole put them so tight they're cutting off the circulation in my hands." Once free of the cuffs, Jason motioned Michelle toward the van. "I need some glov—" He took the pair she held out to him. "Smart." He looked around at the three of them. "No names."

Jason pulled on the black gloves as he crouched down. He removed the man's radio, pepper spray, three spare magazines, and a knife. "No bodycam?"

The man rolled his head slightly. "You've just assaulted an officer. You'll rot in prison if we don't hang you first." He tried to sit up, and Aki shocked him again for five seconds, leaving the cop incoherent.

Jason stood up. "Check for other things in his pockets or on his legs," he told Jake. "Come out from under the van," he ordered Aki and then turned to Michelle. "You shock him if he moves."

Jason then ran to the cruiser, climbed into the driver's seat, turned off the flashing lights, and stopped the dashcam. He pulled the memory card from the camera and rushed back to the officer.

Jake looked up from where he knelt. The officer started to regain his senses again. "I found a knife and phone in his pockets, as well as some coins."

"You are all dead," the cop mumbled.

Jason took a deep breath. *We can't kill him.* "Shock him again," he told Michelle. She looked uncomfortable, then after a long hesitation, she bent down and shocked the man's other leg.

Jason rolled the man onto his chest and pulled his hands behind his back. "Cuffs," he demanded from Jake, and then put them tightly around the man's wrists. "We need to get my daughter. We can't take him with us. Let's lock him up in the back of his vehicle."

"He's seen all our faces," Aki said. "He'll send people after us."

Jason nodded his head. "Well aware. But we're not the bad guys. We're trying to stop the bad guys. Perhaps our friend can fix his memory." He motioned to the others to move closer. "He's going to be heavy and hard to move. I'll need all of your help."

The four of them lifted the cop from the ground and brought him around to the back of the patrol car. They opened the rear door and manhandled him into the vehicle, leaving him face down in the footwell.

"You won't get away with it." The officer's voice lacked any strength.

"We're not the bad guys. You should have left us alone." Jason said. He went to the trunk and opened it to look inside. Multiple boxes and tools filled the space. He found a pack of zip-ties and pulled out two of the thick restraints, moved back to the officer, and secured his ankles together to make it harder for him to maneuver in the hard plastic cage of the backseats. He slammed the door shut, hoping they secured the man long enough that they had enough time to rescue Becca and Kyrie before escaping. *Damn, we'll definitely need a new vehicle now.*

Jason looked at the Taser, pepper spray, pistol, and magazines still on the ground. *If we need to fight to get them out.* He moved to the weapons and picked them up. To Jake he said, "Toss the rest of his things in the front seat and turn off the vehicle and lights. We've lost too much time already."

Chapter 30

Kyrie heard the single earbud generate static, chirp, then go silent as she raced down the hallway. She reached under her ski mask , pulled the device from her ear, and put it into her pocket as she tried to open her mind further. However, too much concrete above her prevented her from sensing those approaching. She turned the corner at the end of the hall and ran up the stairs. As she neared the top of the opening, her mind registered multiple people. *Damn it, Mother, we let you trap us. We should have known better. Stupid.* Her heart raced as she tried to determine where she had gone wrong. *Focus!*

She shook her head and turned to the pistol in her hand. It looked similar to what Jake's father had used, so she expected nine shots. *You should have counted when you had a chance.*

She rushed to the center shelving and crouched down behind a four-foot-tall rack with various steel bars and pipes. *You can't take on fourteen Bound at one time all by yourself.* She growled at herself. *Shut up. We defend our friends. We won't be taken.*

She focused on the mass of men and women who had entered the conference room, and who would soon enter the warehouse. The pausing of their movement indicated they likely sensed her as well. Kyrie looked around for other options. The far wall with the rolling door stood out. *Can you get the door open and get Becca up here in time?* She knew that would not work; the Bound would easily overcome the two of them trying to flee.

The shorter steel bars and angle iron in front of her could work as projectiles. She did not relish the thought of how much energy she would need to put into turning those into weapons. However, she slid a dozen pieces of steel bar and angle stock out of the rack. She placed the various pieces of two-and-three-foot-long bars on the partially open shelf above the rack, pointing the makeshift projectiles at the door.

Her attention then moved to the dozen gallon size metal cans of acetone next to where she put the steel stock. *Flammable,* stood out first. *Don't mix that with bleach, right?* The conversations with Michelle and Becca came back to her, though she did not recall what that combination made. *Mix nothing with bleach.*

Kyrie looked at the shelves next to the door; the chlorine she smelled when she first entered the warehouse came from a dozen plastic bottles of bleach and other cleaners stacked in neat order. She stood up and grabbed three cans of acetone, used her mind to slice off the top with a quick burst of gravity, and then levitated the cans across the room and placed them next to the door. *Hopefully, they won't feel the motion. You should have learned how sensitive Bound really are. Stop, we need to focus!*

Not daring to move from her position in case it sparked the Bound to act, she pulled in more energy and carefully used gravitational fields to transport three bottles of bleach from the far shelves to land next to the acetone, ripping the tops off the bottles along the way.

She rubbed the mask, her forehead damp and itchy from sweat. The energy draw, combined with her racing heart, left her feeling overheated already.

What were those chemicals supposed to make? You should remember these things. She took a deep breath and hoped that whatever toxin she intended to create would work quickly. *You should also take control of some of the Bound and force them to fight for you.* She almost chuckled at her optimism. *One Bound at a time might be doable, but trying to take control of multiple seems a bit of wishful thinking, unless you find their stones.*

She crouched down again behind the rack of metal and waited. An agonizing amount of time later, the door opened slowly, and Kyrie trained the pistol into the dark opening, but she held her fire. She had seen a Bound deflect a bullet before and had fewer shots than targets. *The weapon would be for close range only.*

"We are not here to harm you," came a male voice from within the conference room. "Surrender, and we will take you to safety. As well as your friends."

Surrender is not a friendly term. She built gravitational fields around all six containers of chemicals. She launched everything through the open door, sending it up into the air, while at the same time, she pulled more power through her to generate a vortex of rotating wind to mix the chemicals before they splashed onto the people hiding in the room. Her head throbbed from the concentration, but she heard the reward of people screaming in the conference room.

Kyrie shifted her energy, forgoing the vortex in exchange for a gravitational field just on this side of the door to hold it closed. The twenty-five foot distance to the door produced a strain on her mind and body, but she continued to fight several fields challenging her force.

How long will it take for the chemicals to react? She used the back of her glove to wipe away sweat from her forehead. She could sense the growing emotions of those trapped in the room, and their desperation increased the pull on the door. A moment later, their fields overwhelmed hers, and the reinforced door ripped completely away from the wall and flew into the conference room.

Kyrie pulled a handful of river stones from her pouch and held them in her left hand, hoping she could wear out the bound with those projectiles before she resorted to the pistol or the steel bars.

Three people rushed from the room—two men in jeans and t-shirts along with a green-haired woman. All three of them coughed repeatedly as they moved forward. Kyrie, still flush with energy, launched four stones at one of the men through the six-inch gap between the second level of shelves and the rack of steel she hid behind. The first three stones shattered inches from him as he came to a sudden stop, the debris flying back toward Kyrie. The fourth stone struck him in the chest, and he grunted from the impact, and Kyrie saw blood.

She launched the three remaining stones from her left hand at the second man as she brought her left hand up to fire the pistol. She squeezed off one shot, aiming for the first man's head. The bullet struck him through the eye, and he tumbled to the floor just ahead of the other two, bringing them all to a stop.

The second man, who had blocked all three stones, dove to Kyrie's left, moving toward the open space at the end of the center shelves so he could move around them.

"Alive!" a woman shouted between coughs from within the room.

Kyrie grabbed four more stones and launched them at the green-haired woman. All four of the stones shattered inches before hitting the woman, but the potential fear of a bullet caused the woman to jump to Kyrie's right, keeping the shelving and the rack of steel stock between them. Kyrie moved her finger from the trigger, not wanting to waste ammunition on poor targets.

Shit! Four more people came through the door—two women and two men. The first woman with long brown hair ripped her wet shirt over her head. Kyrie sensed the heat of the exothermic reaction of acetone and bleach growing, reaching temperatures that could easily cause second-and-third-degree burns.

Most reactions accelerate with heat. She released some of the energy she held in her at the six people that had already come through the door. The woman who had just removed her shirt shook her head, coughed through a scream, and danced around as she tried to get the chemicals off her skin and hair.

"Get her friend!" the woman still inside the conference room shouted.

Three more men exited the conference room, and an immense weight hit Kyrie from above. Gravity pressed down, trying to crush her into the floor. Her own quickly crafted field countered the effects, though the strain tore at her muscles both physically and mentally. *There's still thirteen of them. Mother, you stacked the odds against us.*

Kyrie watched as the nine still living people who had already come through the door paused to evaluate the situation. Of the first six she had applied heat to, all of them quickly worked to remove their chemical-saturated clothing. The other three held her in place.

Fight or die! Kyrie dropped her field and redirected her power and focus onto the remaining cleaning chemicals. As gravity slammed her into the concrete floor, the dozen remaining cans of acetone exploded their contents into the faces of the eight people closest to the conference room door. The people turned away as the aromatic solvent splashed over them.

The air left her lungs as the weight increased, but she focused on the nine bottles of bleach, as well as the other random cleaning supplies. The liquids erupted from the shelves on the far wall. Cries of pain rang out as the acidic fluids splashed onto their turned faces, mixing with the acetone.

The gravity crushing her diminished significantly, allowing her to fully counter it and roll to the side. She hopped back to her feet, pulled a handful of stones from her pouch and launched eight of them in quick succession. Two stones struck a man wearing tan slacks in his bare chest; the third and fourth stones bounced away. The next four projectiles hit the woman with green hair, who continued to struggle to breathe. Two stones penetrated her gut, and the last two ruptured her skull.

That's only two down. They have action economy; you need to turn one.

"We need her alive," the woman in the other room repeated, her voice having grown stronger.

Gravity's invisible weight crashed down upon her again, dropping her to the floor. She saw the second man who had come out of the conference room, and who had moved around the end of the shelves, approaching her with a cylindrical device in his hands. A tattooed man, one of the last three out of the room, raced to follow him.

Kyrie ignored the pain of her body being flattened onto the dirty concrete and slammed her consciousness into the one with the syringe. The dolunar had not expected the mental attack and struggled to respond. *Mine,* Kyrie swore. Like Gestr, the two mental presences in the body were both fragmented. The typical diminished human, barely discernible as the alien nature of the dolunar occupied the space it had created, but never fully meshing with the human body.

Kyrie figuratively grabbed what had once been a female dolunar by the throat, sinking her teeth into the essence of the beast. *You are mine!*

Never. I'm loyal to Nalitran.

Kyrie tore a piece of the dolunar's soul from the rest, and she felt the creature's agony as the part of its essence disassociated into the surroundings. Pain occupied the dolunar and freed Kyrie to direct the body of a man who no longer knew its name. She turned him around and jammed the syringe into the tattooed man's neck. The surprise attack allowed her to inject all of the substance.

Kyrie winced as she found it harder to breathe because of the pressure holding her down. A rib in her chest seemed to fracture.

No! cried the dolunar she had captured. *We must take you.*

Kyrie ignored the comments as three of the remaining men, mostly undressed and breathing heavily, climbed into an open section of the shelving so they could cut through the space and quickly approach her. She tasted blood in her throat as she ripped the soul of the dolunar she controlled into pieces.

Gorging on power that burned her mind, she blasted the vertical supports for the shelves on either side of the men moving through the open space with a narrow wave of gravity angled at forty-five degrees. The thick steel sheared, buckled, and the thousands of pounds of weight from the building supplies on the upper shelves plummeted straight down.

Kyrie's chest expanded, and she gasped for breath as the three men shifted their attention to try to counter the mass falling on them. She flung herself away from the falling tangle of metal and toward the rolling door as six eighty-pound bags of mortar hit the floor where she had been, sending clouds of dust into the air.

The woman pleaded. "Stop this! We want to protect you."

Kyrie sensed that two of the three men tangled in the mess of the collapsed central shelves no longer lived and that the third radiated extreme pain. She swallowed and wiped the blood from her nose before it could saturate her mask while she reassessed her situation. The end of the center row of shelves had collapsed in a heap. Support beams, building supplies, including the rack of steel, had scattered across the floor.

Her eyes twitched, and sweat poured from her overheated body into the mask. *Seven left.* Significant distress came from three of the remaining Bound. *Turn another.*

Kyrie almost laughed at the thought, but anger stopped her. *You don't have a choice.* Bearing down on the agony of pulling more power through her, she pushed her consciousness at one of the three distressed minds, selecting a woman wearing a tracksuit. She felt the dolunar fight back immediately and rebuff her attempt to dominate it. A snarl from the woman filled the air, followed by a wet cough.

The seven people split up; the four radiating the least amount of distress came around the end of the collapsed shelving to her side of the building. The other three moved along the other side of the shelves that still stood, heading toward the next gap in materials.

"You can't escape," the woman that Kyrie recognized from videos as Nalitran's personal assistant said from behind three men. One of whom coughed twice as they moved in her direction. Another headed toward the stairs going into the basement.

Kyrie slowly backed toward the rolling door, the pistol still in her right hand. *Leave Becca alone.* Rage pulled more energy into her, and blood leaked from her nose. *Focus.*

Through the sections of empty shelving that still stood, Kyrie could see the redness of the face, upper chest, and arms of a woman with long blonde hair. Kyrie slammed her mind into the distressed woman. The physical damage had distracted that dolunar enough that Kyrie easily overcame her mental defenses.

Kyrie did not negotiate. She pressed her will on the foreign presence in the body by sharing her own pain. The dolunar's resistance crumpled under the onslaught. *Kill those next to you!* The dolunar tried to resist her, but Kyrie slowly sliced at the creature's soul, and it immediately grabbed the woman in front of her. Energy and augmented strength broke the neck of the woman in the tracksuit who had initially rebuffed her.

The man in tan slacks, who she had hit with two stones to the chest, reached out and tried to pull the blonde woman off the other woman. Kyrie, still holding her mental control, continued to compel the Bound to fight, and the woman grabbed a box of bolts from the nearby shelf and hit the man in the head.

Gravity slammed into Kyrie, crushing her from the front and back. The pistol flew from her, breaking at least two fingers on her right hand and bruising a third. Kyrie could not cry out as all the air had been forced from her lungs.

"General, is this worth all this mess?" a tall green-eyed man asked.

Nalitran's assistant drifted forward. "When she passes out, sedate her. Vridac can get the friend downstairs."

Kyrie struggled against the pain as the gravitational fields holding her in place applied uneven pressure, breaking the fractured rib and crushing two more. Unable to breathe, she knew she had limited time. She could only maintain control of the other dolunar for so long before she would have to try to counter the force crushing her. *But we need her to take out the others.*

"Zvnic, deal with Uriand," the woman commanded as the blonde woman dropped the injured man in slacks to the floor by giving him another blow to the head.

Kyrie's eyes widened. She pulled back from the Bound just as she felt the pressure build inside the woman's skull. A moment later, the blonde's head exploded as a gravitational field expanded outward, spraying blood, brains, bone, and hair across the room.

Kyrie cried as she pulled more energy into herself. *You're burning out,* she warned herself. Nalitran's assistant and the green-eyed man continued toward her. *Fight!* Kyrie put aside her pain and launched several pieces of debris and parts still on the standing shelves next to her at the two people. All her projectiles bounced off, flying back in her direction. She wanted to snarl, but dug deeper, pulling more power through her. Her arms and legs went numb, but that did not stop the pain.

"She'll burn out!" the green-eyed man yelled as more debris flew at them. "We are dying here. We should be trying to live! This is not worth it."

"Silence, Ontrc," the woman snapped.

The other man, who had exploded the head of the woman, rushed forward to help shield Nalitran's assistant.

Please, Kyrie begged of herself, wishing the pain would subside. The lack of oxygen had already made her dizzy, despite being held in place.

As the three people advanced forward, Kyrie continued her frontal assault with the detached hope that would prevent them from noticing her rear attack. She could not expand her chest to even swallow the blood that filled her throat, but she latched onto three L-shaped steel bars that had fallen to the floor behind them. The pain of expending the energy caused her to cry blood, but she pulled the bars forward with as much force as she could muster. The first of the three-foot-long projectiles accelerated forward and hit the woman, though it did not penetrate her body. The second ripped through the arm of the man who had rushed forward, before the bar continued on to bounce toward the rolling door. The third projectile, moving slower, tore through the woman's spine and burst through her ribs to protrude out her right breast.

"General!" the green-eyed man cried.

The field holding Kyrie in place dropped away immediately. Kyrie fell to her knees and forced herself not to gasp for air, despite the dimming of her sight. She turned her head, located the pistol and pulled it toward her. The weapon flew ten feet and hit her stomach hard. She pushed energy into her broken fingers, healing enough of the damage that she could hold the pistol in both hands, and she fired.

Four shots left the barrel, the first two missing the injured man's head, the third one deflected off to the left, but the fourth broke through his temple.

"Don't kill me!" the green-eyed man cried, dropping to his knees and raising his hands in the air as his companion fell backwards. "I don't want to die!"

Kyrie forced herself to swallow all the blood in her throat and then gasped for air as her body compensated for the damage firing the pistol did to her hearing.

Her heart raced, trying to burst from her chest, pumping more blood down her face, soaking the mask. She breathed for several moments; the sweet and pungent odor of the toxins she created mixed with the unreacted remnants of acetone and bleach burned her lungs. Dimly, she hoped the volume of air in the warehouse, and her distance to the mess, would limit her exposure. She swallowed more blood and then wiped her lips and nose onto her sleeve. However, she kept the pistol trained on the man with her finger on the trigger. *All Dolunar must die! They killed Zvarncr!*

"Please," the man pleaded. "I was never in favor of this."

She winced as she probed her surroundings. She could not feel the man who went into the basement after Becca, but aside from the man on his knees, the woman still clung to life. *A ploy to buy time? How many bullets do you have left?*

"I only want to live," he said. "If you kill me, I'll never be reborn. Even if Povnrcac would come to this world, Nalitran has fractured my tugmor. I will truly die if you kill me. Let me go and I'll never bother you or your friends."

"Nalitran controls you," Kyrie growled as she wiped more blood from her face.

"He doesn't control you," came the quick response. "You must be a powerful warlord. You defeated Yrginda, a warlord in his own right, before Nalitran betrayed us."

Kyrie tried to focus, but her thoughts remained sluggish.

"Yrginda has our binding stones. If you give me mine, Nalitran won't control me anymore."

Kyrie's thoughts immediately perked up. "Where?"

"Yrginda keeps them in the bag at her side."

Kyrie shifted her focus. The woman lay partially on her side, her legs twisted and the three-foot long angled steel preventing her from lying flat. Blood oozed from her mouth and around the wound. A large leather bag hung from her shoulder.

"We always follow the most powerful warlord. You have proven yourself the superior." He bowed his head. "I just want to live."

If you get the stones, you can protect Becca. Kyrie forced herself to her feet and shuffled around the debris and the man to the woman. She moved to the far side of the woman so she could continue facing the man before she knelt down, avoiding the large pool of blood under the woman. Her head spun from the movement, but she forced herself to open the bag. Kyrie pulled out a tablet computer, a pistol, a smaller cosmetic bag, and then a long, metal, rectangular box.

She coughed. The chemicals irritated her throat, and the blood in her stomach made her nauseous. "How many have you killed?" Kyrie demanded.

The man's features hardened. "You've killed at least twelve here today and more before that. I've not had a choice."

The woman opened her eyes, and Kyrie felt the pain and frustration from the being dying on the floor. Eventually she felt the weak mental connection the woman directed at her. Kyrie drew in a trickle of energy for self-defense as the alien thoughts coalesced into words. *I told Nalitran we wouldn't be able to contain you.* The woman seemed aware of what Kyrie did. *Ontrc's is the red one at the end. Code is seven, five, eight, zero. Free him. Don't screw up the code twice, or all the stones will be destroyed.*

Kyrie picked up the thoughts and the physical distress, thou she held the presence of the creature at the periphery of her mind. Not trusting either of them, or the Bound still in the basement going after Becca, Kyrie put the box on the floor and kept the pistol in her right hand. The side facing her had a keypad and a small display. The recessed lid remained flush with the edges of the long container. The man who had surrendered had not moved, so she entered the numbers into the keypad. The device clicked, and the lid popped open. Wires and electronics filled the edges of the container. In the center, twenty stones were clasped to small hooks and secured in holders that appeared to have spring loaded hammers ready to strike the stones. A red one sat on the far side.

More blood oozed from her nose. The flow had slowed significantly, but it had not stopped. She wiped away the fresh streak and then put a finger on the stone. *Jump up and turn around three times,* she demanded with as much compulsion as she could muster.

The man winced as he leaped to his feet and complied with her request. He stopped and looked at her, pleading with his entire body. "Please, give me my stone so that I might live out my days in peace."

The stone for the man in the basement, Kyrie sent to the dolunar dying before her.

Green one next to Ontrc's.

Kyrie grabbed Ontrc's stone, released the clasp, and held the stones in her hand. "You will stand guard and protect me and my friends until I tell you otherwise." She pulled the second stone from the box. *Do not harm my friend!* she thought at the stone. *Stop where you are and wait.* She slid both stones into her pocket, hoping Nalitran's assistant had not lied to her.

Kyrie turned her focus back to the dolunar on the floor, took a deep breath through her mouth, and carefully strengthened her connection to the creature's mind, sensing nothing of the human that had once owned the body. *What does Nalitran want with me? How can I stop him?*

The dolunar did not fight the mental intrusion. *That was an effective use of chemicals. It numbed us and slowed our response.*

Answer my questions.

A detached pain flowed through the mental connection as well as righteous anger. *I'm Yrginda. You've damaged this body beyond my ability to repair it, but you should greet me with respect and not condescension. I was a powerful warlord over large swaths of the empire. Who are you that defeated me?*

Kyrie took a moment to center herself, though she knew she had little time. *I don't know my other name, but dolunar do not deserve my respect. You killed too many of my kin to earn it.*

Yrginda's surprise registered clearly to her. *You're corvlian!* A sharp spike of pain surfaced before Yrginda suppressed it. *The dolunar do not have a concept of irony, but this host taught it to me before she died. It is your people who created this problem.* The dolunar pushed contempt into his mental projection. *Your ability to take over the dolunar under my command tells me you are of the same caste that chose to preserve Nalitran, flinging him to this world, instead of actually destroying his tugmor. Were you one of the foolish ones who created this blasphemy?*

Kyrie shook her head as she watched more blood flow out of the woman's body. *I never heard of you and only learned of Nalitran from my mother. Please just tell me what he wants with me before you die.*

You must be very young. Perhaps that's how you survived. Yrginda sighed mentally. *Death comes to me. Because of your people, Nalitran's tugmor has thrived. Now, instead of waiting to be reborn when our bodies die, he is certain he can shift to another host. He wants a youthful body that has had time for the proper pathways to develop so he will not lose power during the transfer. Even without Povnrcac to guide our rebirth, he will have immortality.* Yrginda snarled his next thoughts. *Your people have led to my true death and the true deaths of so many others.* The woman's face formed a small, bloody smile. *Including your own true death.*

Kyrie felt cold. *He thinks he can invade my body? Kick me out of my own body?*

Yrginda let out a mental laugh. *He wants a male body, not a female body, like he bound me to.* The dolunar grew serious. *I don't think it would work on you. Unlike all the other Bound, I can't sense a separation in your mind. The rest of us inhabit, destroy the human, but you seem integrated.* He laughed again, but much weaker this time. *I wonder if his plan will always fail, either in the Bound dying or merging too completely.*

Kyrie hesitated, uncertain she wanted to know how easily another human could be taken over. *And why don't you move to a different body?*

Yrginda took a while to reply, and his voice was very weak. *The ripping of our tugmors and fixing it in the binding stones makes it impossible.* He said nothing more for a long time, but Kyrie knew he had more to say. *Nalitran has over a thousand binding stones in his vault. Like the box, the vault is designed to destroy the stones if he does not enter a code every so many days or he triggers the self-destruct. Insurance that those closest to him will never betray him. You must destroy him, regardless of the others.*

The woman's body convulsed. *I have little time left. When Nalitran realizes I'm dead, he will have my primary accesses removed. I have secondary access to the systems he is unaware of, but the accounts are more restricted. I will share those details with you. Have your hacker friend extract the data. Whatever you thought to get here, there is nothing that will bring down his empire.*

Kyrie staggered slightly as Yrginda forced memories through her defenses and into her head. Accounts and pass phases based upon the dying dolunar's family members.

Why give me this?

If Nalitran only used his ability to destroy corvlians, I would not have. But he's bound more dolunar than your people because they will resist him less. Yrginda's presence grew very faint. *Your people deserve their fate. But he lies to the dolunar, promising a restoration of their tugmor and a return to our world. Sadly, too many dolunar are as stupid as corvlians. They are only useful as pawns, but still, they are my people. Promise me!*

Kyrie felt her own anger. *You've supported him and the chaos he spreads. I do this for me and not for you.*

She sensed the presence of Yrginda grin. *Even though I die, at least I know you've created more chaos. I was the only thing keeping Nalitran from rampaging across the world. If you fail, there will be nothing left.* Slowly Yrginda's presence faded away and ceased to exist.

Chapter 31

Kyrie used the back of her bloodstained glove to wipe more blood from her nose. *Keep focused*, she told herself. With her nose clogged, she panted shallowly through her mouth, trying to cool herself down while not succumbing to the toxins in the air or sending shooting pain through her chest because of her broken ribs.

"What's the man's name?" she asked as she followed the green-eyed man down the stairs with her finger resting on the trigger guard of the pistol in her hand.

"Vridac," the green-eyed man said. "I'm Ontrc."

Kyrie shifted the straps of the large leather bag further up her shoulder after it bumped her side. She had returned the tablet and box of binding stones to the tan designer bag, now stained red with Elsa Donaldson's blood. Yrginda's pistol she had stuffed into the back of her pants, though she doubted she could grab it quickly with her injuries.

Kyrie turned the corner and looked at the empty hallway. Her mind hurt too much for her to expand her senses. She focused on the stones in her pocket, but she had no idea of how she might send different commands to different Bound when she carried multiple stones. However, she tried to focus on the stones in her pocket and not those in the box. *You will not harm me or my friends*, she demanded. *You will both raise your hands and move to the middle of the hall. Now!*

She saw Ontrc jerk slightly as though he tried to resist the compulsion, but the man moved forward. The door to the server room opened, and a short Hispanic man walked out with his hands in the air. Kyrie wanted to breathe a sigh of relief knowing Yrginda had not lied about the two stones, but her chest hurt too much.

"Becca?" Kyrie called out, her voice strained even to her own ears.

"Kyrie? You're okay?" Becca called from inside the server room, but she did not emerge.

Kyrie wished they had established a code. *Next time.* "I didn't crit, but didn't roll a one either."

Becca came out of the server room and looked at the two men who stood with their hands raised. "What's going on?"

"We're getting out of here," Kyrie said. "Give her room," she told the two Bound.

Becca looked at the two men. "I damn near shit myself when he forced open the door. I take it you're in control."

The Hispanic man looked at Ontrc for guidance, and the tall man cleared his throat. "The girl defeated Yrginda. She is a warlord free of Nalitran." The man turned around to face Kyrie. "There are some of us who know the truth. That Nalitran is a failure and has no mandate from Povnrcac to rule. He is a disgrace. Please release us. Give us our binding stones and allow us to live out the sentence of death he gave us. We won't bother you again."

Becca moved quickly past the two men and to the other side of Kyrie. "You look like shit, but we need to get to the gate. There was a problem with a local cop. Dad's hoping you can erase his memory or we'll have a lot of cops after us."

Kyrie motioned for Becca to move up the stairs. "Go to the rolling door."

"Please," both men begged.

Kyrie backed up to the stairs; her pistol again pointed in their direction. "Come this way slowly," she said aloud, releasing her mental attention on their binding stones. *They should die,* she told herself. She started to move up the steps and struggled to control the pain in her broken ribs.

Becca came down a couple of steps, took her arm, and helped her ascend. At the top, Becca coughed from the chemical smell and then looked around at the carnage Kyrie had left. "My God," Becca mumbled. "I ..." Becca shook her head. "No, Michelle, not now," she said into the earbud.

Kyrie ignored the bodies and started walking toward the rolling door at the far end. She had moved fifty feet when the two Bound reached the top of the steps.

"We just want to be free," Ontrc pleaded again. "If you release us, we can tell you all about the northern site. I was one of Nalitran's personal guards. He always assumed our loyalty was unquestionable. He often conducted his business in front of me. I'll trade everything I know for my freedom. Even where they took your lawyer friend. It is possible he's still alive."

Kyrie turned around and looked at the two Bound. She felt the hate from her childhood rage and almost snarled in response of their ask. However, Becca put a hand on her right arm, pushing down the pistol in her hand.

"We're only murder hobos in-game," Becca said. "Stay with me and don't go barbarian rage. We really need to get out of here now."

Kyrie nodded. *Perhaps you can save Lars.* She took a moment to breathe. "I will keep your binding stones. I will command you to call a number later, and you can tell me what you know."

"Then you'll free us? Give us our stones?" the shorter man asked.

"Don't betray me, ever, and I will consider it. I would suggest finding someplace to hide from Nalitran until then. Wait two minutes, then leave." Kyrie turned back toward the door. She hoped their distance to any farms and the walls of the warehouse had muffled the gunshots enough to prevent someone calling the police, but she did not want to risk waiting around to see. "I need to rest," she mumbled to Becca as they slightly increased their pace to the door.

Becca found the controls and activated the motor, which started rolling up the twenty-foot-wide door. The two of them moved toward the outer gate, where Becca's father had just arrived with the van.

"Yeah, Michelle, she needs a cleric," Becca said into her earbud. "No, you don't want to see what happened."

Becca's father pulled up to them, and Jake, Aki, and Michelle jumped out of the back to help Kyrie climb inside.

"You're covered in blood," they said.

Becca pulled the door shut behind her. "She's burning up. Her skin's on fire."

Aki pulled open one of the coolers and scooped out handfuls of ice from the water onto a towel. "Here, this will help."

Kyrie allowed them to lay her on the floor as Mr. Williams spun the van around and quickly exited the compound. "There's nothing in the computer systems here," she mumbled as she allowed them to pull off her mask and press the towel against her head. The towel initially dulled the chill of the ice, but it helped. "Water. Just dump some water on me," she told Michelle.

"We have a cop problem," Mr. Williams said as he drove down the road. "If you can't do anything about it, then I'll try to put as much distance between us and him as we can before someone finds him and we have a manhunt looking for us."

"I shocked the shit out of the cop," Aki said. "I really don't want to go to jail."

Michelle filled a cup with water from the chest. "Where do you want it?" She asked as she moved between the seats. "I also shocked him."

"Everywhere," Kyrie moaned. "Head, chest. I'm so hot."

The water started as a trickle, but Kyrie reached up and twisted the cup in Michelle's hand to empty the contents into her face. "More."

"The cop?" Mr. Williams asked again.

Kyrie continued to breathe shallow, not wanting to exacerbate the sharp pain in her side. "I'll try." She closed her eyes as another cup of water splashed onto her face. "The bag I took from Nalitran's general. There's a tablet. I have logins. You have to get in before Nalitran realizes Yrginda is dead and locks the access."

"I've got the tablet," Jake said, bracing himself as the van made a right turn. "There's a phone and other things in the bag. Do we need to worry about trackers?"

"Get back on the drone, Jake," Mr. Williams said as he drove down the road. "Fly back to the police car and see if anyone has found him. We don't want to drive into an ambush."

Jake sat down in front of the computer, picked up the controller and attempted to fly it in what he believed was the correct direction.

"Not seeing any lights, but I'm not sure how to adjust all the cameras."

Mr. Williams sped down the road with each bounce over a rough spot shooting pain into Kyrie. After less than three minutes, he brought the van to a sudden stop.

"Trackers?" Jake asked again.

Mr. Williams waved his hand in the air. "Yeah, trackers, but first let's deal with the cop. If Kyrie can erase his memories, we won't end up on the FBI's most wanted list. Then we can see what's what with the tablet and things in the bag."

Michelle poured another cup of water onto Kyrie's chest, with the excess spreading across the floor. Kyrie raised her left hand. The short time in the back of the van zapped the adrenaline that had kept the pain of her injuries at bay. "Help me up, but watch my ribs and fingers."

Becca, Michelle, and Aki lifted her carefully until she could get her feet under her. The pain in her side burned like someone had stabbed her, but she forced herself not to pass out. *Just a little more. You can do it.*

Mr. Williams came around the back of the van and opened the rear doors. "The cop's still handcuffed in the back of the car. We need to make him forget what happened tonight."

Kyrie nodded. *Prohibitions disappear when there is something important at stake.* She allowed Michelle and Becca to help her walk to the back of the police car.

"You're all going to rot in prison for this!" the officer screamed from where he lay in the secure part of the car. Much of his vigor having returned to his voice.

Kyrie closed her eyes and used Michelle and Becca for support. She allowed a trickle of energy to pass through her. The effort felt like pouring boiling water on her head. *Do it and be done with it.*

More power entered her body, and she pushed her consciousness into the man. "Sleep," she demanded, sharing her own sense of exhaustion through the mental link. The man immediately sagged, and his head lulled forward. Kyrie slipped further into the man's memories, looking for something she could leverage as a means to make him forget what happened.

"Jake," Mr. Williams called. "We'll need to move him out of the back and put him in the front with all his gear where it belongs." He turned to Kyrie. "Can we move him?"

Kyrie felt bloody tears leak from her eyes. The energy continued to damage her, but the man carried significant guilt and self-loathing. She struggled to keep the emotions out of her own head, and the feeling bubbled up in the man as well as his physical pain and discomfort. *You need a story,* she told herself as her own body trembled from the pain.

Simpson, you never saw a van tonight. You never saw those kids or any black man. You pulled over and parked because you had to take a piss. You stumbled in the dark and hurt yourself because you're feeling unwell. You have the flu. You need to sleep. You got the flu from your girlfriend. There was nobody here. Just you. You need to sleep. You need to call in sick.

Kyrie repeated the story three more times before she broke her connection to the man, her legs giving way so that Michelle and Becca had to fully support her weight.

"Are you okay?" everyone asked.

Kyrie swallowed the blood in her throat. "I need to rest."

Mr. Williams nodded his head. "Get her back in the van and then retrieve the drone. He nodded his head to Jake and Aki. "I'm going to need both of your muscles to move him before taking off the restraints. Then, I need to erase the memory card and put it back in the camera."

Michelle drove the van northwest along US Highway 14 with dark cornfields on both sides of the road. Mr. Williams worked on the Yrginda's tablet in the back of the van with Becca as they installed a backdoor they controlled in Nalitran's systems. The layered security systems that protected the dolunar's empire already had weaknesses that Yrginda factored into the infrastructure.

By two in the morning, they had their own set of admin accounts and had begun mapping out the servers on the network. While the impulse to immediately begin extracting data remained high, Mr.

Williams wanted to avoid triggering any alarms that might exist to alert someone of a breach.

When done, they put their burner phone, the tablet, the phone from the bag, and the shielded rectangular box into a larger Faraday cage. As they crossed a tall bridge, they stopped to dispose of the remainder of Yrginda's possessions into the river below.

At four, they arrived in Madison, found a strip mall with some vehicles in the parking lot and stopped to rest. Mr. Williams called in an anonymous police report of gunfire at the Durten Industries Complex using his VoIP software while Michelle and Becca bought snacks, sugar, and caffeine from a gas station convenience store.

Powered with chemicals, Michelle resumed driving to the northwest until well after the sun rose.

Chapter 32

Two days later, Kyrie looked out onto Green Bay from a campsite in Door County, Wisconsin. The dense tree cover and the lapping of water against the rocks on the stone-filled beach below her calmed her. A few birds flew overhead, gliding lazily on the breeze.

"Hey there," Michelle said, dropping down to sit next to her on the fallen log. "You doing better? You've been distant these last couple of days."

Kyrie shrugged. She had healed her ribs and fingers because the pain of the breaks had kept her from getting any rest. However, she avoid using her abilities for almost everything else. The damage from overextending herself needed more time to heal. "I've been fighting a decision," she admitted after nearly a minute of silence.

Michelle nodded in understanding, though uncertainty filled her face. "You don't have to do it on your own. We're here for you."

Kyrie smiled to reassure her friend. "I'm not leaving. We're not done with Nalitran. Perhaps not even with Hurlington." She turned back to the bay and stared. "Parts of me that are waking up despise the dolunar. I want to make them suffer for what they did to my people. But I'm realizing my people aren't innocent in this either."

"You're not to blame for what others did," Michelle insisted.

"It's not that," Kyrie said, her eyes on her hands. She felt the two binding stones of the Dolunar in her pocket. "I have to decide if I will destroy those beings and what's left of the humans." Rage conflicted with guilt in her stomach. "Do they die or do they live? If they live, what if they end up harming others?"

"You said there are eight stones that still feel alive."

Kyrie remained certain that the twelve dead stones from Yrginda's box had belonged to those that died in the warehouse. *Dolunar we killed.* She looked over to Michelle. "Two of them begged for life. I wanted to kill them. Becca stopped me and I let them go. I let them go knowing how evil their species can be. Knowing what they had done to the humans whose bodies they possessed." *Did we hollow out our own mind? Not according to the dolunar.* She tossed her hands into the air. "Part of me thinks it was the right thing to do. Part of me still wants to smash their stones."

Michelle leaned forward and put a hand on her leg. "Letting them live is the human thing to do. You can't judge someone just because of their birth. You have to understand the circumstances of their actions. If they had no choice in what they did, is what happened their fault?"

Not destiny, please, Kyrie begged silently. Neither Michelle, nor Becca, expressed any strong religious sentiments, but Michelle had mentioned fate more than once and it had shown up in the campaign she was running. Kyrie's thoughts drifted to Ontrc's pleas. The man had not appeared to attack her at any point in the conflict, arguing against what his general commanded. *But is it enough? They seem to respect power.* She snorted. *They think we are dolunar, which is the only reason they decided to surrender. What happens when they figure out you're not one of them?*

"You think it is their fault?" Michelle asked, not aware of Kyrie's internal monologue.

Kyrie shook her head. "I'm worried about them turning on us once they figure out I'm corvlian."

Noises from behind them drew their attention and Kyrie winced as instinct caused her to reach out mentally to look for threats. Becca and the others raced in their direction. "What is it?" Kyrie demanded, jumping to her feet, sensing their excitement despite her reluctance to use her power.

Becca carried a laptop in her hands. "It's all over the news. Reports of the FBI raiding Bishop's offices and home." Becca glanced at her father, who had followed the group more slowly. "With the ton of documents we anonymously released yesterday," she turned back to

Kyrie, "plus the carnage at Durten Industries, we did the cops job for them and connected Elsa Donaldson with Michael Rodgers and the false flag campaign to pin all the killings on Hurlington. Nalitran is squirming."

"Don't get ahead of yourself," Mr. Williams said. "He's denying any personal involvement and saying he had no idea his assistant had anything to do with the terrorism, and his actions in the market were either planned in advance, or a reaction to changing conditions. Slick bastards have a tendency to get away with things too often. Plus, I only got a small amount of data before Nalitran's team realized I was downloading things. I've not been able to get back in, though I still have a lot more to go through. But most of that appears encoded in that language of theirs, so it might not be of use for the cops."

Becca glared at her father. "Let me have at least some small amount of hope that we're starting to win."

He chuckled. "Small amount. I'll allow a small amount."

"Kyrie, Michelle, you want to watch the video?" Becca asked, her expression smug.

"Yes," Michelle said. "I want to see it."

"I'm at least a little happy," Aki said. "I'd love to call my parents and say we might be able to come home soon."

"Same," Jake agreed.

"We need to celebrate," Michelle declared.

Kyrie did not join in their excitement. *Just sending Steven Bishop to jail won't stop the threat. Nalitran had to be destroyed or he'll just transfer his essence to a new body.* Her thoughts went to Lars and Ontrc's claim her parents' friend still lived. *We keep the Bound alive so we can get more intel.*

"You okay, Kyrie?" Michelle asked.

Kyrie nodded her head. "Yeah, just a little tired still." *Which is not a lie.*

Michelle smiled. "Then it's settled. We'll celebrate with some D&D. We can roll you up a character too, Mr. Williams," Michelle offered as Becca turned the laptop around to show her the screen.

"You all can call me Jason," he said. "And sure, I might as well try your nerd games."

The relief all of them shared penetrated Kyrie's thoughts and she let out the breath she had held, allowing herself a moment to enjoy the calm of her surroundings. She embraced the exuberance and confidence of her friends, using that to tether her to her purpose. *Protect the party. Protect your friends.* She would deal with the particulars on how to achieve those tasks later.

www.ingramcontent.com/pod-product-compliance
Lightning Source LLC
Chambersburg PA
CBHW030643260626
47157CB00007B/2472